please do [book on / along to] read when you are finished.

The Finest Moment

Erin:

It's great knowing you. I hope that you enjoy this book as much as I enjoyed writing it.

Rob

Copyright © 2005 Robert W. Britt
All rights reserved.
ISBN: 1-4196-1631-5

To order additional copies, please contact us.
BookSurge, LLC
www.booksurge.com
1-866-308-6235
orders@booksurge.com

The Finest Moment

Robert W. Britt

2005

The Finest Moment

To Leland James Dimond. I Love You Brother. May God Rest Your Soul.

PRELUDE

December, 1989, Panama, South America

As the rough waves of the southern Atlantic Ocean slammed against the LPH Navy ship, the men of Seal Team 5 disembarked from the freight elevator that lowered them out of the bowels of the ship into the ocean. Jimmy O'Neal, Mike St. Claire, and Allad Azheen had no time to think as the ship spit them out into the crashing waves as their rubber Zodiac boat plunged into the Atlantic Ocean. Although they did not know where they were, they knew what their mission was: to rescue a group of American tourists who were in danger of being captured. The SEAL team was somewhere about 50 miles off the coast of Panama, and it was about 0100. Zero dark thirty is what they had called it. The 30 foot waves were unforgiving, and the cold ocean slammed the boat around nearly knocking the men overboard. Jimmy was the alert man and had to ride right up on the bow of the boat. He had to pry his sleepy eyes open to see what was ahead, while Allad navigated from the stern. As they worked their way through the rough seas, the water flew up stinging Jimmy so fiercely he could barely see. In spite of his efforts to drink fresh water from his canteen, salt water splashed into his mouth. He wiped his lips and looked over at his friends in the other boats to see that the rough ocean was winning the battle, as his comrades lost their breakfasts into the great blue sea.

The team had arrived safely at the shore line and dragged their boats up to a dense tree line. Mitchell, the Seal Team Leader, approached Jimmy and his fire team, and said,

"O'Neal, you are going to stay here and watch the boats. Look out to the ocean..." Mitchell handed Jimmy a radio, and said, "If you see anybody, tap the handset 3 times. Do not, I repeat, do not, speak on the radio or the whole world will hear. Got it?"

Jimmy nodded his head that he understood and gripped the radio with his trembling hands. The taste of fear moved up into his throat as his stomach churned. Mitchell told Mike, "St. Claire, if something goes wrong, you'll hear us running back. That's your cue to get the boats in the water. O'Neal will help you. Got it?" "I got it." Mike couldn't sit still; but rocked back and forth anxiously. "Azeen, we're going in about a couple of hundred yards to find the air strip; and you'll be in the back trying to pick up some radio contact. I need you to concentrate and find out what their activity is. You're in the back in case the shit hits the fan. I don't want us losing radio contact. If anything happens, you beat feet to the boats and help get 'em ready. Then you call an air strike back to the U.S.S. Independence. We can't use the Air Force because they're up north dropping loads. So, you call the *Indy* for support. Got it?" "Got it."

An hour had passed with no sign of the rest of the team. Jimmy and Mike had to fight to stay awake. An hour later as the sun began to rise; the men could see the thick brush and landscape of their surroundings. Jimmy waved his hand around to get rid of a mosquito that buzzed around his head. The distant sound of birds was the only sound the men heard as they waited. Although they waited patiently the team hadn't come back.

Jimmy buried his head in the ground when he heard an explosion. Kabamm! Then a series of explosions cut through the silence; then gunfire.

Mike low crawled to Jimmy.

"What the hell we gonna do?"

"We have to stay here, Mike. Drag the boats down to the..."

Allad appeared panting and pointing in the direction of where the rest of the team was. "We have to...We gotta...they're all over the place. Looks like a battalion of them. At least a thousand and they've spotted us. Got us all spread out all over the place. We're pinned, trapped. They're just throwing grenades and shooting...Our guys...They're hiding like trapped rats, but they keep shooting. Oh, shit, what do we do?"

Jimmy pointed to the boats. "We have to get the boats on shore for hasty deployment. First of all, we have to stay calm. When we finish, we'll go up and join the others. Allad, I need you to call for an air strike. Make sure you get the right co-ordinates. I don't want to be barbecued. But first, let's take care of the boats and go up and assess the situation."

The men hurried furiously in spite of the explosions and gunfire that was rapidly getting closer. When they finished, they headed cautiously toward the sound of the gunfire. Jimmy pointed to the ground and told his friends to look for any land mines or trip wire. They finally got to the point where the fires from the explosions illuminated the air strip. There appeared to be hundreds of men running around shooting into bushes and trees.

Jimmy ordered Allad to call the Indy for help. Allad radioed for help and waited. Ten minutes later, a few F-16 jets dropped bombs and then departed. There was a quiet, peaceful stillness and everything was back in order.

One of the pilots had made contact with Allad, and reassured him that the Air Force was heading back from their mission. Allad contacted the lead pilot and told them to drop a few more cans on the airfield. He was told to hang tight.

Jimmy and the others slowly got up to check out the situation. There was smoke everywhere and trees were burning. Although the men could barely see anything, they persevered in the direction where the fighting had been. They started looking around for wounded but couldn't find anyone. It was difficult to see so they moved slowly. They continued walking until, out of nowhere, a small contingency of rebels began running towards them shooting. Jimmy and the others hit the ground and aimed their M-16 rifles in the direction of the air strip.

"Okay boys, we have to just keep firing and mowing a few of them down until we run out of ammo. Hopefully, we'll be dead before that happens. Mike, work your magic with the M-60. Just keep shooting."

The men started shooting frantically and throwing grenades; yet the rebels kept coming like ants in your kitchen. The Seal Team was running out of Ammo.

Jimmy pointed to the left and yelled, "Okay, on the quick step, Mike, move around and flank the bastards. We've got no other choice."

Mike worked his away around some bushes and trees and climbed up a hill until he had reached a point where he could fire.

Jimmy and Allad were holding ground, but slowly losing it.

Jimmy motioned to the left and hollered to Allad, "You go to where Mike is and tell him to work his way to the rear. We gotta make 'em think there are more of us than there really is. Gotta make 'em think we've got them surrounded. Tell him to pop a smoke grenade just before he starts firing so that I know to get my ass down. Be careful that the two of you don't get caught in a cross fire. I want you to pop smoke after he does to let him know where you are. Okay? Stay low and shoot like hell. Go now!" Jimmy ordered.

Allad ran as fast as he could and tripped on a rock, but quickly got back up. Because Mike had distracted their attention, the rebels had let up on Jimmy. After a few minutes, Jimmy saw the smoke. When he did, he put his head down and lifted the muzzle of his rifle up in the air. He pointed it in the direction of the airstrip and continued to shoot. The rebels were now headed to the rear to take Mike out so Jimmy stood up, ignoring the fact that his friend was shooting in his direction and began charging furiously.

Without warning, a group of Air Force Jets flew by and dropped five more bombs just north of the strip. Jimmy hit the deck; put his hands over his head; and lay in the fetal position. The rebels began fleeing desperately as the bombs kept coming until the airstrip was like a pot of boiling tar.

When everything was quiet, Jimmy and his friends collected themselves; drifted from the air strip; and searched the woods for the rest of the team.

Mike spotted one of his teammates, Allen King, whose legs were blown off and yelled to him.

"Allen? Allen?" Mike stood over him. "My God! What has? Oh...Shit."

Allen looked at Mike and groaned. Mike let out a loud scream. "Ah, Shit, Allen, where are your legs? Ah. They're all over...Oh Jesus, what do I do?"

Allen's eyes opened wide and he stopped breathing.

Mike went over to him, got on his knees, and put his arms around him. Mike sobbed and shook uncontrollably. He finally picked his head up; wiped the tears and sweat from his brow; looked around and saw that John Richardson's head was next to his body. Jimmy saw Mike sitting next to his dead friend.

"Come on Mike. Let's get outta here."

"No Jimmy, I gotta save him. He can't die. Let me save him."

Jimmy slapped Mike in the face and said, "They're all dead, we checked. Shot to shit, lights out. It's done." Jimmy's voice got louder with each syllable until he was yelling. "Now we need to get our asses out of here. This place is full of booby traps and land mines. It's 06:30. The sun is out and it's bright. The place will be crawling with wetbacks in no time. We gotta go now."

In the distance there were a series of explosions on the shore, so the men ran to the boats only to see them going up in flames.

Allad fired at some people fleeing from the scene and killed three of them. Jimmy and Mike had polished off five of the rebels who had just incinerated their only means of transportation out of there. The radio still worked so Allad called the Indy to send helicopters to get them out.

The sailor on the other end asked for their co-ordinates and told them to hang in there. Jimmy grabbed his friends and led them away from the shore. They grabbed the dead men's weapons and ammunition. They figured that the fleeing men were headed for rebel territory so Jimmy took his men in the opposite direction. They finally found a spot to hide in the thick brush and radioed for help. No relief came and the sun was shining brightly. Six hours later, Allad radioed for help again. No response.

Mike looked at Jimmy and asked, "What do we do?"

"We have to keep running south. That is where the Air Force base is. It's southwest of here, I think. We gotta keep moving under the cover of darkness; and about 4:00 am, we'll sleep for a few hours and then keep running. By then we should be safe enough to run during the day, but we gotta stick together."

Jimmy stood up and began walking along a small trail and his friends followed.

The men walked for many days in the jungle until they reached the Air Force base. Jimmy O'Neal was awarded the Congressional Medal of Honor and a field promotion for leading the remaining two men of Seal Team 5 to safety.

THE FINEST MOMENT

OUTCAST

On Saturday when Jimmy got to his sister, Jennifer's house, he noticed a BMW parked in the driveway. It was his sister Rachel and her husband, Raymond's car. Nobody was inside the house so Jimmy went out back and saw his nieces, Anita and Becca riding a brand-new four wheeler. Rachel and Raymond were standing next to Jennifer and her husband, Jonathon. Their kids were all running around playing. Jimmy was met by Jennifer who had a big smile on her face.

"Hey Jimmy. Look at the four wheeler that Ray bought Anita for her birthday."

"It's nice," said Jimmy with half of a smile.

"Hey, Jimmy how ya doin'?" asked Rachel.

"I'm doin'."

"So, Jimmy," said Rachel, "Ya dating anybody?"

"Ah, no, nothin' serious yet."

"Well, I'm sure something will come along."

"Yeah, I'm sure."

Ray jumped in. "You'd better hurry up. You're not getting any younger."

"Yeah, either that or Cupid missed when he shot the arrow at me."

They all laughed.

Jennifer stood in Jimmy's defense. "Don't listen to them, Jimmy. Will you guys, lay off my baby brother? We're all working hard to find Jimmy a nice girl. She's gonna come when he least expects it. I got Jimmy on a low carb diet and he's gonna lose some weight. He'll be back in shape in no time."

"He'd better hurry." Rachel poked Jimmy. "We're just teasin' you big brother. I just want to see you in shape again and the clock is ticking. How much do you weigh now Jimmy?"

"Oh, about 250 pounds."

"So, how's the job at the, what is it, the ah, Rent a Video place?" asked Ray.

Jimmy, embarrassed smiled. "It's goin'."

"You ought to try the airport. I'm sure that..."

"I applied...twice in the last year and there aren't any openings. If I were a pilot for Delta Airlines I'd have no problems, now would I."

"Hey. I chose to be an Air Force Pilot long ago. I worked hard to get where I am. That's why I work for Delta. You should have thought about that when you signed up to play Rambo."

Rachel shook her head. "No. God has a plan for Jimmy. Maybe you should get back into shape and join the Navy again as an officer."

Ray looked at Rachel and rolled his eyes. "He doesn't want to do that. How about trying..."

Rachel and Raymond's nine year old son, Eric, ran over to Jimmy and said, "Hey Uncle Jimmy!" He smiled and gave Jimmy a hug. "Uncle Jimmy, let's play tackle football."

Jimmy and Eric played rough until Rachel came over and said, "Jimmy, I told you.....No Rough Play! He's just a little thing. You're gonna hurt him. When you have kids of your own you can play with them however you want to." She walked away and mumbled, "If you ever have any kids."

Becca came over and gave Jimmy a big hug. She asked Jimmy if he wanted to play hide and seek. He told her that he had to get Anita to the mall before it closed. She was disappointed, but Jimmy had always made sure he played with her whenever he came over so she would get over it quickly.

Anita finished riding and gave Ray a big hug and said, "Oh, thank you so much Uncle Ray. This is the best birthday present I could ever have."

"No problem kid, don't mention it."

Jimmy went over to Anita and asked, "Anita, are you ready to go shopping?"

THE FINEST MOMENT

She paused and asked, "Ah, can we go another time? I want to invite some friends over and take them for a ride."

"Yeah, sure, maybe next weekend."

The adults had retired to the front deck for a cookout. Ray talked about his Air Force missions in the Persian Gulf and Desert Storm. He also talked about his missions in Panama.

He recalled a mission in Somalia. "I remember when a team of Army Rangers were trapped, but the Air Force dropped some cans and saved them. I don't know what this country would do without the Air Force. Pretty soon ground troops will be obsolete. The Air Force is better than all the other branches because they have more men, machines and technology."

Jimmy looked at Ray and barked, "Ground troops are better because it takes three pilots and a jet to equal one Navy Seal, one Marine, or an Army Ranger for that matter."

Rachel jumped in, "Okay, okay, boys, take it easy." She looked at Ray with a disapproving look. "Raymond, my brother was there. He lost some friends there you know. That wasn't fair."

Ray looked at her with the look of a child who had been reprimanded for spilling milk. "I'm sorry Rachel. I didn't know. You never told me. I thought he was a cook on the ship. You never.. He never..."

"It's really not something that he likes to talk about a lot. Anyway, let's leave it alone. Okay? Let's talk about the new cottage we bought on Lake Tahoe. We're going to stay there during the summers and go back to our Condo on Miami Beach during the winter."

Ray perched his head with pride. "I am taking an early retirement. I've invested in land development and I'm going to take it easy."

Jimmy stood up and said, "I have to get going. I have plans with friends."

Jimmy didn't have any plans and all of his friends had abandoned him when he stopped drinking. However, he still had hope so when he got home he decided to call his buddy, Bill, to see if he wanted to hang out and maybe go to a movie.

Jimmy dialed the number and Bill answered, "Hello?"

"Hey, Bill, this is Jimmy."

"Hey, what's goin' on?"

"Just calling to see if you wanted to check out a movie."

"Oh no, man, I'm goin' to Jillian's to shoot pool. You ought to come along. I'll buy you a beer."

"Well, I stopped drinking a couple of years ago. But I can still have a good time."

"Oh, why'd ya quit?"

"Just getting' too fat, feel like shit."

"Oh, man just work out. Go to the gym. Sweat it out. You can't shoot pool sober. You know that. What the hell ya gonna do during the super bowl? Just can't see you sober. Maybe one beer? Can you have a few?"

"Ah, maybe, I'll meet ya there."

Jimmy decided not to go because he had had the same conversation with other friends and they told him same thing. Whenever he hung out with them, he felt like a third person at a table for two. He did meet a few friends in Alcoholics Anonymous a couple of years ago when he first got sober. However, he had drifted from the meetings so now he was trying to survive on his own.

Jimmy took a drive around town to clear his head. When he returned he saw his two neighbors, Jack and Tiny, sitting in Jack's van drinking beer and smoking ganja.

Tiny leaned out of the front window and said, "Hey Jimmy, what's up? Come on over and join us."

Jimmy went over to the van and said, "Hey guys, not tonight. Gotta get up early." Tiny had greasy gray hair and a red face. He was missing two teeth and looked as if he had just crawled out from under the hood of a car. He lit a cigarette and began blowing smoke in Jimmy's face.

Jack popped his face out and said, "Hey Jim, you think you could lend me ten bucks? I'm starting a job tomorrow as a dishwasher so I have a job, man. Can you help me?"

Jack had rusty colored hair that was long. He was younger and

THE FINEST MOMENT

cleaner than Tiny but tended to get nasty when he drank. Jim had lent both men money on many occasions and had never seen it. He knew they were only going to get another 12 pack.

"Ah, I'm broke myself. I don't have a dime."

"Good enough. Take it easy Jim."

Jimmy patted Tiny on the shoulder and said, "Take it easy, all right?"

When Jimmy got to the hall leading to his apartment, his stomach churned at the sight of the dirty, torn-up carpet. There were black marks on the wall as if a motorcycle had done burnouts on them. As he walked down the hall, he heard one of the men in an apartment yelling at his girlfriend that he was going to break her neck. As he got to his door he heard a **SLAP** and the woman screamed. When he opened his door, he could smell a strong odor in his living room. The man next door had a cat he never cleaned up after and most of the time you could smell it all the way down the hall as you came in. Tonight it smelled as if the cat had taken a shit right in Jimmy's apartment. He lit a couple of candles and sprayed his apartment, but it only helped for a while.

He tried lying down to sleep; but the heat, the smell of the cat. and the sulfur in the water pipes made him nauseous. He had to get up a couple of times to throw up. He was also kept awake by his other next door neighbor who had brought his girlfriend over. Their bed was banging against the wall and the girl was howling like a bitch in heat. Jimmy tried to sleep, but couldn't. He tried to daydream about better days to come. He used to fall asleep by thinking about having a family, a home, and the finer things in life. Tonight, however, he just couldn't manage so he lay there alone and began to cry until he fell asleep.

The following Monday Jimmy found his boss, Nick Stephenson, the district manager of Rent a Video, in his office. At about 350 pounds, Nick was squeezed tightly into Jimmy's chair. His hair was black and greasy and he had glasses. He had pimples on his face and craters where others had been. Nick breathed heavily and had sweat on his brow as well as dark, wet spots on his shirt at the pit of his arms.

He chain-smoked a pack of Viceroy cigarettes, shook his head, and sighed. As he studied some papers that he held out in front of him, he made humming, grunt sounds. A belch, followed by a hiccup, forced its way out of his mouth. A muffled, farting noise, worked its way from the seat, and the smell...worse than a dead cat.

He looked at Jimmy. "It doesn't look good James."

There weren't many things in this world that Jimmy disliked, but there was nothing he hated more than being called James.

Nick continued, "James, James. We have some problems. You're not keeping good records, and you're not managing your people."

Nick lit a fresh cigarette with one that was in the ash tray. He blew a breath of smoke in Jimmy's direction and Jimmy waved it away.

"Jimmy, you need to keep better records. Okay? You've got people who were overdue on movies for over a week and I don't even see any proof that you tried to notify them. When and if,you ever call those people, you need to log it in here." He pointed to a book.

"Well, that is my assistant manager's job."

Nick leaned forward and took a few deep breaths. "Well how about keeping track of the book and making sure that your assistant is doing her job?"

"Yes, you're right. I'll have to start micro managing her more."

"Don't be a smart ass. I'm serious Jimmy. You got to keep records. We have employees taking videos for days and they aren't paying. They can take them at cost, but they still have to pay. You need to sit on your people, Jimmy."

"Yeah, you're right. I'll have to pay more attention."

"That brings me to the next topic. I got here at ten a.m. That is when the store opens and there was nobody here." Nick looked at his watch and said, "It's eleven a.m. now. This store has been closed for an hour when it is supposed to be open. Oh yeah, the alarm wasn't on either. We're lucky we didn't get robbed."

Jimmy protested, "Wait. The cleaning people come as my people are leaving at night. They're supposed to set the alarm."

"Well how about getting on the God damned phone and calling their manager. No shit huh?"

THE FINEST MOMENT

Jimmy looked at Nick as if to say *look at you, you fat piece of shit, who are you to talk to me that way?* But instead, he refrained. "Yeah, okay, don't get your panties up in a bunch."

Nick pointed at Jimmy with the hand that his cigarette was in and said, "Look Jimmy, I'm serious. I shouldn't be down here. I've got more important things to do than to school you on how to do your job. Don't forget who's buttering your bread. There are a lot of people out there who are dying to be managers. You'd better show a little respect. I'm gonna be stopping in often and checking your files to make sure everything is in order." He waved the book in the air. "If this book is indicative of how you keep your records; then we've got a lot of un-fucking of bad files to do. You'll be working Saturdays and Sundays for a month if necessary. Do you follow me smart ass?"

Jimmy rendered him a lazy salute and leaned forward. "Yes sir. Chief Sir. You got it BOSS!" Then he walked out to the front. He figured that Nick, in his present physical shape, wouldn't be chasing him and would calm down before he came out of the office, so Jimmy went to work inventorying his shelves.

After about an hour or so, Nick finally left without saying a word. A few minutes later, Amanda Farley, the assistant manager came in. Amanda was in her last year of college. Although she was ambitious and courteous, she was somewhat forgetful. She came in and walked over to Jimmy.

"Hey, Jim. How'z it goin'?"

"Ah, I'm not good."

"I saw Nick. What's up?"

"He's got himself worked up as usual. Who was supposed to open this morning?"

"Ah, I think Kyle is. I'll have to check the schedule. Whoever it is, I'll call them. Don't worry. I'll get someone to come in."

"Okay, but first, I have to tell you that we gotta really sit on everybody. It seems that these kids are really slacking off and it's affecting the way we keep our books."

"What do you mean?"

Jimmy repeated the information that Nick had given him and

explained to her how important it was to keep Nick happy; because when he was happy, he stayed away. After Jennifer took care of finding out who was supposed to come in and work, Jimmy brought her into the office and went over again the proper way to keep the records.

On Saturday, Jimmy wanted to spend some time with Anita and Becca so he woke up early on Saturday, grabbed his fishing poles, and headed out the door. When he got to the parking lot of his apartment complex, he saw a young man waxing his red 1965 Mustang.

Jimmy walked past the car slowly and said, "Wow, that looks good."

The man stopped what he was doing, wiped the sweat from his brow, and ran his hair through his dirty blond hair. He had on a pair of dirty jeans and an old Ozzy Ozbourne t-shirt. "Hey, thanks man."

"You're up awfully early."

"Yeah, so are you."

"Goin' fishing with my nieces."

"I'm picking my girlfriend and her daughter up."

The man extended his hand and introduced himself. "I'm Joe. Joe Richards."

Jimmy reached his hand out and shook Joe's hand. "I'm Jimmy O'Neil."

Joe smiled and said, "I've seen you around. How long have you been living at this pit?"

Jimmy looked up and thought, then answered, "Ah, I don't know. A couple of years I guess. It seems like forever."

"Yeah, me too. I'd like to get out of here."

The men talked while Jimmy put his poles and tackle gear in the bed of his truck. When they finished, Jimmy scooted along the highway and headed for his nieces' house.

When he got there, Jon's Ford pickup was in the driveway and so was the Caravan. Jimmy walked into the garage and rang the doorbell. There was no answer so he walked around to the front. When he did, Becca stuck her head out into the garage and saw nobody so she went back inside. Jimmy went to the front door and rang the bell. He

THE FINEST MOMENT

waited and again, there was no answer. He decided to go out to the back. When he did he heard Becca yelling in the front.

"Hello? Who's there?"

Jimmy turned around and headed back to the front and saw Becca.

Her eyes lit up when she saw Jimmy. "Whoa, you're here early Uncle Jimmy."

Jimmy walked toward her and said, "Yeah, I should have called first, but I figured I'd just come up. I wanted to see if you and Anita wanted to go fishing."

"Yeah, come in. Let me get Becca."

Jimmy walked into the kitchen where Jennifer was standing. She was in her nightgown and her sandy blond hair was a mess. She was pouring herself a cup of coffee.

She looked at him and walked over to the kitchen table. She pointed to the chair next to her and told him to sit down.

"So what brings you up here so early?"

"I just wanted to see if Becca and Anita wanted to go fishing."

"Well, Anita's in bed; but I'm sure she'd like to go. I know Becca would. She always does."

Just then Anita came out of her room with her hands in the air, stretching, reaching for the ceiling. She yawned and rubbed her eyes. "Hey, Uncle Jimmy. What are you doing here?"

"I came over to see if you wanted to go fishing."

She took a seat next to him and put her head on the table. She labored to lift it up and looked at him. "Yeah, let me get something to eat and then we can go. Dad got me a new pole. I'd love to try it out. Where do you want to go?"

"Well, we could go up to Lake Winnepausakee. There's a good spot on the bridge."

"Yeah. That'll be cool."

Becca grabbed a box of cereal, discovered that it was empty, walked over and saw that Anita's jumbo sized bowl was full.

Becca slapped Anita on the arm and protested. "Do you have enough cereal?"

Anita returned the slap and said, "No, I wanted more but we ran out."

Becca ran back over to the cupboard and searched for another box. "Well, thanks a lot. Now what am I gonna have to eat? You hog."

"There's some dog food in there?"

"Ha. Ha. You're so funny. I'll just have some toast."

As the girls ate Jimmy and Jennifer talked.

Jennifer was filling him in on the events at church. "There's a big Knights of Columbus dance in the Gym tonight. You ought to check it out."

"Ah, those dances are boring and they play fifties music."

"Yeah, but you ought to check it out. There are a lot of single women that go there."

"Ah, I'm not sure what I'm doing. What are you guys up to tonight?"

"I'm supposed to go shopping later with Rene, and then, I think I'm gonna order a pizza and get a couple of movies."

"Sounds like fun."

Jennifer smiled. "You should come to church some time. There are a lot of cute women there. We're getting a new priest. He did missionary work in India as well. He's met Mother Theresa. He came to our church last week and spoke of the work he did."

Jimmy changed the subject in a hurry. He had blamed God for all of his problems and wasn't doing any business with him at the present moment. "Oh neat, so are you girls all pumped up to go fishing?"

They both shook their head to indicate that they were ready.

They finished up, got in Jimmy's beat-up old Ford pickup and headed for the bridge to catch some fish. They set their poles up and Jimmy helped Becca get the bait on her hook. When he finished, he stood behind her to help her cast.

She nudged him and said, "I think I got it, Uncle Jimmy. You showed me this a few times. Can I try it on my own?"

"Yeah, sure kid."

THE FINEST MOMENT

Jimmy watched as Becca leaned forward on the bridge and heaved her hook forward.

Jimmy patted her on the shoulder. "Hey, that's awesome kid. Good job."

"Thanks."

"How you doin' over there Anita?"

"Good."

"Okay, let me get my line out."

Jimmy baited his hook and cast his line. There was silence as they waited for the fish to bite. All of a sudden Becca felt tension on her line, and her pole nearly slipped out of her hand.

She looked over at her uncle and yelled, "Uncle Jimmy. I think I got one. Can you..?"

Jimmy got behind her and helped her pull her catch. "That's it Becca, steady pulls. That's a girl. That's my girl."

Becca's tongue was hanging out and she had a look of strain on her face as she continued to pull. She grunted and yelled, "I got it. I caught one. He looks like a big one."

The fish had surfaced and was swaying back and forth under the bridge. Jimmy pulled the line and brought him to the bridge. It was a large trout and Jimmy brought him to the sidewalk where he was standing. He unhooked him and threw him into the cooler.

He patted Becca on the back and said, "Congrats, kid. Good job. Now go ahead. Bait your hook again and cast your line."

Becca did so and, the three of them again stood on the bridge waiting in silence for more fish to bite.

Jimmy looked over at Anita and asked, "How ya doin' kid?"

"Good, I just wish they'd bite."

"Oh, they will. Just be patient."

As they waited Jimmy talked about all the things that he had planned for the summer. He had managed to put some money away and wanted to take his nieces somewhere nice during their break.

"Do you guys want to go to Canobie Lake Park sometime?"

Becca's eyes lit up as she shouted, "Yeah! Yes! When Uncle Jimmy?"

"Well, I'm not sure. I'll have to check my social calendar. It probably won't be for a few weeks. I'll give you a heads up."

The girls told him that they would make sure they didn't have any plans when he was ready to take them. By the time they left they had a cooler full of nearly a dozen fish that they took home, cleaned, and froze.

The following weekend Jimmy went up to Jennifer's for a cookout. He felt out of place because everyone there was married with children and as always he came by himself. Lisa, Jennifer's neighbor, had wanted to fix Jimmy up with her sister, but Jimmy declined. Blind dates had always turned out to be catastrophic for him.

Lisa's husband, Rick, who had been drinking beer all day commented, " Hey, Lisa, we could always fix him up with your brother. They'd be compatible."

Jimmy's face turned red and he said, "Rick, I wouldn't want to be with anyone that you've already juiced."

Rick went over and pointed in Jimmy's face and asked, "What the fuck's that supposed to mean?"

Jennifer jumped in indignantly saying, "Listen to me Rick, you're cut off, no more beers for you. I mean it."

Rick waved his hand and said, "Lisa was just trying to be helpful. She just wanted to find him a date. The guy hasn't had a date in about three years. He always comes over by himself. We're all beginning to wonder about him."

One of the other guests hollered out, "He could always be a priest or a monk. He might fit in with those guys."

The other guests laughed. Jimmy's eyes were bloodshot and his face was red. Although he wanted to drive his fist into Rick's head, he walked away. Jennifer chased him and told him to come back; but he jumped into his beat-up old Chevy pickup truck and squealed out of there. The guests went on with the cookout as if nothing had happened. Jennifer just rubbed her hand through her hair erratically and went to her kitchen where she paced her kitchen floor. Finally, she went out and told them that she wanted them all to go home. She told them never to come back if they planned on being rude to her brother. She tried to call Jimmy but he wasn't home.

THE FINEST MOMENT

She continued to call him and left a message on his voice mail.

The next day Jimmy called and let Jennifer know that he was okay.

"Jennifer!"

"Hey Jimmy. I was worried about you. You were so angry when you left. Look I threw those drunkards out of my yard and told them not to come back."

"Thanks, I appreciate it."

"Jimmy? Why don't you come over for dinner tonight? I'd hate to see you alone."

"Oh, I'll be okay."

"Are you sure? I'm worried about you, Jimmy. You look down. You don't look happy anymore."

"Oh, I'll be okay."

"Yeah, sure!"

"I'm fine. Look, I just wanted to return your call and let you know that I was okay. I have to get going now. Okay? I'll try to get up this weekend."

"Okay. The girls are looking forward to seeing you."

Two days later Jennifer's old high school friend, Barbara, called and invited her and Jon to a party next weekend.

"Hey, Jennifer, I'm sorry about what happened today. I can see why you were upset. It wasn't nice of those guys to be such assholes to Jimmy."

"Yeah, well thanks, Barbara."

"So, anyway, I'm having a party next week and you and Jon are invited."

"Ah, let me check with Jon and I'll call you this week."

Barbara asked Jennifer if she'd be able to find a babysitter.

Jennifer thought for a second. "Well, maybe I'll see if I can get Jimmy to do it."

Barbara paused for a minute and asked, "Oh, well. Do you have any of the neighborhood girls that might want to babysit?"

"No, Jimmy loves to hang out with the children. He'll be fine."

"Okay, I guess, but..."

"But, what?"

"Oh, nothing."

"Tell me...what's on your mind?

"Quite frankly, as misguided as they were...don't take this the wrong way but.. Rick had a point. I mean...Most guys would say yes to a date, especially, if they hadn't been with someone for...Well, you know...as long as Jimmy has...I mean, can he be trusted with the girls? I'm sorry Jennifer. I'm out of line"

"I know what you mean, and I think Jon and I have plans next weekend. As a matter of fact we do. I gotta get going. I have to clean up the place. We had a big cookout today. Goodbye."

"I'm sorry if I..."

Jennifer hung up and went about her business.

Anita's friend Kelsey stayed the night and they were just sitting around by the pool out in the back yard talking. Kelsey asked, "Is your uncle married?"

Anita paused and said, "No."

"Does he have a girlfriend or kids?"

"No."

"How come?"

"I don't know. Come on let's go outside."

That night Jennifer called Jimmy to see how he was doing.

"Hey, big brother. What's going on?"

"Nothing much. Just hangin' around."

"You can't let those people get to you. I just hate to see you by yourself. You have got to get out and do something."

"Yeah, I suppose."

"Look, Jimmy. I have a friend, Marissa, my hair dresser. Divorced. No kids. She's a nice..."

"No, Jennifer. I don't want a blind date."

"Try it. If it doesn't work out...Then, it doesn't work out. You've got nothing to lose."

The only sound was the humming of the phone.

"Oh, Okay. I'll try it."

"Great. I'll call her tonight."

THE FINEST MOMENT

"See ya."

The next weekend Jimmy wanted to make his apartment look nice so he went to the flower shop and bought some flowers and plants. He set them on the table where his high school football helmet, jersey, trophies, and medals of honor from the military were. He sat down next to the table and admired the plants and flowers. Their pink and white pedals enhanced the old table. Their thick vibrant texture made his dusty old medals shine. He wiped the dust off everything on the table, then looked at his football helmet and jersey and slipped back in time. He escaped to a place where he was at his finest in life. He put his Jersey on. It was tight but still fit. Then he put his football helmet on his head. He imagined himself running down the football field after he had picked up a fumble. This wasn't your typical trip down memory lane. This was a serious blast from the past. This memory was real. Jimmy actually felt himself in the spot he was in about 13 years before. He looked at his congressional medal of honor and again found himself drifting. He dreamed of running through the jungle with his friends.

He remembered well how fearless he had felt. He was amazed at the strength he had possessed at that very moment. He felt invincible and without a doubt, confident. In Panama, his confidence rubbed off on his comrades and enabled them to feel a power that they normally would not have possessed. It was the same confidence that one might have felt playing high school sports or being in the drama club on the night of a big play. Or perhaps how a young adolescent who was in a band felt when playing in front of a hundred people or so. He felt as invincible as he had felt in college. He awoke wondering why and how he had lost his edge. He opened his photo album that sat on the table. In it he found a thin, broad shouldered, image of himself when he was at his best in life. He had never looked at his trophy table with such intensity as he did now. In fact, he had never looked at them at all. He felt a burst of energy, a burst of power—- sort of the way one might feel just after watching the Rocky movies. Jimmy felt a surge of strength that he had not felt in many years. He continued to look at the pictures and the trophies as well as the plants and flowers that made them shine. He fell into a dream-like trance and had visions of himself during his adolescent years when he thought that he was afraid of nothing. It was that edge that had won the hearts and the minds of many beautiful young women. He awoke from his dream state again, feeling a greater power than he had ever felt—- a power that was beyond explanation.

He cleaned his apartment with great enthusiasm and sprayed it so that the odor next door couldn't be noticed. It had been the first date he had had in a long time and he wanted everything to look nice.

At about five o'clock, Marissa knocked at the door. She was wearing a tight black skirt and was well endowed. Her blond hair was pulled back in a ponytail. She had hazel eyes and fair skin. She extended her hand and smiled.

"Hi. I'm Marissa."

"Hi, Marissa. I'm Jimmy. Please come in."

On the table was a chicken and rice dinner. He pulled a chair out for her and she sat down at the table. As they ate, Marissa paused, and looked around. She looked at Jimmy and asked, "What is that smell?"

"What smell?"

"That horrid smell. It smells like a dirty cat litter box or cat piss or something. What the hell is it? Do you have a cat?"

"No, but the next door neighbor does. He doesn't clean up after it."

Jimmy got up and lit a candle. He went to the bathroom and got a can of deodorizer and started spraying it. The cat smell was strong so he emptied the bottle.

"There that's better," he said with a smile.

"Now it smells like candles, perfume, and cat shit."

She headed for the door and said, "It was nice knowin' ya. Jimmy boy." She never looked back.

Jimmy wanted to go next door and choke his neighbor within every inch of his life; but instead sat there, put his face in his hands, and tears began to roll along his cheeks.

THE FINEST MOMENT

A couple of weeks had passed and Jimmy was in a good mood because he would be taking his nieces to Canobie Lake next week. He decided to call Becca to touch base with her about their trip.

Becca answered with a cheerful, "Hello?"

"Hey Becca. What's goin' on?"

"Oh, nothin' just hangin' out."

"So, are you psyched to go to Canobie Lake next weekend?"

"Oh, Umm."

"What?"

"Well, Uncle Jimmy. We can't go."

"Why what's up?"

Jimmy heard Jennifer's voice in the background asking who was on the phone.

Becca responded with hesitation. "It's. It's Uncle Jimmy."

Just then Jennifer got on the phone and said, "Hey, what's up?"

"Nothing. Why can't the kids go to Canobie Lake?"

"Their Uncle Ray has invited them to go to Disney World. It was a last minute thing and…you know. Disney World. The girls figured that they don't get the chance to go to Disney too often and they can always go to Canobie Lake anytime."

"Yeah, I suppose you're right. Wow! Disney."

"Yeah. Maybe when they get back we can all go to Canobie Lake."

"Yeah. We can do that."

Jimmy and Jennifer talked for a while. She could detect disappointment and hurt in his tone as he could never in his wildest dreams afford to go to Disney World.

THE FINEST MOMENT

SALVAGING DIGNITY

Nine months later, in an early morning in March, Jimmy was headed to Racquet Club where he had begun working out again. Before he left, he went over to his trophy table and, again, was compelled to look at his old photo albums and yearbooks. He thought that he looked good and the number of girls he had dated was indicative of how attractive he really was in the early years. He missed being in shape and felt lousy now that he was so overweight so he had decided to take action and get motivated again. He had joined the gym and was back in the fitness mode again. He thought to himself that if he had not bought that flowers and plant, he may not have really noticed how well his trophies and medals looked. And, he would not have been inspired to look at his photo albums. He was happy that he bought the plants. Pondering on the past would indeed help him to solve the problems of the future. He had begun doing aerobics, lifting weights, and swimming. The aerobics classes were lively and some of the people there were friendly. For the most part, he had found a good social outlet there. But the most important aspect of working out was that he began getting his confidence back.

He took a picture of himself with a white tank top on and shorts out of the photo album. He was about 22 years old in the picture and muscular. He also took out a picture of one of the girls he had dated while he was in the Navy and taped them to the refrigerator. He had written the words, "Are you sure you want that Peanut butter and Jelly sandwich?" on a piece of paper and taped it above the pictures. He had a small bowl of low carbohydrate cereal. On his way to his truck, he saw Joe Richards in the parking lot shining up his 1965 Mustang.

Joe stopped what he was doing and looked up. "Hey, Jimmy, what's goin' on?"

"Just goin to pump a little iron. Chase a little ass around the gym."

Joe, who was about 30, laughed and said, "Oh, yep, nothin' wrong with that."

Jimmy looked at the mustang. "Wow, that shine looks good."

"Yeah, just throwin' an extra coat on it."

"Man, don't you have a new Jeep and a motorcycle?"

"Yeah."

"So, what are you doing living in this shit hole, if you can afford to have those nice things?"

"That's why I'm living in this shit hole; because I've put so much money into my vehicles. Ah, I'm doin' all right. Waiting for an opening at work for an 18 wheeler driver."

"Where do you work now?"

"International Movers. I drive the local trucks. I do okay."

"Maybe an opening will come soon and you can get out of here." Jimmy looked up at the roof of his apartment complex where the shingles sagged and the siding was stained and peeling.

Joe wiped his hands on his rag and said, "Well, either way, I'm hoping to move in with my fiancé soon."

The men talked for a while and then parted ways.

Later that morning, Jimmy had finished lifting weights and doing aerobics so he went to the hot tub that was situated in the swimming pool area and relaxed. A woman who was perhaps 30 something, came over toward the hot tub. She was skinny but had a decent shape. As she entered the hot tub, Jimmy said, "Hello."

She looked at him, then quickly looked away and took a seat. Jimmy figured that she didn't hear him, so he repeated himself.

"Hi, how, ya doin?"

She looked at him and rolled her eyes. She then leaned her head back and closed her eyes. A few minutes later she got up without even looking at Jimmy or saying a word and walked out of the hot tub. Jimmy had wondered what part of the word hello she had a problem with. There was a burley man of about 40 who was sitting in the hot tub who smiled and said, "Oh, you're not the only one who has scared that bitch away."

THE FINEST MOMENT

The man extended his had out and introduced himself. "My name is Pete. Don't worry Pal, there are a lot of women here."

Over the course of the next 6 months or so, Jimmy deflected the "better than thou" attitudes that sometimes dominate the atmosphere of a gym and persevered with his workouts. He had lost another 30 pounds and was feeling confident. The Racquet Club had become a focal point where he and his new friends would meet and talk about sports, weather, and the never ending scenario of *why woman love to date losers*, that has been the topic of debate since the beginning of time.

Jimmy had been talking to Amy, one of the women in his class for a couple of months. She had the build of a gymnast. The twenty-five year old woman had blond hair and was blessed by God with robust breasts. She was friendly to Jimmy and to many of the other guys. Although Jimmy had gotten up enough nerve to ask her on a date, he never got one. She had always told him that she was interested; but when it came to setting a day and time to go out, she ended up having plans. After a month of that charade, Jimmy got the hint and stopped asking her; but he continued to talk to her. He figured maybe she'd come around, but she never did.

Jimmy's job was equally fruitless, as he was hoping to get a promotion to district manager. It would set the tone for his success in the Video rental business. He figured that by the time he was in his late 30's, he could eventually open up his own store. However, his plans were hindered by his boss. Although Jimmy had told Nick that he was willing to relocate anywhere in the U.S. where there were openings, Nick had passed Jimmy over a number of times over the past couple of years.

One morning Jimmy went to his office and saw Nick sitting in his chair. Nick was eating an egg and cheese sandwich and drinking milk. He had a cigarette smoldering in the ash tray and motioned for Jimmy to come in. He sucked down his sandwich and opened up another.

"Come on in, Jimmy," Nick said, with his mouth wide open. He had mashed egg and cheese ready to jump off his tongue; and because his mouth was full, his words were muffled. "Would you like a sandwich?"

Jimmy gave him a look of disgust. "No thanks, Nick." Jimmy pulled out a bag,
took out a piece of celery and munched on it. He took a drink of Gatorade and wiped his mouth. "What brings you to these parts?"

"Well, James. I'm just checking up on you. It seems as though things have been going smoothly since we last talk. I must have said something inspiring. Well, there's going to be an opening for district manager in the Western Massachusetts area. The main office is in Newton."

Jimmy sat down and now had a look of interest on his face. "When...When does the position open?"

"Don't get too excited, Jimmy." Nick took another bite of his sandwich and gulped down some milk. "It's not for another six months. The guy who's there now is getting promoted. Johnny DeLanie is applying for the position and his numbers are good and he's got no turnovers. You've got a lot."

"That's because my kids are all high school students, Nick. They're still figuring out how to stroke their Johnson's. They don't even know where they're going in life. They can't even get out of bed in the morning, much less keep a job. Johnny's store is in a retirement community. He has some reliable people. It's not me, Nick, who drives these nose ring wearing punks out after two weeks. I take care of my employees. Ask the ones who stay. They'll tell you."

Nick put his head down and waved his hand in the air. "Save it pal. I know, I know. But try telling that to the brass. They're the ones who make the final decision."

Jimmy waved his hand and said, "Ah, bahh, that's bullshit and you know it Nick. Why the fuck do you even come down here, get my hopes up, and then shoot 'em down?"

Nick took a handkerchief from his pocket and wiped the sweat from his brow and face. "James, my friend, relax. You still have a chance. I tell you what. You just impress the hell out me for the next few months and you might stand a shot. Okay?"

Jimmy stood up and walked out.

A few weeks had passed and one day Jimmy was at the gym

THE FINEST MOMENT

giving Amy friendly punches and pretending to pour water from his water bottle on her. Amy grabbed his arm and returned the punch
She looked at him and smiled. "You're crazy Jimmy."
"I'm crazy about you," he said.
"So, how are things at work? Any news on the promotion?"
"No. No word yet. I should hear something in a week or so."
"Something will come along. You're still young."
"Yeah. Hey, listen, wanna do lunch sometime?"
"Well, maybe. This week is kinda tight. Are you gonna be here Monday?"
"Yeah."
"Come see me then. I'd love to get together. I'm just so pressed for time now." She looked at her watch and then looked at Jimmy. "I gotta get going. I'll talk to ya...". Just then, Kevin Dunstan, a young lawyer fresh out of law school walked by and Amy followed him.
"Hey Kevin," Amy said flirtatiously.
"Oh, what's goin' on Amy?"
Kevin was tall and muscular. He looked as though he had played basketball in college. He had fluffy blond/black hair on the top and his sides were faded. He sported side burns and was clean shaven. Many of the women at the club had asked him out, but he had only gone out with a few of them. Although he was about 26, he didn't look much older than 20.
Amy's eyes lit up and she had a big Kool-Aid smile on her face. "Hey Kevin. How are you?"
"Just chillin'. Ya know, just starting my workout."
The two just kept talking and Jimmy was left standing by himself so he went over to where his towel was and grabbed it. As he was walking away, he heard Kevin ask. "Hey girl, what's up for the weekend?"
"Nothing. I've got no plans."
"Well, let's get together. Have a drink."
Her smile got bigger and her voice was a bit shaky with excitement. "Yeah, that'll be great...."
Jimmy headed for the steam room and just sat there with his hands in his head.

Jimmy's disappointment only lasted a couple of days because he had also been talking to Delia, one of the aerobics instructors there and she seemed interested in him. She had light brown hair and an athletic frame. She was friendly and always seemed happy.

The following week came and Nick Stephenson called Jimmy at the office to tell him that Johnny Delanie had been chosen to become district Manager.

Jimmy held the phone tightly. "I figured he'd get the job."

Nick tried reassuring Jimmy by saying, "Look, there are a dozen guys retiring next September. There are bound to be spots for ya."

"Yeah, okay, I suppose. All right. I gotta go Nick. Got a lot of work to do."

That night he waited for Delia to finish teaching her aerobics class to talk to her.

"Hey, Delia, how are you?"

Delia smiled as if she were genuinely happy to see Jimmy. "I'm doing fine. How are you Jimmy?"

"Good. You must be tired tonight. Didn't you teach the kick boxing class before you did the step class?"

She took a towel, wiped the sweat off her brow, and gave a sigh. "Yeah, but I'm really not all that tired. It's usually when I teach two step classes in row. So how are things going for you? You are a manager at The Rent a Video right?"

Jimmy looked a bit embarrassed. "Yeah, but I'm up for district manager in a little while though."

"Wow. Sounds good."

"So, how was work for you today."

"Well, ya know Jimmy, some times I get so tired of the kids and other times I love them to death."

"So, you teach kindergarten?"

"Yeah."

"How do you like teaching?"

"I love it. There's nothing else I like doing better than teaching."

"I thought about teaching before I got out of the Navy, but chose the business profession instead."

THE FINEST MOMENT

"What made you think about becoming a teacher?"

"Well, they were always having us do some promo stuff at the Y so part of our duty when we weren't deployed was to help young kids with swimming. The Navy wanted to appeal to the public so they had us do that. Well, I enjoyed working with the kids."

"Why didn't you pursue that dream?"

"Well I didn't think I could do it. I figured that I couldn't make a career out of it. Also, I wanted to run a corporation or own my own business. Wanted to make 'lots of money. I needed experience to do that so I took a job as a manager at a video rental store. Now I regret it because I can't even get a business loan with my bad credit due to my student loans. Oh, I don't know if I could deal with kids. If I did teach, I'd have to teach at the high school level."

"You ought to pursue it, Jimmy. I think you'd be good with the kids."

"Do ya think?"

"Yup, I think."

"Maybe I could coach football, and maybe swimming."

"You'll never know until you try it."

They talked for a while and got acquainted a little bit more. Over the next few months Jimmy and Delia began dating. Delia had recently gotten out of a bad relationship so she wanted to simply just go out to a movie or to dinner; but she made it clear that she wasn't into any funny business.

THE FINEST MOMENT

PAINFUL REVELATION

Jimmy began having trouble sleeping and when he did sleep, he had bad dreams about Panama. He often awoke after seeing his friends dying on the air strip that dreadful day in 1989. The dreams began shortly after he began looking at his trophy table and photo albums. Although he was inspired by the sight them, the dreams of terrible things came. He continued to have nightmares every night; but, one night after he looked at his photo album and saw a picture of his first communion, he drifted into a really bad dream. Jimmy woke up in a cold sweat. He had had a nightmare, but couldn't remember what it was about. All he knew was that he felt scared and angry after he had them. His sleeplessness caused night tremors and eventually he woke up with cold sweats. It got so bad that he had to seek counseling. He went to the VA Hospital after work and spoke with Anne Shelton.

She greeted him with a smile. "How are you Jimmy?"

"I'm okay. I guess."

"What brings you here?" She bent over and removed some books that were on a chair and told him to have a seat.

"Well, I've been having nightmares and trouble sleeping."

"Okay." She jotted some notes down in her notebook. "Tell me about the dreams."

"I don't remember what they were about. I just know that they were bad enough to make me shake and sweat."

"Do you remember what you were thinking about before you went to bed?"

"I dunno. I guess, I. Ahh. I was looking at some old photo albums. I've been looking at my trophies a lot and thinking about the past."

"How far back were you thinking? Concentrate, Jimmy."

"I dunno. I don't know, I tell you."

"Jimmy? We're going to go back to the time when you can last remember. Okay? How far back can you remember?"

"I. Ah. when I was about 10, I guess."

"Tell me about the times when you were 10 years old."

"I went to school and played baseball."

"Did you like school?"

"Yes. I loved it."

"Tell me about your friends."

"I had a lot of them."

"Were they all boys or did you have any girls that you liked?"

"Mostly boys. There was one girl who was very cute. But, I was too shy to talk to her."

"How about the adults in your life. Who were they?"

"My parents. aunts and uncles. I was also an alter boy. There was a priest who was very friendly. He used to..."

"He used to...What?

"He used to hug me, and give me kisses on the cheek."

"How often did he hug you?"

"Every time he saw me."

"How often did he kiss you?"

"All the time."

"Did you ever spend any time alone with him?"

Jimmy put his head down, and began crying.

She looked up from her notes. "Let's end for now. We'll talk about this later.

I'm going to prescribe an anti-depressant and some anti-anxiety medication for you. Come see me in a week. "

Jimmy finished up and went home. The medication worked well. It helped him fall asleep quickly and the next day he felt better

His paychecks got smaller and he had to take on a second job working at UPS at night as a package handler. This extra income was still not enough to pay his bills. One morning, Nick was waiting in Jimmy's office and he didn't look very happy. He motioned for Jimmy to come in and sit down. As usual, he was chain smoking and the sweat was pouring off his body.

THE FINEST MOMENT

"Jimmy." Nick said. "I got this…Let's see." He pulled out a piece of paper and looked at it. I got this letter from the home office. It's telling me that the government is garnishing your wages."

Jimmy shook his head and said, "Yeah, so what's your point?"

Nick stood up and walked over to Jimmy and pointed in his face. "Well, this explains your performance. Do you know how much paperwork and headaches this is gonna be for me?" Nick let out a sigh and lit another cigarette. "This is such a hassle for me. Do you know how much trouble you've caused me? Do ya James? It's a no brainer that you've probably taken on a second job to compensate for the lost wages. Do you have a second Job? The room was silent. Where ya workin' Jimmy?"

"UPS. Nights. Okay?"

"No, it's not okay. God damned it. You know the policy James." His voice got louder and bolder with each syllable. "You know that you are not, I repeat, not allowed to have a second job. It is totally against regulation. I could terminate you right now. Listen to me and listen good. A second job hinders your performance as a manager, not to mention your chances of becoming a district manager."

"Oh, save it. You don't give a rat's ass about my promotion. Someone complained that I've been slacking and you're here to cover your own ass. Isn't that right Nick?"

Nick drew on another cigarette and demanded, "If you must know. Your turnover rate is at an ultimate high. The cleaning company you hired is incompetent. You've got the record for having the most late video returns. Business is bad. The numbers are low. This office is not making any money. Some of it's not your fault. I know that. Sometimes it's just bad luck. You're not a lucky guy. We may have to shut this office down. If we do that, guess what, pal? You're demoted to assistant manager."

"I have to keep this second job. I have to. I need the money. I promise I'll work harder. I'll get everything back to order. You'll see. Please don't make me quit my second job."

"Then you'd better pay attention to detail around here. Do I make myself clear?"

Jimmy sighed and then said, "Yeah, no problem. I'll put more effort into running the store."

"Don't make me come back here again Jimmy, unless it's to promote you. I'm afraid I've already put in the names of 12 candidates to fill the positions of District Managers in New England. The old Managers have been promoted due to retirements. I'm afraid I couldn't recommend you Jimmy. Not now. You'd better start taking care of business here. You need to show some responsibility."

Jimmy rolled his eyes, sighed, and fought the tears that were breaking. "Come on, Nick, I told you. Can't you put my name in? If you do that, I'll be making about 35 thousand dollars a year. I could quit my other job."

"I've got to go, James. Remember what I said. Don't be such a fuck-up. Maybe if you'd pay your bills..."

"Maybe if I got paid..."

Nick put his hand up. "I gotta go. Remember, get your shit together, you piss ant. I've got you under my thumb, tough guy." He walked away mumbling."I'll show that tough military guy who's boss."

Jimmy just sat in his chair with his head in his hands as he wondered what his next move was going to be. That night Jimmy went back to his apartment and looked at his football helmet. He picked it up, held it in his hands, and remembered a time when he put an un-Godly hit on an opponent and knocked him down. The kid hit the ground so hard, he broke his collar bone. Jimmy remembered the time in Panama when he aimed his rifle at his enemy and squeezed the trigger. He could literally see them dropping one by one. He took pleasure in knowing that he had power. He had the power of life or death over his opponent and now his energy was focused on Nick. He thought out loud," I hope that fucker burns in hell." He felt an enormous amount of strength. It was a feeling of absolute power. He felt the same way he felt when he knocked his opponent on the ground and mowed down his enemy one by one. Jimmy was certain that he would some day have the same power to break free of the hold Nick had on him.

THE FINEST MOMENT

Jimmy woke up the next day to the sound of the phone ringing. He picked it up, and wiped his face. "Hello?"

"Hey, Uncle Jimmy. It's Anita."

"Hey kid. What's goin on?"

"We don't have school today and I was wondering if you had to work."

"No, today is my day off."

"What are you doing?"

"Well, I gotta go to the bank. I want to try to get a checking account. What are you doing?"

"Just hangin' around. I'm bored."

"Well, do you want to go to the bank, and then maybe go to the mall?"

"Yeah, sure. Let me see if mom will let me go. Hold on."

Jimmy waited and continued to rub the sleep out of his eyes.

"Uncle Jimmy? I can go with you. Can you pick me up?"

"Yeah sure, I'll be over in a while."

"Okay. See ya then."

Jimmy got ready and headed over to pick Anita up. When they got to the bank, they waited in the lobby for about a half an hour. Anita jumped from chair to chair restlessly. "How long is it going to take? We've been here forever."

A woman came over. "Hi, my name is Patrice Longfellow. How may I help you?"

Jimmy stood up from his chair and motioned for Anita to follow. "My name is Jimmy O'Neal and I'd like to get a checking account."

"Sure. Right this way Mr. O'Neal." She looked at Anita and smiled. "Is this your daughter, sir? We do have special offers for families."

"Ah, no. This is my niece, Anita. Do you have special offers for single people?"

"I'm afraid not." She leaned over and whispered in Anita's ear. "How are you today? No school?"

Anita looked up at her and shook her head. "No, ma'am. No school today."

"You are such a polite young girl. I'll bet your uncle is very proud of you."

"Yes, ma'am."

She led them to a corner desk and pointed to the chairs in front, then went over and sat down. "Okay, Mr. O'Neal, do you have some I.D.?"

Jimmy pulled his driver's license and Social Security card out and gave it to her. She turned to her computer and began typing. She looked at the screen, and the smile left her face. "Ah, I see that you have a low credit score, Mr. O'Neal."

Jimmy's face turned red and he squirmed in his seat. "Ah, yes ma'am. My college loans are crazy high. They want a thousand dollars a month, and I can't afford to...Well, I've defaulted."

"Oh, I see. Isn't that the purpose for going to college? To get a job that will allow you to pay your bills?" She took a deep breath. "Well, I wish that there was something I could do, Mr. O'Neal, but I'm afraid that..."

Jimmy stood up and sighed. "That's all right, I totally understand. I'm sorry to have wasted your time."

"Well, you haven't wasted my time, but I suggest that you don't bother going to any other banks. They will tell you the same."

"Yes, ma'am."

"Well, at least Anita learned something valuable today."

"And what's that?" Jimmy asked, impatiently.

She placed her finger on Anita's nose. "Well. To start planning for your future, of course. You don't want to end up like your uncle and have a bad credit report."

Anita pulled away, stood up, and pointed to the woman. "Did you go to college?"

"Ah, no, I didn't."

"At least my uncle has a college degree. He has got a good education. He's a lot smarter than you. And I hope I end up being just like him."

"Yes. I mean...I didn't...No, no...Don't get me wrong...I didn't..."

THE FINEST MOMENT

Jimmy grabbed Anita's hand. "Come on, Anita. Let's get outta here."

Delia was supposed to call Jimmy the same night to arrange plans for the weekend. Jimmy waited up until midnight but the call never came. The next day he decided to go ahead and call her, but when he went to pick up the phone it had been disconnected.

"Shit!" he yelled, "Couldn't pay the bill this month, Fuck!"

He jumped in his truck and went to use the payphone at the Cumberland Farms convenient store. He figured he could work a deal out with the phone company. He waited for about 10 minutes to hear the recorded message before he got through to a representative.

A girl named Shelley answered, "Good afternoon, can I have the number of the phone you're calling about?"

Jimmy gave her all of the information and asked if she could extend the service until Friday when he got paid.

She didn't have good news for him. "I'm sorry Mr. O'Neal, but I need the money now." "Would you like to pay your bill with a phone check?" Her question was asked in a presumptuous, *as if he was going to pay it today*, tone of voice,

"Lady, have you not been listening to me? Hello, I don't get paid till Friday. I cannot pay you until Friday. Hold on. Let me run to the bathroom. Maybe I can shit out the money. Can you cut me some slack?"

"I'm sorry sir, you've been late on payments too many times, and..."

"Oh spare me the details, I make 10 bucks an hour not 20 like you, because that's the only job I can find. Give me a break. You'll have the money on Friday."

"Sir, you don't have to use profanity. If you'd pay your bills..."

"Don't lecture me Bitch. I'm not a kid—I'm just poor."

"This conversation is over, you deadbeat."

She hung up on him so he started banging the payphone against the booth. He drove home; went inside; grabbed a couple of dining room chairs; and hurled them across the room. He hollered, "Those bastards shut me off. I hope they rot in hell. They're gonna pay for this."

Jimmy went to the library and used the computer to email Delia. He had written her to apologize for what had happened. "Delia. I'm sorry that I was not able to take your call. Perhaps you are right. Maybe I should become a teacher and get out of the mess that I am in. I will see you at the gym this week. Can we talk about this? See ya. Jimmy."

That evening at the gym, Delia stopped Jimmy. "Hey Jimmy. I got your email."

"Hey, Dee. Sorry about all of this."

"That's okay. I understand. There may be some positions opening at some of the high schools for next January. They are desperate for teachers and they can arrange something for certification. I gotta run, but call me just before Christmas and I'll let you know about any openings. You're degree is in business, right?"

"Yeah."

"Okay. Gotta run. Call me in."

"Yeah. Gotcha."

"See ya Jimmy."

Jimmy met with his counselor again; but hated having to tell his story even though he knew that it was the only way to begin the healing.

Anne looked at him with sincerity. "Are you doing any better?"

"Yes. Thanks."

"Let's go back to the priest. Tell me what happened."

"Father Flarity took a shining to me. He would hug me and kiss me. Hold me close. One day he called and asked if I could come and help him paint."

Anne handed him a glass of water.

"He was drunk. He pulled my pants down and." Jimmy knew that the only way to get rid of his anxiety was to spit it all out at once. "He was drunk. Beer breath and cigarettes. He had oral sex with me and forced me to get naked and that's when he did it. He had sex with me. He told me that God had a special plan for me and that if I told anybody I would go to hell. So I went over to the rectory every day that summer and did my Godly duties."

THE FINEST MOMENT

"Did you tell anybody?"

"I was too embarrassed and afraid to tell anybody, so I blocked it out."

"How much did you drink with the priest?

"I drank a few beers, then a 6 pack—to deal with it. I drank a case of beer every night when I was in the Navy. I stopped for a year in college. Then I got into pot and Crystal Meth and did that for a year or so."

"How much do you drink now?"

"I don't. It's been about 5 years. I started getting fat and pale and decided to stop. Now that I quit, I can't stop eating."

"Are you going to AA?"

"I used to when I first stopped, but I hate those meetings."

"Jimmy. You need to go to meetings if you want to get better. I want you to go to Sex and love addicts anonymous. There are people there who have been through the same thing as you. I want to meet with you once a week until we can start dealing with this."

That night he called in sick so he go to a Sex and Love addicts anonymous meeting but was disgusted by the things he heard there. Jimmy felt uncomfortable because one of the guys telling his story was Bennet, a priest at St. Katherine's church. Jimmy listened to his story.

"My name is Bennet and I am a Sex addict. I broke my bottom line last weekend when I was in Boston. I drove down the road and saw a young man...He was a prostitute. Well, we had anal and oral sex all night. I felt guilty because I had to say Mass the next day at four pm. Oh, what a mess."

The next man to speak was Jonothan, a priest from Boston. "I broke my bottom line, too. I was traveling to go to a meeting and I stopped at a rest stop. I went in the stall and had oral and anal sex with a man that I never met before."

During the break, Bennet walked up to Jimmy. "Hi. You're new here aren't you? You will like this meeting?" Bennett was smiling at Jimmy. "We are all having coffee at Friendly's after. You should join us. What is your name?"

Jimmy's mouth dropped. "Ah. I'm all set. I have plans after the meeting."

Jonathon walked up to Jimmy and put his arm around him. "Hey, you're new here. What is your name?"

Jimmy looked at Jonathon and then looked at his arm that was around Jimmy's shoulder. "You'd better take your fuckin' hand off me or I'm gonna check you neck size."

"Sorry. I didn't mean to."

Jimmy stormed out of the hall and jumped into his car. When he got home, he checked his mail and saw a letter from the Department of Education's student loan division. They had written him for months demanding payment and finally, last month, they had demanded a payment in full of $60,000 or else they would begin garnishing his wages. There was nothing he could do and he wanted to ignore the letter; but he could not because they had finally begun to take action. The letter read: "Notice of right to garnish wages: According to..."

Jimmy read the letter stating that they would begin taking 40% of his weekly net income beginning June 15th. Jimmy put the letter down ;grabbed his medication; guzzled some water; and fell fast asleep.

Before work he went to see Peter Impollito, a lawyer who was working on other law suits against the Diocese of Boston and Manchester for sexual abuse. Peter was a tall, athletic-looking man in his late 40's. He had graying black hair and wore a polo shirt and khaki pants.

"Jimmy. My name is Peter," he said, extended his hand out. "Come on in to my office and my secretary will take notes." Jimmy sat down and made himself comfortable.

Peter pulled a chair up next to Jimmy. "Okay. I know it's probably painful, but I need to hear your story. You can stop and take a break if you need to."

Jimmy put his head on his hand and looked down. "I was molested," he took a deep breath and continued, "by a group of priests."

Peter removed his glasses from His face and set them on his desk.

THE FINEST MOMENT

He waited a few minutes and watched as Jimmy sobbed and shook.

"Okay. Go on."

Jimmy wiped the tears from his eyes and took a deep breath. "I was an alter boy when I was nine years old and the priest took a shining to me." He continued with his story.

The summer passed quickly because Jimmy was working day and night to keep up but he it was proving impossible. He was two months behind on his truck payment and a month behind on rent. Before he knew it, October had arrived and Jimmy hadn't paid his rent since July. Jimmy had gotten a number of overdue notices from Arlando Spinelli, the complex owner, and it was time to meet with him. It was a Monday and was raining harder than it had in months when Jimmy went to talk to Arlando. Jimmy walked into the office and heard voices in the back. The sound of a woman giggling and a man laughing was clear. Jimmy rang the bell and a minute or so later a pretty woman of about 35 came dashing out. The buttons on her shirt were not aligned and her hair was messed up. She appeared a bit frazzled and short of breath.

She smiled. "Hi, what can I do for you?"

Jimmy looked at her shirt, then at her, and gave her a pathetic look. "Yeah, get me Arlando Spinelli. I need to talk to him."

Her mouth opened, but nothing came out. She combed her fingers through her hair in a feeble attempt to straighten it out. "Ah, and you are?"

"Tell him Jimmy. Jimmy O'Neal is here to see him. He'll know who I am."

"Okay. Be right back."

Jimmy went over to the glass door and looked out at the rain falling onto the pavement. Little white drops of ice hit the pavement steadily. Although it was around two p.m., it was dark and it looked as though night would fall soon. Suddenly, the woman came out and told Jimmy that Arlando would see him. Miraculously, her buttons were straightened and her hair was pulled up. She showed Jimmy into the office; and when he walked in, Arlando was sitting at his desk Arlando was about 40 years old. He was thin and had short, dark black hair. His eyes were hazel and his skin was dark.

He motioned for Jimmy to come in and then pointed to the seat. "Hey Jimmy. How ya doin'?"

"Good."

"I wasn't sure if you was gonna come down and see me."

"Yeah, I've been real busy."

"Jimmy, I don't got a lotta time. I'll get right to it pal. I need all your rent, now. You owe..."

He rifled through his files; found a folder; and opened it. He studied it carefully and then looked up. "You owe me four months rent pal. I need it all A S A P! Kapish?"

"Arlando, I can give you two months rent now and give you the third month's rent on November first."

"Then, that'll still leave you with November's balance and another month's worth."

"Yeah, I know. I can pay you everything in December."

"Ya' know Jimmy? If this were May or June, I could work out a deal. I'm getting too close to the first of the year and all accounts have to be brought up to date by December first."

"Can't you just give me until the middle of December?"

"Look, pal, I'd like to help, but I can't so...,"He laughed and pointed to the door. "I won't. There's the door. I'm pressed for time here and you need to move on. I want all the rent now, Jimmy. I can't be makin' deals with everybody. I got a business to run."

Jimmy stood up. "Oh, come on man, can't you give me a break. I'm working two jobs, because the Department of Ed has garnished all of my..."

Arlando stood up ,adjusted his shirt, and then pointed to the door. "Look, pal, I'd love to listen to your sob story; but I got things I gotta do. You had enough chances, now it's time to pay the piper. I want all my money by the end of the week. Now run along."

"You're an asshole, Spinelli."

"So I hear. Now get the fuck outta here, before you find out what an asshole I am with a shotgun in my hand."

THE FINEST MOMENT

Jimmy looked at him and said, "It's okay that you have shit bags who haven't paid in a year..."

Arlando walked over and stood toe to toe with Jimmy. "Look pal, last warning. You got two seconds to disappear, or I pop ya one right in the eye."

Jimmy stood there and looked into his eyes for a moment, then realized that it wasn't worth fighting a battle he'd never win so he walked away and never looked back.

When Jimmy checked his mail, he saw a letter from his lawyer and opened it:

"Dear Mr. O'Neil:

We hope this letter finds you doing well. We are writing to inform you that your perpetrator, Father Joseph S. Flarity, has passed away and left some incriminating videos in his place of residence. After careful review, the state of N.H. has issued a demand of payment summons in the amount of three million dollars for the damages you've incurred..."

Jim thought for a few minutes about what he had gone through from ages 10 to 14. He remembered how Flarity had taken him on weekend fishing trips and had sex with him repeatedly. Flarity had also prostituted Jimmy to other priests. Flarity told Jimmy that he was serving the Lord. "Our father in heaven created sex for our joy, Jimmy," said Flarity. "And it pleases him that you are being the dutiful son by serving his Godly men's needs. Your rewards will be great if you remain silent and your punishment will be severe if you tell anyone. Do you understand Jimmy?"

Jimmy remained silent and submitted to the Holy Catholic Church for four years. He told his parents that the priests were taking him to the movies or to the arcade. Flarity had made video tapes and sold them to supplement his income. When Jimmy turned 14, his parents moved away and he never saw the priests again. He also shut the incident out completely and never thought about it again until he had gone through an alcohol treatment center while he was in the Navy. Jimmy never blamed God for what had happened. In fact, he had been close to God for many years after that. It wasn't until he had to face the incident that he became bitter. Jimmy continued to read the letter from his lawyer.

"...We do know, however that this money will never heal your spirit."

Jimmy thought of how he would spend his money. He remembered how he had talked with some of his college professors many years ago. They had advised him to buy a duplex home and rent out the one half so that he could pay his mortgage with it. His grandmother had done the same and made quite a profit. He thought about doing the research on this so he decided that he would spend the next day in the library doing an internet search on the market value of vacation rentals. For the first time in many years, Jimmy had feeling of hope.

He thought for a moment and realized that he would need some help managing the money that he would get from his settlement. Suddenly it dawned on him to call Shawn Foley, a college buddy whom he hadn't talked to in years who was sure to help. After everything that they had been through together and the friendship they had, he was certain that Shawn would offer him some good advice. The two of them roomed together in college and studied business. They also had a common bond. Shawn was in the Marine Corps force Reconnaissance team and had trained with the Seals so the two fighting men used to go back and forth about which branch of service was better.

They were both in business management and reaching for the same goal. Jimmy and Shawn had been like brothers during college. Jimmy trusted him and wanted to see him reach his goal. He missed spending time with Shawn and wanted to hang out again. The next day Jimmy went to the library, and looked Shawn's name up on the internet under a people search and found his phone number. As soon as he got it, he went to a pay phone and called him with a pre-paid phone card.

The phone rang and Shawn answered, "Hello."

"Hey, jar head, when you gonna get a real job?" asked Jimmy.

"O'Neal? Is that you?"

"Of course it's me. I'm the only one who could get away with calling you a jar head aint I?"

THE FINEST MOMENT

"How the hell are you, pal?"

"I'm hangin' in there. You know."

"So, what are you up to?"

"I'm a manager at prestigious resort here in Connecticut. The money is real good. I've always wanted to own my own business, but I just got so caught up with climbing my way up the corporate latter here. I woke up one morning; realized I was 30 years old and too damned scared to go out on my own especially with the job security going the way it is. I bought a house about 6 years ago and sold it for more than twice the amount it was worth. I got hooked and have been flipping real estate since. I just passed my test and got my license so I'm just riding the wave. What about you?"

"I'm struggling at a video store right now, but things are going to get better real soon. I'm going to start my own business. Things are going to be good. I can feel it."

"Wow! What's going on?"

"I'm gonna open up my own hotel and make lots of money."

"Whoa!, Slow down, tiger...Where did you get all the money to do this?"

"I'm going to get a settlement around Christmas time

Jimmy took a deep breath. "You know all the hype about the child molestations in the church?"

"Yeah?"

"Remember when I told you that I was,. ." Jimmy paused. "You know...By a priest."

"No way. Get out."

"Seriously."

"Sorry about what happened, but maybe it's time you get paid in full for what happened. Tell me about your plans. Give me the details."

"Well. I'd like to open a hotel and maybe a restaurant. Buy a couple of homes. I'm not quite sure yet."

"Okay. Sounds all right. Just take it slow. How much money are you going to be getting?"

"Two million dollars, Shawn."

"Whoa. That's a lot of coin. Can you handle all of that money?"

"Well, no. That's why I called you. I figured that you could help me."

"When you get the money, put it all in the bank for God's sake. Don't start so big. Maybe you can just buy a duplex home and rent it out for starters so you can get an income from there. Then, you can buy another one and see how that goes. You wanna wait on opening hotels up. You don't want to dive in too deeply just yet."

"That's a lot of money, and I figured we could be partners. You could help me manage my empire."

"Yes, and I will, but you don't even have the money yet."

"I know, but it's a sure bet. The money will be here by Christmas. My lawyer assured me of that."

"Yes, I know. But you want to take it slowly, or you'll lose all that money."

"I know, but I was figuring that we could…."

"I'd like to sit down with you and hash everything out."

"Yeah, that'll be good. I figured that with your marketing skills, you could set up a website and maybe even get an 800 number as well as* advertise in the paper and in the yellow pages. I can give you whatever percentage that you would think would be reasonable."

"That would be good. Maybe the two of us could have a little something to work with. Let's figure out a time to meet."

"Okay. Do you want to go into Boston? Maybe go to O'Mally's and have some grub?"

"That sounds good. Let me see…How about next Saturday?"

"Yeah, around five?"

"Good to go. Hey. How did you find me after all these years?"

"Looked ya up on the internet. Sorry I never called or wrote; but my life was shit and it's just starting to get normal. Whatever that is."

"I understand. I'll see ya next weekend."

"All right, boss, talk to ya later."

Saturday morning had arrived and Jimmy headed out the door

THE FINEST MOMENT

to go to Boston. On his way out, a young woman of about 30 was leaving the apartment down the hall from him. She wore her blond hair in a pigtail and had a tight pair of spandex warm-up pants on. She caught Jimmy by surprise. He gave her a quick hello and she smiled as she hurried toward the front door of the common area. The traffic on I-95 was slow. Everyone was getting an early start on St. Patty's Day. Jimmy parked in one of the garages and headed to O'Mally's Pub that was situated in the basement of Quincy Market. The lights were dim and the air was warm yet stale. The smell of Irish ale brought pleasure to Jimmy's nose, but the ramifications of consuming the libations were sour enough to impel him to have a ginger ale on the rocks. He met Shawn with a strong bear hug and offered him a seat at the table.

"Hey, chief. It's good to see ya."

Shawn looked around as he took his seat. "I see the old place hasn't changed a bit."

"Yup. Still the old place."

"Let me buy you a cold one Shawn."

"Sammie Adams, partner?"

"Oh, yeah.. My good friend Sam."

Jimmy put his hand up and motioned for the waitress to come over.

A young woman of about 24 came over. She was wearing Liz Claybourne perfume which was Jimmy's favorite.

"How ah ya. My name is Sarah. What ya havin'?"

"I'll take another ginger and my friend will have a Sammy."

"Okay. Shoah. Want me to sta't a tab fo-ya?"

"Yes, please and can you bring us a menu?"

"Shoah. Be right back."

Jimmy looked around and had a smile on his face. "Wow. This place sure brings back some memories. Let me tell you what. Remember the time when Shorty bagged that fat waitress who used to work here?"

Shawn laughed and covered his mouth. "Oh, shit. She was nasty. Shorty did like the ones with meat on their bones."

"Do you remember how red started talking trash to those MIT Brats. Oh, those pricks thought they knew it all. Between them and the Harvard pricks..."

"Well, Jimmy, I remember well. Those guys were minding their own business, and Red had a hair across his ass that night."

"Oh, yeah. Old Man O'Mally had to toss him out."

Sarah came with the menus and Jimmy saw instantly what he wanted. Shawn looked at his carefully and they both ordered the steak tips and fries.

Sarah took their order and said, "Okay. I'll bring the ketchup and mustid fo-ya."

Jimmy and Shawn continued to take a drive down memory lane until their meals came.

The smell of the mushrooms, the sauté on the steak and the French fries were pleasing to the senses.

Jimmy cut his steak tips up and said, "Oh. I sure hope it tastes as good as it smells."

The men ate as if they hadn't eaten in a long time.

Shawn paused and chewed his sirloin until his mouth was empty.

Jimmy was anxious to hear about how Shawn could help him create his new empire. "So, tell me more about this Duplex deal."

"Put all of your money in the bank and don't go spending it all. You could buy a duplex in Florida or something—near Disney. I read in money magazine how people buy these homes and rent them out to vacationers coming to Disney. They usually get a couple grand, sometimes even three grand during the busy season. That's three grand a week sometimes."

Jimmy took a bite out of his last fry and swallowed hard. "Wow. That's a lot of green. How much do you think I could get from the house in Florida?"

"The Disney area is big all year round. You might get most of your money in the summer and during school vacations. You'd be surprised how many people visit central Florida during summer vacation and during the holidays. Hell you may even make that much

THE FINEST MOMENT

money during the summer alone. I read an article on how every hotel was full one summer. It's said that even the roach motels were getting over a hundred dollars a night. Oh, yeah. During these times, you could charge three to four hundred a night. The economy is picking up. People are feeling safer now that George W. Bush is opening a can of whoop-ass on terrorism. And when the people feel safe, they travel and spend lots of money."

"Okay, I'm liking what I hear. How are you gonna market this?"

"Networking Jimmy. I create a couple of Web sites, marketed for snow mobilers and skiers. I create a pop up add or send it to various email addresses. It would say something like, "Ski, snowmobile, and enjoy the winter wonderland. Oh I don't know. It would be something catchy. Most of the time, people will be searching vacation rentals anyway and will do a google search My website will pop up with my phone number and boom, it's done. If the guests like their homes, they will tell their friends and so on."

"Wow. Sounds like you know what you're doing. I'm leaving it all up to you. You're the expert."

"Yeah. When you get your money, go to a realtor and buy a house. You'll have to go online to look for places. You can start right away by doing the research. Call the town hall of the Chamber of Commerce and get a listing on the profits from vacation homes. I could probably even give you a website to go to. When you get the house, give me a call. You can email me all the details of your home and maybe a picture so that I can post it."

"Yeah, that sounds fair."

"What about the hotel and restaurants?"

"One thing at a time. See how this goes. Invest your money, so that it will increase, and we'll cross that bridge when we get there."

"Yes. I can feel it. I'm gonna be rich, rich."

"Slow down, Jimmy. Not so fast. Haste makes waste. Try this deal with the vacation rentals and then see how it goes."

"Okay. I know. I'm just so psyched. I can't wait to get started. It's gonna be..."

"I know. It'll be good to have some money at last."

"So, Shawn...How come you never got married?"

"I haven't found the right girl I guess. I've dated a lot and have had a few relationships, but they just never work out. What about you, Jimmy?"

"Well, to be quite honest with you...I've lost my magic. There was a time in my life when I couldn't beat the girls off with a stick. Ah. Now, I don't know. Women just aren't attracted to me."

"Oh, come on now. I'm sure there are lots of women who want you."

"No. Every time I see an opportunity, I end up striking out."

"Well, you can't hit, if you don't swing. Just keep on shooting and you'll make a basket one of these days."

"That's my problem. I have to stop shooting. I've been trying too hard. They see that. Right now, I guess I just want to make a lot of money and have some fun. What do you say that we go out to the ocean sometime and do some fishing? We can go out to Portsmouth. There's also plenty of fishing in my back yard."

"That sounds like fun. Just like old times." Shawn took a swig of his beer and slammed the bottle on the table.

"Let's plan to do some fishing soon."

"Sounds good. Give me a call."

"I will."

Shawn looked at his watch. "I gotta run. One of my buddies has me hooked up with some whore. It's been a long time since I've pounded some skins. I'm gonna bust a new asshole in her."

"You go do that. Make sure you wear you rain coat."

"Yeah. No problem."

A week had passed with Jimmy not being unable to come up with all the money to pay his back rent. So one afternoon when he pulled into the parking lot of his apartment complex, he saw a sheriff's cruiser parked in front of main door. There were two men standing next to the cruiser.

One of the men put his hand out and said, "Are you Jimmy O'Neil?"

THE FINEST MOMENT

"Yes, what's going on?"

"Let me see some I.D."

Jimmy pulled out his driver's license and showed the man.

The man reached in his car and pulled two documents out of a brief case. The first one was an eviction notice and the second was summons to go to court in February of next year to take care of all the back rent Jimmy owed. Most of his neighbors were coming home now and saw the officers standing outside talking to Jimmy. The flashing blue lights on the cruiser didn't eliminate any attention that was brought on to Jimmy already.

He had nowhere to live and had until the end of tomorrow to move. The bank was getting ready to take his truck and he was wondering if it was going to get worse. When Jimmy had finished packing a few personal items into his truck, he went over to Jennifer and Jon's house showed them the letter from the lawyer. He asked if he could stay there until December and borrow a thousand dollars. He promised to repay them when he got his check. He also offered to help out around the house and babysit the kids. They accepted without any hesitation.

Near December, Ford Credit reclaimed Jimmy's truck, but he didn't resent what had happened. His creditor had given him fair warning and the men who took the truck were polite. One of them had commented on how he, too, had lost a car years ago to repossession.

THE FINEST MOMENT

LOSING GROUND

December arrived and Jimmy received a letter from his attorney. His hand shook as he opened it and a chill overcame him. He looked up at the sky and said, "Thank you Lord. I'm sorry I've not done business with you, but I've been so frustrated." He had to sit down and breathe as he began hyperventilating. He thought out loud, "Yes, a check for two million dollars. I don't know what on earth I'll do with so much money. It's only a couple of weeks until Christmas. I can get my shopping done, and get everyone the gifts that they deserve. Jimmy continued to open it as he jumped up and down, bounced around, and paced the floor. He thought out loud, "I gotta take care of my bills. I gotta pay Jon. I want to buy mom and Dad..." When he finally opened the envelope, he didn't see anything that resembled a check. He only saw a letter. It was from his lawyer. As he read, the sweat beaded on his brow.

"Dear Mr. O'Neal: We are sorry to inform you that you will not be receiving compensation at this time. The Catholic Church has reneged on their deal. We are taking them to court and all of their assets will be garnished. Unfortunately, this may take some time. We will know more in a couple of months. The earliest anything may happen will be sometime in the spring. We apologize for the inconvenience."

Jimmy took the letter and ripped it up. He wailed and began crying. He hollered the way a man would if he had just had his leg snapped in half. "What am I gonna do?" He thought out loud. "What am I gonna do?" He lay in his bed and thought about killing himself. His hand was heavy and he just didn't want to live anymore. He thought obsessively about ending his life as he cried himself to sleep.

The next morning when Jimmy awoke, he drove to Portsmouth where he was going to throw himself into the icy ocean. On the way he stopped at one of the country stores along the way to put gas into the old Chevy that John had lent him. He wanted to get drunk enough to be out of his mind so that he would have no fear when he dove into his icy grave. He walked down the aisle of the store and opened the beer cooler. He pulled out a 12 pack of tall boy Budweiser and went to the counter. He placed the beer down and paid for it. As he walked out, he saw a young girl who was about seven years old. She looked up at Jimmy and smiled. Her two front baby teeth had fallen out and she had chocolate on her mouth. Jimmy stopped for a second, and listened.

"Daddy. Can I get something?"
"No, sweetie. You've had enough sweets."
"Come on, Daddy. Please."
"No. Come on, kiddo."

Jimmy headed for the truck and drove to Rye beach where he had gone as a child. There was a spot there that was overwhelmed with rocks. He pulled his truck over and sat there. The sun was going down so Jimmy grabbed the beer and walked out to the rocks where he saw the waves crashing. He looked out at the ocean and popped open a beer. He put his nose over the top and took a sniff. He looked out at the ocean and in the back of his mind, he saw the little girl at the store. He thought about his own nieces and nephews; and, although he had given up hope on ever having his own children, he knew that he had a reason to live. He hurled the bottle into the ocean and threw the rest of the 12 pack in as well. He turned around and got back into the truck; but, the truck didn't start. Jimmy continued to try to ignite it but the old truck failed him. Jimmy walked two miles in the bitter cold until he found a pay phone at a gas station along the road and called Jon to pick him up.

Jimmy spent the next day in his room thinking about what he had tried to do the night before. It was cold and dark outside; and the snow was thickening. Jimmy had to get out of the house. He couldn't take the insanity of the cabin fever so he walked to the convenient store to get some junk food. When he got there, he stood in front of the counter and asked the man for a lottery ticket. Jimmy paid for it

THE FINEST MOMENT

and took a quarter out of his pocket and scratched the gray area. It read, "You are not a winner."

Jimmy laughed and said, "Bull shit. I am a winner," and threw the ticket in the trash.

He remembered the conversation that he had with Delia and realized that he wanted to see if he could find a teaching job.

THE FINEST MOMENT

RAY OF HOPE

Jimmy called her and she told him that she knew of a position at the high school as a business teacher. She said there was a shortage of teachers and that the school district would give him a year or so to get his teaching certification.

He paced the floor as he waited for her call. Finally the phone rang.

Jimmy picked it up and said, "Delia?"

"No, sir, this is Doctor Sharadon, of the Concorde County School District. Is this Jimmy O'Neal?"

"Oh, ah, sorry sir. Yes, sir, what can I do for you?"

"Well, can you get a resume to me this afternoon. I spoke to Delia and she said that you have a degree in business."

"Yes, sir. I do."

"She also said that you are a veteran."

"Yes, sir."

"I am a Vietnam Veteran. I was in the Marines. What branch were you in Jimmy?"

"A Navy Seal, sir."

"Outstanding. I was Force Recon. I fought with Seal Team 3 over in Southeast Asia."

"Did you swim in high school Jimmy?"

"Yes sir, and in college. I also played high school football."

"Outstanding, we are looking for a head swimming coach for the spring and summer. I tell ya what Jimmy...Can you be in my office with your resume at one o'clock?"

"Yes sir."

"I'll look forward to seeing you there."

Jimmy rifled through his closet to find a nice tie and shirt. He got dressed and headed for Dr. Sharadon's office. When he got there, Dr.

Sharadon welcomed him with a death grip of a handshake. He was a tiny man but his arms were solid. He had a goatee and a short haircut. He had that thousand yard stare that the old vets talk about.

He pointed to the chair and told Jimmy to relax. He asked Jimmy to tell him all about his experiences in Panama and Central America. The men shared war stories and talked.

Dr. Sharadon took out a piece of paper and wrote down the number $30,000.

"Jimmy, I'd like to offer you a position as business teacher at Lincoln Academy. I'm going to pay you as a teacher with a few years of experience because you have a military background. The swim coach position will be $1,000.00 a season. It pays well because it is intense; and, frankly, I need a coach that I can keep." He walked over to a trophy case and picked up a football. He looked at it for a moment and put it down. We are state champs at the varsity level you know. We've been winning ball games since I played."

"How about the swim team?" Jimmy asked reluctantly.

"Ah, ha, ha. We haven't won a championship in..." He looked up at the ceiling and closed his eyes. "Oh, about 38 years. ha, ha. We haven't had a winning season in probably 25 years. We win about two or three meets a season. Just can't get the coaching staff to commit themselves. With basketball and Hockey...nobody wants to coach a swim team. So, I have raised the salary Jimmy. I want a Navy seal who has been a competitive swimmer in high school and college to at least get me a few winning meets. I'm not asking for a trophy. Just get my head above water." He patted Jimmy on the back and said, "No pun intended."

"Anyway, Jimmy. If you get the job done, I will raise your coaching salary. What do you say? Do you want the job or not?"

"Yes sir...I'll take it."

"Good, you give me a call after Christmas and get yourself ready to teach."

"And the teaching certification, sir?"

"Yes, you'll have two years to get it. We'll talk about this later."

THE FINEST MOMENT

Dr. Sheradon showed Jimmy the door and said, "Thank you Jimmy. You have a Merry Christmas."

Jimmy went back to the house and told everyone the good news. He called Delia and thanked her. The next morning Jimmy slept in but his telephone woke him. It was Nick at the Video store.

"Hello, Jimmy?"

"Hey, Nick, how are you?"

"Jimmy, what the hell...Where the hell have you been? I tried to reach you and your phone is disconnected. I tried calling your sister but I got a message that the number had been changed and was unlisted." He spoke in his usually condescending tone. "Do you know what time it is?"

"Well, Nick, I'm finished working for you."

"Nice of you to let me know. You could have called. Good luck trying to find a job anywhere, pal. I'll put your name out as being a derelict."

"I'm just extending to you the courtesy you've given me over the years."

"What are you talking about?"

"What am I talking about? Well, to put it lightly...Go jack off to a good magazine, I'm finished putting up with your bull shit. Have a nice life, fat ass," Jimmy said as he hung up the phone.

When Jimmy went to Dr. Sheradon's office later that day to sign his contract, he met with the Principal of Lincoln High School where he would begin teaching. When he finished, he went to see a good friend of Jon's who was a manager at the auto dealer in town. After about an hour, Jimmy was in a new Jeep with no money down. As he drove through town, he decided to take a leap in the dark and went to a local Wachovia bank to try getting a checking account. He met with Teresa Tanyatta. She told him that although his credit was bad, he had enough points to get a checking account with her bank.

She smiled and said, "Well, you are approved. Our bank gives people with poor credit a chance. A lot of banks have been burned because there are a lot of deadbeats who give honest people such as you a bad name. So you are approved if you'll just sign here."

"Great. You're the best."

"Don't worry, Jimmy. You'll get that student loan paid off. I can feel it."

"Thanks. You have a good holiday."

"Merry Christmas."

Jon also had a good friend who had a furnished studio apartment available and was more than happy to let Jimmy stay there for a hundred dollars a week. Christmas was good for Jimmy and he knew that the next Christmas would be even better for him.

THE FINEST MOMENT

THE CHALLENGE

It was Jimmy's first day of teaching, and his first period class was full of seniors. He had about 20 students in the class. As they arrived he greeted them. When the bell rang, they all looked up at Jimmy as he stood in front of the class.

"My name is Mr. O'Neal, and I will be your business law teacher for the rest of the semester." He paced back and forth slowly, stopping from time to time to turn and look at his students. "I want to go over the rules with you. Well actually, there is really one rule that I want to enforce and that is to treat others with respect. When I'm talking, you're not talking. When you're talking, I'm not talking. When another student is talking, we will all show respect and listen to the other student. We will not make harsh comments about anybody here. You will leave the profanity and negative attitude at the door. Are there any questions?"

Kaitlin Blake, a tall, skinny, blonde whose makeup was caked on her face like clay raised her hand and asked, "Do you have any kids Mr. O'Neal?"

Jimmy looked at her with a patient smile. "No, I don't."

"Do you have a girlfriend?"

"Ah, no I don't?"

"How old are you?"

Jimmy walked over, and stood near her desk. "Do these questions have anything to do with my class?"

"Well, I was just wondering. I have an aunt about your age." She turned around and whispered, but was loud enough for everyone to hear, including Jimmy. "When she sees what a nice ass he has she'll..."

"Thank you for sharing Kaitlin, but we need to get back to business." Jimmy went around the room and asked each student to tell him a little bit about himself. It seemed as though these kids were caught up in the simplest dilemmas like, 'how should I break up with my girlfriend, or should I keep cheating on my boyfriend.' He understood these simple dilemmas as he was still caught up in a dilemma that was similar to theirs. Like 'how can I get the girl at the gym to notice me.' Jimmy lived vicariously through his students' eyes and remembered well the peer pressure and adolescent turmoil that they were going through. His memories of high school served him all too well and he felt as though he were a high school student again. The kids felt the compassion of Jimmy. Only children can understand the difference between true compassion and bull shit. Because they were the biggest bull shitters in the world they knew the difference between honest caring and false empathy. Jimmy's was true and it was indicative of the type of teacher that he would become; and the kids knew it.

When he met his team at the pool later that afternoon, he did not have many words for them because the former coaches before were all about fun and games and the 'feel good' coaching method that is not conducive to a winning season. So, he went on the deck of the pool and hollered out, "Okay, let's go...It's time to work."

The kids were all sitting on the far end of the pool jibber jabbering and ignored his command. He remembered talking to the athletic director about why the team always had losing seasons. He learned that the coaches before him were too laid back. They were too easy on the kids and allowed the kids to run their own workouts. He went into the coaching office and came out with a whistle in his mouth. Walking over to the team, he began blowing it and pointed to the pool. They all scurried jumping into the pool and swimming to the shallow end. He trotted over to them the way an angry drill instructor would walk over to a recruit who did not obey his order. He pointed to the clock and said, "We have two hours tonight. We're gonna work. If you don't want to work then hit the shower and I don't ever want to see your face in the pool." He pulled the inkboard over to him and wrote down a few drills that they would do.

"Okay, you are gonna start with a 500 meter Individual medley

THE FINEST MOMENT

warm up. I will look at your strokes and tell you which need the most improvement. Then we will work on those strokes until we get them right. I am Coach O'Neal and that is how you will address me. If we have a losing season, it will not be because I have failed to train you. You will work day and night; and if you lose, it will be because you failed to be disciplined. Now get going." He blew his whistle and pointed to the lanes. As the kids were swimming he took notes. When they were done, he pointed at one swimmer and asked, "What is your name?"

"Brian."

"Okay Brian, hop over into the first lane." He pointed to four other boys and told them to do the same. He separated each swimmer into various lanes. The swimmers in the first lane needed work on the crawl stroke. The swimmers in the second lane needed work on the breast stroke and so on. He learned their names and showed them how to do the strokes properly. From time to time he jumped in and had the kids hop out and watch as he did the stroke correctly. Occasionally he had them do a dry land drill by going to the mats on the deck to practice the stroke movements outside of the pool.

Practice was finally over and he certainly had made no friends. However, he wasn't there to make friends. He was there to win meets. By the look of things, he wasn't sure if he wanted this job. He didn't see any potential in any of the kids and was sure he was doomed to another shit storm he knew all too well. "However," he thought, "what else do have to do with my time? I might as well make the best of it."

The next day at school went smoothly and that night practice was the same. He maintained a stone cold face and an angry disposition about him. Kayleigh Turner, a sophomore, was floundering in the pool when Jimmy tapped her.

"Kayleigh! Hop out. Hop out kid."

He dove into the pool. He surfaced and spit up a little bit of water.

"Watch me Kayleigh. I'm gonna show you what you are doing; then I'm gonna show you how you are suppose to do it." He floundered around and slapped the water down the lane; did a flip turn; and then did a near perfect butterfly stroke.

He jumped out of the pool and looked at Kayleigh. "You see, kid, you gotta work the hips." He began a hip motion that looked like a belly dancer and told her to grab a kick board to work on the Dolphin kick. "If you get your kick down, you will be a master at the fly; but you gotta walk before you run. Okay?"

She wiped her face and nodded in agreement.

"Okay, do it to it!"

He walked over to Phillip Bradley, another sophomore, and tapped him.

"Phillip, slow down, boss, slow down. Your haste is making waste."

He walked around to the other side of the pool and tapped Bill Haley.

"Bill. Bill. Hey. Listen."

Jimmy knelt down and looked Bill in the eye. "You gotta point your toes chief. Ya gotta point your toes. Grab the kickboard and work on it for the rest of the night. Just kick. Kick, kick, kick. Okay?"

Billy nodded and hustled to the kick board.

Jimmy hustled over to Kisha Thompson and tapped her.

"No, Kisha. No, no, no."

"What, what, what? Coach O'Neal?"

"Look at your pull..." He made a reaching and pulling movement with his arm. "You have to form a question mark in the air. Come out."

She looked at him and rolled her eyes, and sighed. "Whaaat, coach?"

"Make the movement with me, now, okay. Ready?"

"Ah, okay, already, okay...."

"Reach, Kisha, reach and pull. That way you can pull the water and the mass of the water will glide you through so you don't have to work so much."

"Oh, whatever."

She went over to grab a kick board and hopped in and worked on that single movement with her arm.

THE FINEST MOMENT

"Ray..." Jimmy yelled. "Ray!" Jimmy went over and tapped Raymond Dionne. "Ray?"

"Ah, yeah coach?"

"Why are you bending your legs?"

"Was I bending them?"

"Ah....yup."

"Yeah, I know coach. Grab a kickboard.. Gotcha."

Jimmy walked around the pool and grabbed his face. "Oh, shit, what have I gotten myself into?"

He looked at the clock and noticed that it was getting close to 8:00 and wondered where the time went.

The next couple of weeks passed and Jimmy felt that things were going well with the teaching; however, he was taking two steps forward and 20 steps back in the pool. He was ready to throw in the towel when he looked in his mailbox at school and found a card addressed to him. It read, "Thanks coach. I've never been much of a swimmer and probably never will be; but you haven't given up on me." Kayleigh. Jimmy sat in the chair in the teachers lounge and realized how much power this simple card had. He was ready to give up on himself and he got a thank you card from a kid whom he had not given up on. This was a pleasant surprise and a good way to begin his February vacation.

The next day he got up and checked his mail. He opened a letter from his lawyer stating that he would be getting a check within the next few days. He raced to the library and went online to look at duplex homes on Lake Winnepesaukee. He was certain that the check from his lawyer would find him soon. As he browsed, he saw a good deal for $200,000.00. It was a real fixer upper and he had no carpentry skills by any stretch of the imagination. He did, however, have brothers-in-law who did so he figured he would call them and have them go with him to look at the place.

Jimmy called Jennifer's house to see if Jon was home and Becca answered,

"Hello."

"Hey, kid. What's new?"

"Hey, Uncle Jimmy. When are you coming over?"

"Well, I was going to come over today. I wanted to see if your daddy was home."

"What time are you coming?"

"Oh, in about an hour. Is your dad there?"

"Yeah, hold on. Hey, I'm getting a new rabbit this weekend."

"No way, get out."

"Yes, and he is white and has a little spot on his face."

"So, what are you gonna name him?"

"I don't know. I'm still thinking about that."

"How about Bugs Bunny?"

"No, silly, there is already a rabbit with that name."

"Hey, how do you catch an unusual rabbit?"

"Ah, um. I don't know."

"U-nique up on him."

"Huh? I don't get it."

"I'll explain it to you later. Can you get your Dad?"

"Yup. Hold on. I love you."

"I love ya too kid. Bye."

Jimmy heard Becca in the background yelling for her dad. A few minutes later Jon got on the phone.

"Hello."

"Jon…"

"What's new?"

"I've got a deal for you."

"Oh, yeah. What's the deal, Wheel?"

"Well, I am thinking of buying a fixer upper duplex. I just got my settlement and I wanted you to come look at it with me."

"Where is it?"

"It's on Lake Winnipesauke."

"Oh, yeah? How much is it?"

"It's $200,000.00."

"Okay. Who's gonna fix it up for you?"

"Well, I don't know anyone who does such a fine job at fixing places up like you Jon."

THE FINEST MOMENT

"Okay, I get the point. Come on over and we'll take a look at it."

"Okay. Be over in about an hour. See ya."

Jimmy called the Lakes View Real Estate office in Laconia and set up an appointment with Roger Thurman, one of the local agents.

Jimmy and Jon arrived home that was rundown but had a bird's eye view of Lake Winnipesauke. The snow plow hadn't been there and they had to walk trough 2 feet of snow to get to the porch. Roger Thurman arrived and met the two men on the porch.

"I see ya found the place all right." He put his hand out and said, "I'm Roger. Nice to meet you."

Jimmy and Jon shook his hand and moved to the side to let him open the door.

"As you can see, gentlemen, the place needs some work," said Roger, as he pounded on the walls and stomped his foot on the floor, "..but it's solid. Solid, I tell you. It was built about 20 years ago and was only used for the summer season."

Jon walked around feeling and grabbing every nook and cranny in the place.

Jimmy walked over to the sink and asked, "How's the plumbing?"

Roger walked over and said, "It's good. I had the utility company turn it on." He turned the faucet knob and hot water came out. There's plenty of hot water. There's an Artesian well in the back. The toilets work and so do the showers. A little paint and cleaning and this place will be in good shape."

Jon continued to look around and banged on the walls and saw that they were solid. He went outside and looked at the siding that was falling off and saw that the paint was peeling.

He walked back in said, "Well, the siding is toast and the shingles on the roof have seen better days."

Roger looked around and said, "Yes. That is true. But the house is solid with a good foundation."

Jimmy pointed to the door and said, "Roger, just give me a few minutes while I go outside and talk to my brother in law."

"Sure. You guys take your time."

"Well, Jon. What do you think?"

"Well. Tell him you'll give him 150 even. It needs a lot of work."

Jimmy looked around and scratched his head. "Okay. Yup. I'll tell him."

Jimmy walked inside. "Well, Mr. Thurman, my brother-in-law has been in the business of carpentry for a long time and says this place needs a lot of work. I'll give you $150,000.00 for it."

Roger put his hand on Jimmy's back and said, "Well, ya know Jimmy. This house is right on the lake and I got an offer last week for $200,000.00."

"Okay. Well, thank you for your time, Mr. Thurman. I know that I can find a better deal if I look hard enough."

Roger paused for a few minutes and said, "Well, I like ya Jimmy. How about $195,000.00?"

"You have a nice day, Mr. Thurman. If someone has claimed the place for 200, then you should take it."

"Well, Mr. O'Neal, it's not a sure thing yet. I tell ya what, 190, and the place is yours."

Jimmy grabbed Jon and they started heading for Jon's pickup. He turned around and said, "Mr. Thurman. Give me a call if you want to sell the place for a 150. See ya."

Jimmy got back to his apartment, and felt as though he should have said okay to the 190 deal. He felt discouraged knowing that he probably would not find a better deal anywhere else.

A week later, Thurman called. "Hey Jimmy. Give me 200 for the place. I gotta make a profit. It's business. I just can't sell it to you for 150. I want to be completely honest with you. I need to break even and I won't do it for 150."

"Not a problem, Mr. Thurman."

"I'm losing my shirt on it, but you got a deal. Come on down and sign the papers when you get time

"Okay, thanks, Roger."

Jimmy, however, did not receive his long awaited check from the

THE FINEST MOMENT

lawyer. Instead, 2 days later, he received a letter stating that he would only be getting $50,000.00 sometime in early June. Jimmy picked up the phone and called his mother. She always knew how to make him feel good when he was feeling down.

"Hey, Mom. It's Jimmy."

"Hey, Jimmy. How are you?"

"Good. How is the weather up there?"

"It's not bad."

"So, when are you going to move down here?"

"I don't know——- maybe someday. Where is Dad?"

"He's working part-time at Jiffy's grocery. You know, to get a little extra money."

"I just wish there was something that I could do so that he doesn't have to work any more. I just want you guys to be fully retired."

"Well. He doesn't mind it, and it keeps him busy."

Jimmy and his mother talked for a while until he had to go because he had another call.

February vacation was over and the following week was routine. He lectured and gave out some activities for his students to do. He had wondered why things were going well for him in the classroom, but terrible in the pool. His team had lost their first few meets. After all, he had never taught before; but he had spent a lot of his time in the water. Yet this was the area in his new career that hurt the most. Suddenly it dawned on him. I need to teach my swim team. Instead of practice, he held a class. He showed a video with Olympic swimmers demonstrating their techniques. Over the course of the next couple of weeks, he held classes instead of swim sessions. The students took notes on the aspects of swimming that were difficult for them. He had talked Dr. Sheraton into hiring two former college swimmers who swam for the Master's swim team at the local YMCA. He told Dr. Sheradon that he could pull the money from his coaching salary and pay them; but Dr. Sheradon somehow found the money to pay them and did not have to take the money from Jimmy's salary.

Although the team was on its way to having a winless season, Jimmy had seen a great deal of improvement in his swimmers. He continued to persist, and at the end of each practice session, he had wondered where the time went. He was enjoying spending the time with his kids. It filled the empty void that he had in his life and he liked the way his team was improving.

THE FINEST MOMENT

GOOD THINGS JUST KEEP GETTING BETTER.

The fifth swim meet had arrived and Jimmy gave his team one simple suggestion. "I want you to go out there and have fun. This is what it's all about. You have been working diligently over the past few weeks. You have worked long hours tirelessly. Now you are in shape and you are good. Let all of that hard work pay off tonight and just enjoy swimming because you love to swim.

Well, they took his advice and won the meet. Over the course of the next few weeks, his team had won 5 swim meets in a row. That was the first time they had done this in many years. He was glad that he hadn't given up on them. In fact, he was living vicariously through them. He found that he had an energy that he hadn't possessed since college. He would stay after school grading papers or preparing assignments; then workout at the gym before going to practice. He was working at his career and on his personal growth nearly a hundred hours a week. He had lost about 40 pounds and was feeling invincible.

His team had only six more meets left until the season ended. He wanted them to win so badly that he wanted to swim in the meet with them and help them to win. Instead, he went to the gym and swam in the pool with the same intensity that he would have if he was swimming in those meets next to those kids. Jimmy's determination level had elevated higher than ever before. He looked at his trophies and the plants that made them shine. He felt as though his students were the flowers and plants of his own life. He was a dusty old medal or trophy that just sat there until he began teaching and coaching. Now they made him shine. He touched an azalea plant that sat on the table and put his football shirt on. He grabbed his helmet and again thought of the times when he had been at his best in life. He closed his eyes and visualized his kids winning their meets.

ROBERT W. BRITT

It was a windy Saturday when he and his team got on the bus and headed to Bentley High school for a meet against six schools. Everyone was nervous and jittery that day. As the team got on deck, Jimmy huddled them together and they all reached out their hands to touch his. He felt a great deal of power and energy being released from his body. He felt as though the courage and strength had transcended to their hands. Sort of they way his buddies must have felt when he led them into the relentless jungle of Panama. The fear had left his swimmers as Jimmy exerted his enthusiasm. "Okay, okay...We can do this. You can do it. Yes, there is no reason why you cannot win today. Go get em."

Kayleigh was on the starting block and looked over at Jimmy. He walked over to her and reaching out, shook her hand. He had tears in his eyes and they rolled down his face.

"Kayleigh, you told me earlier in the season that you probably won't ever be much of a swimmer. Well, kid, you were wrong. Dead wrong. You are the best damned swimmer that I have and I am proud of you. Give 'em hell today." Although Kayleigh was far from the best swimmer with her techniques (in fact, she had the worst technique on the team), she was the most dedicated person he had ever seen. He felt sincere and honest when he told her that she was the best swimmer on the team. He meant it because she practiced with the most tenacious attitude he had ever seen. She was determined to get better and had done everything Jimmy had asked of her.

She smiled and fought the tears as her lip crunched up. She looked up at her dad who had just won a bout with cancer as he sat on the bleachers earnestly watching. "Thanks coach. This is for my dad and this is for you. I want to thank you both so much for showing great courage through tough times."

The buzzer sounded and she dove in. Amazingly enough, something about Jimmy's touch made all the difference in the world. She had felt the power of belief that he had in her and had felt the weight of her father's stare so somehow a miracle was performed today. She did a perfect dolphin kick and eased her fingers into the water to perform a near perfect butterfly. She pounded the water with everything

THE FINEST MOMENT

she had—with all her love, all her frustration, all her passion, and all of her skill. She had left her opponents way behind and, for the first time in her life, she ended her race victoriously.

The season had ended with the team winning 10 meets and losing 8. Jimmy had done what Dr. Sheradon had asked him to do. He had trained these young athletes to simply have a winning season. However, at the banquet he gave praise to his young assistance coaches and the parents who helped along the way. He also thanked Dr. Sheradon and his friend Delia for giving him the opportunity to coach. But, most of all, he thanked the kids for sticking with it and believing in themselves.

Jimmy had a couple of weeks off before the summer season began so he called Shawn and invited him down for a couple of days. Shawn arrived with a bear hug and a smile and, of course, a six pack.

"Jimmy. It's good to see you. Where is the fridge?"

Jimmy pointed in the direction of the sink. "It's right over there. It's small, but it'll do."

Shawn opened the fridge and put began placing his cans neatly in the refrigerator. "Where's all the food Jim?"

"Ah. I haven't had a chance to go shopping yet. I eat out a lot and maybe have a sandwich once in a while."

"You still teaching?"

"Yeah."

"Ya gonna stick with it?"

"For a while. I figure that now...Well, I'm not going to get what I thought I'd get from the settlement and I can't start the hotel business so I'll stick with the teaching. I'll try to get someone to rent the other half of the duplex nine months out of the year." Jimmy sighed. "I suppose that's what I'll do."

"It's all for the better."

"What's that?"

"It's good that you didn't get as much as you thought you would. This way, it forces you to move slowly."

"Well, I'm still grappling at trying to understand that concept, but I can see where you're going."

Shawn took a slug of his beer. "Yup. Trust me. Slow and easy wins the race."

"Come on. Let's get outta here and go do something."

The summer season started and there were only about a fourth of the winter team members that went out for it. However, the summer season was more or less an extended practice for the fall and didn't count for anything except the feeling of winning a few meets here and there. Jimmy wanted to convince Dr. Sheradon that Kayleigh, Brian, and Kisha had a great deal of potential and that they should go to a swim camp in Rhode Island for the summer; but it would be costly.

Jimmy went to his office and met with him about the matter. Dr. Sheradon met Jimmy with a smile and a pat on the back.

"Come on in, Jimmy. Come on in. Take a seat."

"Thank you, sir, don't mind if I do."

"Can I get you some coffee? Tea?"

"No thanks. I'm all set."

"Congrats on a great season. You did a fine job with those kids."

"Thanks. They worked really hard."

"Yes, indeed. What's on your mind Jimmy?"

"I have a couple of athletes with enormous potential and there's a camp in Rhode Island that is run by Olympic and collegiate swim coaches. There are also former Olympic swimmers there to assist them. My athletes would benefit from this."

"Yeah. Okay. What is the name of it, Jimmy?"

"It's called the URI, International Training Camp."

"Well, you see a great deal of potential in these kids?"

"Yes, sir. I do."

"Okay, how much is in going to cost me?"

"Two thousand dollars each."

"Wow! That is a great deal of money."

"Yes, sir, but these kids are good athletes and it would benefit the team."

"Okay, Jimmy. I'll check my funding. Perhaps there is money

THE FINEST MOMENT

somewhere in the budget. Yes, I'm going to take your word for it. Let me get back to you on that. Okay?"

"All right. Thank you, sir."

"No...Thank you Jimmy. You have put our swim team on the map and I expect great things from you next season. I'll call you."

"Thanks. Take care."

"See ya, Jimmy."

Jimmy spent the early part of his summer swimming laps at school and coaching his team in the afternoon. Kayleigh, Brian, and Kisha were approved for summer camp and the rest of his swimmers were training diligently for the fall season.

Summer ended and school had started in the usual way. Jimmy was happy to see his new students. Now that he had a semester of teaching under his belt, he was relaxed and confident. He introduced himself and laid out the ground rules right away. He was anxious to get to know each of his students and to develop a rapport with them. During lunch, however, a couple of the seniors had gotten into a fight. They had some unfinished business that wasn't resolved during the summer months so they decided to hold trial and conviction right in the cafeteria when Jimmy was on duty. Jimmy pushed his way through the mob while Jake Summers and Russ Calvin were exchanging blows. Russ grabbed Jake and threw him into a student who was sitting next to the glass pane. The kid tried to stand up but his chair and his ass broke the glass pane. Russ was getting ready to deliver another blow when Jimmy grabbed him from behind. Russ was about 6 feet 3 inches and had a muscular physique. A burst of adrenaline enabled Jimmy to put Russ into a head lock. Jimmy pulled Russ back and called out his name.

"Russ. Russ. Russ. Calm down, kid. Calm down." Jimmy marched backward, as Russ stomped on his feet. Jimmy finally got Russ in a neutral area and continued to call out his name. "Russ. Russ. Calm down." Russ continued to swing left and right into the air until he could swing no more. Jimmy led him into the hall where Bryson Bennet, the school security police, took hold of the angry young man. Jimmy ran back over and fought his way through the mob.

"Everybody get back! Get back!" Jimmy aid as he pushed through the mob and directed them to their seats.

"Go back. Get back to your seats right now. Get back." Some of the other teachers were pushing through the crowd as Jake wiped himself off. He had blood all over his shirt and his face was mangled. Blood was pouring from his nose so the school nurse rushed over to him.

Swim practice that night went much smoother for Jimmy than his day at school. The kids were happy to see him and were already programmed to Jimmy's coaching style so they knew what was expected of them. Jimmy ended practice early and had the kids go to one of the classrooms where they would write down the name of the person whom they thought would make a good captain. He met with each of them one on one in a separate classroom to discuss their choices. The person with the most votes was Kayleigh Turner. She was the most improved swimmer on the team and her determination from last season as well as the summer season had earned her the position of team captain. Jimmy was happy to announce her victory and reminded the team that they needed to listen to their new captain the same way they would listen to him.

The next day in school Jimmy was giving a lecture to his senior class on personal management. He remembered how his former boss, Nick, at the video store had treated him and he wanted to stress to his students that they needed to be fair to all of their employees. Veronica Patten kept tapping Virginia Diez on the shoulder to show her a love note that she had gotten from Jason Keniston. Virginia was trying to listen to what Jimmy was saying and kept pushing Veronica's hand away. Jimmy walked over to Veronica and snatched the note from her hand. He looked at her and said, "Veronica, leave Virginia alone. Just…Just leave Virginia alone. He began singing the song by Rod Stewart. 'Leave Virginia alone.'

The entire class began laughing and singing, "leave Virginia alone. Just leave Virginia alone."

That night at practice Jimmy ended up in the pool working with individual swimmers on their strokes. He swam over to Kisha

THE FINEST MOMENT

Thompson and told her to kick her feet. "Come on Kisha. I know you had a great summer, but I expect a lot of great things from you this season. Now straighten out your legs. She just rolled her eyes at him and said,

"Whatever, coach O'Neal. I got it. Kick the feet. Point the toes."

"That a girl."

He swam over to Brian Bishop and scolded him. "Brian. Brian. No, no, no. You have got to slow down a little. Extend your body. You were doing so well last season to correct this. What happened?"

"Was I going too fast coach?"

"Yes. Now slow it down....And reach....Reach....Reach. Okay?"

"Got it coach...Reach."

"Now you got it."

Jimmy got out of the pool and on the deck and hustled over to Phillip Bradley who was gasping for air and crying.

"Phillip. Phillip. Are you okay?"

Phillip was wheezing and leaning over the side of the pool. "Ahhh, I need my spray. I can't breathe."

Jimmy ran into the coach's office and grabbed a bottle of spray. Phillip was having an asthma attack so Jimmy rushed over to him and gave the spray to him.

"Here ya go, kiddo. Take this."

Phillip inhaled a couple of times and began breathing normally. Jimmy patted him on the head and said, "Go over to the bench and relax. Catch your breath."

Jimmy continued to walk around tapping his swimmers out and correcting their mistakes.

THE FINEST MOMENT

A WINNING EDGE

The day of the swim team's first meet of the season fell on a warm September Saturday morning. Before Jimmy got dressed he put his Aerosmith C.D. in and played the song "Dream On." He held onto his football helmet as he listened to the words: "Sing winner, sing for the years. Sing for the laughter sing for the tears. Sing winner just for today. Never tomorrow, the good Lord will take you away. Dream on...Dream on...Dream until your dreams come true."

Jimmy held on tightly to his medal and realized that there was a time in his life that he had been so brave and yet more afraid than any other time. He remembered how well he hid his fear while leading his comrades to safety. He then realized that the mark of a hero had nothing to do with bravery but had everything to do with how well a hero can put his fears aside and do what he is supposed to do. He knew that today was a big day for him and his team. If they lost, then they would lose the psychological edge that they had gotten last season and that would put them back on a losing mentality again. He knew that today was the day that mattered most in his career.

He looked at his medals and his photos and wondered what his dreams were. He thought about the dreams he had as a 10 year-old boy. He had wanted to be a pro football player. Then, his dreams changed in high school when he wanted to be a fearless warrior in the United States Military. When he became that Warrior, he didn't feel so fearless. He didn't even feel like a warrior. He thought about how when he had fulfilled his dream of being a Navy Seal, he didn't truly fulfill his dream. It wasn't as glamorous as he had imagined when he was daydreaming and fantasizing about it. Then, when he was ready to get out of the Navy, he had dreamed about graduating from college. While in school, he did not feel the magic that he had felt while daydreaming about being in school. His ideals and goals didn't have that sweet flavor while he was in the middle of achieving them. He then realized what he had accomplished in life. He had been a decorated war veteran with a college degree. Now he was a teacher on his way to making a lucrative income in real estate.

Although he hadn't fulfilled his dream of having a home on the lake, he had a classroom full of students to educate. He also had a swim team that looked up to him, no matter how they despised the way he pushed them. He made a vow to find the sweetness in all of this. He vowed to himself to savor the sweet tastes of what little piece of the pie he did have and to enjoy the moment to savor the sweet aroma of immeasurable, intangible prosperity. However prosperity be measured in his case, he knew that he was at the peak of great things. He had climbed mountains, but never looked around at the beauty around them. He was always too busy thinking that the mountain he had climbed was not big enough; that he should climb the bigger mountain above him. Because of that, he missed out on the journey. He listened to the words of the song and realized that he was truly a winner. "Dream on. Dream on. Dream on..Dream until your dreams come true."

He felt psyched and pumped with adrenaline as he headed for the pool. He went to his office and for the first time in many years said a short prayer, "Oh, Lord, I am not worthy of your prayers, but the kids are. Let them do their best today. That's all I can ask of them. Your will be done today. For whatever it is worth."

There was a certain harmony in the sound of lockers opening and closing and the shouting of excited adolescents. . Jimmy smiled as he listened to the rhythm of it. This was music to his ears. The sound of innocence was what he loved the most about his job. He could re-live his adolescent years—- his forming years On a daily basis, he could go back and correct the mistakes of his own youth.

Jimmy opened his door and walked towards the lockers. "Okay, okay. Let's go." He clapped his hands. "Big day today, guys. Come on. Stop the grab ass and let's move."

He opened the door to the girls' locker room and yelled out, "Kayleigh. Get out here right now."

THE FINEST MOMENT

Kayleigh came screaming out of the locker room as if her coach had yelled, "Fire."

"Yes, coach."

"Get the girls moving. Come on. You're the captain. You are in charge. Get some fire under them. Okay?"

"Yes, coach."

All the kids came bailing out of the locker rooms, pushing and shoving each other. Kayleigh pointed to the bleachers as she told them to be quiet and wait for the coach. Jimmy was wearing a suit and tie. He walked up to the team and looked at them. They all looked at him silently. He was filled with joy at their presence for he knew that they were going to win this meet. He felt proud of them and felt proud that he was their coach.

"Okay. Okay. Today is a big day for all of us....We had an excellent season, and we need to stop and savor that sweet taste. However..." He pointed to the pool. "We have a big meet today. If we win this meet, it will give us a psychological edge. A victory will set the tone for the rest of the season. Everyone thinks that it was luck that got us a winning season. Everyone thinks that we don't have what it takes to win another meet..." He paused for a moment. "I am proud of each and every one of you. You have been working your tails off. Now go out there and have fun. Enjoy the swimming and enjoy the water. Enjoy the victory once it's yours. Remember, one meet at a time until the championship is yours. Okay. Now kick some butt. Huddle up."

The team put their hands together and yelled out..."Go Lincoln High, pride, victory, defeat....."

They jumped in the pool and warmed up until the other team came.

Jimmy was running around trying to get all of his swimmers signed up for their races. Brian Bishop's name wasn't on any of the rosters so Jimmy went over to the official to see what was going on. "Why isn't my junior boys fly swimmer on the list?"

The official looked at her sheet and said, "I don't know, coach. Did you submit his name?"

"Of course I did. I gave it to the athletic director last month. Come on, you guys need to get with the program."

"Well, sir, we don't have his name down and he can't race without the proper clearance."

"Oh, come on Sharron. What proper clearance. This is high school, this isn't the God damned Olympics."

"Coach O'Neil. I'm not gonna put up with your…"

"Sharron. I am so sorry. I'm under a lot of strain these days. It's not your fault. I'll call Ted and see why his name wasn't on the list."

"Okay, Jimmy. Just relax. I'll pencil his name in. you make your phone call and have Ted give the clearance. Your boy can race."

Jimmy pulled out his cell phone as he went into the locker room and called Ted Brighten, Lincoln High School's athletic director.

"Hello."

"Ted, this is Jimmy. Brian Bishop's name is not on the list to swim. What is the deal?"

"Jimmy. I submitted the paperwork into the state last month. Call Bill Kenton. He will give approval. I'll be right down. Relax."

Jimmy dialed Bill Kenton, The state commissioner of athletics.

"Mr. Kenton, this is Jimmy O'Neal, and one of my kids is not on the swim roster."

"Okay Jimmy. Who is it?"

"Brian Bishop."

"Hold on."

Jimmy pounded his fist on the desk in his office as he waited.

"Yes, Jimmy, his name is on my list."

"Can you tell Sharron to put his name on her roster?"

"Yeah, sure. Let me talk to her."

Jimmy went back out to the pool deck and handed the phone to Sharron.

She grabbed her pen and wrote over Brian's name so that it would be official. "You're all set Jimmy. Give 'em hell."

"Thanks."

Jimmy went over to the outer edge of the deck and watched Kisha as she dove in to do the 500 yard medley. She was way behind her

THE FINEST MOMENT

opponent, but Jimmy wasn't worried because she always waited for the last two laps to put on the turbo. She did a flip turn and pushed fiercely off the edge of the pool. The push alone allowed her to be even with her opponents. She stretched her arms and pointed her toes perfectly. She grabbed the water in the way that an apple picker would grab for apples in a hurry. She reached and stretched and did another flip turn. She pushed again fiercely off the edge of the pool and the push was enough to get her in the lead.

"Come on Kisha. Don't' stop, kid. Keep pushing. Keep pushing," Jimmy yelled in excitement.

Kisha had reached the last lap and, although she was way ahead of everyone else, she put on the turbo booster anyway. Now, it wasn't about her beating her opponent. It was all about her beating her own time. She reached the edge of the pool and was victorious. She beat her own time by an eighth of a second. That was big. It was a big win for her both physically and psychologically.

Jimmy met her at the edge of the pool and slapped her a high five. "Way to go Kisha. Good job."

"Thanks coach. I beat my own time. Yes?"

It was Brian's turn to swim and he looked around to see if his parents were there, but they were not. They had never missed any of his meets before and he was concerned. "Coach, I don't see my family."

"Relax, Brian. They'll be here. Come on. Get your head into it."

"Okay. Coach. Got it."

The buzzer sounded and Brian dove in way ahead of his opponents. He looked good as he executed his moves with great precision. It was as if he had been training with Dolphins to look at him. He was graceful and didn't make too much of a splash. He wiggled and bounced in the pool. He did his flip turn with near perfect timing. He swam as though he was trying to get away from a great white. He too, was looking to beat his own time. He reached the edge of the pool and won the race. He also beat his time by a quarter of a second. He jumped out and slapped Jimmy's hand.

Jimmy grabbed Brian's arms and said, "I knew you could do it kid. You're going all the way baby."

It was Kayleigh's turn and her father was watching her intently. She looked at him, then at Jimmy and gave them both a thumb's up. The buzzer sounded and she dove in with great distance between her and the pool's edge. She had a good lead over her opponents and persisted with everything she had. Although she was tired, she remembered the words of Coach O'Neal. "Just when you have nothing left to give, you will find that you have everything to give. Go get 'em."

She reached the edge of the pool victoriously. She jumped up and hugged Jimmy. "Thank you, coach. I'm goin' all the way baby."

"All Right. Kayleigh. Good job."

The meet had ended and Brian was sitting outside of the locker room waiting for his parents. "I don't know why they didn't come."

"I'm sure they had a good reason Brian," Jimmy reassured him. "Do you have a way home?"

"Well, a friend of mine dropped me off and I thought my parents were gonna be here, but…"

Just then, Brian's cell phone rang. "Hello? Yeah? Okay. When? Is, Is? Is he gonna be all right? Okay? Yeah. We won. Yup. I'm here with Coach. Okay. Okay. Hold on." Brian's face turned red and his lower lip covered his upper lip as he tried to be brave and hold back the tears.

"What's the matter Brian?"

"Coach, can you take me to the hospital. It's my Dad. He's had a heart attack…He's okay…but can…"

"Come on, boss, let's get you to the hospital."

Brian said goodbye to whomever he was talking to and walked with Jimmy.

"Everything is gonna be okay, kiddo. Just come with me."

Jimmy put his arm around Brian and gave him a reassuring pat on the back. "You know Brian. I've seen grown men cry. I've seen myself cry on many occasions. Don't be ashamed. Just let it all out kid. Let it all out. I won't think any less of you." Jimmy grabbed Brian's shoulder and gave it a tug as the flood gates opened and Brian began to cry.

THE FINEST MOMENT

"It's gonna be okay kid. I tell ya what I'll say a little prayer with you if you want me too. If you don't want to, I will keep the prayer to myself. What do ya say?"

Brian shook his head in agreement as they got into Jimmy's car.

"Okay kid. Say it along with me. Our Father who art in Heaven...."

They prayed all the way to the hospital and Brian felt a little better. Jimmy walked Brian into the waiting room where his family was. Brian was met with open arms by Priscilla, his mother.

"Oh, Brian. It's gonna be okay. Your father is awake and he is okay. He had a silent heart attack. He's gonna be just fine." Priscilla turned to Jimmy as she wiped the tears from her face. "You must be Coach O'Neil. Thank you so much for bringing Brian here."

Jimmy shook her hand and smiled. "No problem ma'am. Is your husband okay?"

"Yes, thank you. My husband is an over achiever and spent the entire morning in the yard. He was complaining of chest pains, so I brought him here. Thank you so much sir."

"Not a problem ma'am. I'm happy to see that your husband is okay."

"Thank you so much."

Just then a young nurse came out and asked for Mrs. Bishop.

"I'm Priscilla Bishop."

"Priscilla? My name is Jessica Heimlick. I'm Richard's nurse. He is doing fine and wants to see all of you."

"Okay, thank you Jessica."

Jessica had sandy blond hair, and wore it up in a bun. Her blue eyes sparkled and reflected the sunlight. Her eyes reminded Jimmy of the ocean upon which he had spent many a day. Her smile was sincere and filled with compassion. She had a genuine, caring look on her face and a gentle voice that made Jimmy feel a bit sedated—- like a gentle breeze blowing upon your face. Her athletic figure filled her uniform completely. The curves of her body were an indication that she worked out frequently. Her skin was a natural bronze color, unlike most women who had the tanning booth coloration.

Jimmy's eyes followed her to a cot where she was tending to a young child who was crying. She comforted him in a motherly way with caring affection and authentic concern.

Jimmy said goodbye to the family and watched as Jessica made the young child laugh. She wiped his snotty nose and gave him a hug. Jimmy was paralyzed from the neck down and could not move as he watched and listen to her sing the little boy a song. "Oooh child, things are gonna get better. Oooh child things are gonna get brighter...."

Jimmy pulled himself away from the song and hurried to his car. He sang the song all the way home and prayed to God that he would somehow have an opportunity to meet that young woman again on better terms. That night Shawn called and Jimmy was happy to hear from him because it had been a while since they had talked. "Hey Jimmy, what's goin' on?"

"Hey pal, how's it goin'?"

"Great, just great. I was talking to an old Marine Corps buddy of mine. Anyway, he's gained a lot of weight. So, he was tellin' me that he saw a gym and outside on the window it says, 'Lose 10 pounds in five days.' He said that every guy that walked outta the place was as thin as a rail. So he said he kept going by the place and one day he decided to stop in. He got in and they put him in shorts and a t-shirt and brought him to this room. Well, this chick with the tits the size of Mt. Everest walks in. She was hot. She was wearin' a t-shirt that said 'If you can catch me, you can fuck me. So he starts chasin' her around the room and couldn't catch her. He kept going and realized he was losing a few pounds. When he went on Friday he knew for sure that he'd catch her. So, he gets in the room and this giant Gorilla comes out. And he was wearin' a t-shirt that said, 'if I catch you, I get to fuck you.'" Shawn laughed until he was out of breath.

"Holy, shit, Shawn. That's unbelievable. You really had me going for a minute."

"Oh, yeah. Anyway, Jimmy. A lot's been happening lately and I have been mad busy. I'm sorry I haven't gotten back to you sooner."

"Well, what's goin' on?"

THE FINEST MOMENT

"I've just been busy with the swim team. I got $50,000.00 from the lawsuit. I'm caught up with my student loan and all my other bills now. I've put the rest of the money into a 401K, I have a thousand left.

"I'm going to Las Vegas this weekend. I was wondering if you'd like to go with me. Maybe try your luck."

The idea of going to Las Vegas was tempting, but Jimmy did not want to squander his chances with Jessica. He thought, however, if he could win some money he could take her out on a nice date. "Okay," he said reluctantly " I have a swim meet on Friday but we can leave Saturday morning and spend the day there."

"Yeah. I can feel it in my bones. We're gonna win big."

"Okay. Go ahead and book flights at Logan. Call me when you get the details."

The next morning Jimmy was walking down the corridor as Angela Hoffman and Jessica Johanson, two of his students, passed by.

They gave him a wave and said in synch, "Hi, Mr. O'Neil."

"Hey ladies, how are you?"

Angela's eyes sparkled when he said hello. "Good. Hey Mr. O'Neal, can we have an easy day today. Just sit and talk about politics or something. My brain is really fried."

Jimmy stopped and looked at her. "Well, I tell you what Miss Hoffman, if you can somehow tie the conversation into world trade and global economy, I would be happy to oblige."

She rolled her eyes and put her hand over her mouth. "Oh, brother, not one of those adult conversations that make you think."

"Well, ya know Angela, a thinking brain is a healthy one. I'll see you first period."

"Bye Mr. O'Neal."

Jimmy began practice with all of his athletes laying flat on their backs on the mats. "Okay, okay. Time to work those legs. We have a big meet on Wednesday and I want you to get those legs ready. Okay. Get up up....six inches. don't drop 'em until I say. Well, come on get 'em up."

The team was all moaning and groaning saying, "Come on coach."

"Come on nothing. Get 'em up."

Everyone lifted their legs six inches. Ray Shepherd was squinting like he was constipated and Joe Langly was moaning an awful sound.

"Ah, coach. Coach."

"Come on, Joe. What's going on? Are you going to give birth? Come on. Get 'em up. We're not gonna practice 'til everyone has them up for 1 minute."

Kayleigh was breathing heavily yet had enough energy to shout, "Come on. Get your damned legs up. Let's go, stop doggin' it."

Jimmy walked around and watched as his kids all looked like they were going to die. "Okay, down."

A loud "oh" sound came out of everyone's mouth. And it sounded as though they were in a giant delivery room.

Jimmy looked at his stop watch. "I can't believe you guys are having such trouble with this. We need to work on more dry land drills I see. Now get 'em up. Get 'em up. That's it. Now flutter kick. I said, flutter kick. Stop being so lazy. All of you. We have got a championship to win. You need to practice like champions. Let's go Phillip, get those legs up!"

"I am coach. Ah, I am."

"Flutter kicks. Do it now. Flutter kicks. Come on. Stop doggin' it."

Kisha let out a big cry of pain as she chastised her teammates "Come on you lazy slackers, get your freakin' legs up, I want to swim. Let's go. Ah!"

"Okay, down. We have a lot of work to do guys. Get into the pool and do a 300m IM. Do it now."

The practice and hard work paid off because the team won their 2nd and 3rd meet of the season. The efforts of the team were not appreciated by many of the faculty. One day when Jimmy came into the teacher's lounge to check his mailbox, he interrupted Jake Stanley, Roger Philman, Denise Hartman, and a couple other faculty members talking.

Jake was the ring leader in the conversation. "Ya know, I ha'dly

THE FINEST MOMENT

think that swim team is as great as everyone is sayin'. I don't know I think they just got lucky last season and they definitely got lucky over the past couple of weeks."

Denise put her thoughts out to the conversation. "Well how long do ya think it'll be before they blow it out theyah asses?"

"Oh, I dunno. Seems as though they'll get to the finals and choke."

Roger jumped into the conversation. "Well, I dunno. I think O'Neal's doing pretty good. It's just that I don't think that there is enough talent theyah. I mean look who he picked as a captain. Kayleigh something or rather. Is she any good?"

Jimmy walked over with a smile. "She's the best and hardest worker I've ever seen. She doesn't sit around talking about what could happen, or what should happen. She's a go-getter. You ought to come see her swim on Friday. You may just have something solid to base your opinion on."

"Yeah. Maybe. What time is the meet?" asked Roger.

"It's at six o'clock. Be there. See ya."

Jimmy went back into the corridor and heard them whispering, "I didn't know the coach was standing there."

The team was victorious on Friday and Jimmy was proud of his troopers. He went home and called Shawn to get the details about where he was supposed to meet him at Logan tomorrow. Jimmy took his medication and fell quickly to sleep. The next day he drove down to Logan Airport where he parked his car and headed for the Delta Terminal where Shawn was waiting.

Shawn looked at his clock and ran his hand through his hair. "Hey Jimmy. You all ready to make some money?"

Jimmy reluctantly said, "Well, I've never been too lucky."

"How much did you bring?"

"Oh, I cleaned out my savings. A grand is all."

"That's fine, you will triple that. I got a few thousand myself."

They boarded the plane and Jimmy was struggling to get his bag into the compartment when a flight attendant bumped him.

"Excuse me sir. You need to move. I've got to get to first class. I have some customers waiting for me."

"Well, sorry ma'am. I'm trying to…"

She smiled an "I'm working really hard to be polite, but you need to move your ass" kind of smile at him. "Here, let me do that for you before you hurt yourself."

Jimmy looked at her, let out a frustrating sigh, and sat down.

He made himself comfortable and couldn't help but thinking about how rude the flight attendant was. He looked to the front and seeing how friendly she was to the business men in first class, rolled his eyes.

When they arrived they got situated in their hotel room and headed for the roulette tables down stairs. Jimmy walked up to the table and placed his money down. He threw the dice and hit the winning number. He put another hundred dollar bill down and, boom, he won again. After he had won a couple of grand, he walked around because he didn't want to be the center of attention. He cashed in a hundred dollars for quarters and played the slot machines. He couldn't do anything wrong tonight. By the end of the night, he walked out of there $2,000.00 richer than when he walked in. Shawn was just as lucky for he won about $5,000.00 in a matter of hours. The men decided to rent a limo and Shawn made a couple of phone calls. When the men arrived back at the hotel, they were met by two beautiful women.

Jimmy looked at Shawn with a puzzled look. "What's this?"

"Well, Jimmy. Do you want to have a good time tonight?"

"Well, Yeah."

"Well, I've hired these ladies to take care of our manly desires tonight. You can do what ever you want to your whore, all night long."

Jimmy smiled, but hesitated. "Oh, what the hell. It's been a long time."

The following Monday during practice, he continued to be stern and persisted with the dry land exercises. He even got his aerobic instructor from the gym to come over to the Lincoln Academy Gym to do teach the kids aerobics once a week. They also did some light weight lifting in the weight room. They won their next couple of meets and Jimmy walked the hallways proudly and posted up the newspaper articles about each and every victory.

THE FINEST MOMENT

Thanksgiving break had arrived without warning and Jennifer called to ask Jimmy if he wanted to spend Thanksgiving at her house.

"Hey Jimmy. How are you?"

"Good. How ya doin?"

"I'm pretty good. I just wanted to see if you were coming over for Thanksgiving."

"Yeah. That would be nice."

"We're all going to church in the morning. Did you want to come?"

"Ah, I'll pass. I'll meet you guys at your house in the afternoon."

"Well, Jimmy. A lot of good things are happening to you and I thought you might come and give the Lord thanks."

"Well, I am grateful and I thank God every night; but I'm just not up to going to church with the crowd and all. Thanks anyway."

"Well...Okay...We'll see you in the afternoon."

"Okay. 'lots of love."

"Love you too. Bye."

Jennifer hung up and sat next to Jon on the couch. "I just wish he would believe again like he used to."

Jon reached over and stroked her long brown hair. "How do you know he doesn't believe?"

"Well, when we were in high school he used to go to church all the time. I remember his best friend Todd Druin would come to church with us. Todd didn't believe in God and had a rough home life. His stepfather and father used to beat him. Anyway Jimmy taught Todd about Jesus and Todd wanted to get baptized in the Catholic Church. But then he died. He drowned. But he accepted Jesus into his heart. He was saved and he wouldn't have been saved before he died if it hadn't been for Jimmy. Jimmy always led people to God. He's been real good at teaching the girls to pray, but he has his moments. One day a drug and alcohol abuse counselor filled his head with hatred for the church for being abused when he was little and now he's down on the church. I don't understand how people can go astray."

"Well, you have to take a look at what Jimmy's been through in his life. He's seen war, death, and poverty. He's seen rough times. I think that once God is in a person's heart, he is always there. It just takes time. When Jimmy's ready to come back he will. Have you ever thought about how difficult it is to see us and other families in church when he has nobody. Jimmy probably thinks that God is punishing him and he's afraid that he will spend the rest of his life alone. It's probably painful for him to see people with families and joy in their hearts, and he can't share that."

"Well, if he'd go to church, he might find a good woman there."

"Well, if you look around the pews, there aren't a lot of single women his age going to church."

"I never thought of it that way. I just wish he'd find somebody so that he could be happy again."

"In time He will. I know there is someone out there for him.. In God's time.

The following day when Jimmy entered his class he overheard some of the students talking about how good the swim team was this year. Jim Ortiz was going on about how he didn't think they could do it. "Ya know. They used to suck. I didn't think they had a chance to win a single meet."

John Tollino jumped into the conversation. "Well, what about last year. I thought they just got lucky but they are undefeated now. I guess they do have some talent."

Jimmy walked over and said, "I think it has something to do with the great coach that they have."

Jim threw a paper ball at Jimmy and laughed. "Not. I think it's all about Kayleigh. She is a hottie. She is the balls. I'd like to..."

Jimmy threw the paper ball back at him and asked, "You'd like to what?"

"Um. I'd like to...tell her what an awesome job she is doing."

"That's what I thought you said." Jimmy went up to his desk and grabbed a pile of papers. "Okay. Open up to Chapter 5."

The entire class moaned in unison. "Come on Mr. O'Neal. Give us a break."

THE FINEST MOMENT

"Come on now. You've had a long break and it's time to get the engines running again."

The next three meets were disappointing and frustrating for Jimmy. His team had gone up against the three toughest teams in the state: Concorde Academy, Dartmouth Christian School, and the Lakes Region Trinity School; and had lost. They only had 4 more meets left before they would be going to the semi finals.

It was a cold, rainy Monday evening and his team came into his classroom with their heads dragging. Jimmy could feel the frustration that his kids were feeling; but he did not have the words to make them feel better. He looked at them as he walked back and forth in the front of the classroom.

"Do you want to give up? Do you want to throw in the towel? Tell me now and I will walk out the door and go home."

They all looked up at him and no words came.

He walked over to Brian. "I know you have all had some tough times this season. I know life has not been easy. But for God's sake, do not give up on yourselves. So we lost to some great teams. So we had a tough time. I'm not asking for anything from you but your best effort. I want you all to do well. But if we are gonna lose; then we are going to do it together. We have a mission to execute. The chips are down, and we have nothing left to give. But when you have nothing left to give..."

Every one of his students stood up and said, "That is when you have everything to give."

Jimmy smiled and said, "Well, then do it. Give it 100 percent. Go and have fun and finish the rest of the season out victoriously. Let the Finals take care of themselves. We'll cross that bridge when we get there. For now, I want you to focus on one meet at a time. Okay? Now be in the pool in 10 minutes, ready to do some leg lifts. No bitching and moaning either. Enjoy the pain. Enjoy it now, because it is going to make the victory that much sweeter. Now get moving."

The next three meets were a success and they came close to winning their fourth meet. They had a 14 and 5 record as they began preparing for the semi-finals on Saturday. On Friday the day before the big meet, Jimmy lined them up to play Sharks and minnows. He chose Kayleigh to be the shark and the rest of the team had to swim past her without getting tagged. They had fun and forgot all about the meet that they had ahead of them. Jimmy was pleased because they played so hard that they had given themselves a tougher workout than Jimmy could ever have done.

The next morning Jimmy looked over at his football helmet and medals. Today, however, was their day. The day belonged to his teammates and they were going to win it without the help of Jimmy's intercession. He drove to the pool and went into his office. He did not need to hurry his athletes as they were already suited up and warming up in the pool. When the other team arrived, Kayleigh commanded her team to go over to the mats and stretch out until the coaches got on deck. Jimmy was accompanied by Ray Polanski and Seth Franklin, his assistant coaches from last season. Their schedules had been tight this season and they had been unable to help; but today they volunteered and helped with all the paperwork and the rest of the stuff that gave Jimmy a migraine. He pulled the team together and said, "Okay. It's all up to you. The winner of this meet will be the team that wants it the most. The winner will be the team who swims with more heart and more spirit. Which of you is it gonna be? Okay. Get out there and have a good day."

The meet started well with Brian's victorious race and Kayleigh and Kisha's shocking wins. However, the rest of the team was unable to help them out and they were disappointed. They would not be going to the state meet over Christmas break. But, Jimmy was proud of them and he told them when he got them together after they shook the other teams' hands.

"Okay. Okay." He pointed to the other team. "They did well and we have to give credit where credit is due. They swam with great intensity. Listen. You guys had an awesome season and you will all be coming back for the spring. If we don't do it then, there is always next year. All of you will be seniors and you will take the Championship. I know this in my heart. You have the ability and that I can work on. I can help you with your technique, but I cannot teach "WANT."

THE FINEST MOMENT

I cannot give you the heart and the desire to win. You all have the ability, but now over the break you have to ask yourselves if you have the want. Go on now. Have a wonderful holiday, and I will see you in January. Good job this season."

It was Christmas Eve and Jennifer called Jimmy to see if he was going to mid-night Mass.

"Hey Jimmy. Great job with the swim team."

"Thanks, sis. They were good."

"Yes they were and you have a great deal to be thankful about this Christmas. Are you going to Mass?"

"Oh, I dunno. Midnight is kinda late."

"Well, we're all going to the five p.m. Mass at St. Joseph's. Are you gonna be there?"

"Ah, I don't know Jennifer. I mean, I believe and all but I'm just not a church person anymore."

"Well, Jimmy, so many good things have happened to you this past year, and I don't want you to punish God for what happened to you a long time ago. It's not his fault. Bad things happen to good people. Maybe we'll see ya there."

"Okay. Five pm?"

"Get there early. It's gonna be packed. We'll look for you."

"Okay. Bye."

Jennifer didn't realize that Jimmy was indeed grateful to God. She didn't understand that the reason Jimmy didn't like to go to church was because it was too painful to see all the young families there with children and he had no family of his own to share it with. It was just too lonely for Jimmy, but he promised her and didn't want to back down on his promise so he decided that he would go. However, it was still early and he looked out his window and saw a young woman outside jogging. She lived in the house down the road and Jimmy had seen her from time to time. He wanted to talk to her and get to know her so he put on his wind pants and sneakers and went out. He jogged passed her and said hello. She looked down to the ground saying nothing as she kept on running. Jimmy's mouth dropped and he felt like a horse's ass. He turned around and headed back to his apartment. Now that the season was over he had a lot of time to think. He thought about going to the hospital and trying to find Jessica Heimlick, the beautiful nurse he had seen at the hospital a couple of months ago; but he faltered as he felt discouraged at what had just happened. He felt that he was not destined to meet anyone special. He thought for sure that his past failures at relationships, his rejections, and today's blow off were indicative of his destiny of dying a lonely old man. Instead, he dove into bed and put the covers over his head until 3:30 when it was time to get ready for church. He didn't want to go, but a promise is a promise he thought and went anyway.

When he got there the pews were filled with young families and their children. He found Jennifer and sat next to her. Anita and Becca gave Jimmy a hug and wished him a Merry Christmas. There was a stunning brunette sitting with her husband and new born baby. Her eyes were icy blue but she had a warm smile. She held her infant and rocked him to the music. Jimmy began feeling resentful as he looked around and saw all these mothers and fathers with their children. Although he was happy and grateful for the things God had given him, he felt slighted. He felt as though God had given him so much, yet so little. Jimmy watched the happy people of the church as they sang with joy. Jimmy was upset that he could not experience the happiness they all felt.

He began to get angry and thought that God had abandoned him. When the collection came, Jimmy put 50 cents in the basket. He thought to himself. "Well, I should give back to God what he has given me. He has given me half of my dream. He has given me a good job and a nice place to live. He has fulfilled 50 percent of what I have prayed for so I should give him 50 cents of a dollar that I would have normally given him. Jimmy began thinking about the priest who had molested him and ugly thoughts began filling his mind. Hateful thoughts overwhelmed his heart and he felt like a horse's ass, standing there in the church all alone without a wife and children to be with. Jimmy felt disgusted. He felt as though church should be a place where he could find Christ especially on Christmas; yet the only thing he found that day was resentment, bitterness, and sorrow.

THE FINEST MOMENT

He fought the tears of loneliness and felt a lump in his throat. He couldn't handle it anymore so he dashed out the door and got into his car. As he drove away, he began crying—crying the way he cried when he buried his good friend Todd.

As Jimmy drove down the road, he saw a van pulled off to the side. Next to the van was a young family carrying a sign that said, "We are stranded and will do anything for oil and gas." Jimmy turned around and pulled behind the beat-up old van. He approached the van where a young man, his wife, and 3 snotty-nosed, dirty-faced children of about the ages 3-11 were standing. The kids were playing in the snow and the mother and father were huddled together keeping each other warm. For the first time in Jimmy's life, he had wanted what the impoverished had. He desired the love that they shared and wanted to experience the joy of snotty-nosed, dirty-faced children running around. Jimmy walked up to them and asked them what the trouble was. The young man shook Jimmy's hand.

"Thank you for stopping, sir. We were headed to the nursing home down the road to visit my mother and my van shit the bed. I think there's a gas leak and my oil is dry."

"Okay. No problem. Been there, done that. What is your name?"

"I'm Ken and this is my wife Judy."

Jimmy looked at their vanity plate and it read, "Jesus."

"Okay, Ken. My name is Jimmy." He put his hand out and shook Ken's hand. "I'll take you to the nursing home and I have triple A. I will call them and have them tow your van to the nearest garage. I will take care of the bill. Don't you worry."

"Oh, thank you." Ken grabbed his wife tightly and tugged at her shoulder. "We thank you very much. How can we repay you?"

"Well, Ken, right now, I need you more than you need me. What I mean is I need your prayers. Please just pray that I may have a loving family like yours someday. That is how you can repay me."

"Oh, yes, I will pray for you my brother."

Jimmy made a phone call on his cell phone and then packed the young family into the car and they drove down the road. "So, tell me Ken, what do you do for work?"

"Well, I am on disability for the next six months for my back. I have a good job working for Coca Cola. I'm a driver and I was lifting some crates when bang! Pulled my back and have been out of work for a year."

"Ouch. That's gotta be tough."

"Yes. We had to sell our car and the bank took our house; but we are surviving. Coca Cola has been good. They will have a place for me when I get better. I've been with them for 15 years and have done a good job. They want me back; but, it just takes time, ya know?"

"Oh, yeah, I understand."

Jimmy dropped them off at the nursing home and handed them a 20 dollar bill. "Here. Call a cab when you are done. Your van will be at Jake's auto downtown. You can call them to see when your van is ready."

"Thanks, we will pray for you. Count on our blessing."

"Merry Christmas, Ken. God bless."

Jimmy felt good and his sadness had disappeared for he knew that Ken's family was in good hands. Jimmy was happy to do something nice for someone on Christmas. He knew that they would be praying for him and that everything would be all right. "Things are gonna get better," he whispered out loud. About 10 minutes later, a car in a hurry passed him and fishtailed on some black ice. There was an oncoming car going just as fast so Jimmy slammed on his brakes and did a 360 on the road. His car went into a ditch and capsized.

The next thing Jimmy knew was that he was lying in a hospital bed with his sisters and nieces standing over him. He fell asleep and awoke in the early hours of morning when a young nurse came in to check on him.

"Hello, my name is Pamela. I passed by and heard you moaning. Are you okay?"

Jimmy looked at Pamela. She had short curly hair and a pleasant smile. She grabbed his hand and he noticed a diamond ring on her left hand. He looked up at her and said, "Thanks Pamela." He pointed at her engagement ring and said, "Your man is very lucky to have someone like you."

THE FINEST MOMENT

"Thanks."

"I hope he appreciates you."

"Oh, he does." She blushed and bashfully tucked her head in her shoulders.

"Ah, oh. Oh, my aching head."

She grabbed Jimmy's hand and held onto it. The tears rolled down Jimmy's face and he began sobbing.

"Oh, you poor thing, you must be in a lot of pain. Can I get you another pain reliever?"

Jimmy shook his head. "No. Thanks. I'm okay. I'll be okay."

What Pamela did not realize was that Jimmy's pain had nothing to do with his accident, but had everything to do with the loneliness he felt in his heart this Christmas morning.

THE FINEST MOMENT

A NEW BEGINNING

The holiday had passed and Jimmy was recovering well. The insurance company had given him the money to get a new car so he could get on with his life. That night at practice was routine. He had his athletes jump in and do a 500 meter individual Medley. Jimmy looked over and saw Ray Polanski and Seth Franklin walking toward him. He stood up and shook their hands.

"Hey guys. Good to see you."

Seth had a smile on his face and gave Jimmy a strong handshake. "Hey Jimmy. How goes it?"

"Good. Good. We're gonna have a good team this year. I can feel it."

Ray put his hand out and gave Jimmy a firm handshake. "Good to be back with you, Jimmy. How ya been?"

"Awesome. Can't think of anywhere in the world where I'd rather be."

"You been workin' out Jimmy?" Seth asked.

"Yeah, when I can."

Jimmy pointed to the pool and said, "they're warming up right now; then we're gonna jump right into dry land endurance exercises."

The men nodded their heads and said in unison, "Sounds good."

Just then Miranda Miles let out a horrifying scream. "Ah. Coach! Coach!"

Jimmy and the other coaches ran over to her at the other end of the pool where she was holding her ankle.

Jimmy knelt down beside her. "What happened, Miranda?"

"My foot." Miranda was crying and holding her ankle. "I banged it on the corner. Ah. Shit. Shit."

Jimmy looked at Ray and said, "Ray, can you go into the office and call for an ambulance. There's also a phone list. Can you call Miranda's parents?"

Ray looked at Miranda and then at Jimmy. "Yeah. Sure."

Jimmy looked down at Miranda. "Okay. Relax. Relax. You're okay. Just sit tight."

"Ah. Coach it hurts."

"I know, sweetie, relax. An ambulance is on the way. Hold tight."

Jimmy turned to Seth and told him to conduct the remainder of the practice as he waited for the ambulance to come. The kids were all huddled around Miranda so Jimmy pointed to the pool. "Okay. She's okay. Get back to work. You've got a lot of work to do. Listen to Coach Franklin. Let's go."

The team hopped back into the pool and finished their warm-up. The paramedics came quickly and put Miranda on a stretcher and wrapped blankets around her. Jimmy jumped in his car and followed the ambulance to the hospital. When he arrived he saw Jessica Hiemlick at the desk in the emergency room. However, this time he had no intentions of getting to know who she was. He just wanted to see how Miranda was doing.

"Hi, my name is Jimmy O'Neal and I'm the swim coach at Lincoln. One of my kids is here. Miranda…"

Jessica smiled at Jimmy and typed quickly on her computer. "Yes, coach. Miranda is in the 3rd room over." She pointed to where he was supposed to go. Jimmy thanked her and headed in the room. He opened the door and Miranda was lying on the bed shivering. He walked in and put the blankets on her. "Oh, sweetie you are as cold as ice. Let me get the nurse to get a robe for you and some dry blankets."

Miranda's lips were purple and she was shivering uncontrollably. Jimmy walked out to where Jessica was and approached her.

"Excuse me, ma'am."

Jessica turned and smiled. "Yes?"

"Can I get you to put a dry robe on Miranda and get her some dry blankets? She's freezing."

THE FINEST MOMENT

"Why certainly. I apologize. We are so swamped here tonight. A lot of snowmobile accidents. I will get right on it. I apologize."

Jimmy put his hand up and smiled. "No problem. I understand. Things must be hectic for you here."

Jimmy went back to the room where Miranda was and sat next to her. He grabbed her hand and comforted her. "The nurse is getting a dry robe and some blankets for ya, kiddo. You'll be nice and dry."

Miranda began crying. "It hurts...coach. Oh, it hurts so bad. I think I broke something. Oh. Ah, shit, Coach it hurts."

Jimmy squeezed her hand and began singing, "Oooh child things are gonna get easier. Oooh child things are gonna get better."

Just then, Jessica walked in and heard Jimmy singing. She smiled and walked over to him. "That is a lovely song, Jimmy." She put the blankets and gurney on a table next to the bed. "If you will excuse us, coach. I've got to get her out of this wet bathing suit."

"Oh, I'm sorry. Sure." Jimmy stood up and walked into the corridor while Jessica gingerly undressed Miranda.

Jimmy was met by Susan and Jeff Miles, Miranda's parents, as they came into the emergency room. Susan came over to Jimmy and asked, "How is she?"

Jimmy smiled and put his hand on her shoulder. "She's okay. She's in a lot of pain and the nurse is putting a robe and blankets on her now. We're waiting for them to take an X-Ray."

"Oh, my poor baby!"

Jessica opened the door; introduced herself to Susan and Jeff; and invited them in. Jimmy excused himself and told them that he would be waiting in the lobby. Jessica followed him and asked, "Can I get you some coffee, Jimmy?"

Jimmy rubbed his head and let out a sigh of frustration. "Oh. Thank you. I'm all set."

She led him to the sofa in the lobby and said, "Well, it's finally quieted down in here. Oh, what a night." She stretched her arms out, and yawned.

"You must be tired. Looks like you guys were really busy earlier."

"Yeah. We were. I only work here part-time. I come in when it's busy or when one of the other nurses is out sick. I work full-time at Oak Ridge Elementary School. I'm the school nurse there."

Jimmy made himself comfortable in the chair. "So, this is like a second job?"

"Well, actually it was my first job. I started here when I graduated from nursing school. Then I went to the Peace Corps for a year before I landed the job at Oak Ridge full-time."

"Wow, you are really straight out. How do you do it?"

"Well, a lot of coffee, and a little sleep." She smiled and looked at the front door to make sure that there weren't anymore patients coming in. "It's really not so bad. I enjoy what I do. I guess you could say it's sort of like you with the coaching. I'll bet coaching a high school swim team takes up a great deal of your time."

"Actually you know, I always end up looking up at the clock and realizing there is only 15 minutes left of practice, and I haven't done nearly enough with the team as I want. I guess you could say that time flies. I like the kids. They keep me motivated."

"I'll bet they do. How long have you been coaching?"

"Not very long. This is my second season. I just got into teaching a year ago. To make a long story short, I graduated with a Business degree; but did not find what I was looking for. I always thought about teaching but never really pursued it. I enjoy it and think I'll keep at it."

"Well, that is good that you enjoy what you are doing. I'm sure the kids really love you. I know Miranda kept asking for you when she wasn't asking for her parents. You seem to have connected well in there. You made her smile a little bit with the song."

Jimmy blushed and said, "Well. I really care about those kids. They bring me back to my younger days. I get to live through their eyes."

Just then, an older man walked in and stood in front of the nurse's desk.

Jessica looked at him and then back at Jimmy, She smiled as she said, "Well, duty calls, I gotta get back to work."

THE FINEST MOMENT

"Yes, it's getting late."

"So….Ah…when is your next meet?"

"This Saturday at Lincoln Academy. 10 o'clock."

"Well, I'd like to get in there and see your team. I hear they had a really good season last year."

"Yes. I'd love to have you there. That would be great. I'll see you Saturday at 10:00."

"It was really nice talking to you Jimmy."

"It was nice talking to you, too, Jessica. See you later."

The next day in school Jimmy was approached by Dr. Prescott, the Principal. "Hey coach. How is Miranda? I heard she banged her leg pretty badly."

"Yes, sir. She has a fracture. She'll be out for the rest of the season; but that kid is good. She'll be back in the summer and will do great things for us next year."

"That's good, Jimmy. I wanted to tell you what a fine job you are doing here. I've been so bloody busy lately, I have not had time to come in and observe you. But Mr. Croteau has said that you are doing great work in the classroom."

"Thanks. I enjoy working with the kids. I think that teaching is the right move for me."

"And how is the certification coming?"

"Well, sir, I have to take the test in February and then I'll find out from there."

"Good. I know you will do well. When is your next meet?"

"On Saturday. It's right here. At 10."

"I'll have to bring the Missus and the kids. I know they would enjoy it."

"Yes, sir. It will be good for the morale of the kids to see you there giving them support."

"Will do, Jimmy. Keep up the good work."

"Thank you. I will."

Jimmy was on his way to study hall when Brian Bishop passed him in the hall. "Hey coach. How's it goin?"

"Good Brian. How's your Dad?"

"He's good. He had to slow down a little. He's taking it easy."
"Good to hear that. Send him my best."
"See ya coach."

On Saturday, Jimmy was dressed in the new suit that his parents had bought him from Giovani's Gallery at the mall. It was dark blue and he had a nice white shirt with a navy blue tie on. He was wearing Opeche due Shurn cologne that Jennifer had bought him. He was feeling confident and was looking forward to seeing Jessica there. He had his doubts, though. He knew that his conversation with her seemed too good to be true. He was sure that she would blow him off and he was okay with that. He was happy knowing that he still had his kids and that was all the love he needed. Seth and Ray came out to the pool deck. They were dressed in suit and tie as well. They looked sharp because Jimmy had set a precedent in high school swim coaching. Coaches usually never dress up for meets, but Jimmy made sure that he and his staff shone above everybody else.

The team came out and jumped into their lanes. Jimmy had arranged for one of the students to play music while they were warming up. There was a variety of songs being played to get the fans pumped up. Eminem, Snoop Doggy Dog, Shaggy, and even the old school such as AC/DC and of course, Aerosmith's "Dream On." Jimmy listened to the words with all of his heart and soul as they played. "Sing winner, sing for the year, sing for the laughter, sing for the tear. Dream on, dream on. Dream on. Dream until your dreams come true." Jimmy felt a tear forming in his eye as he realized that he was a winner. His teammates, his coaching staff, and the fans were all winners. They all had a dream, and Jimmy felt that his dreams were all coming true. For the first time in a long time, he felt happy to be a part of this crowd. There wasn't anybody here today that he resented for being happy. He was the happiest of them all and he was certain that this was his finest hour because today was the day when he was at his best. He looked up and saw a woman waving at him. He walked toward the bleachers and saw that it was Jessica who was waving. He went over to her and waved.

"Hey!"

THE FINEST MOMENT

She smiled and sat down. "Hey yourself!" Her eyes ran up and down Jimmy in his new suit and she nodded her head in approval. "Not bad. Not bad at all. You look nice."

Jimmy's face turned red as he smiled. "Glad to see that you could make it."

"Thank you. Glad that I made it."

"Hey. The team and their families are all getting together at Angelina's Restaurant after the meet. I was wondering if you'd like to tag along."

"Sure. I'd love to."

"Great." Jimmy looked at his watch and then pointed at the pool. "I gotta run. I'll talk to you after."

"Okay. Good luck coach."

"Thanks. See ya."

Jimmy walked back and told Seth and Ray to get the kids in the gym. Jimmy walked in and looked at his team. "Oh. You guys look good out there today. But we can't get too cocky. Right now is the time when all the hard work pays off. All the pain and suffering that you have gone through will pay off today. Remember, keep your focus. And please, please, for goodness sake, go out there and enjoy yourselves. Remember…When you are tired, and you feel like you have nothing left to give…"

The kids stood up and screamed, "THAT IS WHEN YOU WILL FIND THAT YOU HAVE EVERYTHING TO GIVE!"

"All right then, what are you waiting for. Break 'em down."

The team joined hands and shouted, "Go, fight, win. Win, win, win."

Jimmy pointed to Seth and Ray. "Coaches, break them down into their individual groups." He shook the men's hands and wished them luck today.

Jimmy stood over near the stands with his arms folded. Occasionally he would put one of his hands up on his face, and leave the other hand across his chest supporting his arm. This was the way Don Shula, the former head coach of the Miami Dolphins and one of the most winning-est coaches in the NFL, stood during a game.

Calm, cool, and collected, Jimmy stood with great composure as he watched his troops from a distance. He had a blank look on his face and stood stoically without any emotion. He had excellent assistant coaches who knew what they were doing, so today Jimmy stood and let them do all the screaming. Jimmy was happy to be competing against Lakes Region Trinity and Dartmouth Christian Academy today. This way, his team would get the tough teams out of the way; and, even if they lost, they would have the rest of the season the redeem themselves. The first race was ready to begin as Brian Bishop looked over at Jimmy and gave him a thumb's up. Jimmy put his hand in the air and returned the gesture. Brian was going up against Chazz Hartman, a senior, and the number one Fly swimmer in the state. Jimmy saw this as an advantage for Brian. He knew that even if he did not win the race, at least a half dozen college recruiters would be here to see Chazz so they would also have a chance to see the boy that would give him a run for his money. Jimmy was beginning to see the positives in everything. His cup was beginning to flow half full rather than half empty. Jimmy knew that whatever the outcome of the meet, he and his team were at their best so their best performance was going to have to do—- win or lose.

Brian stood on his block and wound his arms around. The way a softball pitcher would wind around before pitching a strike. He shook his head back and forth and danced on the block until he heard. "Swimmers take your marks. Swimmers get set…." The buzzer rang and Brian leapt out to the pool further than Chazz could even piss. Brian immersed his body into each stroke as he went up, then went down, then up again. He was ahead of Chazz by a long shot. Jimmy whispered to himself, "Slow down, Brian. You've got a whole lap to do."

Just then he heard Seth screaming at the top of his lungs "Slow down, Brian. Pace yourself. Slow down." Seth ran along the side of the pool and hollered out. "Slow down. Pace. Pace." He cupped his hands over his face. "Slow down, Brian. Pace yourself." Brian did not slow down, and was way ahead of Chaz at the turn. Unfortunately, Chazz pushed off with such a thrust that he was even with Brian. To-

THE FINEST MOMENT

wards the end, Brian began to slow down and run out of steam. Chazz stretched his body out as far as he could and won the race by an eight of an inch. Seth ran over to Brian and helped him out of the pool.

Brian looked at him and said, "I know. I started too quickly."

Seth pointed to the water bubbler and told him to get a drink.

As Kisha mounted the board Ray kept repeating himself, "Start slow. Start slow. Pace yourself. Pace yourself. Extend your body. Let the water do the work, Kisha. Let the water do the work. "

Kisha stretched out as she too faced the best swimmer in the state, Mariah O'Connely. Mariah had been picked to enter the national Olympic trials last year but declined because she wanted to stay with her team. Again, Jimmy saw this as an opportunity for the eyes that were on Mariah to be on Kisha as well. Kisha had trained at camp with Mariah and the too had become good friends. Kisha was reluctant to compete against her friend; but Mariah informed her many times that she wasn't competing against her friend, she was competing against her own time. Mariah told Kisha what Jimmy had been trying to tell her all along. A swimmer is constantly trying to improve her own time. It's not about winning the race, but beating your time.

Kisha shook Mariah's hand and said, "Good luck."

Mariah reached over and said, "Remember, you've got to beat your time. Okay?"

Kisha looked at her and nodded. Ray repeated one last time. "Pace yourself."

"Swimmers take your mark. Swimmers get set...." The buzzer sounded and Kisha had an enormous form in her dive. The distance was not good, but both Jimmy and Ray were impressed at how her form had improved. Seth looked over at Jimmy and gave him a thumb's up. Kisha reached as far as she could go. She kept hearing Jimmy yelling at her, "Reach for the gold; reach for the gold; and when you have nothing left to give...." Kisha, for the first time ever, let the water do all the work as she glided with great finesse by reaching and controlling her breath. Again, she heard Jimmy yelling, "Come on kid, control that breathing or you're gonna choke. Let's go damned it." Kisha had enormous composure and control over herself. She was surprised to feel that she was doing little of the work. It was incredible how the water pushed her along. Although Mariah was ahead on the second turn, Kisha did not panic. She continued to let the water push her along at the lowest drag possible. Suddenly she saw Mariah's shadow ahead of her on the 3rd turn. Again, she remained steady and continued to glide through the water with the least amount of exertion possible. She felt a powerful feeling in her body. It was the best she had ever felt. The after-burners kicked in and she thrust to the edge of the pool finishing victoriously. Ray pulled her out and she gave him a hug.

"I did it Coach. I beat Mariah. Holy shit, I beat Mariah."

"You beat your own time, too, kiddo," Ray reminded her.

"Holy shit, Mariah. I can't believe it. I did it."

Mariah picked Kisha up and said, "Damn. You beat your own time."

"Holy shit, I did it, Coach. Coach O'Neal. Holy shit. Ah. I did it."

She ran over to Jimmy and gave him a hug. "Coach, I did it. Holy shhhh. I did it. I did what you told me. I could hear you screaming, "Point your toes, glide, relax, pace, breath and reach, and let the water do the work. I did it coach, I beat Mariah.."

Jimmy held her tightly. "You did it kid. I knew you could."

"Oh, thank you Coach." She began crying and said, "Thank you Coach O'Neal. I love you man. Ah. I did it."

Jimmy felt the lump in his throat and grabbed her hands. "That is the way you gotta do it. Just like that."

Jimmy looked around at everyone in the stands who were watching as Kisha had her finest moment. She was at her best today and he felt proud that the eyes were on him too..Kisha was truly grateful that Jimmy had helped her to reach her potential. He looked up and saw Jessica smiling at Kisha and the coach that she truly admired. There was a love here that was unlike any love ever. Children love their parents and their families; but the love a child has for her coach somehow stands out above and beyond any love at all.

THE FINEST MOMENT

Kisha ran over to the stands and shouted to her parents and brothers. "I did it. I beat my time. I did it."

Her Dad stood up and gave her a thumbs up. "You go girlfriend, you go. Haa, haaa, awesome job Kisha. Just great."

Kayleigh was up next and looked nervous. Her dad wasn't in the stands and when she looked over to where he might have been sitting, a look of doom filled her face. Jimmy walked over to her. "Kayleigh. Look at me kid. Look at me. You can do this. You can do this. Have faith in yourself."

"Yes, Coach." Her lower lip began trembling as she fought the tears.

"Swimmers take your mark. Swimmers get set." Kayleigh dove into the pool before the buzzer and was disqualified. Ray helped her out of the pool and she ran toward the locker room crying. Kisha and Mariah ran in after her. The next events were victorious for Lincoln Academy so they won the meet. Jimmy ran to his team and congratulated them. He went over to Jill Bennedict, the head coach of Trinity, and congratulated her.

"Good job Jill. Great work."

"You too, Jimmy. You have a great team this year. You will go far."

"Thank you. That means a lot."

Jimmy finished shaking the other coaches' hands and went over to the girl's locker room.

"Marissa, can you ask Kayleigh to come out here please?"

"Yes Coach."

A few minutes later when Kayleigh came out her eyes and face were red.

Jimmy took a seat on the bleacher and motioned for her to do the same. He looked at her and asked, "What's going on Kayleigh?"

"My dad. He's not doing too well. He was in the hospital a few days ago. He's back home, but he's...."

Jimmy grabbed Kayleigh's chin and said, "Listen. Your dad is a strong man. He's a fighter. He doesn't want to see you lay down like this. I know mistakes happen, but today's mistake happened because you did not have your chin up. You've got to be strong for your dad. You've got to be strong for the team. And if nothing else, you've got to be strong for yourself. You have got a bright future ahead of you no matter what. Listen to me, Kayleigh. No matter what happens, your dad wants you to strive and be the best. Okay?"

"Yes, Coach. Thank you."

"Okay. Send your Dad my love and tell him to get better and get his butt back to the meets."

"Coach, can you come and visit Dad? He would really appreciate that."

"You bet. After dinner though, because we are all meeting at Angelina's now; but after that I will go see him."

"Thanks Coach."

"Now get in the damned locker room and get showered. Come on move it."

Jessica came over and sat down next to Jimmy. She looked at him with great sincerity. She smiled as she looked into his eyes. "Great job, Coach. You sure do have a way with these kids."

"Ah, it's nothing. Anyone would do the same."

"Ah, yes, but not everyone would do it quite the way you do. They really admire you Jimmy. You are doing a great job. It was a good meet."

"Thanks."

A group of men and women were headed towards Jimmy. They were racing each other trying to get to him first. The first man who approached him was Derek Bradley, a scout from the University of Connecticut. "Coach O'Neil, I want to tell you what a good job you've done with the kids. You got a minute?"

"Yeah, sure. Hold on a second." He turned to Jessica and asked, "Can you start without me and please save me a seat?"

She smilingly said, "Sure thing. What do you want?"

"Huh?"

"Do you want me to order for you?"

"Yes. That would be good. I'll have a big steak with fries and lots of ginger ale."

THE FINEST MOMENT

"Ah, okay. I'll see you there. Bye."

"See ya there, Jessica. Bye."

Derek pulled out his card and gave it to Jimmy. "I'd like to meet with Kisha and Brian. Can you give them my card? I know you don't have a lot of time, but can you give them a video of today's meet and ask them to send it to me?"

The next person waiting was Pat Sullivan from Penn State. "Jimmy, I actually came here to look at Kayleigh. I saw her a year ago when I was scouting her opponents and have noticed her improvement. I came last season and saw what a great job she did. I would still like to set up an interview with her. She's got great potential for a junior. Can you give her my card?"

"Sure can. We'll be in touch."

Jimmy met with all the scouts as well as the newspaper and when he was finished he headed over to Angelina's Restaurant. Jimmy was happy to see that all of his athletes and most of the parents made it. He looked around and saw Jessica sitting with Ray and Seth. He walked over and sat down next to her.

"Thanks for saving me a seat."

"No problem. After all, you're the man of the hour."

"Naw. I couldn't have done it without these two guys. I see you guys have already met."

Jessica lifted her glass and drank her water. "Yes, and Seth tells me that Liz went to UMass Amherst. That's where I went."

"Really. I didn't know that. So, when are you and Liz gonna tie the knot?"

"Well, hopefully by this time next year."

Jimmy nodded his head and smiled, "Good. She might think twice when she really gets to know you."

"Now, now, Jimmy. When I get to be as old as you and develop bad habits, well, then, she will be too old herself to find anyone new."

"Okay, okay. Ya got me. I stepped into that one."

Ray lifted his cola and laughed. "Yes, I was wondering what the hell that smell was."

"Okay, now Ray. I've been nice to you. So, what about you pal? When is Maria gonna be an unlucky woman?"

"Not for a while. She's doing her graduate work. It'll be a while."

Jimmy lifted his ginger ale toward Ray and looked at Jessica. "Ray has been dating Maria for a couple of years now. She's studying psychology at UMass, Bowston. She'll need a degree to figure this guy out."

Jessica laughed and held onto every word that Jimmy said as if they were a basket of eggs that she did not want to drop. She smiled and continued to look at him. "Seth tells me that you are going to have his bachelor party."

Jimmy had a look of confusion on his face. "Oh? Is that so Seth?"

"Well, Jimmy," laughed Seth. "You're the head coach. You're getting the big bucks now."

"Yeah, Right."

Jessica looked at Jimmy and winked. "He tells me that you are gonna have it at your place and it's just gonna be the guys. Right, Seth?"

"Yeah. Just the guys. No women invited. Although I know Jimmy and, to my disapproval, he'll invite women there but I won't even pay any attention to them because Liz will be the only person on my mind."

"Yeah, Right. Get outta here you dog. Nottttt!"

Kisha, Kayleigh, and Brian came over and shook their coaches' hands and thanked them. The girls gave Jimmy a big hug and Brian gave him a strong handshake. "Thanks again, Coach."

"No problem kid. Take care. Kayleigh, I'll stop by later."

"Okay, coach. I'll see ya."

Marissa, Jenna, Patrick and Stacey came over to thank the coaches and say goodbye. Kisha's parents came over and said goodbye. Her Dad patted Jimmy on the back. "Way to go, Coach. You're doing a fine job with these kids. My Kisha is so happy. She did real well today. Thank you."

THE FINEST MOMENT

Jimmy stood up and shook his hand. "Oh, no problem. She's come a long way. I'm just glad she took my advice. She's on her way to great things."

"Yes, sir. You take care now."

Jimmy said goodbye to all of his kids and their parents and got back to his friends. The waitress came over and asked if there would be anything else. Jimmy looked at his friends. "Yup. Now you can give Ray a beer." Jimmy looked around to see if all of the kids and the parents were gone. "Yup, I know he's been drooling over there. Been going through withdrawals. He's ready for a beer."

They laughed and talked for a while until it was time for Ray and Seth to go home. "Well, Jimmy. Thanks for a good time. But, I've got to get going. Liz went to visit her mother today and she should be home."

"Yup. I gotta get going too. Maria is waiting for me. She's been knee deep in the books all day and I told her I'd spend some time with her."

"Okay, guys. You take care now. Congrats on a good meet. See ya Monday evening."

Jimmy looked at Jessica and asked, "You don't have to get running do you?"

"Well." She looked at her watch. "As a matter of fact, I do...not have to go anywhere."

"Great. Can I get you a tonic. Ginger ale?"

"Sure."

He motioned for the waitress to come over. "Can you get a couple more ginger ale's please?"

Jimmy looked at Jessica and smiled. "Thank you for coming. I'm having a real good time."

"Yeah, me too. You're friends are hilarious."

"Yes. That they are."

"So, how long have you guys been coaching together?"

"Not long. Just under a year now but they are the type of guys who seem to have been your friends for a long time."

"Yes, I could tell. I hardly knew them and it was if I had known them for a long time."

"So, Jessica, did you enjoy the meet today?"

"Yes. You have a good team. I've heard that it hasn't always been this way."

"Yeah. It's tough to get people to commit to such long hours."

"I can imagine. It must be difficult."

"Yes."

There was silence for a minute as the waitress brought the drinks over. Jimmy began to get nervous at the silence even before she left.

"So, Jessica, you said you were in the Peace Corps?"

"Yes. For about a year."

"Where did you go?"

"Well, just after college I went over to India. I was a nurse there. I worked with Mother Theresa."

"Wow! No kidding. I've always admired her work."

"Yes, she was something else. She had a genuine love for people. She treated everyone no matter how ill they were with great love and respect."

"It must have been a thrill to work with her."

"Well. It was a challenge at first. But I adapted. I enjoyed it a great deal. Yes."

"Amazing. It takes an amazing person to be able to do that."

"Thanks."

Jessica and Jimmy talked for about an hour and he looked at his watch. "Well. Now I really must get going. I told Kayleigh that I would go visit her Dad. He's dying of cancer and he may not make it to see next season."

"Oh. I'm sorry. Was Kayleigh the one..."

"Yes. She is one of my best swimmers, but today she had much more on her mind than swimming."

"Oh. That's so sad for such a young girl to have to go through that."

"Yeah. It really is. I'm worried about her. I really am."

Jessica looked at Jimmy and smiled. "Oh. Well, it seems that she really looks up to you. I'm sure that you will be there for her."

"Yes. I hope so."

THE FINEST MOMENT

Jessica got up from the table.

"Can I walk you to your car, Jessica?"

"Sure, Jimmy. Yeah."

Jimmy walked her to her car and said goodbye. "Jessica?"

"Yeah?"

"Can I call you? Maybe we can catch a movie or something?"

"Yeah, sure. I'd like that. Yes."

"Great."

She pulled a piece of paper out of her purse; searched for a pen; wrote her number down; and handed it to him. "If I'm not home, just leave a message on my voice mail."

"Sure. I'll call you this week. Maybe we can grab dinner and go see a movie."

"Yeah. Sure. I'd like that."

"Okay. I gotta get going now. I'll talk to you."

"Bye Jimmy. Congrats on your meet today."

"Thanks. Bye."

Jimmy drove over to Kayleigh's house and knocked on the door. Kayleigh's mother, Donna answered. "Hi, Coach O'Neal. Kayleigh told me you'd be stopping by. Come on in."

"How is Mark, doing, Ma'am?"

"He's much better. I'm not sure if Kayleigh gave you all the details. It wasn't as bad as we thought."

"No. She didn't tell me much."

"Well, Mark was clipping his fingernails, and—.well, he went a little bit too deep so he got an infection in his hand. His body wasn't able to fight the infection. But he's doing fine now." She led Jimmy toward the living room. "He's relaxing in his easy chair watching college football. Come on in."

"Thanks."

"Mark?"

Mark looked up and smiled when he saw Jimmy. "Hey Coach. Good job today. I understand you won a hell of a meet."

"Yes, sir. The kids were great."

"Kayleigh told me what happened. I had a little talk with her."

"Where is Kayleigh?"

"Oh, she's next door watching a movie with her friend." Mark pointed to an empty chair. "Take a seat Jimmy. Can I get the misses to get some coffee for you? A beer?"

"No, I'm all set. Thank you." Jimmy sat down and made himself comfortable. "How are you doing?"

Mark took a long swig of his Budweiser. "Never better. I'm feeling good. Donna, can you grab me another beer? You sure I can't get you something Jimmy?"

"I'm all set. I can't stay too long. It's been a long day, and I gotta get heading home after a bit."

"Sure. I'm sorry about what happened to Kayleigh today, Jimmy."

"I understand Mark. She's got a lot on her mind with you being sick and all."

"Well, Jimmy, I had to give her a reality check today. You know, I've put the cancer behind me, but there are no guarantees in life. I could get really sick and I may not be here so Kayleigh needs to realize that she has to push on. You see, Jimmy, we don't have a lot of money; and as it is, I've been in and out of work. I'm really counting on Kayleigh getting a scholarship somewhere."

"Well, sir, I wanted Kayleigh to be here when I told you the good news; but a scout from Penn. State was at the meet today to see Kayleigh."

Mark sat up in his chair and listened. "Are you serious? A scout from...Donna? Donna."

Donna came in as if Mark were yelling for help. "Yes, dear, what is it?"

"Jimmy says that a scout was at the meet today to watch Kayleigh."

"No kidding? Our Kayleigh?"

"Yes. Our Kayleigh."

"Oh, I'm sorry I haven't been to any of the meets. I have had to work so many long hours at the grocery store. I promise I'll get over and see her. So, a scout from Penn. State came today? I have got to call Kayleigh. She can put her movie on pause. Hold on."

THE FINEST MOMENT

Donna went into the kitchen and called the next door neighbor and told Kayleigh to come right over.

A few minutes later Kayleigh came in. "Hi Coach. How's it goin'?"

"Good."

Mark motioned for Kayleigh to take a seat. "Sit down, sweetie. Your coach has some incredible news."

Jimmy adjusted himself in his chair. "Well. A scout from Penn. State came to see you today."

Kayleigh had a look of shock on her face, the way a person would after winning the lottery. "No way." She pointed to her chest. "Me? He came to see me?"

"Yes, he's interested in you."

"Oh, no, I bit the bullet today. He must have been disappointed."

"No. Nope, he was interested in watching some tapes on you. He told me to give you his..." Jimmy sat up and reached for his wallet. He rifled through the plastic and money that was in it and found the card. "He wanted me to give you his card."

Kayleigh reached over and took it. She looked at it for a moment. "He's really interested in seeing me?"

"Believe it. He's seen you before and wants to take a look at you."

"Wow, this is big."

Mark motioned for her to come over to where he was. When she did, he put his arm around her. "Now listen, kid. This is the opportunity of a lifetime. I don't want you to lose out."

"I won't Daddy."

"Now, I'm telling you. Don't let me being sick pull you down. I want to see you go to college and do well in life. The Good Lord has plans for you; and, even if I'm not here to see you, you've gotta push on."

"You'll be okay, Dad. You'll be fine."

"I know sugar, but you've got to brace yourself for the worst. Now go on. Get back to your movie and enjoy yourself."

The following Monday, Jimmy looked out on the pool deck and saw his varsity swimmers doggin' it. Kisha and Brian were running around playing tag and jumping in the pool. Carter Becker and Cote Patterson were doing cannonballs in front of the freshman. Jimmy stormed out on deck and blew his whistle.

"What is the meaning of all this? You guys win your first meet against the best teams in the state and all hell breaks loose. Let me tell you what. You aint all that. You guys are no Olympic gold medalists by any stretch of the imagination. J.V. kids, go with Coach Polanski and Coach Franklin. Where is my Captain?" Kayleigh put her hand up. "Right here coach."

"All right, come here. Come here."

He looked at her and led her away from the pool to talk to her in private. "Kayleigh, don't take this the wrong way. You've got way too much on your plate with your dad and all. I'm going to excuse you from your duties as Captain for a while any way. You've got too much to deal with emotionally right now to be dealing with these yahoo's. You'll still be Captain at the meets; but for now, I'm going to pick one of those yahoos to deal with their friends. Okay?"

"Gotcha coach."

"Okay. Now I'm not talking to all of you; but if you lose, you lose as a team, and if your teammates screw up, then all of you have to pay. There is too much grab assin' goin' on here. You guys are too cocky. Okay, everybody outta the pool. Time to have some fun."

Jimmy pointed to the mats. "Let's go. Move. Get on the mats. We don't have all night. Let's go." He waited for everyone to get out of the pool and onto the mats before he began. Jimmy walked over intently. "Everyone...Back in the pool. Now. You want to drag your ass? Get back in the pool and try it again. Let me tell ya what. We can do six inches all night for all I care. You guys want to sloth off. I tell you what. Test my patience."

Carter Becker whispered to Cote Patterson, "What the hell crawled up Coach's ass tonight?"

Jimmy trotted over to where Cote was. "Is there a problem, Carter?"

THE FINEST MOMENT

"Ah, no Coach."

"Coach Franklin, go ahead and work with the J.V. girls. Coach Polanski, you go ahead and take the J.V. boys. Have them do some simple endurance and work on their techniques."

Jimmy walked around and looked at his varsity swimmers in disgust. "You guys are the cream of the crop I hear. Everyone's talking about your big victory. You are preparing for a championship and preparing for college. This is not the attitude of a champion—running around grabbing ass. Again, I'm not talking to all of you; but I might as well because if your teammates are screwing off, then they have cost you the championship. I need some leaders here to take charge when the coaches aren't around. Carter, you are going to be a co-captain to take some of the pressure off Kayleigh, whom I might add is doing an awesome job. Kisha, so will you. And don't you dare roll your eyes at me."

Kisha looked up. "Ah, I didn't.."

"Don't talk back."

"What is your problem?"

"Get 'em up. Six inches. Let's go."

"Ahhhh, ahhhh, ohhh, my ankle, my leg," yelled Marisa.

Jimmy pointed to his varsity team. "You guys are too good to be out here screwin' around. You can screw off in the locker rooms; but when you get out to the pool, it's business. This isn't J.V.'s anymore. You are preparing to win a state championship; and if you don't want to work, then go home now. Get 'em up. six inches….Down."

Jimmy walked over to the J.V. girls and noticed that Rene Mafatado, a freshman, had a huge gouge in her leg. "Rene, see me after practice."

Rene looked up. "Yes, coach."

He returned to his varsity squad. "Get 'em up. Six inches…Flutter kicks. Flutter. Let's go, no doggin' it. Okay coaches, get the J.V.'s in the water please."

Jimmy pointed over to Kisha. "Let's go, get 'em up. You will either love me or you will hate me. It doesn't matter because we still have 14 more meets ahead of us; and we will lose them all if you don't get humble now."

Jimmy had seen enough. "Okay, line up in the deep end and move it."

Everyone scattered to the deep end and lined up. Jimmy stood at the edge and pointed at the lane. "When I say go, you will dive in and swim to the edge. Then get out and walk quickly, no running, and walk quickly back to the line. I promise you after tonight you will have no sass in you. Go."

Jimmy had his varsity squad doing sprints down the fast lane for about an hour and a half. He stood at the edge of the pool in his black mesh shorts and his white Nike t-shirt. He put his hands on his hips as he watched everyone doing their sprint. He stood at the edge of the pool wearing his Teva sandals and stood on the balls of his feet. They were all hanging their tongues out and gasping for air. Finally, he stopped them and said, "Okay everyone take out the lanes and hop in the pool. Sharks and minnows. Okay? Do it now. Have some fun."

After practice was over, Kisha approached Jimmy and apologized. "I'm sorry Coach. Don't be mad at me. I was just having a little too much fun."

Jimmy patted her head and said, "I know Kisha. I know you were. It's my job to see that you learn how to balance the fun with business. I don't want you to get too cocky. I've seen it before, kids get too happy with themselves and they choke. Hit the shower and get a good night's rest."

"Okay, Coach. Thanks for not being mad."

"Go on, girl, go home."

"See ya."

"Take care."

"Rene Mafatado came over to Jimmy. She looked scared to death as if he was going to make her do sprints. "Coach, you wanted to see me?"

Jimmy led Rene to the bench and sat down. "Take a seat, kiddo."

Rene sat next to Jimmy and he patted her on the shoulder. "I just wanted to see what happened to your leg."

She rubbed her leg nervously. "My brother and I were horsing around and my dad swatted me."

THE FINEST MOMENT

"He did?"

"Yup, it was a quick slap as I was trying to get away."

"Well, I'm concerned. That there is a pretty big gouge."

"Yeah, I know. Please don't tell him that you saw it. Please?"

"I can't promise you that. Can I talk to your mother without your Dad knowing?"

"My mother died when I was little."

"Oh, I'm so sorry, angel."

"That's okay."

"Well, do you have an aunt or an uncle I can approach without your dad knowing?"

"Aunt Cecilia, she's my Dad's sister. She's been like a mother to me."

"Can you give me her phone number before you leave?"

"Yup."

"Okay, hit the shower kid. You look good out there. Just keep listening to Coach Franklin, okay?"

"Thanks Coach."

Jimmy went into the locker room and entered his conversation with Rene into his log book. When he was done, he turned to Seth. "Listen, I need you to give Rene's aunt a call tomorrow. She's gonna bring the number in. Did you see that welt on her leg?"

Seth sat down in the chair. "Yeah, I just figured that she was horse playing."

"Well, she said her dad slapped her. It just may be an innocent slap, but it's policy to report it so I need you to talk to her aunt before I take the next step. And do us all a favor—log everything in the log book. If it's not written down, it never happened. Put the date and time and nature of the call. Okay."

"Sure boss."

"All right, I gotta get outta here. I want to give Jessica a call tonight."

"Yeah, she's a looker. How did you meet her?"

Jimmy put his shoes and was tying them. "Well, ya know, I met her at the hospital when Miranda cracked her ankle last week. She's a nurse there. Well....She works there when they're short handed. She's actually," Jimmy tightened his laces, "a nurse at Oak Ridge Elementary School."

"Well good luck to you guys. She's a keeper."

"You got that right. Take care, and remember...."

"I know, log it in the log book. Gotcha."

When Jimmy got home, he dialed Jessica's phone number. His heart was pounding because he couldn't help but feel that this was still too good to be true. He was afraid that she would give him an excuse. He tried to feel that he didn't really care, because then he could go with Shawn. Well, he did care because he wanted to spend time with Jessica. He wanted that a great deal more than gambling. The phone rang and a woman answered.

"Hello?"

"Hi, Jessica?"

"Hold on, this is Christine, her roommate. May I ask who's calling?"

"This is Jimmy."

"Okay, Jimmy, hold on."

"Hello?"

"Jessica?"

"Hey. How are you Jimmy?"

"Good. How are you?"

"I'm okay. Just relaxing a little."

"Oh, yeah? How was your day?"

"Good. Really busy. And how was yours?"

"Really busy, too."

"How was your team today at practice?"

"Very cocky. Very."

"Oh, I can imagine, they must have had heads the size of watermelons."

"Yup, that's for sure. I made sure that they got off their clouds though."

"Oh, I'll bet."

Jimmy and Jessica talked for nearly an hour until it was getting late.

THE FINEST MOMENT

"Listen, Jessica, would you like to go out this weekend?"
"Absolutely, what did you have in mind?"
"Well, what do you like to eat?"
"Let me see. I love seafood."
"Oh, yeah?"
"Yes."
"Maybe we can go to Newick's in Portsmouth and then go check out a movie."
"Yeah, that'll be nice. Where's your meet Saturday?"
"It's home again. Would you like to come?"
"Sure. What time?"
"Same time."
"Yeah, I could meet you there and we could go out after."
"Okay, great, I will see you then."
"Can't wait."
"Take care, Jessica."
"You too, Jimmy. Have a good week."
"You too. Bye."
"Goodbye."

During school the next day Jimmy went to the guidance office to talk to Vic Jakello, Rene's guidance counselor, about the conversation that he had with her. Jimmy knocked on Vic's door and Vic was in the middle of typing something on his computer. When he heard the knock, he stopped and turned around.

"Jimmy. Come on in. What's going on?"
"Hey Vic. I know you're busy, but have you got a minute?"
"Yeah, sure. What's going on?"
"It's Rene Mafatado? I'm concerned about her."

Vic stood up and closed his door. He picked up some books that were on a chair and motioned for Jimmy to sit down. "What's going on?"

"Um. She had a welt on her leg. I talked to her about it and she said that her father cracked her a good one."

"Really? I've met the man and he seems like a good guy. You see Jimmy, Nick Mafatado is an unhappy man and he drinks once in a while. His wife died, ya know. Cancer. A few years back."

"I didn't know that."

"I go to church with him. He never misses a Sunday. He and his wife were a big part of the church. They were really close to the priest, Father Antonio. He went out to the house the day she died and said the last rites just before she died. She was a good woman."

"I didn't know..."

"Yes. I don't think that he is abusive. You know, he probably wrapped his belt on her leg. I don't think it's anything to worry about. Just keep your eyes open, okay Jimmy?"

"Yeah. Sure thing. Take care."

"Take care. Jimmy."

Before practice Seth walked in and let out a sigh. "Oh, what a day..."

Jimmy was in the bathroom putting on his shorts. "What's up?"

"Well, I called Rene's Aunt. She wasn't too happy. She was pissed at her brother. Told me she was gonna ring his neck."

"Oh, yeah. What did she say?"

"Well. Rene's mother died a few years ago, and she said the guy has his moments. Said he was a loving father; but ever since his wife died, he gets crazy on his kids once in a while—especially Rene."

Jimmy opened the door and came out. "Why Rene?"

"Well, I guess she reminds him of his wife and he resents seeing his daughter because it gets him thinking about her. He can get real nasty she said."

Jimmy sighed. "Oh. Great. This is all I need. Log the conversation in. Also write down that I spoke with her Guidance Counselor. I suppose that is all we can do for now, I guess. We've done all we can."

"Yeah, but I'd like to meet the guy and crack him a good one."

"Now, now. Let it go Seth. We'll just keep watching for any more bumps or bruises. We've documented it. If it happens again, we'll call Social Services." Jimmy pointed to the door. "Come on, let's get going. We've got a lot to do tonight."

That night Shawn called and had some good news. "Hey, Jimmy, I bought the place."

THE FINEST MOMENT

"Shawn? Hey, what place?"

"You know. The mill apartment building."

"All right, Shawn that's great."

"Yeah. Hey, can you give me Jon's number so I can call him and see if he wants to fix it up?"

"Yeah, sure," Jimmy gave him the number and they talked for a while. Jimmy was tired so he had to cut his conversation short.

Saturday came and Jimmy had to get up early so that he could take the teaching certification exam at Plymouth State College and then double back to Lincoln Academy for the big meet. The test was three hours long and he dreaded his ride back. When he arrived, he grabbed his suit that was hanging on a hook in the back seat of his car. He went to his office and changed. Jimmy was all decked out in a new suit that he had bought. He had also paid for jump suits for Ray and Seth, as wearing a suit and tie was just not appropriate for them during a meet because they had to get close to the swimmer, as well as bend and kneel down a lot. Jimmy looked sharp and Jessica was sitting in the stands waving. Jimmy walked over to her and said hello.

"Hey, you. Good to see ya here."

"Good luck today, Jimmy."

"Thanks. I'll see you after the meet."

"You look good today."

"Thanks, you too."

Jessica was wearing a white silk dress shirt and a pair of wool dress pants. She wore her hair up in a comb and her blond highlights were illuminated by the lights in the pool area. Here blue eyes sparkled and she did not have to wear makeup because her dark complexion enhanced her beauty.

Kayleigh was standing on the diving block, stretching out. She looked up and waved at her parents who were sitting in the stands. She adjusted her cap and moved her head back and forth. Seth walked over and tapped her.

"Remember Kayleigh. Pace yourself. Get a good dive, and start slowly. Okay?"

"Gotcha Coach."

She looked over at Jimmy and gave him a thumbs up. Jimmy smiled and returned the gesture.

"Swimmers take your marks. Swimmers get set." The buzzer sounded and Kayleigh dove in with near perfect form. She bounced up and down gracefully, skimming the top of the water. She had hit the first turn and pushed off with enormous thrust. She had taken the lead and was diving and kicking with all of her might. She hit the next turn and continued to utilize the water for speed. Finally, she hit the last turn and was on her way to victory. She reached and extended her body to the edge of the pool. She jumped out and looked at her time. It read 2:30:15. She jumped up. She had beaten her old time of 2:30:30. She ran over and gave Jimmy a hug.

"I did it coach. I beat my time."

"Way to go kid. Good job." Jimmy slapped her a high five and shook her hand.

After the meet Pat Sullivan was standing in the lobby waiting for Jimmy. "Great meet coach. You won another one." Pat shook Jimmy's hand. "I was really impressed with your young swimmers. Have to keep my eye on them over the years."

"Yes, indeed, we do have potential." Jimmy looked over and spotted Kayleigh coming out of the locker room. "Please excuse me, Mr. Sullivan. There's Kayleigh over there."

Jimmy walked over to Kayleigh and smiled. "There's someone here who wants to talk to you."

She looked around and pointed to her chest. "Me?"

"No, your twin. Yes, you. Silly. Come on."

Jimmy led her to where Pat was standing, "Mr. Sullivan, I'd like you to meet Kayleigh."

Pat shook her hand and patted her on the back. "Great job today."

"Thanks, I couldn't have done it without Coach."

"Listen Kayleigh. I'd like to talk with you about coming to Penn. State."

Kayleigh had a look of embarrassment on her face, sort of the way a person would look after dropping her tray in the middle of the cafeteria.

THE FINEST MOMENT

"I'm so sorry I never called. You know with studies and a demanding coach," she winked at Jimmy, "I've been so busy."

"That's okay. I've been watching you, and...Well. I like what I see."

"Thanks."

"I'd like to sit down and talk to your parents today over lunch."

"Yeah, sure. My father is pulling the car around and my mother is..." She looked around the crowd. "She's here somewhere."

"Well, name the restaurant and it's my treat. I'd like to talk to you about a swimming scholarship."

"Yeah, that's cool. Umm, we could all go to.."

Jimmy tapped Kayleigh on the shoulder. "I gotta run, kiddo. Good luck." He turned and shook Pat's hand. "Take care Mr. Sullivan."

"Yeah, see ya Coach."

Jimmy met with reporters and talked for a while as he anxiously looked over at Jessica who was talking with some of the swimmers and their parents. She was congratulating them and laughing and smiling. Jimmy was anxious because he wanted to leave and spend some time with her. When he finished up, he walked over and put his hand on Jessica's shoulder.

"Hey. You ready to go?"

"Yeah. Let's get something to eat. I'm starving."

As they drove along Route 4 they talked. Jimmy was interested to hear about Jessica's journey in Calcutta. "So, tell me. Was it as bad as it appeared in the documentaries? The poverty and sickness?"

"Ah. Yeah, it was pretty bad. I remember my first day there. I walked into a large room and the smell. Oh, Jimmy, I've never smelled anything like it. The smell of urine, blood, and....Oh, it was awful. I wanted to turn around and get back on the plane."

"Wow! That bad huh?"

"Yeah, I thought I had made a big mistake. Suddenly a tiny little lady, Sister Gertrude, came over to me and handed me a bunch of towels. I remember she said, 'are ya gonna just stand there or are ya gonna help? You take these towels and dry them off, after I pour water an' soap on 'em.'"

"Oh, that must have been tough."

"Well, I remember I walked over to an elderly man and he looked at me. I have never seen the eyes of Jesus until I looked at him."

"That must have been fulfilling."

"Yes, it was."

They had arrived at Newick's so Jimmy hustled over to Jessica's door and opened it. "There ya go."

She smiled. "Thank you."

Jimmy opened the door to the restaurant for Jessica and they entered. A young college woman led them to their seat and handed them a menu. Jimmy continued to enquire about Jessica's experiences in Calcutta. She talked until their meals came and then it was her turn to ask the questions.

"So, tell me Jimmy. How did you get involved with teaching?"

"I had always thought about it when I was in the Navy."

"The Navy? Wow, where were you stationed?"

"I was with Seal Team 5 in San Diego."

"A Seal. Quite impressive. I'm sorry, you were saying."

"That's okay. I had worked with kids at the YMCA. Taught swim lessons. The Navy wanted to have a good image so they had us go out into the community and work with kids. I liked doing that so I guess that's when I first wanted to be a teacher. Before I got out, I decided that I wanted to follow in my grandmother's footsteps. She was a genius when it came to business management. She did it the old fashioned way. She didn't have any business degrees, but she worked really hard. Anyway, I pursued business in college and swam on the swim team. I worked at the Y part time as a lifeguard and swim instructor. When I graduated, my student loan was sky high. I couldn't get any credit because I defaulted so I took a job at a video store and was miserable. That is when I talked to a friend who was a teacher and decided that I'd like to get into it. And here I am."

She smiled and stopped eating. "Teaching is a very noble and honorable career. Your family must be proud."

THE FINEST MOMENT

"Yes. They are."

"Do you have any siblings?"

"Yes, I have three sisters, four nieces, and two nephews."

"You must be really good with the kids."

"Yeah, I like hanging out with them although I haven't been spending much time with them lately, with the teaching and the swim team."

"I can imagine. And your parents?"

"They are retired and live in Florida. They come to N.H. to visit during the summer and holidays."

"Sounds like you are close to them."

"Pretty close. We are a tight family. How about you?"

"I have a sister. She's a couple of years younger than me. She just got married. She has a 5 year-old girl. My parents are retired. My father was a surgeon in the Army and when he retired he worked at the hospital for a few years, and then opened his own practice. He did that for about 20 years. My mother stayed at home and took care of us kids."

"I take it that you are close to your family as well."

"Very. We've always been close."

"What made you decide to be a nurse and work in the Peace Corps?"

"I always admired the work that my father did and, well, I admired Mother Theresa. I almost became a nun."

"Are you serious?"

"Yes. I wanted to go over to work with Mother Theresa and see what it was like. But, I just didn't have it in me to do what she did. I wanted to have a family of my own; so after a year, I went to work at the Hitchcock hospital."

"I admire Mother Theresa so much. I remember when I was in San Diego she was down in Tijuana, Mexico, visiting the poor. She was supposed to come visit my church in my old town. I used to go to Saint Theresa's Catholic Church there and I was anxious to meet her; but she got sick and had to be rushed to the hospital in La Jolla."

"I remember that. It was a few years before I went over. I think I was a junior or senior in high school. So, do you still go to church?"

"Ah, yeah. I go to St. Peter's in Laconia. It's nice. Where do you go?"

"I go to St. Michael's in Concord but I often visit my parents in Portsmouth. That's where I grew up. When I'm there we go to St. John's."

"Portsmouth is nice. Did you live there all your life?"

"Yes. My grandparents came over from Germany, when my father was just a baby. Just before the war. My grandfather didn't want any part of the Nazi Party so he came over to Portsmouth."

"So, you said you went to nursing school at U Mass, Amherst?"

"Yes. I went on a field hockey scholarship."

"That's a nice school. Field Hockey? My sisters played field hockey. It's fun to watch."

"Yeah, I miss it. I sometimes think about coaching. Maybe next season. I dunno. My schedule is so busy."

"Well. There's nothing like coaching. You get a sense of accomplishment working with the kids."

They talked for a while and then headed to the movie theater. Jimmy led Jessica to the middle of the theater and found a spot next to the wall. They talked some more until the movie began. During the movie, Jimmy was itching to grab Jessica's hand but was nervous. After about 20 minutes or so he grabbed her hand. He thought for sure that she would push him away; but, instead, she held returned the grip. She looked at him and let out a sigh of relief the way a person would sigh after being saved from being stranded on an island for many years. She smiled and stroked his arms gingerly. Goose pumps flooded Jimmy's body and a warm feeling overcame him. He had a sense of relief and a sense of security. They watched the movie and held each other's hand. After the movie, Jimmy drove Jessica back to her house. They talked some more and got better acquainted. When they arrived at her house, she invited him in. She led him up the stairs, opened the door, and turned on the lights.

"Christy, are you home? Christy's my roommate. We share the house. She's a good roommate. I don't think she's home though. Come on in."

THE FINEST MOMENT

Jimmy walked in and took a seat on the couch.

Jessica walked into the kitchen. "Can I get you anything, Jimmy? I have some juice or soda." She searched her refrigerator. "I also have some Gatorade."

"Sounds good."

She came out a few minutes later and after handing him a glass full of orange Gatorade, took a seat next to him. "I had a really good time tonight Jimmy."

"Me too, Jessica. It was fun."

"Good job again, on your meet."

"Thanks."

They talked for a while and Jimmy looked at his watch. He stretched his arms and yawned. "Oh, my. I better get going. It's getting late."

"Yeah, you've had a long day."

"Yes, it's been eventful. Hey, I was wondering if you'd like to go to church tomorrow."

"Sure. I'd like that. Do you want to go to my church or yours?"

"We can go to yours. That would be good."

"Okay. Mass starts at 11:00."

"Yeah. Okay. I'll pick you up at about 10:30."

"Okay."

Jimmy stood up, and headed for the door. Jessica followed him and opened the door.

Jimmy smiled. "I'll see you tomorrow. Thanks for a good time."

"Thank you, Jimmy. I'll look forward to seeing you."

"Okay. Then maybe we can grab a bite to eat after."

"Absolutely."

"Take care."

"Bye."

The next day, Jimmy picked Jessica up and they went to church. They took a seat toward the middle and prayed. Jimmy thanked God for giving him the opportunity to have a desire to go back to church again. He felt whole. He was happy. The two of them sat hand in hand during mass and Jimmy enjoyed it when Jessica ran her fingernails up his arm. After church they went out to Angelina's for lunch and then went shopping at the mall.

They spent the next couple of weeks together, going out to eat, to the movies and shopping. One Sunday, they walked hand in hand looking in the windows of various shops. The young couple spent a great deal of time browsing. Jessica wanted to go into Tour De France and see what they had. She looked at each and every little knick-knack that she passed. Jimmy, a man who hated shopping, actually enjoyed browsing. He was in no hurry to be anywhere and felt at ease. Besides, there was no place else that he would rather be than next to Jessica, holding her hand.

From time to time she'd stop and comment on some of the things she saw. At one point she came across a stuffed animal. It was a little bear with a blue, knitted sweater on. The details on the sweater were precise and showed that much time and effort had been taken on making it. On the bear's head rested a blue winter cap.

Jessica picked the bear up and said, "Oh. Jimmy? Look at him. He's so cute."

She brought the bear to her face as if he were a child of her own and felt the soft fur on her cheeks. "Oh, he's so cute. I think I'm gonna buy him."

Jimmy placed his hands on its fur and stroked it gently. It felt softer than teddy bears that you get in the States. It had a silky, cottony, texture that was almost mesmerizing. Jimmy put his hand on Jessica's shoulder and said, "Yeah, this is nice. How much is it?"

Jessica looked at the price tag and a look of shock overcame her as she put it down. "Ah, I don't think so."

"How much is it, sweetheart?"

"You don't want to know."

"How much?"

"Two...HUNDRED...dollars."

"Well, you know, it's not one of those 50 dollar ones that were thrown together in five minutes at a factory you know. It's hand craft-

THE FINEST MOMENT

ed. The person took a great deal of time putting it together. Much labor went into it. Besides, whoever made it might be a peasant in France who spent all her money on the material. If you buy it, you'd be giving to a great cause."

Jessica picked it up again and re-examined it. Although she wanted it, she could not afford it and on this day, she didn't want to have him buy it. "Yeah, it is nice; but, I'm not paying that much on it."

"Okay."

"Let's go check out some of the other shops." Her eyes lit up much like the wide eyes of the stuffed bear she had put away. "Oh, sweetheart, look..." She pulled Jimmy toward her so that he could see what she was looking at. On the rack was a thick blanket. It seemed to have a million layers. The wool blankets here were far thicker than the ones back in some of the other stores. All of the items here were made by peasants in France and shipped to the United States. The blankets of France were extremely full and rich because the people over there aren't wealthy by any stretch of the imagination. Their small cottages are especially cold at night, so they need thick blankets.

Jessica looked at the price and put the blanket back down. "Oh, my. This is a thousand dollars sweetie. I don't think these people are poor if they're making so much money on these blankets and stuffed animals."

Jimmy rebuked his frugal friend. "Listen. These people labor all month to make these. That means they only make about a thousand a month. They probably have a lot of mouths to feed."

Jessica put the blanket down and followed Jimmy out. She pointed to the pet shop. "Oh, Jimmy. Let's go look at the pets."

Jimmy grabbed her hand and led her to the pet shop. They stopped and looked at a white German shepherd puppy that was looking at them in the window. "Oh, Jimmy. Look at him. He's so cute. Isn't he?"

"He sure is. Let's go inside and see if we can hold him."

"Oh. I hope so."

Jimmy went over to the young woman who was working there

and asked her if she could take the puppy out. She went over to the door of the kennel and unlocked it. She picked the dog up and brought him out. Jessica reached out and held him. She put her face close to his and closed her eyes. "Oh, you are such a sweet little puppy. Yes you are. Yes you are. You're such a cute little baby. Yes." The dog licked her ear and began kissing her. "Yes, you are so cute."

Jimmy pet the puppy and put his face up the puppy's face. "I think he likes you."

"Yes. Oh, you're such a good little puppy."

Jessica pulled her head back and looked at the dog closely. "Oh, Jimmy. He's so cute. Oh, I'd love to have a dog."

"Yeah, me too. Maybe someday when I have a yard."

The next day after school Jimmy sat at his desk and opened a letter he had received from the Department of Education. It read, "We are sorry to inform you, but you have failed the written portion of the praxis exam and will have to take it again in six months. Below is a list of your scores." Jimmy tore the paper up and threw it in the trash. He got up, pretending nothing happened and went about his business in the usual manner. He jumped in his car and headed for the pool. During practice, he worked with Kayleigh, Kisha, and Brian on getting their times better. While he was doing that, Seth was working with the other Varsity swimmers at increasing their time. Ray had taken the Junior Varsity to Hanover Prep for the final meet of their season so the pool was quiet and seemed somewhat empty. Jimmy continued to have Kayleigh work on getting her initial dive perfected.

"Okay, Kayleigh, imagine that you are on a spring board. You have got to LEAP outwards." Jimmy pointed his toes and lifted his body upwards as he pointed his hands in the air. "You have got to imagine that you are diving to the other side of the pool. Let's try it again. Come on. Leap. Leap and reach."

Brian had completed his lap and Jimmy clicked his timer. "That's better Brian, but you still need to pace yourself. We have got one last meet of the season and then we are going to the semi-finals. You've got to work on pacing yourself. You're all over the place. You start off slowly and do well; but you get in a hurry towards the last lap. Come on. Concentrate."

THE FINEST MOMENT

Jimmy went over to where Kisha was and kneeled down. "Okay, Kisha, release." Jimmy reached his arms up and made a giant circle in the air. "You have got to glide that breast stroke. Glide, reach high, then release, and push. Push, Push. Reach for the gold. Reach and let the water take you. You don't need to do anymore work after you have reached. Let the water take you for a minute and then pull around again. Okay? Work on it."

Practice ended so Jimmy called Kisha, Kayleigh, and Brian over and sat them down. "Okay, you three. I'm gonna send you guys to summer camp again. I want you to start the summer practice at the end of April. You will leave as soon as school gets out. But for now, I want to let you know how proud I am of you. You are all on the verge of getting scholarships from some fine schools. I want to make sure that you keep your grades up and do not miss any days of school. I know that I don't have to worry about that with you guys; but continue doing well in school and everything will take care of itself. We have only lost two meets this season and I'd like to have a victory on Thursday. I know there are some easy teams competing. Worry about keeping your time; or better yet, beating it and we will win. Next Saturday is the semi-finals. We go up against Burlington, Mt. Washington, and Portsmouth. These are some good teams, but I know we can beat them. Then we will have the final meet against Proctor, Hampton, and St. Peter's High School. We have to get through those meets and we will face the winner of the Dartmouth, Lakes Region, and Concorde Academy. Proctor is good this year. They beat Lakes Region, and Dartmouth. They came close to beating Concorde so we have to do our best. Okay. You've done great. Tomorrow you will warm up and work on your event. It'll be a very short practice and I want you to get all the rest you can for the meet on Wednesday. Okay, get outta here, and get some rest."

When Jimmy got home, he grabbed a sandwich and called Jessica. "Hey, beautiful. How are you?"

"Are you coming to the meet on Wednesday. It's home."

"Of course. Wouldn't miss it for the world. What time is it?"

"It's at 6. I figure we could grab a bite to eat after school and then…"

"Yeah. I get out at 3:00. I can stop by and pick you up."

"Sounds good. How was your day?"

"Oh, everyone has spring fever. They all just want to go on vacation. They're starting to suddenly get sick and want to go home."

"And go out and enjoy the nice weather?"

"Yeah, right? I mean, there's only a week left until vacation. You'd think they could wait."

"Yeah. My kids are a little antsy as well."

"I'll be glad to see April vacation.

"Is that so?"

"Yes. And you of course."

"Can't wait. Anyway, I've gotta get to bed. I'll see you on Wednesday."

"Okay. Good night."

"Good night."

Wednesday came quickly and after dinner Jessica drove Jimmy up to the front door of the pool house. "I'll park and see you in there." She gave him a kiss and said, "Good luck tonight, sweetheart."

"Thanks."

Jimmy headed for the pool deck to see if the other coaches were there yet. He looked around and the pool was empty. He went to his office, put on his suit jacket, and looked through his paperwork to make sure the rosters were up to date. He was studying the swim times as Ray and Seth came in.

Seth went into the bathroom and got changed. Ray took a seat and looked at Jimmy. "What's up?"

"Oh, nothin' much. Just looking over the stats. Looks like we should do well. The other teams don't have a whole lot to offer. We should do well tonight. I just hope Brian can concentrate."

"He'll do fine Jimmy. How's Jessica?"

"Good. We just had dinner. She should be here any minute now."

Just then, there was a knock on the door.

Jimmy stood up. "That's probably her now." He opened the door and Jessica was standing there. "Speaking of the devil."

THE FINEST MOMENT

"Hey you."

Jimmy gave her a peck on the cheek. "Hey. Come on in. We're all decent."

Ray looked over at Jessica and waved.

They talked for a while until the team came on deck. Ray and Seth hustled out to the pool deck and hurried the kids along. Jessica stayed in the office and talked with Jimmy for a while.

"Jessica, I was wondering if you wanted to spend the weekend together. It's supposed to be nice. I figure we could take go to a little bed and breakfast on Squam lake. We could just relax. I can rent a double suite and I can sleep in the other room."

"Yeah, sure. That would be nice. I'd like to spend some time with you." Jessica got closer to Jimmy and the smile left her face. She looked into his eyes, and then down at his tie. She adjusted it and ran her fingers along his back, and then up his neck. "You look nice today. Um, You smell good too."

"Thanks."

"I love you Jimmy O'Neal. I love you so much."

Jimmy smiled and looked at her. "I love you too Jessica. More than you'll ever know."

She kissed his forehead. "You make me feel so good. I love spending time with you and I am proud of who you are. I truly want to get to know you more each day."

"I'm glad I met you. I'm not glad that Miranda broke her ankle, but I guess something good came out of all of that."

"It's the joy that comes out of sorrow."

"Yes. It is." He gave her a hug and held onto her tightly as if he were never going to let her go.

"Well, we'd better cool it before your kids come out on deck and come knockin' at the door. I don't know. Maybe it's the suit but you look good, Jimmy."

"I think it's the cologne."

She slapped his shoulder gently. "Okay, now. I better get outta here." She kissed him on the cheek. "Good luck. I'll see you out there, handsome."

"I'll see ya."
"I love you."
"I love you too."

Jimmy went on deck and looked on as his young athletes were warming up. He walked around the pool and watched each and every one of them as they swam. He listened to the music that was playing and a sense of pride and dignity overcame him. He had finally felt that sense of accomplishment that he had longed for so many years. He looked up and saw Jessica in the stands. He felt proud to have such a wonderful woman by his side. He gazed at her and a warm, peaceful feeling had made him feel at ease. His eyes probed the stands as he looked over the proud parents and faculty members who had attended. Jimmy had found a balance of being humble and proud.

Seth and Ray dismissed the team from the pool and told them to go to the gym to wait for the head coach. Before Jimmy entered the gymnasium, he knelt down and genuflected. "Thank you, oh Lord, for fulfilling every dream of mine. Please give us strength today."

Jimmy walked over and caught the tail end of Kayleigh's pep talk to her team. "….And when you feel like you have nothing left to give…."

The team stood up raising their hands toward the ceiling and shouted," That is when you have everything to give!"

Jimmy smiled and walked over. Kayleigh looked at him and said, "Good luck today, Coach O'Neil."

"Good luck to you too, Kayleigh."

Jimmy paused for a moment and began walking around in front of the team. "Well. This is it. The last meet of the season. You have all put a great deal of effort into making this season a successful one. Although we will be going to the semi-finals over vacation, you still have one more meet to win. It won't be easy. Winning is not easy and it never will be. If it were easy, then everyone would be winning. A winning season is only for those who are dedicated and you have shown great dedication this season. I want you to go out today and do your best. Remember. Pace yourself and focus; but most of all, go out there and enjoy yourself. Okay? Good luck today and give 'em hell. Break it down."

THE FINEST MOMENT

The team put their hands together and yelled. "Victory, victory. Go, fight, win. HoooH!"

Jimmy went out to the deck and took his spot on the far corner of the pool area so he could watch his team. Seth and Ray situated themselves near the starting blocks. Tisha Mazzaglia, a young sophomore, was waiting on the blocks to begin. She adjusted her cap nervously and stretched her arms to the ceiling. She shook her head around and leaned over as she stretched.

"Swimmers take your marks. Swimmers get set." The buzzer sounded and Tisha had a graceful dive. She began her free-style stroke with great exertion. Seth ran on the edge of the pool and shouted to her. "Slow down, Tisha. Keep a good pace. Reach your arms."

Tisha did her flip turn and pushed off the edge of the pool with amazing force. She had moved through the water with as little splash as possible. She hit her second turn and caught her second wind. She continued to be ahead of her opponents as she reached the next turn. She pushed off again with the same force as she had on the first 2 turns. She was pacing herself pretty well and continued to be in first place. On her final turn she whipped her legs over and slapped the water as she pushed herself off the edge of the pool and glided toward the center where she pushed and reached until she hit her final destination and won the race. She jumped out and gave Ray a high five. Then she looked over at Jimmy and gave him a thumbs up. Jimmy smiled and nodded his head as he returned the gesture.

Lincoln Academy could do no wrong that evening. Everyone on the team had great technique and paced themselves well. Jimmy was proud to see that his team had won the meet; but, it was now time to prepare for the semi-finals next week.

On Friday after work, Jimmy picked Jessica up and took her to the cottage he rented. The landlord offered to let Jimmy stay there year 'round at lower rent than he was paying as long as he looked after the rest of the cottages during the winter months. The weather was getting warmer so they went out to the water and sat along the beach as the sun went down.

Jessica looked up at the sky. "It's so beautiful here. So peaceful."

"Yeah, it's nice. I'm glad I got the place."

"Yeah, it's good being with you, Jimmy." She put her hand on his shoulder and leaned her head on his chest.

Jimmy ran his hands through her hair and put his head on hers. They sat there for a few moments until Jessica trembled from the cold.

"It's getting chilly. Wanna go back in?"

"Yeah, let's curl up on the couch and watch a movie. We can just cuddle."

"Sounds good to me."

Jimmy led her back to the cottage and cooked her a nice dinner of scallops and fries. After dinner, they put a movie in and just sat on his couch arm-in-arm. As the night wore on, he wanted desperately to continue the cuddling, he realized that it would be a sin to even think of what would happen next. She began drifting to sleep so he picked her up and brought her into the bedroom.

Jimmy woke up early the next day and fixed breakfast of scrambled eggs, sausage, and toast. The sun was shining and it was warm. After breakfast they all took a walk on a path out in the woods. They walked along the dirt bike trail a good distance. As they walked, Jessica looked around in amazement.

"It's so beautiful out here. How far back does it go?"

"Oh, pretty far. There's wild life out here."

"Really?"

"Yeah and it'll be getting dark soon. The wild animals come out at night and I couldn't BEAR to see anything happen to you."

She nudged him and said, "Nice try." She looked at her watch. "Yeah, in about 10 hours or so." She pushed him hard and began running back toward the house. "Last one there is a total dead beat."

Jimmy started running, but Jessica had too much of a head start on him.

Jimmy finally caught Jessica and wrestled her to the ground as he began tickling her.

"Jimmy, No, Jimmy please I'm..." She wrapped her arms around him and began kissing his face.

THE FINEST MOMENT

When they were finished playing, they went out by the lake. Jessica just looked at Jimmy like a young girl would look at her dad when she saw Mickey Mouse for the first time. The lake was so calm and peaceful. Morning mist was reaching for the sky and occasionally a fish would jump out and create a ripple in the water. The sun was shining brightly now and it reflected the trees and the sky. Jimmy disturbed the placid lake as he began skipping rocks across on it.

When he was finished, he sat down and opened his legs while patting his right leg in a motion for Jessica to sit down with him. She walked over and situated herself between his legs and turned her body to him. She rested her shoulder on his chest, and placed one of her hands on his shoulder and the other one on his leg.

"Oh, Jimmy. This is so nice. It's so quiet out here. I love it."

"Jimmy began stroking her hair and giving little kisses on her forehead."

"Oh, girl. I love you so much."

Jessica let out a gentle moan as she enjoyed Jimmy's soft caresses. "Um. That feels so good, sweetheart. Umm. I love you too."

Jimmy continued to kiss her so she sat up a little and turned toward him a little bit more. Jimmy began kissing her cheek one kiss at a time. He kissed her slowly and gently. He could feel the chills on her neck as he began kissing her neck slowly one kiss at a time. He whispered softly after each kiss. "You're so very beautiful. Oh, sweetheart. You smell so good. Um."

"Um. Jimmy, this feels so good, sweetheart. Oh, baby I love you so much."

"What are you wearing sweetheart.? It smells so good."

"Um. It's. Oh, Jimmy. It's Liz Claiborne. Sweetheart."

Jimmy placed Jessica gingerly upon a thick blanket of last fall's leaves and made her comfortable. He returned to stroking her hair ever so gently. His body began tingling and he felt warm. He kissed her neck slowly and gently one slow kiss at a time. He worked his way up to her face and kissed her cheek. He pressed his face against hers and began massaging her cheek.

She smiled and closed her eyes. "Oh, sweetheart, this feels so good."

"Oh, Jessica, I love you so much, baby girl."

The only thought, to the contrary, on Jimmy's mind was being gentle with her. He kept thinking about how much he loved her and how he enjoyed spending every second with her. He did not want to let her go. He retired from the kisses and pulled her toward him. He put his arms around her and held tightly. They swayed to the music of the morning doves and the birds. He held her and they rocked back and forth, as if they were dancing slowly. He enjoyed the moment and felt better than he had ever felt with a woman. Jessica was a complete woman, he thought. She was a human being; a person; a friend. He enjoyed hearing the sound of her laugh as he blew gently into her ear. He felt sedated as he listened to her tender voice whispering in his ear.

"I'm so glad I met you Jimmy O'Neal. You are so special to me. I feel so safe in your arms.. Um. So secure." She rubbed his arms gently and worked her way to his chest. "Um. You're so strong. So..."

Jimmy pulled her closer and they held each other.

After a while they got up and walked around for a while. Jimmy headed for the house. "Hey, you wanna sit in the hot tub for a while?"

Jessica got up and wiped the leaves off herself. "Yeah. Is it nice and hot?"

"About 103 degrees. It's nice and steamy."

"Yeah, sure."

She hustled up to the house and grabbed her bag as she went into the bedroom to put on her bathing suit. Jimmy was already waiting for Jessica in the hot tub. "What are you waiting for? Get in."

Jessica went over to take off her bath robe. Jimmy's mouth dropped wide open when he saw her in her two-pieced bathing suit. The curves of her body were round and her cleavage was deep and smooth. She pulled her hair out of her bun and it waved about as she got closer to the tub. Her legs were smooth and tone and her smile was so genuine, so real. Jimmy just looked at her and said, "Wow."

Jessica worked her way in the tub slowly. He reached over and took hold of her so she grabbed him and dunked him under. When

THE FINEST MOMENT

he emerged, he splashed her. The smile left his face and a tear rolled down his face as he said, "I love you Jessica. I love you so much."

She wiped the tear from his face and said, "I love you too Jimmy. More than you know. You make me feel good. I enjoy spending time with you." She put her hands on his head and they kissed. This time Jimmy held her tightly and began sucking on her lower lip as he kissed her. She grabbed his head with great force and aggressively returned the action. Jimmy ran his hands along Jessica's legs and began caressing her buttocks. She ran her fingers through his hair and worked her way to his shoulders.

That night after dinner, Jimmy put some wood in the fireplace and a bright fire burned. He turned the lights down low and put on an Eric Clapton C.D. He held Jessica and their two bodies began swaying. She had one hand on his chest and the other one on his shoulder. Jimmy had his hands on Jessica's hips and he ran his fingers up and down the side of her body. She jerked a little and let out a moan. "Oh, Jimmy. Ahh. That feels so good." She pulled him closely toward her body and began kissing his neck. Jimmy sang along with Clapton. "It's late in the evening. She's wonderin' what clothes to wear. She puts on her makeup and brushes her long blond hair..." They danced and held one another as Jimmy continued singing. "...And the wonder of it all is that you just don't realize how...much.. I.. love...you." They continued swaying to the rhythm of the song, and Jimmy continued to sing. "Oh, my darling...You are wonderful tonight."

When the song ended, Jimmy led Jessica over to the sofa and they laid there kissing and holding each other until the music stopped playing. Jimmy came back to reality and pulled himself away and stopped kissing her. He sat up and looked at her and smiled. "I love you, Jessica."

"Umm. I love you too, Jimmy."

They held each other close as they lay in each other's arms and began to drift into a peaceful sleep.

Jimmy awoke to the sound of the crackling fire and looked around. He gently picked Jessica and carried her to bed. Jimmy turned out the lights and went into the guest room and fell asleep.

Jimmy was the first one awake so he drove into town to get a newspaper and some milk. When he returned, the house was quiet so he walked softly so as to not wake Jessica. He made himself comfortable in on the Laz-E-Boy in the living room and looked through the Boston Globe. He thumbed through it and saw an article about a man who had tried to take his life. He read further and discovered that it was his good friend from the Navy, Mike St. Clair, who was living in Rhode Island. The newspaper article said that Mike had cut himself up because he was lonely and bored and wanted to get attention. All the police could say was "he wasted a great deal of time on getting attention. A lot of personnel were called that could have been used for more important missions."

Jimmy threw the paper down and thought, "more important missions? The man was cut and bleeding and was crying out for help..."

After church, Jimmy took Jessica back to his place; explained to her what had happened; and told her that he had to go visit Mike in the hospital. He gave her a kiss and told her that he would be back later in the evening.

When Jimmy got to the hospital he found his old buddy resting in his bed. He went over and sat down. Mike was asleep so Jimmy just grabbed his hand and looked at him. Mike was pale and thin. He had cuts all over his face and arms. His arms were spread out like Jesus on the cross. There were also huge open wounds in the palms of his hands. The sun was shining brightly on Mike's face illuminating his sickness. A tear fell from Jimmy's face as he looked at his friend lying there helplessly. Jimmy remembered how motivated Mike had been. He was always in the gym building his solid frame. He was never lacking female companionship. In fact, Jimmy used to love going to clubs with Mike because he knew there would be four or five women over at their table. Now, he looked and saw this strong man lying, waiting to die.

Mike had been thrown out of the Navy due to alcohol abuse. He started drinking too much after nearly their entire team was mowed down on an air strip by rebels in Panama in 1989. Mike had desper-

THE FINEST MOMENT

ately tried to put arms, legs, and heads back on the dead carcasses until Jimmy and Allad had pulled him out of the pool of guts. The three of them had escaped to a nearby swamp for three days and would submerge whenever the rebels came. Dealing with death, swamp rats, snakes and hunger had been tough for Mike. The Navy was supposed to send a helicopter to evacuate them at a nearby field, but they never came.

The men had walked for four more days, ducking and hiding. They had no food or extra water so they had to drink river water. They also had to eat rats, mice, snakes, and other varmints. Mike's life went down hill after that and he was sent to an alcohol treatment program at the Naval Hospital. However, he got into another drunken brawl and was thrown out. Jimmy stayed in touch with him and learned that he had gotten sober and found a good job working for Brinks Security driving money to banks. After a year or so he had met a woman and gotten married.

Mike woke up, sat up, and looked at Jimmy. He wiped his eyes and stretched out and yawned. He had a confused look on his face and wiped his eyes again. When he recognized Jimmy, his eyes lit up and he smiled. The tears of joy flowed down his face as he reached out for Jimmy to hug him. Jimmy went towards Mike and gave him a bear hug.

"O'Neil! Jimmy O'Neil! You crazy son of a bitch, how are you?"

Jimmy smiled and wiped his eyes, "I'm great Boss, I'm great."

"Yeah? Good, that's great boss."

"Mike, I never expected to see you here. What the hell happened?"

"I guess it has been a while since we've talked. My life. It's, it's… I've had a tough time." The tears started to fill his eyes. I lost Sandra and my 2 sons a couple of years ago. An 18 wheeler…you know. Kaboom! They were all gone. Goodnight Irene! I've been drunk ever since. I was on the wagon for years and my life was going great, then this. I was doing construction and making some serious coin. Then I got arrested for drunk driving while driving a company truck. I was fired and have been out of work for 6 months."

Mike started to hyperventilate and began crying uncontrollably. Jimmy grabbed his hand and held tightly. "My house will be foreclosed on next week. I'm going to be homeless at the end of the month. I have no car. The happy men took that last month and I have nowhere to go."

Jimmy just looked at Mike and said, "You need a job Mike?"

"Yeah."

"I have got a job for you, but you have to stay here and go through the treatment program and go to AA meetings on a regular basis."

Mike was so desperate that he was willing to do whatever it took to feel better again.

"Yeah, okay Jimmy. I'll do it. What's the job?"

"Well. My friend Shawn has just bought an old apartment complex, and wants to fix it up so that he can have tenants. I figure that you can help re model it for him. I have to talk to my brother-in-law to see if he will do the re modeling and you can help. I'll get a hold of Shawn ASAP. He can pay you minimum wage and you can live in one of the apartments for free for a year. You can stay with me until the place is finished. "But Mike…I won't have someone who is drunk doing this job. I've been sober myself for a few years and you have to get well before I can let you begin."

"You got it chief. I was sober before, I'll do it again."

The men talked about old times and laughed and cried.

"So, Jimmy you married?"

"No."

"Any kids?"

"None that I know of. I am dating a woman."

"Really? Tell me about her."

"Well. She is beautiful. She's a nurse. Oh, words cannot do her justice. You will meet her someday."

"What is her name?"

"Jessica."

"That's nice. I'll bet she's great."

"She's the best."

"Tell me Jim. How's Allad doing? That dirty Muslim. I haven't seen him since I was discharged. I hope he's okay."

THE FINEST MOMENT

"Great. He works for the CIA and has a hottie for a wife. They have two kids. I see him from time to time."

"The CIA? Those bastards. They are all responsible for..."

"He's one of the good guys. He's an auditor. He checks on his agents to make sure they're doing their jobs. He was undercover acting as a terrorist in the Middle East. When he got out of the Navy, he joined and they sent him over to Afghanistan where his parents were born. He lived there for a few years and had to join some obscure terrorist group in order to get information from them."

Mike looked up and sighed. "Sounds like a tough assignment."

"Well, he did so well that they promoted him a number of times."

"Ah, I still don't trust the CIA."

"Listen Mike, I gotta go. I'll get back to you in a little while. You can stay here and go through the three week program. I'll be back to visit you a few times to see how your doing. Then we'll take it from there."

Mike smiled and waved goodbye as Jim walked out the door. "You got it chief."

THE FINEST MOMENT

PICK YOUR HEAD UP AND MARCH FORWARD.

Beads of sweat rested upon Jimmy's forehead as he walked around the quiet pool. Nobody was there and the lights were dim. He looked around and noticed how quiet the place was. It was so empty. But he knew that in an hour or so, it would be full of life. And when the meet was over, it would be silent again until the next meet, and this cycle would continue. Jimmy went to his office and kneeled down. "I thank you Lord for giving us the opportunity to make it this far. Give us all the wisdom to appreciate such a gift. If it hadn't been for you, oh, Lord, I would not be here if it hadn't been for you. Lord to give me the strength to push these kids. They could be staying home tonight. If we do not succeed tonight, Oh, Lord, there will be many people who are disappointed. I beg you that those people will not be my athletes. Thank you."

Jimmy sat in his chair and just listened to the humming of the florescent lights in the pool area for about 20 minutes. Suddenly he had a feeling overcome him. It wasn't a voice and it wasn't a burning bush of any kind. It was feeling that shot through him like a gentle voice. "Go out, and see the light that shines upon the pool."

Jimmy walked out and looked at the pool. The florescent lights took about 30 minutes to warm up and were now shining brightly. They illuminated the still waters of the pool. Jimmy looked around and knew that there was no place on earth that he wanted to be at this very moment more than here by the poolside. There was nobody in the world at this moment that he wanted to be with except for himself and God. He had been so caught up in the excitement of his new life, that he did not have a moment to sit quietly by himself and think. He continued to look at the pool as Ray walked in.

"Jimmy? Is that you?"

"Hey, Ray. Good to see you."

Ray stopped for a second and looked around. "Wow! I've never seen it so peaceful here."

"Yeah. That's why I came early."

Ray walked over to him and stopped. "Well, the J.V. team kicked ass last week. Sorry I didn't call you, but I..."

"They did? That's good."

"Yeah, they were really good. Rene was a shining star. She took all 3 of her events and kicked ass in the fly. You should have seen her Jimmy. She's quite a little scamp."

"Oh, I can imagine. She's so tiny. So small, but has the speed and strength of a varsity swimmer. You can bet we'll be seeing her here during the varsity meets."

"Ya think?"

"Oh, yes. Without a doubt. Without a doubt."

"I certainly hope so."

"Oh, yes. Come on, I want to go over with you the line-up for tonight and let you know what we did at the last practice. The kids had a light workout and they should be ready."

Jimmy and Ray went into the office and one after the other, the young swimmers flooded in the pool area and headed to the locker rooms. Before long, they were out warming up. Seth arrived and went into the office to change. Jimmy and Ray went out to the deck and met the other coaches as they came in. The music began to play and Jimmy listened to it to calm his pre-meet anxiety. The parents, friends, and faculty began filling the bleachers. Jimmy looked up and spied Jessica waving to him. He returned the wave and headed for the gym. As he paced the floor, he again found himself standing in an empty arena where the only sound that could be heard was the humming of the florescent lights. He heard the sound of children's voices and he smiled. He looked up at the ceiling and reflected about what he was going to say. He drew a blank and he was glad that he did because spontaneity is best source of inspirational wisdom. Jimmy walked over to his team and began pacing back and forth.

"This is it. This is the moment we have been waiting for. If we win this meet, we will go to the semi-finals. If we lose this meet, we

THE FINEST MOMENT

will have at least made it this far." Jimmy stopped walking and stood looking at each and every one of his kids. "I want you to know. I will be happier if we do our best and lose than if we do our worst and win. All of you, and I mean every last one of you has earned a right to be here tonight. You have worked your tails off and have put in your time. You go out there tonight and relish in the fact that you have had a winning season. What matters the most to me is that you give everything you have tonight. All I ask of you is that you do your best. Break 'em down."

The team joined hands and Kayleigh hollered out, "When you have nothing left to give..."

The rest of the team hollered out, "That is when you have everything to give."

Brian mounted his block and prepared to go. As the buzzer sounded he dove in and reached. He was ahead of his opponents on the first turn. He pushed off with amazing thrust and reached out. Then he slowed almost to a halt as he grabbed the lane lines and let out a scream. He pulled his way to the edge of the pool where Ray was standing with his hand out to pull him out.

"Ah, my leg. I got a cramp. Ah."

Ray sat him down and motioned for the trainer. Beth Chadwick, a paramedic from the hospital ran over.

"What's wrong?"

"He's all cramped up."

"Ah, my fuckin' leg. Ah it hurts. Holy Christ."

Beth began messaging it. "Sit still Brian. Sit still."

"Oh, I can't."

Jimmy hustled over and knelt down. "Brian. Brian. Look at me."

Brian looked up at Jimmy with tears in his eyes. "Oh, Coach. I'm sorry. I'm so sorry. Ah, I blew it. God damned it to hell."

Jimmy looked at Brian with indignantly. "Brian. Stop it. Stop it now. Right this moment. Zip it. You didn't blow anything. Now relax."

Brian turned over and faced the floor. His voice was muffled.

"Oh, coach. I had a chance to win. I had a chance to go all the way. Now we're gonna lose. Oh."

"Brian. Listen to me." Jimmy crouched closer to Brian. "Listen to me kid. If we lose this thing, we're gonna lose it together. We're a team and when one of us falls, we pick him up and continue marching on. Do you read me loud and clear?"

Brian turned over and wiped the tears from his eyes. "Yes, coach. I think; but I.." He reached over and held onto Jimmy with everything that he had. "But I don't want to lose. I've been losing since I can remember. I had a chance. I lost. I'm a loser and everyone is gonna hate me."

The entire place was silent. As silent if not more silent than when Jimmy first came in a couple of hours earlier. Jimmy held onto Brian and began stroking his head. The sound of the florescent lights was loud now. That was the only thing that Jimmy could hear were those ever loving florescent lights humming like a million bees swarming down ready to sting you in the ass. "You're not a loser, Brian. Come on. Pick yourself up. Pick your damned head up and march on. Let's go." Jimmy's face turned red and his voice got louder. "You know what embarrasses me more than you losing the race?" His voice got even louder. "You sitting here giving up your dignity. Squandering what is left of your self confidence. In the face of your opponent, in the face of your parents, and in the face of your team. Sitting here crying like a baby. Pick your head up and march forward…Do it now." Brian just sat there sobbing. Jimmy pointed to the locker room and he yelled to the top of his voice.. "Okay, you wanna lie down and die? Okay, then, give up.." Jimmy pointed to the locker room again. "Get outta here. Go to the locker room…Now. Get in there and get dressed and get outta here." Brian wiped his eyes and put his hands over his face as he exited the pool. Jimmy yelled out. "You are not a loser, but you are acting like one right now…Get outta my face."

Jimmy walked calmly over to his corner and motioned for the officials to resume the meet. Everyone just looked around and did nothing. They just stared at Jimmy. He motioned again. "Go ahead and start the meet. Let's go." Jimmy rolled his head back and forth

THE FINEST MOMENT

and folded his arms. The incident that just occurred was indicative of the way the rest of the meet turned out. Lincoln Academy lost. Jimmy shook the hands of the other coaches and motioned for his team to take a seat on the floor in the corner. He paced back and forth, but could not find the words. He turned around and looked at the team.

"You are not losers. I don't train losers…If you fall or if you fail…Damned it, pick your ass up and push forward. Pick yourselves up, and march on. Carry on. Move forward. Don't just lie down and in die in front of your enemy." The tears began rolling down his cheeks. "Don't you dare give up on me—-none of you. Don't you ever lie down and die like that. If you do, I will boot your ass off my team in a heartbeat. You are all winners. I don't care what anybody says. Pick your heads up and walk proudly. Get up and continue marching on like your life depended upon it. Now get outta here."

As Jimmy headed out, he was met by Jessica. She gave him tender smile and reached out and gave him a hug. "Hey, you."

"Hey, sweetheart."

Jimmy looked over and saw Brian and his father standing in by the doorway waiting for him.

"Oh, shit. Here we go. I don't need this bullshit."

Jimmy gave Jessica a kiss. "I'll see you in a bit.

"Sure. I love you."

"I love you too."

Jimmy walked over and Brian's father shook his hand. "Good work this season Coach. You are doing one hell of a job."

Brian's dad reached for his son. "Brian, is there something you'd like to tell your coach?"

Brian reached out and shook Jimmy's hand. "Thank you Coach O'Neil. Thank you for giving me a good kick in the ass."

Jimmy grabbed Brian's hand tightly and with his free hand grabbed Brian's arm."

"No sweat, pal. Remember, keep your head up and don't you ever let up. Go home and get some rest."

THE FINEST MOMENT

HOMECOMING

The weather continued to get warmer, and spring fever was in the air. On Saturday Jimmy picked Jessica up and they drove to his sister, Rachel's house. Ray was out of town so Jimmy felt a bit more comfortable being there. Jon and Jennifer were sitting on the back porch. When the couple arrived, they were met by Becca, Anita, and Eric.

"Uncle Jimmy, Uncle Jimmy."

"Hey guys, what's goin' on?"

Eric ran over to Jimmy and gave him a big hug. He looked up and asked, "Can you watch some college football today?"

"Yeah, maybe. Look guys."

Jimmy pointed to Jessica. There's someone I want you to meet."

"Uncle Jimmy?" asked Eric, "Is she going to be your wife?"

Jimmy looked at Jessica and they both smiled.

Anita picked Eric up and spun him around and scolded politely, "Eric, now you know better than to ask those kinds of questions."

Becca extended her hand to Jessica and said a polite hello.

When they finished with the introductions, they headed for the back porch and said hello to Jennifer and Jon. They talked for a while and then Jimmy's parents came.

Jimmy's mother, Ellen, walked right over to Jessica and extended her hand out to Jessica. "Hi, I'm Ellen. I have heard so much about you. It's really nice to meet you."

"It's nice to meet you too."

His father introduced himself and everyone took a seat. They talked and got to know Jessica until the barbecue was ready. They had spare ribs, chicken, steak, hot dogs, hamburgers and of course, corn on the cob. After dinner they continued to talk for a while

"So, Jessica, how did you guys meet?" asked Roland, Jimmy's dad.

"Well, we met at the hospital where I work. One of his swimmers had an accident and was rushed to the emergency room. That's when I met Jimmy."

"So, are you from N.H.?" asked Ellen.

"Yes. Right in Portsmouth."

"So, where did you go to nursing school?" asked Rachel.

"I went to The University of Massachusetts on a field hockey scholarship."

"So, you work at the hospital?" asked Jennifer.

"I'm actually the school nurse at Oak Ridge Elementary. I just work at the hospital when they're short staffed." Jessica's face got flushed and she felt extremely nervous so Jimmy put an end to this interrogation. "So, Jon, how goes the big dig project? Have you started working for Shawn?"

"Yes. It's gonna take forever. There's a lot of work to be done. I'm working 8 days a week."

Jimmy's family got more acquainted with Jessica and they all approved. She told them about the time she had spent with Mother Theresa in India and they were quite impressed. Even Becca had only talked to her for a little while when she realized how special Jessica was. They had to leave so they said their goodbyes.

After they left Rachel's and headed for Portsmouth to Jessica's sister, Alana's house.

When they got there Jessica's niece, Chelsea who was 5 ran out and gave her a big hug. She looked up and Jimmy and said, "Hello," and then ran back inside. Jessica and her sister had a striking resemblance. Alana was a couple of years older, but didn't look it. She invited them in to the living room. They talked for a while until Jessica's parents came in.

Jimmy stood up and extended his hand to Jessica's mother. "Hi, I'm Jim. It's a pleasure to meet you."

Jessica's mother looked young and it was then that Jimmy knew where his new girlfriend had gotten her good looks.

"Hi, I'm Rene. It's nice to meet you too. I've heard so much about you."

THE FINEST MOMENT

Jimmy shook Jessica's father's hand and introduced himself.

Her father smiled and said, "Hi, I'm Paul, I have heard some interesting things about you."

Paul and Irene took a seat and made themselves comfortable. Paul was a short, thin man, but looked healthy. He had light brown hair and hazel eyes. Paul looked at Alana and asked, "Is Barry and Woody coming? Where's Ron?"

Alana thought for a moment and said, "Barry had to meet with a client today..."

"On Saturday?" protested Paul.

"Well, Dad, you know how attorneys are. Sometimes they have to work weekends. Anyway Ron had already made plans months ago to go up to the Cape with his family."

"Oh, that's too bad. I was hoping that Jimmy would meet my grandchildren. So where is Ron?"

"Ron had a little situation at the Restaurant. One of his cooks quit and his manager was frantic so Ron is slaving over a hot stove. He's so short handed there it's not even funny. I keep telling him..."

"So what time do you think he'll be here?" asked Rene. "I can't wait for you to meet her husband. He is so funny. I guarantee he'll keep you in stitches."

"He said he was going to make lunch and one of his other cooks was going to fill in for dinner. He'll be here."

"Well, Rene, let's get to know this fine young gentleman that our daughter's been talking about." Paul looked at Jessica and then at Jimmy and smiled. "Jessica tells me that the two of you met at the hospital. You know nothing happens by mistake. There was a reason that you were there at the same time."

"Yes, sir, I saw her and...I just knew that I had to get to know her."

Irene looked at Jimmy inquisitively and asked, "So, you are a teacher?"

"Yes, ma'm. And a swim coach."

"Interesting. What do you teach?"

"Business."

"Very interesting. High school right?"

"Yes, ma'am."

Phil was interested in learning about Jimmy's time in the Navy. "So tell me, how long were you in the Navy for?"

"Four very long years."

"Navy Seals, Right?"

"Yes, sir, Seal team 5."

"Incredible, I saw a documentary program on television about the Navy Seals. You must have gone through hell."

"Yes sir, it wasn't easy."

Phil asked more questions about the Navy Seals and Jimmy talked about the time he had spent on a ship. He told them that he had been in Panama but closed the subject quickly.

"So Mr. Heimlick, I understand that you were a Doctor."

"Oh, yes, I had an incredible time. I've done a great deal of traveling. Rene and I met in Mexico. We were both in the Peace Corps. She was a school teacher and I was a young physician trying to heal the world. We came back to Portsmouth where I am originally from and settled down. I worked at a free clinic; but with trying to raise a family and all, I took a position as an emergency room M.D. As my family's needs grew, so did my need to earn more money. For the last 10 or so years of my career, I opened up my own practice."

"So, Mrs. Heimlick…"

"Oh, please call me Rene."

"So, what did you teach Rene?"

"I taught 1st grade. I resigned after I had my first one and raised my babies myself. I'm so proud of them all. They're all doing so well for themselves.

They talked for a while and then had lunch. When they finished, Ron slipped in the door. He spotted Jessica and ran over to her and gave her a big hug. "Hey, how's my favorite sister-in-law?"

"I'm your only sister-in-law Ron."

"Well, if I had more, you'd be my favorite."

"I'm fine, how are you?"

"Well, I know how a cooked chicken feels. It was hotter than hell in that kitchen today. I'm gonna have to pay my cooks better."

THE FINEST MOMENT

Ron looked at Paul and Irene and said, "How are the parents of the best looking woman in the world?" Then he reached over and gave Alana a kiss on the cheek.

Paul smiled and said, "We're doing all we can."

"Great, it's so good to see you."

Ron extended his hand out to Jimmy and said, "Hi, you must be Jim. I've heard so much about you. It seems that Jessica is crazy about you. It's nice to finally meet you."

Jimmy shook Ron's hand and said, "I've heard a lot about you. It's nice to meet you."

"Oh, don't believe a word they tell you unless it's good of course."

Ron stood at about six feet and had dark skin. He was balding on the top and had a few extra pounds on him.

Ron motioned for the family to go out to the back yard where he had plastic lawn chairs set up for the occasion. "Let's go out into the yard it's a nice day."

They all talked for a while and Ron asked, "So, you're a teacher and a swim coach?"

"Yes. I enjoy it."

"Where did you go to college?"

"I went to Boston College."

"Good school."

"Yeah, I learned a great deal there."

They talked until it was time to go so Jimmy and Jessica said goodbye.

"Hey, Jimmy, do you golf?" asked Ron.

"To be quite honest, I'm more of a fisherman and woodlands kind of guy."

"Well, listen, maybe we can go fishing some Saturday before the weather gets too cold."

"Absolutely, I'd love to."

"Great, Jess has our number here. Give me a shout."

"Will do."

When Jimmy got home late that evening he realized that he

couldn't hold Shawn off any longer so he called him and they made plans to go to Las Vegas for the weekend.

When Jimmy finished talking he called Jessica and reluctantly told her about his plans with Shawn.

"Hey, sweetheart. How are you?"

"Good. What's goin' on?"

"Well, not a whole lot. I'm just calling to tell you that I'm gonna hang with Shawn this weekend. I've been blowin' him off and he wants to get together with me."

"Oh, that's fine. Christa and the girls wanted to get together and do something anyway. That's fine. What are you guys gonna do?"

"Well, he wants to go to Las Vegas."

"Really? Wow!"

"Yeah, I'm not gonna bring a lot of money with me—- maybe a grand or so. I don't really want to go but he's been bugging me for a long time and…"

"No. You go ahead and have some fun. It'll probably do you good to get away. Really, it's fine. Get away and have some fun."

"Are you sure you're not upset. Because if you are, I could call him and…"

"Not at all. You go and let off some steam."

"Okay. You are right. It might be a good idea to get away."

"Yeah. Go on and have some fun. You disserve it."

"Okay. We should be back Sunday. I'll call you when I get in."

"Okay, sweetheart. Take care. I love you."

"I love you too."

On Friday night Jimmy and Shawn flew to Las Vegas. Jimmy knew he could win some big money there. He was going for broke but knew he'd earn it all back the first week of business.

The men headed straight for the Lucky Seven casino. When they arrived, Shawn headed for the poker table and nearly lost his shirt while Jimmy chose the roulette table. Before he threw the ball he rubbed his good luck tie and was lucky on every spin. Finally, after a couple of hours, he had won 5,000.00 thousand dollars. Suddenly he was tapped by a friendly man in a business suit.

THE FINEST MOMENT

The man looked at him and said, "How ya doin? Come wid me."

The man led Jimmy to an office in the back. They walked down a long, narrow, corridor where some of the light bulbs had been burned out. They finally reached the small office where a group of men were playing cards, drinking beer, and smoking cigars. The lights in the dank room were dim. Smoke filled the air and subsided at the base of the overhead lamp. Next to the office was a laundry room and a small storage room. There were no windows, just mirrors. Jimmy walked in and stood speechless.

An older Gentleman handed Jimmy a bag full of money and said, "My name is Mario Capelli. Congrats, chief, you've won a lot of money. Now I would like to give it to you and escort you to the door. And do yourself a favor, don't come around here no more. Kapish? "

There were two men who were about 6 feet 8 inches tall and all muscle that were standing next to the man so Jimmy didn't argue.

Jimmy looked at the man and shook his head in agreement. "Ah, yes sir. No problem."

The man took a long drag of his cigar and leaned forward and asked, "What's ya name kid? I want the truth pal, because I have ways of findin' out. Ya know what I mean?"

"Yes sir, my name is Jimmy O'Neal."

"Good. Very good Irish name. You a Catholic kid?"

"Ah, yeah."

Mario genuflected and then kissed his hand and said, "Good. That's what I like to hear. It's good to see a nice, honest Catholic boy. So, I'm gonna let ya go widout any problems. I got ya face on camera kid so If I see you heya again. Well, I won't be seeing you again so we won't have to worry about what to do if you come back, do we?"

"No sir. I mean, right, I won't show my face here again."

"Good, that's what I like to hear. Now beat it kid."

The two lugs escorted Jimmy to the bookie's office so he could collect his winnings and then they took him outside and told him to walk. As he walked across the parking lot he tried to reach Shawn on his cell phone, but got no answer so he paged him with a message to meet him outside of the Lucky Seven. Evidently, Shawn did not get the page, because 30 minutes had gone by and still, there was no sign of him. Jimmy frantically pushed the numbers on his cell phone that would hopefully connect him to his friend. Jimmy paced the pavement near the entrance of the Casino and ran his hands nervously through his hair.

He waited while the phone rang. "Come on, come on, come on," he sighed impatiently. "Come on damned it Shawn, pick up."

Finally, Shawn picked up. "Hello?"

"Shawn," Jimmy muttered. Get out of there. I'm outside."

"What's up Jimmy?"

"They threw me out. I won 3 hundred grand brotha. Let's go celebrate. Get out here. I'm out front."

"Okay. Give me a minute."

When Shawn came out, he shook his head and laughed. He punched his friend, who looked a puppy whose nose was rubbed in his own shit, in the stomach and wrapped his arm around his head and gave him a noogie. He bawled, "What the hell happened? You fool. You've been here a million times, you know the scoop. What were you thinking?"

Jimmy's face turned red and his mouth opened but no words came out. He finally choked up an explanation. "I, I, mean, well, you know. Shit man." He drew a deep breath. "I thought those apes were gonna kill me."

"Come on, let's go and let off some steam."

The men went to a few strip clubs and then went dancing. Both Shawn and Jimmy had been hitting the gym so they were in good physical shape. This was certainly conducive to what they were trying to achieve that night. God had somehow given them the same frame except Shawn was a bit taller and had more hair on his head. They were sitting at a table and Jimmy was sipping on a ginger ale while Shawn was nursing a draft. They were swaying to the music and singing. Shawn pointed to the dance floor and licked his lips.

"Damn. Do you see that? Man, she's got some hips."

"I'd like to see those legs wrapped around my neck."

THE FINEST MOMENT

Jimmy looked at Shawn and forced a smile upon his face." Yeah."

At that moment, a light-skinned, black girl tapped Shawn on the shoulder and smiled at him. "Hey, are ya gonna get up or are you gonna sit here all night?"

Shawn looked at her starting with her legs and ending at her smile. "Would you like to dance honey?"

"Well, yeah, let's go."

"What's your name?"

"Natasha, what's yours?

Shawn extended his hand and gingerly grabbed Natasha's as he said, "I'm Shawn.".

"I will be you tour guide for the evening. We'll be going on a long ride and I want to make sure to show you a good time."

Shawn stood up and looked at Jimmy and shrugged his shoulders as if to say, *what can I say? I still got it*, and said, "I'll be back."

When Shawn hit the dance floor, his new friend started grinding her body all over him. Shawn held on to the back of Natasha's neck and did the same. They had to at times pull away from each other so that the sweat would dry from their bodies. Jimmy just sat at the table listening to the music and paid no attention to Shawn and Natasha.

Shawn looked at Natasha then at Jimmy and pointed to the bar. "I'm gonna grab a beer, anybody want anything?"

Natasha hastened to answer as she shouted over the loud music. "I'd like one too. A draft, please."

Jimmy looked up and put his hand out to indicate that he did not need anything and just sat there quietly.

Jimmy started thinking about Jessica and began to feel depressed. He didn't want this life. He had left it behind many years ago and had worked so diligently at creating a new life for himself. He excused himself from the table and went outside. He pulled his cell phone out of its holster and speed dialed Jessica. The phone rang and Jessica answered.

"Hello?"

"Hey sweetheart."

"Jimmy?"

"Hey."

"I thought you were in Las Vegas with Shawn."

"I am. I'm having a lousy time. I miss you."

"What's going on?"

"Well, I won some money and Shawn wanted to celebrate. He's in the club now. Getting his drink on."

"Where are you?"

"I'm outside the club. I'm gonna head back to the hotel. I'm gonna take an earlier flight. I just want to spend the day with you tomorrow."

"I'm sorry you're not having fun."

"I'd rather be next to you all cuddled up."

Jessica laughed. "Oh, Jimmy, that's so sweet. Me, too. What do you want to do tomorrow?"

"Do you want to go to the mall? Maybe do some shopping?"

"Yeah, that sounds good."

"I'll catch an A.M. flight. I'll see you."

"Okay."

"Jessica?"

"Yeah?"

"I love you."

"I love you too. I'll see you tomorrow."

"Bye."

Jimmy went back to the club and motioned for Shawn. He led his friend outside and began talking to him. "I can't do this anymore, Shawn. I love Jessica so much. I just want to be with her right now. I was having fun earlier, but I got to thinking. I'm gonna catch an A.M. flight tomorrow and spend the day with Jessica."

"Are you okay, pal? You look down?"

"I am down. I just want to go home, Shawn. I miss my girlfriend."

"Wow! This is a different Jimmy. You're really hooked bad. You really dig this chick.

THE FINEST MOMENT

"Yeah. My time has come Shawn. I'm crazy about her."

"That's cool boss. Call me this week."

Shawn gave Jimmy a big hug. "You're lucky. You've got a good woman waiting for you. Go and be with her. Okay?"

"All right. I'll see you later."

THE FINEST MOMENT

WAVES OF CHANGE

After school, Jimmy was sitting at his desks grading papers when Dr. Sheradon knocked at his door. He was accompanied by a woman of about the age of 50.

Jimmy motioned for them to come in. Dr. Sheradon walked into Jimmy's classroom and met him with a smile and a hand shake.

"Jimmy. How are you?"

"Good, sir. And yourself?"

"Good. Jimmy, I want you to meet Dr. Parsons." He turned to the woman and put his hand on her shoulder. "You see Jimmy. My doctor told me that it's not good for my heart to continue on so I'm going to be retiring. And well...Dr Parsons is going to be replacing me."

The smile left Jimmy's face for a moment and he labored to get it back. "Oh, really? Is everything okay?"

"Just great Jimmy, but it's time for me to step down."

"I'm sorry to hear that sir. I'm happy for you but you will be missed."

"Thank you, son. I appreciate that. Dr. Parsons here was a teacher years ago and worked her way up in administration. She is very qualified and very capable."

"Yes indeed." Jimmy reached out and shook her hand. "My name is Jimmy O'Neal."

She returned a firm handshake. "Yes, Dr. Sheradon has told me all about you."

"Oh, don't believe a word he says." Jimmy laughed but Dr. Parsons remained expressionless.

"He tells me that you are the head swim coach here at Lincoln."

"Yes. I am. We've got a good swim team. We almost made it all the way this season."

"Well, I'm sure you will next season. At least I hope so."

"Well, we'll have to wait and see."

"Jimmy. I've talked with Dr. Parson's about your certification waver and she has signed the waver extension for another year."

"Yeah, okay. Thank you."

Dr. Parson's gave Jimmy a stern and scolding look. "You do know Mr. O'Neal, that we are striving to have excellent teachers and it is imperative that you get your certification. Where are you regarding that?"

"Well. I took the Praxis exam and passed everything but the written portion."

"And have you rescheduled to re-take it?"

"Ah, yeah. I have to wait a few months."

"Okay, then, keep me posted on your progress."

"Will do."

Dr. Sheradon shook Jimmy's hand and gave him a pat on the shoulder. "Jimmy, this is goodbye." He pulled out his wallet and took a business card out. He walked over to Jimmy's desk and wrote on it. "Jimmy. Here is my home phone number." He handed Jimmy the card. "You stay in touch. I'm certainly gonna be back to watch some of your meets in the fall. Take care and good luck."

"Thanks, Dr. Sheradon. I appreciate that. Good luck to you."

Jimmy drove home and thought about what had happened as he looked out the window at the trees as leaves were growing on them. The grass on the highway was beginning to turn green. The warm breeze blew through his cracked window and refreshed him. He felt disappointed that Dr. Sheradon was leaving and was unsure about what the future held with the new superintendent. Jimmy was expecting good things to happen but was preparing for the worst.

The next day after school, Kayleigh came into Jimmy's classroom with tears in her eyes. She walked over to the desk in the front row and sat down. Jimmy stopped what he was doing and looked up.

"What's going on?"

Kayleigh wiped the tears from her face, and looked up. "My father...He's in the hospital again."

THE FINEST MOMENT

"What is it?"

"He's had a relapse. He's not doing very well. We had to take him yesterday. I didn't get very much sleep last night." She yawned, and put her hands in her face.

"I'm sorry to hear about this Kayleigh. I'm sooo sorry."

"The doctors don't think he's gonna make it, Coach. He's been slipping in and out of a coma. It just came on suddenly."

"Oh. I see."

"How is your mother doing?"

"She's being strong. She's really being good about it."

"Yeah. How about you? How strong are you feeling?"

"Not very. I just don't know what to do. I can't live without my father."

Jimmy stood up and took a seat next to her. "What do you think your father would say if he were here?"

"He would tell me to be strong. He would say 'push on.' But it's tough, you know?"

"Death is never easy, Kayleigh. It's never easy to see the one's we love leave us."

"I know. I just don't know what I'm gonna do."

Jimmy patted her back. "I know what you are going to do. You are going to pick yourself up and make your father strong. No matter what happens, you are going to keep marching forward. That is what your father wants. That is what he said."

"I know. I know." She put her hands in her face and began sobbing.

Jimmy stood up and grabbed her hand. "Come on Kayleigh. Get up. Get up. Go and see your father and let him know that you are going to be strong. Tell him that you are going to continue to strive for the best. You have to let him know that you aren't going to lie down and die. You have to do this Kayleigh. Go and be with him."

Kayleigh stood up and wiped her face. "Okay. Thanks Coach. I will try to be strong for my dad."

"And if nobody else…Do it for him. Do it for your father."

When Jimmy got home that evening he checked his voice mail. "Hey, sweetheart. Just thinking about you. Call me."

"Yes, Jimmy, this is Fran from the office at Lincoln. Please call me."

"Coach, O'Neal. This is Kayleigh. My father..Please call me."

Jimmy dialed Kayleigh's number and her mother answered. "Hello?"

"Mrs. Turner. Kayleigh called me?"

"Yes coach. My husband passed away this afternoon."

"Oh. I'm so sorry, Mrs. Turner."

"Kayleigh had just arrived at the hospital and...Well, soon after she arrived, he said goodbye."

The tears ran down Jimmy's face and he let out a sigh. "Oh. My. How is Kayleigh?"

"She is strong. She's in her bedroom lying down. She's okay. She was able to tell her father goodbye, and that she loved him."

"Oh, Mrs. Turner. Please let me know if there is anything I can do."

"There is one thing, Jimmy."

"Yes?"

"Don't let Kayleigh give up on her dreams. Please. Make sure you push her, and make sure she continues with her dream. The last thing her dad told her was to continue reaching for the gold."

"I promise you...I will be there for your daughter."

"Thank you, Jimmy."

When Jimmy hung up, he called Fran at her house and she told him that there was going to be a faculty meeting early in the morning to discuss the death of Mr. Turner. Jimmy dialed Jessica's number and she picked up on the 2nd ring.

"Hello?"

"Hey, beautiful."

"Hey Jimmy. How are you?"

"Not so good."

"Oh. What's the matter?"

"Kayleigh's father passed away this afternoon. It's just awful."

"Oh, I'm sorry sweetheart. How is Kayleigh?"

"She's doing her best. I just spoke to her mom and it's just awful. I can't believe..."

THE FINEST MOMENT

"Do you want me to come over and be with you?"
"Would you mind?"
"Of course not, honey. I'll be over in about an hour."
"Thanks. I love you."
"I love you too."

During the faculty meeting the next day, Dr. Prescott told the teachers to help their students in anyway they could to deal with the death of Mr. Turner.

"Kayleigh's friends were all very close to Mr. Turner and he has done a lot around the school to help out. He was close to a lot of the kids. So, if they need a pass to the guidance office let them have it. One final note of business. We have a new superintendent and she's all about education. She wants to give the teachers a great deal of training. At the end of the year, we're going to have a staff retreat at Waterville Valley resort for a few days. There will be excellent motivational speakers there and some great projects. All the Department heads will be going to Chicago for a few days before the end of the school year."

John Baker, one of the science teachers, spoke up. "Dr. Preston? You mean to tell me that the students have to pay for their own busing and we need textbooks. As it is now, the kids have to pay to play sports or be in extra curricular organizations; and you are going to send us all up to some expensive ski resort for the week? What about final exams and final grades. Where are we going to find the time to do this?"

"It's not my decision, John. Dr. Parsons is the new superintendent of schools and she's pushing for better quality teachers."

Many of the faculty members spoke amongst themselves.

Sue Richards, the music teacher, spoke up. "And what is wrong with the quality of our teachers now?"

"Nothing is wrong with our educators, Sue. Dr. Parsons just wants to see that we get some good training."

Jimmy stood up. "Excuse me, sir. Couldn't we just go up to Plymouth State and do our training there? I mean, it would save on cost and the facilities there are sufficient."

"I don't know Jimmy. You'd have to run that by Dr. Parsons."

Jake Hinkley, one of the reading specialists, turned and whispered to Jimmy. "Sounds like she's the 'group hug, go team' kind of Superintendent. Our students have to pay for their own education, our salaries suck, and she wants to take a spring ski trip. She's probably got a free family ski pass for taking us all up there."

Jimmy nodded. "Yeah. This is freakin' ridiculous."

Summer practice began with the kids sitting in Jimmy's classroom watching a Sea life video. Jimmy stopped the tape from time to time to point out how graceful the Dolphins glided through the water. He told them that they could take a lesson from the Dolphins who swam so naturally. Linda Lavalley and Monica Hoydt, two of the phsycology teachers, passed by and stopped in to see what the team was doing. Linda shook her head and said loud enough for the team to hear her, "No wonder they can't get into the championship. All they do is sit around and watch movies."

The next morning before the students arrived, Jimmy walked into Linda's classroom and stood in front of her desk with his hands on his hips.

She looked up and said, "Good morning."

Jimmy looked at her as his face turned red. "I would thank you very much to express your little opinions to me directly and not when walking by my classroom where my kids can hear you."

"Excuse me?"

"You know what I'm talking about. You've got a problem with the way I run the swim team?"

"Well, it's just that…Well, the kids should be swimming. They should be in the pool."

"You teach psychology and let me take care of my swim team. Good day to you."

That afternoon when school ended, Jimmy was called to the office. When he got there Fran told him that Dr. Prescott was waiting for him in the conference room. When Jimmy arrived he saw Dr. Prescott, Dr. Parsons, Linda Lavalley, and Monica Hoydt, sitting at the table. Dr. Prescott motioned for Jimmy to take a seat at either end

THE FINEST MOMENT

of the table. Jimmy went over to one of the chairs, pulled it out and sat down. Dr. Prescott took his glasses off and let out a sigh.

"I want to thank you for coming Jimmy. I do appreciate it. The reason why I called you down was because Mrs. Lavalley has some concerns. She said you approached her in an aggressive way this morning and I'd like to find out what happened."

Jimmy shook his head and put his hand in his face. "Oh, brother. Here we go."

"Excuse me Jimmy?"

Jimmy looked up at Dr. Prescott. "Are you serious? Is that what she told you?"

"Well, Jimmy, this is a serious matter. That is what she said. I'd like to hear your side of the story."

"Well. Last night, Mrs. Lavalley walked by my classroom while I was conducting a class on water buoyancy and made a rude comment."

Dr. Parsons tapped Dr. Prescott's hand. "Let me speak if you will. Mr. O'Neal. One of our teachers has reported that you had acted in an aggressive and threatening way toward her. When something like this happens, we have to address it. If you were not aggressive, then you have nothing to worry about." She smiled at him in a motherly, nurturing way. "We just want to make sure that there aren't any problems amongst our family of educators here. That is all. When you were conducting practice, what method of coaching were you using?"

"I was showing a film."

"Yes. Go on. And what was the film about?"

"I was showing the kids how Dolphins swim naturally through the water."

"Well, Mr. O'Neal, forgive me for not seeing the relationship between Dolphins and athletes."

"Well, my kids could learn a lot from the Dolphins."

"Okay. I'll accept that. But I just have one question Mr. O'Neal."

"Yes?"

"Do you think your methods of coaching are working for your athletes?"

"Well. I think so. They've had winning seasons since I've been here and have made it to the semi finals."

"Well. Mr. O'Neal that is quite a major feet, and we are all very proud of you." She continued to smile. "Do you feel that you have been successful with them?"

"Yes I do."

"Do you feel that it is okay for them not to set their sights at winning a State Championship?"

"Excuse me? Of course I want them to win the Championship. That is a ridiculous question."

"Tell me about the games you play in the pool. What is this Sharks and minnows game that I've heard people talking about?"

"It's an age old game. Many coaches use it. It's an endurance game and it gets the kids minds off a big meet. I use it the day before a meet."

"Don't you think that their minds should indeed be on the meet?" Her smile, turned into a look of concern.

"Well, it's kind of the same way before S.A.T. testing or other big tests. You want the kids to study for a long time, but the day before…Well, you want them to keep their minds off the test."

"Kind of the way you had your mind off the Praxis Teacher Certification exam just before you failed it, Mr. O'Neal?"

"You know what? I don't need this harassment. Get to the freakin' point Dr. Parsons. I don't know what I did to give you a hair across your ass. Hell, I don't even know you."

Dr. Prescott stood up and pointed at Jimmy. "You are out of line sir. Do you understand why you are here, Mr. O'Neal?"

"Yes, I do. Because some uptight bitch needs someone to use as a scapegoat to show her faculty members how tough she is and how afraid of her they should be. And she was given this fuel by a teacher who is not happy where she is and looking for a better opportunity so she found a way to polish the superintendent's ass."

Dr. Parsons laughed, and pointed at Jimmy. "You see, Mr.

THE FINEST MOMENT

O'Neal, this is the sort of behavior that I expected from you. You lost your temper at the last meet with Brian Bishop. You had the poor kid pissing in his pants. You embarrassed him by yelling at him in front of hundreds of fans. I'm surprised he's still on the team. He just needed a little TLC. Not a scolding. You contradict yourself by playing pre-school games with the kids and showing them films about dolphins. Then you yell at them like they were a bunch of recruits in boot camp."

"I don't need this shit. I really don't need this."

"Well then, I suggest you change your methods and begin working on preparing to win a state meet."

"You really don't get it do you? I've been busting my ass to give this school a winning season. They hadn't had a victorious season in 20 years."

"Do not rest on your laurels, Mr. O'Neal. You gave us a winning season. That is good, but now it's time to do more. I hope that you can work on making some changes for the fall." She cleared her throat and leaned forward. "You'd better work on your temper as well. I cannot and will not tolerate violent behavior toward faculty. This sort of behavior is seen by the students. Perhaps you are feeling the pressure of not winning the semi-final meet. I just don't want you to lose your temper with one of the children. Let me remind you; and I know that you are aware, that you are on a teaching certification waver..."

"What does that have to do with my coaching?"

"Well, let me just put it bluntly, Mr. O'Neal. If you don't achieve a trophy by this time next year...Well, let's just say that you will be washed up. Pardon the pun."

"Oh, really. Is that so..."

"Don't test me Mr. O'Neal. Just coach the swim team the way a swim coach is supposed to coach. Get them in the pool and practice."

Jimmy got up and walked toward the door and looked back. "This meeting is over. Good day to you."

Later that night when Jimmy got home he looked up Dr. Sheradon's phone number and called him.

"Hello?"

"Dr. Sheradon? This is Jimmy O'Neal."

"Hey Jimmy. How are you?"

"Not good."

"What's troublin' you?"

"Well your replacement...Dr. Parsons. She's stickin' it to me."

"Okay. Okay. What's goin' on?"

"Well, she's in an uproar. I had a meeting with her today and she basically told me that if I didn't win a championship by this time next year, she was gonna give me the boot."

"Oh, Jimmy. I wouldn't worry about her too much. Her bark is bigger than her bite."

"She sounded pretty adamant about it."

"Ah, she's just doing what all new superintendents do. She's trying to play the tough guy. I wouldn't lose any sleep over it."

"You weren't there. You didn't see the look in her eyes. I'm gonna finish my contract and get out next year, win or lose. I don't need this."

"Jimmy, come on. It's not as bad as all that."

"Dr. Sheradon. I think it's time that I move on, anyway."

"Oh, Jimmy, you're doing a super job there. I've heard nothing but good things about you."

"Thank you, but I think it's time to get away. I've always thought about starting a hotel or rental management in Florida. I dunno."

"Jimmy. You are a teacher and a coach. It's not what you do but who you are. Think about that. You've gone too far to let this woman shake you up so. You've worked to hard to just lie down and die in front of her."

"Well, perhaps; but I know that things are gonna get worse before they get better. I just have a bad feeling about it. I failed my exam. I can't get certified and I don't want to take the test again. Maybe I'm not destined to be a teacher. The hurdles are too high and it's too difficult. That's an indication of what I'm destined to be in life."

"Get some rest Jimmy. You'll feel better in the morning. Remember...Just pick yourself up and march forward. Okay. Get some sleep. I'll be in touch."

THE FINEST MOMENT

The birds were chirping for the first time in months and the sun was shining brightly on Saturday morning. Jimmy turned over in bed and saw the sunshine working its way through his bedroom. He looked at the clock and realized he overslept. "Oh, shit. Oh shit." He sat up in his bed and wiped his eyes. I'm supposed to meet Shawn this afternoon. Son of a bitch, I'd better hurry. When he arrived at O'Mally's in Boston he saw Shawn sitting at a table eating some peanuts and nursing a beer.

He hurried over to the table and sat down. "Sorry I'm late. I overslept. How's it going?"

Shawn looked at Jimmy and forced a smile on his face. "Hey,"

During lunch, Shawn didn't talk much but mostly listened and shook his head.

Jimmy looked at Shawn with a serious face and asked, "Is everything all right Shawn? You don't look yourself."

"Yeah, Jimmy, I'm okay. I've just been so...Yeah I'm okay."

"Talk to me Shawn, what's happening?"

"Well, it's been a while since we've talked and I met a woman..."

"That's great, you should be happy."

"Well, I met a woman who's a born-again Christian and we dated for a while. I even went to her church and I got saved."

Jimmy just listened and nodded his head.

"Well, I was brought up Catholic and drifted. I was never really much into God, but I've had a great deal of faith lately and have been reading the scriptures. Anyway, she used to use drugs and got saved and was clean for a long time because of it. Well a couple of weeks ago she went back to her old life and I haven't talked to her in a week. She crashed hard and she's prostituting herself for drug money. I really liked her and..."

"You may have lost her but you found a new spirituality. Another Christian woman who has been straight all of her life will fall in your lap. You just have to believe."

"I know but I had to see a doctor because I couldn't sleep and I have been having panic attacks. My anxiety level is at a Max. Don't get me wrong, I love running the hotel; but Jimmy, I'm just so lonely. I'm 31 years old and I'm still not married. I don't want to sleep around anymore. I want to raise a nice family. It would be nice to come home from work and have a son to take out and play catch with." Shawn paused for a minute and looked at Jimmy and said, "A couple of days after I found out about her going back to drugs, I was invited to a business dinner with a man who was the CEO of some company in Texas. I met him at a business seminar that I attended a while back and he called me out of the blue to invite me to dinner."

Jimmy shook his head and looked at Shawn as if to say, *okay, where is this leading?*

Shawn leaned forward and got closer to Jimmy so that nobody else could hear their conversation and said, "Anyway, we talked for a while. Then suddenly, the guy pulled out a hundred dollar bill and began playing with it. Then—- get this, he asked me if I wanted to go back to his hotel room with him and watch some entertaining movies."

Jimmy's eyes lit up and asked, "What did you say?"

"I told him that I'd give him a 10 second head start and that he'd better run back to his car and drive away and never look back; and that if I ever saw him again, I'd castrate him."

Jimmy's eyes and mouth were wide open.

Shawn continued, "It's frustrating when you're having lady problems and a flamer hits on you. It's as if God is telling me that all I'm good for is being hit on by fags. It's as if that was an indication of what my life will be like: heartache and frustration. That's when the late night shaking and bad dreams came. I felt as though I was ready to fly out of my skin so I went to see a shrink and he gave me a mild antidepressant and some anxiety pills. It's just so tough to push on when you're all alone. Ya know?"

"It will come, Shawn. You know, you're not the only guy who's been hit on by someone who wants to travel down your Hershey highway. Come on, there are a lot of guys in the same boat. I wish there was something I could say or do; but I can only say, stay close to your new church and God will put someone in your life."

THE FINEST MOMENT

"It sounds like you have gotten some spirituality yourself."

"Shawn, I was raised Catholic and had a strong faith at one time; but after I had to deal with the priest thing, I didn't do much business with God. I didn't have a lot of faith in him for a long time especially as far as finding me a woman was concerned. But, I stopped fighting him. I just let go of my anger and boom, when I least expected it, he put the most wonderful woman in my life. Shawn, you are starting to believe and you're my brother, so I guess what I'm trying to say, is, continue believing. God is taking care of me and he'll continue to take care of you 'cause you're a hell of a guy."

Shawn laughed and said, "How are you surviving?"

"Well. Things aren't going so well at school. We got another superintendent and she's a royal bitch. She told me that if I didn't start winning championships, she's gonna give me the boot."

"What a bitch. What did you tell her?"

"Well. I'm keeping quiet, but I think I'm gonna finish another year and get out."

"What do you plan on doing?"

"I'm thinking about asking Jessica to marry me. I'd like to move to Florida. Get a house. I dunno. I'll have to cross that bridge when I get there."

"I'm sorry, Jimmy, that I've been so busy. I haven't had a chance to meet Jessica yet."

"Well. We both have the summer off; maybe one day you can come down."

The men talked for a while and then headed home.

The weather was warm at Hampton Beach. The waves crashed along the beach as Jimmy, Jessica, and Kayleigh walked along the sand

Jessica put her arm around Kayleigh as they walked. "It's so beautiful out here. Oh, the breeze."

Kayleigh looked up at her and smiled. "Yeah. It's so peaceful here, isn't it, Jessica?"

"Yeah, I love the ocean. It's my favorite place to be."

"Yeah, I remember when I was a kid Daddy used to bring us here. This is where I learned how to swim."

"How old were you when you started swimming?"

"About three years old. I dunno. I just took to the water. Whenever we'd come to the ocean or go to the lake or the city pool, I'd stay in the water for hours. That is when daddy insisted that I join the swim team at the YMCA. It was about 5 years old then. We didn't really compete. We just had fun. I think that is why I love Coach so much. He works us to death, but he always makes sure that we have time to have fun."

"Yeah. Jimmy is all about fun."

"You know something Jessica? You guys are lucky to have each other. Coach seems so happy when he is with you. He looks alive and you seem to be very happy to be with him."

"Yes, Kayleigh. I have prayed for many years to find somebody like him. He's a good man. I love him a great deal."

"And without a doubt, he loves you too. You will both make great parents someday."

"Thank you Kayleigh. I hope we will."

"Oh, you will. You are meant for each other."

Jimmy turned in his final grades to the office and cleaned his room before going home. When he finished, he looked at his room and sighed with relief that the school year had finally ended. He headed home and turned in early that night because he had plans with Shawn and Jessica to spend the day at the Isles of Shoals, just off the coast of Portsmouth.

Jimmy was awakened by the sound of a pounding on the door He jumped out of bed and went to see who was at the door. Shawn had his face on the glass window. He had put his mouth up to it and began blowing. Jimmy opened the door.

"Hey, O'Neal. Man you look great kid. Been working out?"

"Yeah. What's up Shawn? Come inside. It's good to see you."

"Yeah, likewise. I'm starving, let's get out of here and get some chow."

The men drove to Jessica's house and picked her up. She jumped in the front seat and gave Jimmy a kiss.

"I want you to meet Shawn."

THE FINEST MOMENT

She turned around and smiled. "Hi, Shawn. Nice to meet you. I've heard a lot about you."

"I've heard a lot about you. Now I finally get to meet the unlucky woman."

"Don't pay any attention to him. Jessica."

They drove along Route 4 with the top down and enjoyed the summer wind in their hair. They went to Newick's and sat down. The hostess handed them menus and brought them water.

"So, how is everything Shawn?" Jimmy asked inquisitively.

"Things are okay. I guess."

"Still going to that church?"

"Ah, every once in a while. I'm not as heavily into it as I used to be."

"You know, I have my moments of spirituality. I always feel closer to God when I'm at the ocean."

"Yeah, I guess I do to. I love it here in Portsmouth. It has so much history."

"Jessica was born here in Portsmouth, you know."

"Really. Did you grow up around this area too?"

"Yes. I went to school here, and lived here most of my life."

They talked for a while and then headed toward the Portsmouth bay to pick up the boat to the Island.

Jimmy was wearing an old faded pair of khaki cargo pocket shorts and a WBCN, Boston's Rock Alternative, T-shirt. He also had his Teva sandals on and hadn't shaved in a couple of days. He felt comfortable and at ease. Shawn was wearing an old pair of military type shorts and a Budweiser t-shirt. He had a Notre Dame baseball cap tipped backwards on his head. Jessica was wearing a tight pair of military khaki shorts. They were olive and fading in color. She had on a loose t-shirt and sandals. Her hair was put up into a comb. As they boarded the Thomas Leighton Steamship, Jimmy nearly tripped on top of the ladder well. Shawn grabbed him.

"Gotta get those sea legs back. You've been away from it way to long."

When they got on, they headed for the top deck and took a seat along the port side railing. As they waited for the ship to get underway, Jimmy rested his foot along the rail and leaned back.

Jimmy and Jessica sat down and held hands as Shawn looked out at the bay. "This is great."

"Yeah, I guess so."

Jimmy took a deep breath and smiled. "Oh, I just love the smell of the ocean."

As they talked, the ship began filling up with people. The steam horn blasted and they were under way. They continued to look at the sights around them. They had to talk loudly because in the background there was a group of of about 8 college students playing the guitar and the harmonica. The guy playing the guitar was wearing olive green khaki shorts and had rings in his ears, nose, tongue, and God only knows where else. They were all singing about world peace and unity.

Shawn became aggravated and started moving around restlessly. "Oh, I wish we would hurry up and get there. Those guys are from another planet."

"Relax Shawn, they're just kids."

Shawn rolled his eyes and stood up looking out at the ocean.

When they arrived on the Island, one of the workers helped them off the boat. The kid was about 20 years old. He sported a dread lock hairdo and he looked like he hadn't bathed in a month.

Shawn looked at him and said, "Thank you. Smell ya later."

They all headed over to the rocks at the edge of the Island. As they sat and looked out at the white water from the waves crashing against the rocks, Shawn led the conversation.

"Jimmy says that you were in the Peace Corps and that you worked with Mother Theresa."

"Yes. I worked over there for a year."

"It must have been quite a spiritual experience working with Mother Theresa. I have always admired her."

Jessica smiled a humble smile. "Yes it was. It wasn't easy, but I did it. So Shawn, Jimmy says you were in the Marines."

"Yes, for four very long years."

THE FINEST MOMENT

"Where have you traveled?"

"I was in Rio for a few days when I was on a ship. I passed by those dung heaps..."

Jessica continued to look at him and said, "What was it like being in the Marines?"

He went on to tell her about his experiences in Central America, Panama, and the Persian Gulf.

Jimmy and Jessica sat arm-in-arm and listen to Shawn as he talked. After about an hour or so, they began walking around the Island. They stopped from time to time to look around at the sights. At one point Jessica was standing on the edge of a rock and Jimmy nudged her a bit as if to push her; then quickly pulled her into his arms.

He held her and smiled. "I saved your life. You almost went into the drink but I saved you."

She slapped his shoulder and said, "If I fall, I'm taking you with me."

She tickled him and then he tickled her back. They swayed in each other's arms and giggled.

Shawn was ahead of them saying, "Come on, that's enough of that. Let's go."

Shawn reached for his bag and gave Jimmy a wink. He had pulled out a long bungee cord and some spikes. He walked over to one of the cliffs and drove spikes into 2 bungee cords and let them hang over the side. Jimmy worked his way down to the side of the cliff and tied the cord around his waist. He sat along the rocks at the bottom and waited for the waves to hit him. He waited, waited, and suddenly, SMACK! A horrendous wave hit him and pulled him down the side of the cliff into the ocean. Jimmy floundered around for a few seconds and the cord pulled him back to the spot where he was sitting.

Jimmy let out a big Hoo, Hoo and said, "Wow, what a rush Shawn. Get your butt down here."

Shawn reluctantly come down and sat next to Jimmy and said, "You know, it's been a long time since I've bungeed and even then I never did anything like this." Shawn went and came back.

He let out a big yelp and yelled. "Oh, yeah, baby, oh yeah. This is awesome."

Jimmy went again and when he got himself together he looked up and saw Jessica sitting at the top of the cliff waving to him. She cupped her hands over her mouth and yelled, "You're crazy, James O'Neil. You're gonna get yourself killed." She smiled and then began laughing.

"Come on down and join us" yelled Jimmy.

"Not for a million bucks."

Shawn looked at Jimmy and smiled and yelled up. "How 'bout 10 million?"

"Never." She continued to smile.

Later in the day a bunch of the young workers on the Island played tackle football. Jimmy and Shawn joined in while Jessica watched. That evening they had a big cookout. Then they played a game of chase. Jimmy and Jessica were on the opposite team so he made sure he chased her until he caught her and held her in his arms. They swayed around and he tackled her gently to the ground and gave her a kiss on the cheek. She grabbed a hold of him and they wrestled. They continued to hold each other and Jimmy looked her in the eyes and said, "I'm crazy about you. I'm just so darned crazy about you."

She tickled him and ran until he caught her again.

She grabbed the back of his head and looked into his eyes and said, "I'm a little nuts over you as a matter of fact."

They kissed for a while and then rejoined the game.

That night they stood at the ocean's edge and held each other."

"I love the ocean, Jessica. And being here with you makes it even better. I feel as though this is where God's permanent residence is."

The next morning Jimmy awoke and saw Shawn walking along the beach. Jimmy caught up to him and they walked quietly. Shawn stopped and looked out at the placid water and said, "I love this place early in the morning. It's so peaceful."

"Yeah, me too."

"You know, you don't appreciate something like this unless you've been through hell."

THE FINEST MOMENT

"I guess your right. Life has that special flavor to it."

"Yeah. You know, there are times when I feel as though I never made a difference."

"What do you mean?"

"Well, it seems that every mission I ever went on turned out to be a disaster. I mean, we used to have to go into villages and find out if there were any death squads around. Most of the time we were too late. We'd have to march all over the hillside trying to find them, but the only thing that we could find were mutilated bodies of women and children. It seemed that we'd wander aimlessly for days, for miles and had no clue where they were; but yet there were bodies all over the place. We were always a day late and a dollar short. They were always one step in front of us. When we did catch the scent of those bastards, we'd always get called out on some other mission and have to go through it all over again."

"It was like walking through hell, Shawn. I know pal. I was there, too. We were probably within miles of each other. I remember one time we had to hide in a sewer in Columbia for three days."

"No way."

"Way. We were off trying to show our muscle in the world by intercepting the phone lines of a major drug dealer. The only problem was we were working with civilians. We had the CIA, the DEA, oh, everyone you could imagine had their hand in on the deal. Well, anyway, a bunch of DEA's had been captured and our cover was blown. We had to get out of there in a hurry, but the place was crawling with Drug Lord Soldiers. We had to hide in a sewage treatment suppository until we could figure a way out."

"Get out."

"Oh, it gets better. We had to share the small space with some real live ones. Dead Carcasses everywhere. The smell...."

"Oh, no way. Check this out. Down in Honduras, we had a lead that the rebels were stealing cattle so we had to check out the lead. We went to every barn around and found nothing until one day we found a barn that didn't have cattle, but people were hanging on meat hooks. Our cover was blown and we couldn't leave. We were stuck there for two days. Now, you want to talk about smell. I don't know, but it seems as though we wandered aimlessly and accomplished nothing."

"Yeah, I know. I know. But, we're accomplishing a lot these days."

"Yup. I guess you're right."

The following weekend Shawn stayed the night at Jimmy's and in the morning they packed their gear and headed for the basin of the Old Man on the Mountain. They walked to the river and saw a group of teenagers jumping from a 20 foot rock so they did the same. Although the water was ice cold, they continued to jump. When they got back up, they headed back and went for a late night dip in the lake.

They woke up early on Sunday and headed to Boston. They stopped and had lunch at Quincy market; then took the T over to Copley square where they went shopping at the mall. They also sat and talked at the commons as they watched the ladies jog by. The trip ended at Fenway Park. Because they had gone there in college, they were accustomed to the atmosphere of sitting on the bleachers. They could very easily enjoy the VIP seats; but there was nothing like the smell of hot dogs, French fries, and beer. There was also nothing like the sound of faithful Bostonians yelling and routing for their team.

Jessica wore a light blue dress that enhanced the blueness of her eyes when Jimmy picked her up late on a sunny Saturday afternoon, She had her hair pulled up and she was wearing a silver crucifix. The scent of her Liz Claybourne perfume filled the air and Jimmy looked at her in amazement.

He walked over to her, gave her a big hug and held her before opening her door. He ran his hands gently along the back of her hair and said, "Oh, I am so glad that you are my special lady. Oh, girl you look so good." As they drove down the road, the song, "Cherish" by Madonna was playing on the radio. Jimmy sang along. "…Romeo and Juliet…They never felt this way I bet…So don't under——-estimate—- my point of view…Oh, cherish the joy…You keep bringin' it…into my life. You've got the power…To make me feel good." Jimmy moved his head and shoulders back and forth as he swayed to the music. Jessica picked her hands up and waved them in the air and sang.

THE FINEST MOMENT

"Cherish is the word I use to remind me of..your love...Ya givin' it. You're givin' it. You keep givin' it to me. Ah, ah, ah, the joy, my boy. Give me faith...Romeo and Juliet...They never felt this way I'll bet...." She let her hair down and it blew in the wind. The two of them swayed to the music as they drove along the highway.

When the song ended, Jimmy leaned over and gave her a kiss. "I love you so much Jessica. Oh, I love you."

"I love you too sweetheart."

They got to Rye beach at about five o'clock and there were a few people throwing rocks into the water. Jimmy grabbed Jessica's hand and led her out to the beach. They walked for a while and then he picked her up in his arms. She let out a big scream. "Jimmy. Don't drop me. What are you doing? Jimmy?" He carried her over the rocks to the waters edge. They took their shoes off and waded. She looked puzzled and asked, "This is a pleasant surprise? Where are we?"

"This is Rye beach. I used to come here when I was younger. I felt closer to God here. I felt as though he really heard me here. I often talked to God here when I was a boy and threw rocks out." Jimmy picked up a giant rock. "These rocks represent the burdens of my life and I throw them out..." He hurled the rock into the ocean. "I throw them out and cast my worries and my prayers to God. He has always listened to my request and today I have a big one."

He stopped, kneeled, and genuflected. He looked up at Jessica and smiled. Then he reached out for her left hand. He pulled a black case from his pocket but could barely hold onto it. He was trembling uncontrollably and his face was flushed. The tears flowed from his face as he remained on his knees.

"Jessica? I ah...I want to. I want to spend the rest of my life with you. I love you so much and cannot live without you."

He took out a diamond ring and handed it to her. Tears filled her eyes as she smiled and put it on.

He smiled and asked, "Jessica, will you marry me?"

The tears began flowing from her face as she put the ring on her finger. "Oh, Jimmy, I love you so much. Yes, sweetheart, I would love to marry you."

Jimmy stood up and put his arms around her. He began crying into her shoulders. "Oh. I'm so happy that you said yes. I was so afraid that you might not. Oh, you have no idea how this makes me feel."

Jessica leaned her head on his shoulder as the wind blew her hair around her face, and said, "Oh sweetheart." She sniffled a bit and drew a quick breath. "Oh honey. I love you too. There's nobody in this world that I'd rather spend my life with. I can't wait to begin a family with you."

Jimmy lifted his new bride-to-be over his shoulders and carried her across the rocks. They drove to Rizzodo's Restaurant and had dinner. While there they discussed their plans for the future.

"Jessica, I wanted to ask you something?"

"Well, I know it's not for my hand in marriage because you already did that, so what is the question?"

"Well, I was wondering if you'd like to live in Florida..." Jimmy played with his hand nervously. "I was wondering if you'd like to buy a home in Florida and come back to New Hampshire and live during our school vacations."

Jessica looked at Jimmy and grabbed his hands. She pulled him closer to him. "Come here." Jimmy leaned toward her and waited for her reply. "Jimmy O'Neal...I would go anywhere in the world with you."

Jimmy gave her a kiss and returned to his seat. "Really? You mean you wouldn't mind...? I mean, you would do that?"

"Well, I love it here, but it would be nice to go out on your deck in January and be able to have dinner. Yes, the warm weather would be nice. I mean, we could spend the summers up here and come up during thanksgiving and Christmas break. Yeah, I think that would be nice. What about your job at the school?"

"Well. A good friend of mine told me that they were always looking for teachers and school nurses in Florida, and that is when I started thinking about it. The pay is better there and the cost of living is much lower, too."

"Yeah, it would be nice to get away during the cold winters and come back here for a couple of months during the summer. We can have the best of both worlds."

THE FINEST MOMENT

"We can have our cake and eat it too." Jimmy looked at Jessica and smiled. "It'll be nice to see the snow at Christmas time and then get on a plane and be poolside a few days later. You know, I have always wondered what it would be like to have my cake and eat it too. It always seems sweetest when you long for it."

The Boston Red Sox were playing the New York Yankees at Fenway Park and Jimmy had gotten tickets. He and Jessica had taken his nieces and nephews to see the game. They had fought their way through the crowd and found their seats. The smells of popcorn, hot dogs, and ice cold beer danced through the air. The steam from the concession stands worked its up into the stands and spread out in waves with the warm New England air. Jimmy tapped Becca and asked, "Have you ever read the book called *Under the Bleachers?*"

Becca took her eyes away from her Cracker Jacks and said, "No. Who wrote it?"

"Well, I think his name is Mr. Butts. I can't remember his first…Oh, yeah, it's Seymore. Yes. Have you heard of it?"

"It's called *Under the Bleachers* by Seymore Butts?" She paused for a moment and said, "No, never heard of it." It was quiet for a while and Becca punched Jimmy in the arm.

"That is so gross. See more butts. Ha Ha real funny." Becca scratched her head and thought for a moment. She took a wiff of the hot dogs and popcorn and looked at the smoke in the air. "Okay. What kind of grill can't you cook from?"

Jimmy and Jessica looked at each other and Jessica answered. "I don't know."

"A Grill-Ah. You get it? A Gorilla."

"He tapped her in the arm. "Ha, ha."

Tony jerked Jimmy. "Uncle Jimmy, it's Pedro. He's up to bat."

Jimmy leaned forward. "Ah, yes, he's gonna hit a grand slam."

Pedro Martinez looked up at the crown and dug his foot into the ground. He bent over and reached for the dirt. He spit into his hand, and choked his bat. He began swinging his bat back and forth. He positioned himself and waited for the ball. It was a strike. He waited again and swung to no avail. Strike two.

Tony put his hands over his mouth. "Come on Pedro. Keep your eye on it."

"Crack." The ball sailed through the air into left field for a single run.

The next weekend Jessica and Jimmy paid a visit to Jennifer's house. When they got there, the girls were outside on the porch, talking to some friends. The couple headed towards the house and onto the porch.

Becca looked up from her conversation and smiled. "Hey, Uncle Jimmy, Hi Aunnie Jessica."

Jessica smiled and waved. Jimmy walked over and said, "So, Anita, how'z school going?"

"It's okay, I guess."

"I met one of your teachers."

"Oh, really, which one."

Jimmy looked up at the ceiling and thought for a few moments. "Ah, let me see, I can't remember. Oh yes, a, ah...Mr. Dover. He said his name was Mr. Dover. I can't remember his first...Oh, yes, his first name is Benjamin, but he said to call him Ben. Do you know him?"

"Mr. Dover? Ben? No I don't know any Ben Dover."

"Did you say you didn't know any one who one by the name of Bend Over?"

Anita put her hand over her eyes; sunk into her chair; shook her head; and said "you are weird, I don't know this stranger who is walking in my house."

She put her head down in embarrassment.

Jennifer came out and gave Jessica a big hug. "Hey, girl. How are you?"

"Good. Real good. How have you been?"

"Great. Just relaxing. It sure is a nice day, huh? Come on to the back. I have some iced-tea."

The women headed to the pool area and sat down. A few minutes later, Jimmy came running out with Becca in his arms and did a cannon ball in the deep end. He made a splash big enough to get the women wet and then surfaced blowing water all over the place.

THE FINEST MOMENT

"Come on in, girls. The water is beautiful."

Jessica stood up and wiped her seat. "I'll be in in a while. I'm just relaxing."

"Suit yourself." Jimmy went under and chased Becca around. She screamed and jumped out of the pool and ran over to the side. She paused and then ran toward the pool and did a cannon ball next to Jimmy.

Jimmy slept in the next morning. He tossed and turned and looked out his window at the blue sky. Although it was a nice day, he felt depressed. It was his birthday, and he had made no plans for the day. He didn't want to be reminded of how old he was getting. He figured Jessica, Shawn, and his family would concoct a scheme to get him out of the house so that he wouldn't sit around sitting in his stew. As he lay there, the peaceful sound of the birds was interrupted by a voice that had been all too familiar to him. It was a voice he hadn't heard in years, but seemed as though he had heard it only yesterday. "Could it be?" Jimmy thought, "Naw, not possible." He stood up and looked out the window. To Jimmy's surprise, a slender, man with dark hair and cocoa butter colored skin was standing in his driveway. Jimmy had to exert himself to make out the features of the man. After a minute, Jimmy recognized him. It was Allad Azheen, his old Seal buddy from years past. Next to him was Jessica, Mike and Shawn. Jimmy hadn't asked for anything special for his birthday but anything that he might have asked for could never compare to what he saw.

The man walked up to the front porch and waited for Jessica to open the door. Jimmy threw on a pair of shorts and a t-shirt. He went to the door and opened his arms.

"Hey, you son of bitch." The tears filled Jimmy's eyes and goose bumps deluged his body. He wrapped his arms around Allad and held tightly. "How the hell have you been, brother?"

"Hey, Jimmy. It's good to see ya, pal." Allad took a step back and looked Jimmy up and down. "Look at you, boss. You look great, kid."

"Oh, man. Jessica, Mike, Shawn. How did you know?"

Mike reached up and put Jimmy into a headlock. "How else,

chief? I figured that you might want to see your old buddy on your birthday."

Jimmy worked his way out of the headlock and ran over to Jessica and gave her a big hug. "Oh, baby. Thank you so much."

Jimmy pointed to the couch. "Take a seat, my man. Take a seat. Man it's good to see you. I didn't know what happened to you. I mean, I figured you..."

Allad sat down next to Jimmy and grabbed his hand. "It's been a long time." The tears began streaming from his face as he looked at Jimmy."

Jimmy picked his hands up. " "

"How have you been, brother? It's been a long time." Tears streamed down Jimmy's face as he looked at Allad whose face revealed years of anguish and pain. "How are things, pal?"

Allad wiped the tears from his face and paused for a few moments. "Things are going great Jimmy. I'm glad to see that things are going well for you. Jessica tells me that you are a teacher and the swim coach of a winning team."

"Yes. Things are going smoothly. How was your flight?"

"It was good. Jessica, Mike, and Shawn here have been telling me how nice it is up here and I just had to see for myself. I'm anxious to see Port's Mouth."

Jimmy looked at Jessica, and they both chuckled at Allad's pronunciation of Portsmouth. "So, you're gonna hang out with head banger." "

Allad pointed at Mike. "Yeah, Mike told me what you and Shawn have done for him. He says you bailed him out of a tough time."

"Naw. He'd do it for me in a heart beat. He's doing real well for himself. He loves his new job."

"Yeah, he told me. That is a good thing that you did for him. You were always taking care of us."

"Well, somebody has to."

"Well, Jimmy. It wouldn't have been the first time you saved someone's ass. I remember how you helped out the children and their

THE FINEST MOMENT

teachers in El Salvador. Remember when I intercepted a conversation that the death squads were having? They were talking about going to sweep through and mow down all the teachers and their students in an elementary school?"

"Yeah. I remember all too well."

Jessica put her hand over her mouth and had a puzzled look on her face. "Why on earth were they going to go after the children?"

"Well," Jimmy responded. "They weren't really after the children. They wanted to eliminate all the teachers and take a few of the kids with them and use them as examples."

"Examples for what?" she said in bewilderment.

"Well, it was like this..." answered Allad. "They were going to liberate El Salvador and create a new educational system. They were going to brainwash young people into believing in their cause. They had to do this by using fear. Fear of death. They had it all backwards. I stopped trying to figure it out a long time ago."

"Yeah, I guess so."

Allad continued to look at Jessica. "Well, this guy here..." he pointed to Jimmy. "This guy here compromised our position when we got word that the Marines weren't able to secure the school because they were pinned down by some Leftist guerrilla snipers. So anyway, there were about 10 of us and over 2 dozen death squad soldiers heading for the school. So Jimmy, who was our team leader at the time, carefully leapfrog's us to the school one by one. He got all of the kids in the gymnasium and hid them under the bleachers while the rest of us made a quick hasty booby trap of the entire schoolyard and school."

"Yeah, you should have seen some of the creative things they did with a little bungee cord, chicken wire and gasoline," interrupted Mike.

Allad looked over at Jessica and said, "It's nice to see that Jimmy has finally met somebody who cares about him. He certainly deserves a break." "You see Jessica," Allad added, "Jimmy acted quickly during a disaster and saved me and Mike. During that time, I had fallen and twisted my ankle. We had to walk miles in the swamps and jungle and I had a broken ankle. I remember I told Jimmy to just go on without me. He told me, and I remember it to this day, he said, 'fine, then just lay here and die. Maybe they will come and torture you.' and Jimmy began walking away. Well, I got up and followed him. I would follow him anywhere."

Jimmy broke in quickly to put an end to the sentiments. "The last time I spoke with you, you had just gotten a promotion in the CIA."

"Yeah. It's kept me busy. So busy I haven't had time for my wife and children."

"How are they doing, Allad?"

"Oh, they're great. It's just that I've been out of the country a great deal in the last couple of years. It's been tough. After September 11th, I've been spending my time in the Middle East. Oh, it's a mess over there. A big mess."

"Yeah, I can imagine. How long are you back for?"

Allad paused for a moment and looked down as he ran his hand through his hair. "Well, I'm back for good. I'm teaching young recruits. The CIA put me on administrative duty. It was stress related. I was suffering from serious insomnia for years and then came the night tremors and cold sweats. I was having dreams of being trapped inside of a sewer with dead bodies. All I could dream of was watching snipers shooting at little kids and my hands were tied. Anyway, one night I woke up and found myself choking my wife." Allad trembled. "Jimmy, I never meant to hurt her."

"It's okay, boss. You're all right."

"Oh listen to me. I came here to wish you a happy birthday and I'm blubbering all over you."

"That's okay, man. Talk to me."

"Anyway, my wife took the kids and went to stay with her mother. I checked into a clinic and they've been treating me for my depression and anxiety. I've been going to counseling and I have my family back again."

"Wow, I never realized you had it so tough pal. You had always seemed as though nothing bothered you."

THE FINEST MOMENT

"Well, that's just it. I never reacted to any of the stress we went through. The panic began when I felt helpless. I mean, we were supposed to be the world's finest fighting force, but all we could do is just sit back and watch as the shit hit the fan."

"That was our job. Our only purpose in life was to observe; to gather information for the infantry; to do surveillance; to gather intelligence; and if we had to, fight for our lives. I guess I felt like a trapped rat. I just felt so powerless. It took a great deal of discipline."

"And you had it. You see, the military only needed you to restrain yourself for 4 years. They didn't care what happened to you after that. They figured they'd let the V.A. figure that out. And, oh, what restrain you had. What discipline you had." Jimmy looked over at Jessica. "You should have seen this guy. He could de-code anything. He knew when, where, why, and how the bad guys were going to do things before they did it; and because of that, a lot of people were saved."

Jessica yawned and motioned to the door. "Oh, my goodness. It's getting late. I'd better be going now."

Allad stood up and shook Jessica's hand. "It was nice meeting you Jessica."

"Likewise. Take care." Jessica leaned toward Jimmy and gave him a good night kiss.

On Labor Day weekend, Jessica had asked Jimmy if he'd take her fishing with him. She knew that he loved doing it and she wanted to be a part of how Jimmy enjoyed spending his time. She was reluctant at first because her dad really never took her fishing and she had only been a few times. They arrived at the East Portsmouth Bridge near Strawberry Banke. Jimmy unloaded his jeep and handed a tackle box and pole to Jessica. The couple walked to the middle of the bridge and set their things down. Jessica looked like a little girl who was being taught the skill of fishing for the first time.

Jimmy baited the hooks and showed Jessica how to cast the line out. "Now, sweetheart, you want to give it a good nudge and get it out as far as it will go."

She shook her head and asked, "What do I do then?"

Jimmy shook the pole and said, "Wait until you feel tension, then pull steadily. You'll want to pull quickly."

"Okay, I think I got it."

Jimmy handed her the pole and pointed to a spot on the pavement. "Here, honey. Stand right here and face the water."

Jessica took the pole and faced the water. "Okay, what do I do now?"

Jimmy stood behind her and put one hand on the pole and manipulated her hands to where she was supposed to grab. "Okay, now you want to cast it out." He helped her to cast the line out. "Like this, there you go. You got it sweetheart."

"I got it. That's a girl. Now I just sit here and wait?"

"Yeah, basically. You can nudge on it from time to time. Move it around. You wanna make the fish think your bait is alive. You can reel it in from time to time if the current brings it in."

Jessica stood there and looked out at the water. She concentrated as if she were in the middle of an S.A.T. test or something. Jimmy baited his hook and cast it out. He looked over at Jessica who had a death grip on the pool. Her body was tense and she didn't appear to be enjoying herself.

Jimmy laughed and said, "Hey, relax, loosen up. This is supposed to be fun."

She loosened her grip a bit and looked over at Jimmy. "So, what do you usually talk about when you go fishing?"

Jimmy smiled and answered her question half heartedly, "The Patriots, sports, the weather, politics, girls."

Jessica protested, "Girls?"

"Well, you know. Guy things."

"Okay, so do you think Brady is gonna have a good season this year?"

"Yeah, I think so."

Jimmy pulled out a Slim Jim and put one in his mouth. He handed one to Jessica. "Want a Slim Jim?"

She put her hand out. "Yeah, sure."

They sat there quietly until suddenly Jimmy picked something

THE FINEST MOMENT

up and began reeling it in. It was a mackerel. Jimmy was hoping to catch a Striped Bass so he wasn't as excited as his new fishing partner.

Jessica put her pole down and went over to Jimmy who was hooking the fish onto his line. She bent down beside him and said, "Wow, you caught one already."

"Yeah, sure did."

"What are you doing?"

Jimmy was fighting with the fish as it floundered about.

"Hooking him to my line. Gonna use him as live bait. Live bait is better than dead bait."

"Doesn't the hook hurt him?"

"No baby, it doesn't. He'll be all right."

"Wow, I've never seen live bait before."

"Yeah, it works better."

Jessica went back to what she was doing and stood there for a few minutes until she felt some tension on her line. She screamed, "Jimmy. Jimmy."

Jimmy fixed his pole so that it would rest upon the rail of the bridge and rushed over to Jessica's side. "Oh, you got one baby girl. Hold on."

He got behind her and held on to the pole. "Okay, sweetheart. Just like I showed you. Keep reeling him in. That's it. That's my girl! You got it."

"I don't want him to get away."

"Just hold it steady. There you go."

The fish was finally out of the water and swaying near the edge of the bridge.

Jimmy tapped her hand and demanded, "Don't let him hit the bridge, he'll get tangled. Gotta pull faster. Faster."

Jessica pulled with all her might, quickly and steadily until the fish reached the bridge. "I got it. I got it."

Jimmy grabbed the fish and unhooked it. "Now you just have to unhook him and throw him in the cooler."

"I can't believe it I caught one. Yes. I got one."

"Yeah, now bait up another and throw it in."

He helped her re-bait her hook and she threw in the line. They stayed on the bridge for another hour or so, and by the time they were ready to leave, they had a dozen Mackerel in their cooler. They brought the fish over to Jimmy's cottage and cleaned them. When they finished, they put them in bags and froze them.

School had started in the usual way. The school had gone on a double block schedule so that they students could finish their courses by the end of the semester instead of having to take them for an entire year. The teachers were flocked in the guidance office getting their schedules. While Jimmy waited he talked to Derek Brimmer, the head football coach. Derek was tall and had a stocky frame. He looked at his watch impatiently and let out a sigh.

"I wish these boner breaths would hurry up. I've got one more day of double sessions and I need to get out to the field. I wish they didn't go to double blocks. It's messed up my whole schedule."

"Ah, you know how it goes, bull dog. Hurry up and wait. I'm sure your coaches will have the boys draggin' their dicks in the dirt. They'll be all right. I kind of like the double blocks. It gives me less students to concentrate on."

"This is true, but the freakin' classes are so long—an hour and a half."

"Yeah, but instead of having a hundred kids, you only have 45. And you only have to teach 3 classes as opposed to 5. If you have a study hall, you only have to prepare for 2."

"Yeah, but I can't teach for an hour and a half."

"Well, by the time they get settled down and you get their attention, half the class will be over with and you don't have to worry about rushing through. I think it's good. I only have to deal with half the kids and I get more time to teach them."

"True..true. Oh, I wish these assholes would hurry up."

Jimmy had the ideal classes. He had first period free and then had a group of about 15 freshmen. He introduced himself, passed out a course syllabus, and got to know his students. He felt at ease, because he didn't have to rush through and cover a lot of material before the bell rang.

THE FINEST MOMENT

When he got to the pool, Ray was standing on deck with his arms folded. He was wearing a beat up old baseball cap and a pair of white mesh shorts, and an Abercrombe t-shirt on. Jimmy walked over to him and nudged him.

"Hey, stud. What's new?"

"We've got a hundred freshmen. That's what's new."

"Good, deal. That's what I like to see."

"Well, actually there are about 20 and there are at least a dozen sophomores who came out this season."

"Where's my varsity squad?"

"They're in the gym warming up. Kayleigh's fired up this season. I tell ya what, she's on fire. She's got them all lined up doing something I've never seen before. I think she learned it at the camp she went to this summer."

"Amazing. I feel badly, I never followed up to see how she was doing after her dad died."

"Well, I think he's been resurrected, because she is pumped up for sure."

Jimmy entered the gym quietly so as not to be detected by his team. He stood along the wall and watched as Kayleigh and Kisha were conducting calisthenics. Kayleigh, Kisha, and Brian were situated in the middle of the gymnasium as the rest of the team circled around them. Kayleigh bent down on all four legs and lifted herself up slowly as the rest of the team followed her. She reached and jumped, and then went back to her stance. Occasionally she yell at them.

"Get your damned hands up. Get 'em up." She stopped and walked around. "You need to get down low, reach for the sky and jump. This will help you with your dives and your flip turn recovery thrusts. Now push. Come on, push like you mean it. Give it everything you have. Stop doggin' it, Miranda. I know you've been out of it for a while, but push yourselves. We are gonna win the gold come Christmas. I can promise you that. If you don't want to win, then get the hell out of the gym. There is no room for slackers on this team. Now, let's go. Let's do it again."

Jimmy walked over and watched his captains take charge of the team. Although he stood there with a stern look as if he were pissed and ready to lay into each and every one of them, he felt like jumping for joy knowing that his captains had finally taken charge of the team. He couldn't be certain of the future of the team, but he could be sure that his captains had finally figured out what to do. To him, he had accomplished everything he had set out to accomplish. When they finished, Kayleigh got in their faces and pointed toward the pool. "Now get out there and warm up. I don't wanna see any grab ass from anyone. Let me tell ya what. If I do, I'm gonna ask Coach to boot ya outta here. Now, let's go."

Kayleigh ran over and stood in front of Jimmy. "Coach...How are ya?" She gave Jimmy a nudge on the shoulder and threw air punches at him."

"Not as good as you. I'm impressed, girl. Looks like you learned a lot this summer. How have you been? I'm sorry that I didn't get hold of you, but...," he paused and smiled. "I asked Jessica to marry me."

Kayleigh's eyes lit up and she gave Jimmy a hug. "Coach! All right! Good for you."

"Thanks. How are you?"

She pulled away and took a step back. "Well, I have my ups and downs. I have my moments, but I'm hangin' in there. I decided that there's a time for livin' and a time for dyin', and I'm not ready to lay down my head yet. My dad wants to see me shine this year and I'm gonna take the state title this year for him."

"That's my girl. That's what I wanna see."

She pointed to the pool. "Well, I gotta get out there. Got a lot of work to do." She ran off and yelled, "Good to see you again Coach. I'll see you out there."

The next day after school, Dr. Prescott walked into Jimmy's classroom. "Jimmy. Jimmy. How did the interview go down in Florida?"

"It went very well, Dr. Prescott."

"You know Jimmy, when they called me I was a little surprised. I didn't know what to say. I didn't realize that you were looking elsewhere.

THE FINEST MOMENT

"I got to thinking about that little meeting that we all had back before school ended and I thought that it would be best for you and your school if you didn't have such a violent loser teaching at your school. I felt that it would be good for the team if they had a coach who could help them win the state title, so I sent my resume out." Jimmy felt like dancing on the table and saying, "I got a new job. I got a new job, and you'd better kiss my ass." But Jimmy felt as though there was some poetic justice in Dr. Prescott having a good coach being pulled out from under him.

Dr. Prescott scratched his head and began playing nervously with his hands. "Well, Jimmy. I got a complaint from one of the teachers and I had to act on it. You know how it is. I'm in a position to..."

"I understand sir. I completely understand."

"Did you take the job?"

Jimmy walked over and straightened his desks one by one. "Well, sir. I haven't made up my mind. I tell you what, when I do you'll be the first to know."

"I hope you stay on. I know that you have potential to win a state meet."

"You see, you just don't get it do you."

He looked at Jimmy with a puzzled look on his face and scratched his head.

"It's not about winning the state meet. It's about teaching the kids respect, discipline, teamwork. It's about teaching them how to succeed in life. And if they do all of those things, they may or may not just win the state meet."

"Well, yes, I agree, but you are doing a good job here; and if it's the salary, well, we can..."

"No, no, no. It's not about the salary. It's about taking care of the kids. You know at the meeting last year, when the teachers protested not going on that week long retreat in Waterville Valley, you didn't agree with them."

"Dr. Parsons has her mind made up and I can't..."

"Why? Why can't you go to bat for your teachers and students?

They had a valid argument. We have to photocopy pages from a beat-up old text book; we could use a new library; and the kids have to pay for their own transportation."

"Yes, I understand that, but you have to see Dr. Parson's point of view. She wants to have the best trained educators to…"

"And why can't they get the training at no cost to the community? Why can't they go to Plymouth State or something?"

"Because, you can't get the same quality of training there."

"Our dropout prevention program is suffering. You had to lay the career specialist off last winter. The poor kids don't have money to go to night school. They need transportation to get from job to job. As it is, all the departments have to raise money to go on all of their field trips. All the kids who play sports have to pay. What about the kids who can't afford to play? Sports are their only way out of their shit hole. Now, only the rich kids can play sports. They don't need scholarships like the poor kids do. Those kids need a principal who will go to bat for them and sit in front of the school board and tell them to find the money. It sucks when the kids who are dropping out have to go before the state legislature and beg for money, and then their program is cut. For God's sake Dr. Preston, these kids need the money and you guys are sending your staff on these expensive trips. How about the trip to Chicago that the administration was supposed to take this summer? I'll bet they went. You see, you cannot run education like a corporation. I'm sorry, but the money needs to go to the programs that help the kids. You are spending the money the wrong way. And the more you stay silent and shake your head in agreement, the more you take away from the kids." Jimmy finished straightening the rows and walked over to his desk. He looked Dr. Prescott in the eyes. "He who is silent is giving consent. Think about that."

"You don't understand my position. I've got the school board and the state Department of Education saying 'we need quality teachers.' They haunt me day and night with their bullshit about how the quality of educators is diminishing. They demand that we spend every waking hour thinking of ways to improve it. Do you think for one minute that those clowns at the capital will think that going to a

THE FINEST MOMENT

second rate college for the day will be sufficient?" His voice got louder and his face was turning red. "Don't you think that I know we could save money and help the kids? Try walking in my shoes for a day. See how it is?"

"If enough people stand together, they will hear you."

Dr. Prescott shook his head and rolled his eyes. "We are in a new society, Jimmy. I think you're fixated on the U.S. History that you read in college. This isn't Bunker Hill, Jimmy. And I'm not George fucking Washington. I'm just a God damned piss ant who is retiring in 5 years. I just want to collect my freakin' pension and get the fuck out."

"Then do it."

Dr. Prescott took a deep breath. "Do what?"

Jimmy pointed to the door and yelled, "GET THE HELL OUT!"

"Okay, Jimmy. I get the picture. You haven't heard the last from me pal."

Jimmy locked his classroom up door and was headed down the hall when he heard a loud noise coming from the other end of the corridor.

"Coach O'Neal. Coach O'Neal." Kayleigh ran up the stairs and down the hall. "Coach. Coach." She stopped in front of Jimmy and took a deep breath. She had a piece of paper in her hand. She continued to breathe heavily. "Coach, I'm in." She pointed to the paper. "I'm in, coach. I've been accepted to Penn. State on a full scholarship. I did it coach. I did it." She jumped up into Jimmy's arms and held onto him tightly. "Oh, Coach. You're the best. Oh. I'm so excited. Oh, I love you Coach O'Neal. I love you soooo much."

"That's great kiddo. You are the best. Oh. Hot shit. I love you too, kid."

Before practice that day, Jimmy grabbed Rene Mafatado and pulled her aside. "How are you kid?"

"Good, thank you."

"Rene, you had a good season last year and you've worked hard this summer. I'm going to have you practice with the varsity and see how you do. Okay?"

She smiled and looked at him with doubt. "Are you sure? I dunno. Do you really think...?"

"Of course I do. You can do it. Go on. Jump in the fast lanes with the older kids."

"Okay."

Jimmy stood at the edge of the deck with a pair of navy blue, mesh basketball shorts and a New England Patriots football shirt topped off with a Boston Red Sox baseball cap. He folded his arms and looked proudly at his team.

"Okay, okay. Let's go. Everyone over to the mats. It's time to work those legs. Let's go."

After the warm-ups, Jimmy had Seth work with the J.V. squad while Ray timed the varsity swimmers. Jimmy took Rene into one of the lanes and he jumped in and worked with her.

"Okay, Rene. We're going to work on setting your pace. Okay?"

She shook her head. "Yes, coach."

"Okay, you want to get a good strong dive. Now, I'm gonna have Kayleigh show you some things that she has learned at camp. She's been doing a great job at springing off the starting block and thrusting off the edge for a good flip turn recovery. Now, what I want you to do is block out your opponent. You have to remember to ignore your opponent. You are not racing against another person. You are racing against yourself. You want to start off slowly, very slowly and increase your speed as you go. You don't want to make the mistake of going too slowly now, and giving all of your energy at the end. You want to slowly and carefully increase your speed, no matter how far ahead your opponent is. Now, what will happen is that you will be tempted to see your opponent ahead of you and speed up. You do not, I repeat, you do not want to do that. Let your opponent get as far ahead of you as you want. Do not try to catch up. It won't help you win the race if you do because you will be working so frantically to win that you will squander your techniques. I have watched your techniques and they are good. Those are the things that will help you win. Now, what I'm going to do is race you. I'm going to swim at a fast pace and will be ahead of you. I don't want you to pay any attention to me. Okay?"

THE FINEST MOMENT

"Yes, coach."

"Let's do it."

They mounted their blocks and Jimmy yelled out. "Take your marks, get set....Go." Jimmy dove in way in front of Rene and swam ahead of her. When the race was done, they surfaced. "Okay. We're going to do that again, and again, and again. Later this week, I'm gonna get some of the varsity kids to race you and I want to make sure that you are paying more attention to your pace and not to the race. In time, we will work on establishing your times; but for now, I just want you to learn how to race against somebody without having them affect the way you swim."

Before practice started the next day, a small, stocky man of about 45 years stood at the door. He had on a pair of gray, wool, dress casual pants and a white oxford dress shirt. He wore a leather jacket and his face was as dull and uncheerful as his attire. He had short, dark hair and bags under his eyes. Jimmy walked over to see who he was. He put out his hand but the man did not return the gesture. Jimmy looked at him inquisitively.

"My name is Jimmy O'Neal. I am the..."

"I know who you awh."

"What can I do for you sir?"

"You can stawt by taking that shit-eating grin off ya sorry face."

"Excuse me? Do I know you?"

"No. My name is Nicolas Mafatado."

"Oh, yes. Your daughter is Rene?"

"Dats right. My dawta is Rene."

"What can I do for you?"

"She says you put hah on the vawsity swim team."

"Yes. That's correct."

"Well, you can take hah off the team. She's not that great."

"I think she is."

"And you know hah so well do ya?"

"Well, I do know a good swimmer with potential when I see one."

"Well, she needs to be at the J.V. level where she can improve."

"Well, she's not being challenged at the J.V. level. She won't improve unless she is pushed."

"Well, she'll just get frustrated and give up. She gives up too damned easily. I know thes things. She'll give up I tell ya."

"Okay. I tell you what. Let me try to see how she does with the varsity. If it's too much, I will take her off and put her back on the J.V."

"Do you have any children, coach?"

"No, I don't."

"Then, you don't know nothin' about kids the way a fatha knows about his little girl."

"Well, you're absolutely right, Nick. I don't know Rene the way you know her, but please. Please let me at least see how she does."

"Okay. But if she gives up, I'm comin' down heyah and I'm gonna teach you a thing or two. She'd betta nowt quit this. Swimmin' is the last strawer. I sawhr her give up too many times and I don' wanna see her quit any mo'. I want what's best fa' my lihhle goil. Kappish?"

"Gotcha. I won't let her get in over her head." Jimmy laughed. "You get it? In over her...Okay. Gotcha."

"I'm tellin' ya right now, pal. You'd betta nowt frustrate hah."

"I won't."

Over the next couple of weeks, Jimmy watched Rene carefully to make sure that he had done the right thing. Nick Mafatado had made Jimmy question his decision and he battled with the thought that his decision may not be conducive to her succeeding as a swimmer. He would have her racing the 200 yard free-style against Miranda and Rene had a competitive time of 1:25:19. One night as practice was ending, Jimmy went over to Rene and complimented her on her performance.

"Rene. You have a great time. I think you are doing well."

"Thanks, coach."

"I'd like to have you start on Saturday against Newfound High School. Okay?"

She looked a bit self conscious and nervous. "Do you think I can do it?"

THE FINEST MOMENT

"Well, there is only one way to see. If you are not comfortable after Saturday, then I will put you back on the J.V. squad. All we can do is try. Okay?"

"Okay, coach. Thanks."

"No…thank you, Rene. You are an asset for our team. I think you will go far."

On Saturday Kayleigh, Miranda, Kisha, Brian, and Billy had all placed first in their events to lead their team way to victory over Newfound. Rene had stood up to her block for the final event. She looked up at her Aunt Cecilia who was in the stands waving at her. Cecilia held a pair of rosary beads in the air and genuflected. Rene reached her tiny arms in the air and rotated her neck back and forth.

"Swimmers take your marks. Swimmers get set." The buzzer sounded and Rene dove in. She had dove further than the other opponents and surfaced. She reached her arms out and rolled her body in synch with her shoulders. She took quick breaths, reached and pulled. She utilized the water to pull her to her first turn. She flipped with great force for someone her size. Although she was small, she was powerful. The definition of her muscles were well formed. She pushed off the side of the pool with the force of a tug boat, but with the speed of a jet ski. She glided through the water and continued to reach and pull. She hit her first turn with greater force than the last one. She was ahead of her senior opponent by a good distance. As she reached, she glided gracefully in the water without much of a splash at all. She continued to push her way through the next few turns with a greater force than before. Ray looked at her with astonishment. He didn't say a word as she had paced herself perfectly. She pulled and reached until she had reached her destination victoriously. She jumped out and gave Ray a high five. He knelt down and put his arm around her. They looked up at her score and then they both jumped up when they saw it was a 1:15:28. She had beaten her opponent and Lincoln Academy had won their first meet victoriously.

Rene's aunt had come down and greeted her with a hug. She gave her kisses on the cheek and lifted her up. She grabbed Rene and brought her over to Jimmy. "Coach O'Neal? I just wanna say, thank you fa helpin' Rene out. She is doing such a good job." She put her hand out and shook Jimmy's. "Oh, I'm sorry. My name is Celia. I'm Rene's Aunt. They call me Cee fa showt."

Celia was a small woman. She stood about 5'3 at best. Her hair was dark and short. She had dark eyes and a look of many years of struggle and hard work. She was pleasantly friendly and had an aura of compassion about her.

Jimmy shook her hand and smiled. "Well. You are absolutely right. Rene is going to be an all-star on my swim team."

"Oh, yes. I do think she has found something she likes. We are all so proud of hah."

"It's good to see that you came by." Jimmy looked around. "I don't see Nick anywhere."

"No. He's nowt heyah. He's...Well, you cewtainly have a nice team." She looked around and smiled. "This is such a nice arener heeyahh. It's so big. This is really a nice pool."

"Yes, it is. These kids are really good this year. They're going all the way."

"Well I hope so." She looked at her watch nervously. "I betta get goin'. Gowtta get Rene back. Take cayah, coach."

"Take care. Thanks for coming."

The next few meets were victorious for Lincoln Academy and Jimmy continued to push his team the way he had been pushing them all along. He spent a great deal of time with helping Rene improve her time. He had seen her potential and understood how painful it must be to have to live under the same roof as Nick Mafatado. Jimmy trusted his assistant coaches and his captains to take up the slack while he gave Rene most of his attention. One night Jimmy hopped into the lane and explained to her how important it was to keep her focus.

"Okay, Rene. What you have to do is block out your opponents. Pretend they are not there. Even if they are winning, you still have to maintain composure. You see, they might have a faster time than you. They may even beat you. Winning the race is not important. What is important to you is that you continue to work on your time.

THE FINEST MOMENT

On the Saturday before Thanksgiving, Lincoln had to face Dartmouth Academy. They had lost much of their talent in June when half of their team graduated. However, they looked good that day. They had placed 2nd in 5 events and 1st place in 7 events. But, they were falling behind when it came to the back-stroke and the breast stroke. Rene stood on her block and stretched out. She looked up at her Aunt Celia and her father, who were both smiling and waving. She took a deep breath and gave Jimmy a thumb's up. Jimmy smiled and put his finger up to indicate that she was number one. The buzzer sounded and Rene dove in. She surfaced and reached with great intensity. In spite of her diligent efforts, Asley Hamilton was ahead of her. Rene tried desperately not to look at her opponent, but was tempted to search for her shadow out of the corner of her eye. She continued to reach and heard Jimmy's voice echo in her mind. 'Don't look at the other swimmers. You are not racing the other swimmers. You are racing to beat your own time, kiddo. Just relax and keep reaching. She hit her first 2 turns with incredible force. She continued to work her way slowly to Ashley; but, she could not catch her and came in 2nd place. She jumped out of the pool, put her head down like a puppy that had just gone number 2 on the rug, and walked over to the bench. Jimmy came over and knelt down before her.

"Rene. You beat your time, kid. You have a 1:06:35. That is great, considering you only had a 1:08 during practice. You are doing a good job. Ashley is a senior and has been doing this for a lot of years. You have to be proud that you, as a sophomore, went the distance. Come on, kid. Don't be so hard on yourself. You gave our team enough points to blow Dartmouth outta the water. Come on. Pick your head up."

She let out a big sigh. "Yeah. I suppose. I did beat my time. And Ashley is a senior. It wasn't bad."

THE FINEST MOMENT

CHRISTMAS BREAK

One night over dinner at The Olive Garden Restaurant, Jessica reached out and put her hand on Jimmy's. "Jimmy? How did you get to be such a wonderful person?"

"Oh, naw. I'm not. Well, I'm not really a..."

"Don't be so humble. You are a great guy. You are doing so much to help young people and you are doing a great job. I mean, you have been like a big brother to Kayleigh. You are a wonderful man."

"Thanks. I guess I am dedicated to what I do. I mean, when I really enjoy something, I work really hard at it."

"Have you always been this way?"

"Not really. I mean, I was kind of lazy growing up."

"What happened for you to get so motivated?"

"Well, I learned my work ethic from my grandparents and my mom and Dad. You see, my parents were hard workers, but they just weren't lucky. I mean, they busted their tails for us kids; but it just never seemed to be enough. They both worked overtime. We'd never see them. But we just never had much money. We never had nice cars or homes. My dad and I never cut enough wood so we'd have to go trudging through the snow to get some. The only problem was it would be wet. That's why the house was always smoky."

Jessica looked at him with a less than pitiful, but more than concerned frown and stroked his arms and hands gently. "It must have been tough for all of you."

"Yeah, it was. It seemed that there was never any end to the stacking of wood. I had to lug wood out of the woods. There were always chores to do. We had to buy our clothes from good will. I was embarrassed to bring girls over. Anyway, we had some good times. We used to walk out to the river and go swimming. It was kind of nice living in the woods. It was quiet and life was simple." He let out a sigh and looked at Jessica with a serious look. "Oh, I don't ever want to be poor again."

"Well, I don't think you have to worry about that." She paused for a moment and had a look of deep concentration on her face and asked, "Jimmy?"

"Yeah, sweetheart?"

"You know, there are a lot of people who could use your help."

Jimmy looked puzzled. "What do you mean?"

"Well, there are a number of charities that could use some help. I work at a soup kitchen during the holidays and it would be nice if you would come down and help out this Christmas. You'd get a chance to meet some real neat people."

Jimmy felt a warm glow as he looked at Jessica and wondered how on earth he deserved to be with such a saintly, compassionate woman. He leaned closer to her and held her hands tightly. When he did this he felt an energy, a power that he'd never felt in his life. Everything that he had worried about earlier in the day was gone in an instant. He felt secure and his tension had succumbed to an inner peace. There was only one thing in life that Jimmy was certain about: that he would do anything and everything in his power to make this woman happy.

He held her hand tightly and said, "Hmmm, ya sure that would be great baby girl.

I'd love to help the less fortunate."

"You're the best, Jimmy O'Neil."

"Just don't let that get out."

"I promise."

On Thanksgiving Day, Jimmy and Jessica helped out at one of the soup kitchens in town. They ate Thanksgiving dinner there and enjoyed the company of many desperate souls. Jimmy sat next to a man who had a long beard, an old Army fatigue shirt, and jeans on. Although he had no home or possessions, he looked grateful. He sipped on his milk and took small bites of his turkey. He looked over at Jimmy and gave him a wink.

"I want to thank ya, young buck fa helpin' me out the way ya been doin'. I appreciate that."

THE FINEST MOMENT

"No problem. It's the least I could do."

The man extended his hand and introduced himself, "My name is Frank Fletcher."

Jimmy returned the gesture. "I'm Jimmy O'Neal. Nice to meet you."

"It sure is nice to have a warm place to rest my head tonight. Lost yeeahh, I spent my Thanksgivin' in an old beat up Chevy truck. Tawlk about cowld. Oh, Jesis, must've been about 10 degrees out theyah. All alone in the truck." He wiped the gravy from his beard. "Ayuh. Been outta work since the old lady left me a couple a yeeahs agow. Yuh. Been strugglin'."

"I'm sorry to hear that, sir."

"Oh, please. Don't call me sir. I was in the Ahhmy in Nam and I hated those little pricks. Ya know those officas. Frag a few of them pecka heads."

Jimmy continued to eat his dinner as he looked up to see where Jessica was. He smiled when he saw her at another table talking with some of the elderly women. "Yeah, I would have liked to have fragged a few of them myself."

Frank smiled a cool aid smile. "You a war vet?"

"Ah, yeah."

"Wehay did ya sewve?"

"Panama, Central America."

"No shit. I mean no foolin'. Wow. It's good to be talkin' to one of my own. What outfit?"

"Seal Team 5."

"No foolin'. Them crazy sons a bitches, I tell ya. Oh, boy. War is hell. I smoked more weed and drank a hundred times more afta I got back. I couldn't work. I got this temper. I memba my last job. Threw the snot nosed punk of a boss out a window. Damned neeyah killed the son'bitch. I got this freakin post traumatic shit. I don't know. Anyway, stopped drinkin'. It's been a few months, but can't hold a job. Get so stressed. So angry. I dunno."

"The longer you stay sober, the better you'll get. I promise you. Got a few years myself. Things are just starting to go well for me. I think."

"Well. Hope sooowww. Don't wanna be livin' in this heeyah soup kitchen fa' the rest ah my days. Ya know?"

"It'll get better. This too shall pass."

"I hope so."

Jimmy and Jessica went to some of the shops downtown to do their Christmas shopping. As they walked, they would occasionally see a homeless person bundled up in a blanket on the sidewalk. Each time he saw someone in need he gave him 20 dollars. When they finished downtown, they drove to Wal-Mart. As they entered, Jimmy threw a 10 spot into Santa Clause's pot. He continued ringing his bell and thanked Jimmy. At Mass on Sunday when the second collection came around, Jimmy never hesitated to reach deeply into his wallet and found a 20 dollar bill so he threw it in. He felt good giving his money away. He was grateful that he had some money to give away. He was grateful for the life he was living, and it was his way of thanking God.

THE FINEST MOMENT

TIES THE BIND

During warm-up stretches the following Monday, Jimmy noticed that Rene's eye had a dark, shiny spot around it. He told Ray to take over and pulled Rene over to the side. "What happened to your eye?"

She covered her eye nervously and looked down. "Ah, me and my brother were wrestling. It's nothing."

Jimmy knelt down beside her. "Did your dad do this?"

"No. He ah...No."

"Okay. You can go back now."

After practice, Jimmy called Rene's Aunt to see what was going on. He wasn't happy with what he heard; and although he tried to be as objective about it, he was unable to.

"Hello, Cee?"

"Yeah, this is she."

"Hi, Cee, this is Jimmy O'Neal."

"Hey coach. How'z it goin'?"

"Well, I just wanted to call to tell you that I saw the remnant of a black eye when I saw Rene at practice tonight."

"Ohhh. That bastid. That freakin' cowid. I told him nowt to...Yes, Jimmy. It's Rene's Fatha. He gets drunk from time to time and wants to hit on Rene. He probably had a few too many over the Hawliday and smacked Rene."

"How long has he been doing this?"

"Since hah motha died a few yeeahs agow. Oh I tell ya, I'm gonna strangle him."

"Well, you know I have to report this to the social services."

"Oh shoah. I know. But, he's been reported to them a lowt of times and it didn't do him any goowd. When they come out, he puts on a dog and pony show for 'em. He knows how to beat the system.

Oh, I tell ya, he's a complete asshole. He doesn't deserve a dauhtah like Rene."

"Okay, Cecilia, I have to go, but I just wanted to let you know that I'm going to call DCYF tomorrow during my free period."

"Yup, go ahead. I got ya back a hundret percent. Call the lawyer on him. Take care Jimmy…and thanks alowt."

After practice the next day, Jimmy saw Nick Mafatado waiting by the door to the outside of the pool. He walked over to Jimmy and shook his head in disgust.

"Ya know somethin' pal, you're causin' a lowt of trouble for me."

"I think you're the one who's created this problem."

"Let me tell ya what, howt shot. You need to keep ya nose outta my affayahs. You're got notin' on me. Rene was wrestling wid hah brotha. That's how she gowt the black eye."

"Is that so?"

"Yes, it is."

"Well then, you've got nothing to worry about."

"Well, why'd you cawl the DCYF. I don't need them callin' my work place. I am an upstanding citizen. And, my sista's awll worked up ova nothin'."

"Like I said, you should have nothing to worry about. I called them because it's my job to report it whenever one of my students has any bumps or bruises. It's DCYF's job to figure out where they came from."

"Well, let me tell you something, you punk. You ain't nothin' but a first class bum who should be cleanin' toilets somewhere."

"Maybe. But this conversation is over, pal. I've got nothing to say to you."

Nick put his hand on Jimmy's shoulder. "Let's get somethin' strait, pal."

Jimmy looked down at Nick's hand and then looked him in the eye. "I would thank you to take your dirty paw off my shoulder or else this is going to get ugly. Now go home. Get outta my face and get outta my pool. I got your number pal and I've got my eyes on you like a hawk."

THE FINEST MOMENT

"Is that so?"

"Yes, now if you will excuse me, I must be getting along now. Good day to you."

Over the next couple of weeks, Lincoln Academy was victorious and would soon be headed into the semi-finals with an undefeated record.

Jimmy got to the empty pool, looked around and didn't see his team. He walked to his office and put his hand on the door.

"Surprise!"

Jimmy jumped back. "Ah!"

He turned around, and saw his team standing behind him. Kayleigh walked up to him. "Surprise! Coach."

"What? What on earth is..."

"We have something for you Coach."

"Isn't this a pleasant surprise? What do you have?"

Kayleigh had a bag in her hand, and lifted it up. "Go ahead, Coach. Take it."

Jimmy looked around, and took the bag. He pulled out a suit coat, a pair of pants, a collared shirt, and a tie. He set the bag down and held the suit coat up and looked at it. "Wow! This is nice. For me?"

"Of course. Who else?"

"You guys didn't have to do this."

"We thought it would be nice for our coach to have a nice suit for the semi-finals. We all pitched in. It was nothing."

"Thank you. Thank you for this. I don't know what to say."

"How about saying, 'get in the pool and warm up.'"

"Okay. Get in the pool and warm up."

Seth walked over to Jimmy and shook his hand. "This is the least we can do, Jimmy. You've earned it."

Ray shook Jimmy's hand as well. "I hope it fits. We tried to guess your size."

"Thank you. I'm sure it will."

THE FINEST MOMENT

ROUGH SEAS

The Lincoln Academy Swim Team sat in the gymnasium waiting for their head coach to offer some words of encouragement. Jimmy, who was wearing his new suit, paced the floor in front of them. He looked up at the sky and then at the team.

"We've been here before. We have had a victorious season and there is no reason why we cannot win this meet. You are all fine athletes and I have no doubt in my mind that you will all do well. We have to get over the hump. We have to get past this one meet—one meet at a time, until the championship is ours. We must not be defeated. You have all worked very hard; and all the sweat, tears, and pain will pay off right here, right now. Pace yourselves and don't think about your opponent. Work on beating your own time. Relax and concentrate. Let the rest take care of itself. Now go out there and give it your best shot. Break 'em down."

"One meet at a time until victory is ours. Lincoln Academy... Go, fight, win..."

Fans continued to pour into the bleachers holding VICTORY signs in the air. The music played loudly as Jimmy paced back and fourth. Jimmy stood proudly as the National Anthem played. This was his finest moment. He had never been as proud of his team as he was today. This was their finest moment. No matter what the outcome of the meet was, they would all be champions in his heart.

Kayleigh toppled her opponent in the first race. Kisha, Brian, and Billy scored first place. Miranda waited anxiously on her starting block. She looked over at Jimmy and put both hands in the air. Her index fingers stood high indicating the #one sign, and she smiled.

"Swimmers take your marks. Swimmers get set."

She dove in, surfaced forcefully, and began swimming. She moved with great ease and agility. Working her way to the edge, she turned her body and flipped with great might. She had pushed off way ahead of her opponents. She continued to glide and breathe, letting the water do most of the work. She continued in the lead. As she stroked, she felt an overwhelming power that she had never possessed. One stroke, two strokes, then three. She continued to move through the water. Her head went into the water and out and in, then out. She hit her last flip turn and pushed off. She continued to stay in the lead but her focus was now on beating her own time. She gritted her teeth, pulled, pushed, pulled, pushed. She extended her arm out and kicked frantically to the edge of the pool. She jumped out victoriously and ran over to Seth. Slapping him a high five, she looked up at her time, 1:01:23.

"I beat my time. Holy shit. I beat my time."

Seth grabbed her hand. "Way to go kiddo. You did it."

Lincoln Academy was way ahead of Dartmouth, when Rene approached her starting block. She didn't feel pressed to win because even if she lost, her team would still win.

"Swimmers, take your marks..."

Rene dove in and worked her way through the lane. She closed her eyes and shut out her opponent who was ahead of her. She thought to herself, "Gotta beat my time. Don't worry about the girl next to you. Just beat your time. Pull and push. Pace yourself, kiddo." She stretched her short arms as far as she could reach them. She pulled, pushed, and breathed. She approached the edge of the pool and flipped. As she thrust, she felt a cramp in her leg. "Ignore it." She thought." Shut it out. Don't think about it." She worked her body frantically to the center of the lane. "Push and pull. Push and pull. Get to the edge." The cramp worked itself out and she continued to push forward. Although her opponent was ahead, Rene continued to exert herself as little as possible. She used the water as leverage to pull herself forward one stroke at a time until she hit the last turn. She pushed off the side harder than she had ever pushed. She gritted her teeth and continued one stroke at a time. Now she was swimming next to her opponent. "Can't think about her," she thought. "Keep pushing." She pushed and pulled frantically with every ounce

THE FINEST MOMENT

of energy she had. "Now, it's time to put on the thrusters." Her little body felt like it couldn't give anymore than it was already giving; but she thought, "When you have nothing left to give..." She pulled and pushed ahead of her opponent so that as she reached the edge of the pool, she extended her arm out. She jumped out victoriously, ran over to where Ray was and slapped him a high five."

"I won, Coach. I won."

Ray grabbed her and picked her up. "We did it, Kid. We won, we won!"

"We did it, Coach. We're going to the finals next week!"

THE FINEST MOMENT

THEY GAVE ALL

The stands were packed with supportive fans that were waving signs that read, "Go Lincoln #1." Jimmy paced the deck as he watched his team warm up. He listened proudly to the music that echoed throughout the building. He looked up and saw Jessica sitting next to Kayleigh's mother. They were apparently involved in a serious conversation because Jessica didn't wave to Jimmy as she normally did. When the team finished, they went to the gym and waited for their head coach. The sound of Jimmy's footsteps broke the silence of the humming florescent light. He approached the team and looked at them proudly.

"This is it. This is the day that we have all been waiting for. Many of you have trained for many years to get to this point. Remember how you feel today. Remember this feeling. You will be able to talk to your grandchildren about this day. This is your finest hour. This is your finest moment. Enjoy it because some people never get to this place in their lives. Only the chosen few have what it takes to win a championship. All that I am asking of you is to give it your best. Give it your all. Go out there and perform like you've never performed before. Do your best and that is all I ask of you. Break 'em down."

The team huddled together and let out a big, "Lincoln Academy Number 1. Go, fight, win!"

Jimmy took his spot at the other end of the pool. He put his hands behind his back and watched as Ray and Seth stood at the starting blocks talking to the swimmers who were ready to compete. Brian Bishop was the first person from Lincoln to race. He stood on his starting block and wiggled his head around. He bent over and stretched his arms out to the edge of the starting block. Jimmy had given him a bottle of Tums to loosen up the acid in his system so that he wouldn't cramp up.

"Swimmers take your marks. Swimmers get set." The buzzer sounded and Brian leapt into the pool further than his competitors. He wiggled through the water one stroke at a time. He reached, pulled, and then pushed. Reached, pulled and pushed until he reached his first turn. When he flipped, his feet slammed into the water and he pushed with all of his might off the edge of the pool. He glided a few yards and began pushing and pulling with everything he had. He reached and extended his body as far as it would go. He was ahead of his competitors by a long shot when he turned for the second time. Again he flipped and pushed off the edge with a great amount of force. He glided, pulled, and reached until he hit the next turn. He continued to maintain the lead. He reached, and pulled with every bit of energy he had. He glided out of his next turn and continued to stay in the lead. He pushed and pulled with all of his strength and reached the edge of the pool a winner. He jumped out of the pool and gave Seth and Ray a high five. He hustled over to the bench and looked at his time. He leaped in the air when he saw that it was 2:17:01. He had beaten his time and had placed first in the race. He continued to jump up and down and hugged his teammates.

Kayleigh waited on the starting block. She looked up at the sky and said, "Be with me, Daddy. Be with me."

"Swimmers take your marks. Swimmers get set." The buzzer sounded and Kayleigh leapt into the air with such a spring, she landed far ahead of her opponents. She reached with every stroke and turned her body. She rolled her shoulders with great finesse. She continued to reach and push, and reach and push. She rounded the first turned and pushed off the pool's edge with incomparable thrust. She glided for about a fourth the distance of the lane. She continued to reach and push. Her breath control was perfect as she rolled her head and shoulders with synchronized precision. She continued to push and pull until she reached the next turn. She flipped and pushed off the edge and glided even further than the last time. As she continued down the lane, she focused her energy on each and every stroke. She reached and pulled one stroke at a time. Finally, she hit her last turn and was way ahead of the other swimmers. She continued to utilize

THE FINEST MOMENT

the water to push her along to a victorious win. She jumped out and gave Seth and Ray a high five. She ran over to Jimmy and jumped into the air. Jimmy's hands met hers in the air.

He gave her a big hug. "Way to go. You won. Super job. Super."

She grabbed him tightly and squeezed with all of her might. "I did it coach. I did it."

Kisha and Miranda had also taken first place in their events. As the meet progressed, Lincoln Academy continued to stay in the lead. Lakes Region Trinity managed to pull ahead toward the end taking first in the boy's 100 meter crawl and the back stroke. The score was tied when the final race had begun. Rene was standing on the starting blocks when Jimmy came over to her.

"Rene, kid, I just want to let you know that you have been doing an awesome job this season. You are one of the best kids I have and you will go a long way. Right now, what I want from you is to continue doing your best. I don't want you to feel as though you are the one responsible for winning or losing this meet. Your team has gotten you to this point; and whatever the result, I want you to know that I am damned proud of you. Just do your best and that is all I ask of you.

She shook her head and looked at her lane with great intensity. "Yes, coach. Thank you."

"Swimmers take your marks. Swimmers get set." The buzzer sounded and Rene sprung into the pool like a frog jumping for a fly. She reached and pulled, and took quick breaths. She remained focused and was ahead. She reached, pulled, and glided. Reached, pulled, and glided. She hit the first turn and was ahead. She glided as far as her tiny body would take her. Then, she continued to reach and pull. Marissa Miles, from Lakes Region, was slowly gaining on her. Ray yelled out, "Pace yourself, Rene. Pace yourself. Take it slowly. Pace yourself. That's it. Keep reaching for the gold. Keep reaching."

She reached her final turn and pushed off with all the strength she had. She could hear Jimmy yelling out, 'even when you are tired... Even when you hurt all over...Even when you have got absolutely nothing left to give...That is when you will find....You have everything to give.' She continued reaching frantically until she reached the edge. She got out and gave Ray a high five. She looked up and saw her score. It was 1:03:21. She, then, looked at Marissa's score. It was 1:03:20. Her head dropped and she slowly walked over to her teammates. They greeted her with a hug. She continued to hold her head down and began crying.

"I lost. I lost. Oh. She beat me."

Jimmy came over to her and put his hand on her shoulder. "Rene. You beat your time. You beat your time. I am so proud of you."

She continued crying. "I lost, coach. She beat me."

"Rene. You beat your time. You beat your time. That is all that matters." He grabbed her chin and squatted down. "Listen to me, kid. You beat your time. You are a sophomore, racing in a varsity championship meet. You are a winner. You beat your time and I am proud of you. Pick your head up and be proud."

The awards were handed out and Kayleigh, Kisha, Brian, and Miranda had taken gold medals in their events. Rene took a silver medal and ran over to Jimmy. "Well, Coach. You are right. I did beat my time. I came close to beating an all-state senior as well. Thank you, Coach."

Jimmy looked at her with tears in his eyes and pulled her close to him. "Come here. Way to go. You are awesome."

All of the kids on The Lakes Region Trinity School team jumped up and down when they were announced the winner in the all around. They had won by two points and carried the winning trophy proudly. The excitement was ended when the announcer stood at the top of the winner's block.

"Okay. I need everyone to sit down please. Everyone take your seats for this special award. Please take your seats."

The crowd got quiet as the announcer stood and waited for a minute. "Okay. I have a special award to give out this evening." A young woman carried a gold trophy that was nearly as big as she was over to the announcer and gave it to him. He held the trophy in his hand and said, "The winner of the Rene Julian Parker award for the best girl's swimmer in the state will be invited to the New England

THE FINEST MOMENT

Invitational at Springfield College in May. She will also be going to the University of California in San Francisco, to compete in the National High School Swim meet in June. The award for the best girl's all around swimmer in New Hampshire goes to...Kayleigh Turner of Lincoln Academy. Come on up here, Kayleigh, and receive your trophy."

Kayleigh put her hands over her mouth and screamed. "Oh. Ah." She jumped up and gave Jimmy a high five and a hug. She reached out and slapped the hands of Ray, Seth, and the rest of her team. She began crying. "I did it. I won. I got the trophy. Ahh." She ran over to the winner's box and stood proudly as she took the trophy. The announcer whispered in her ear and put the microphone up to her mouth.

"Oh, my. Ah. Thank you so much. I just want to thank my team for helping me along. I also want to thank Penn. State for awarding me a four-year scholarship. I want to thank my coaches. But I especially want to thank Coach O'Neal for believing in me, when I didn't believe in myself." The tears rolled down her face and splashed onto the microphone. "Oh, my...I can't believe. I want to thank my mother. But I especially want to thank...Ah. Oh." She screamed out to the top of her voice. "Oh, Daddy..." She lifted the trophy up in the air. "Oh, Daddy...This is for you!"

After the meet, Rene's father grabbed her by the arm with great force and ordered, "You hurry up and get dressed. You could've won...You blew it."

She began crying. "Ah. Daddy. Let go of me.. You're hurting me."

"You'd better get dressed and get your fuckin' ass out of..."

Jimmy hustled over and put his hands on Nick's back. "Mr. Mafatado. Can I talk to you in my office?"

He let go and pointed to the locker room. "Get your ass in there and get dressed." He looked at Jimmy with contempt in his eyes. "What. What do you want?"

Jimmy smiled at him and said, "I just have to talk to you for a minute. Can you come to my office?"

"Ohh. I suppose. This better be quick."

"It will be. Come on."

Jimmy opened his door and led him in. He closed the door, locked it, and looked at Nick. "Let me tell you what." Jimmy, took off his coat and tie, and rolled his sleeves up. He grabbed Nick by the shirt. "Let me tell you what. You worthless piece of shit. You lay another hand on that child and I promise you…" His voice got louder. "I promise you a trip to the morgue you worthless coward." Jimmy pulled him closer and then pushed him against the wall. He put his hands around Nick's neck.

Nick's face turned blue and he gasped for air. "Please don't kill me. Please."

Jimmy let go and threw him across the office until he landed on the floor. Jimmy put his foot on Nick's chest. "I want you to call your sister now and tell her to come pick Rene up."

Nick put his hands up to shield himself. "Please don't kill me. Please don't kill me." He started crying. "Ah, please don't kill me. I need help. I don't want mean to hurt her. I just get so drunk. I get feeling lonely. I miss my wife desperately. Please, I need your help."

Jimmy looked into Nick's eyes and saw years of pain and desperation in them. He almost felt sorry for him; but realized at this moment, he didn't care about him. He only cared about the pain and suffering that he had put his daughter through.

"You have to help yourself. I can't help you. You have to make the effort."

The next day, Jimmy walked into the conference room where Dr. Prescott and the school board were and took a seat.

He looked at everyone with contempt. "You can save it. Save your breath, I know what you are going to say."

Dr. Prescott pulled the chair out for Dr. Parsons to sit down and then took a seat himself.

"Jimmy, I'm sorry that we have to do this; but, we have no choice."

"Yeah, no problem."

"We also want to address our concerns regarding Kayleigh Turner."

THE FINEST MOMENT

"And what concerns are those?"

"I have seen the way you look at her; and I have seen you fondling and caressing her in the halls after school."

Jimmy sat up. "Excuse you? Come again?"

"I'm not sure that I'm comfortable with the way you..."

"The way I what? What the hell are you talking about?"

"I'm going to call her mother...and I am going to get Kayleigh down here to testify that you have been..."

Jimmy stood up and walked over to where Dr. Prescott was sitting and pointed to him. "Don't you dare. Don't you dare pull Kayleigh into your bull-shit lies. Isn't it enough that you have destroyed me? She's got a free ride to Penn State and you will not jeopardize that. Why on earth are you doing this?"

Dr. Prescott stood up. "Don't you dare put your hand in my face." His voice got louder and his face turned red. He began shouting and spitting when he yelled, "Don't you dare, you worthless piece of shit. Let me tell you something."

Jimmy grabbed him by the neck tie and began choking him. Dr. Prescott stood there begging for his life.

"Get him off me. Please don't let him kill me."

"Don't you dare destroy Kayleigh. Don't you dare."

Two of the security officers came in and jumped on Jimmy. They pulled him up to the table and held him there until the police arrived.

Jimmy sat in an empty cell wondering where he had gone wrong in his life. He had looked at these bars and never realized he'd be the one behind them.

THE FINEST MOMENT

COACH O'NEAL. COACH O'NEAL

The pool was empty when Richard Foster, the new head swim coach, went on deck. He walked around and looked at the pool. He paced the floors and went into an empty locker room wondering where his team was. He went back out on deck and took a seat on one of the benches. As he sat there, he listened to the sound of the humming florescent lights. The silence was remarkably powerful and spoke as loud as war. He began to pace the floor and then looked up and saw the swim team as they took seats on the bleachers. They were all wearing their street clothes and sat silently. Ray and Seth came out and took a seat in the front row. Richard looked up at them, then looked at his watch and hollered to them.

"It's time for practice. Why isn't anybody suited up?"

The team just sat there quietly without saying a word. He pulled out his cell phone and called Dr. Prescott, and talked with him. After about 20 minutes, Dr. Prescott came out to the pool deck and looked up.

"It's way past 3:00. Everybody needs to get dressed and get out to the pool."

The sound of the humming lights got louder and louder and louder, until Kayleigh Turner stood up and walked to the edge of the bleachers.

"When our head coach gets here, we will practice."

Dr. Prescott pointed to Richard and said, "Your new head coach is here. Let's go. Get out on deck."

She repeated herself, "When our head coach gets here, we will practice."

Dr. Prescott walked over to her. "Well, you have a new coach and you need to get out here and practice."

"We will not practice until Coach O'Neil gets here."

"Well, you can forget it. That will never happen. Not here, not now."

"Then, we are not going to practice. When you bring Coach O'Neil here, we will practice."

"Well then, you are all off the team. Go home. Get outta here."

Kayleigh's mother came out to the pool deck and stood toe to toe with Dr. Prescott.

"Let me tell you something. I've heard the lies that you have been spreading about my daughter and her coach." She began crying. "Coach O'Neal has been nothing but a father to my Kayleigh. He has loved her like nobody else, except for her own father who is no longer with us. You are hurtful, and hateful, and I will not stand by and watch you destroy my daughter like you've tried to destroy Coach O'Neal. You are a pathetic excuse for a human being."

The rest of the team stood up and began chanting, "Coach O'Neil, Coach O'Neil, Coach O'Neil. They began stomping on the bleachers and yelled louder, "Coach O'Neil, Coach O'Neil, Coach O'Neil."

They continued for about 20 minutes and then left. They went to the Boy's and Girl's Club where they started their own team. Seth and Ray were the new head coaches and would continue to be their coaches indefinitely.

Shawn and Jessica came to the police station, and paid Jimmy's bail so they released him. Jessica tried to reach out for Jimmy, but he pulled away from her. They drove along the highway without saying a word. When they got to Jimmy's house, Shawn looked at him and said, "You need to get to Florida, kid. You have a good job waiting for you there. You have your whole life ahead of you."

Jessica followed Jimmy to the house and reached out for him. Jimmy pushed her away and said, "You probably think that Prescott is right."

"Of course not. Don't be foolish. No, Jimmy. He is a fool. There's no way he could be..."

"Well, then, you probably think that I am a loser."

"Of course not, sweetheart."

THE FINEST MOMENT

"I've done nothing wrong. I have done absolutely nothing wrong."

Jessica wiped a tear that was forming in her eye. "I know you haven't, sweetheart."

"No. I mean, I have never done anything wrong. All my life since I was a child, I never deserved any of the bad things that happened to me. I never did anything wrong for those people to hurt me."

"What people, Jimmy? What are you talking about?"

"My life. I was always a good boy. I did what was right. I was a good Catholic boy and...Well, I never started the freakin' war in Panama. I never did anything wrong to deserve..." Jimmy leaned on his door and put his head down. "Ya know. I went to college. I went to college to better myself because I didn't want to have to struggle like my parents, and what did I get? Years and years of shame. I was shamed and ostracized by society for doing something good for myself. People laughed at me, Jessica. People laughed at me and called me a loser." He lifted his head up and looked at her. "It's a paradox. Life is a paradox. Now, I do something good for young people...," His voice got louder, "and I am attacked." He punched his chest and then punched the wall. "I have been a slave to that school and all those people there. I have done nothing but bust my ass. And people like Nick have a wonderful child and does not deserve her. What about people like Kayleigh's father? He deserves life more than that coward Nick. I just don't understand the way the world turns."

"And nobody else does either. We have to stay on and enjoy what good it has to offer."

Jimmy tenderly reached out for Jessica's chin and rested his palms under it. "That is why I love you so much. You can find the good in any shit storm."

"So can you Jimmy. I have seen the good in you. You've just been knocked down. Get back up. Pick your head up and continue marching on."

"How did you get to be so strong?"

"By watching you, Jimmy."

Jimmy stood in his doorway and then looked at Jessica. "I'll call you later. I have to get some rest."

"Okay, Jimmy. What are you going to do?"

"I don't know. I don't know right now. I just need some time alone."

"Okay, but will you call me later?"

"Yeah."

Jimmy went inside and turned his laptop on. He clicked on the Travel site and hastily reserved an online ticket with Southwest Airlines to Las Vegas. He mumbled, "I'm not gonna be poor again. No way. Never again."

Jimmy spent the next few days in Las Vegas before he had gotten up the nerve to call Jessica. His stomach churned as he listened to the phone ring.

Jessica answered. "Hello?"

"I am so sorry I haven't called you. Oh girl, things are going very well. I've got a lot of money."

"Jimmy, what's happening? Your sisters and your parents are looking for you. Shawn has also been…How did you get the money? How did you get the money? Are you doing something illegal?"

"No. Not at all."

"Jimmy, we need to communicate. Are you in some sort of trouble?"

"No, I just, I just…"

"Jimmy, you need to talk to me. You need to let me know what's going on. We're getting ready to be married and you need to be up front with me."

"Okay, okay. I've been gambling. I'm trying to get enough money so that I don't lose my shirt."

"Sweetheart, don't put yourself through this. Get on the plane. All we need is each other."

Jimmy became irate and said, "No, I will not go back to a life of poverty. I will not lose everything that I've worked so hard for."

"Jimmy, I need you here. You've worked so hard at our relationship. Isn't that more important?"

"Yes, but I want you to have nice things."

"They're not important. Jimmy I don't want to lose US."

THE FINEST MOMENT

"Give me a couple more days. Baby, I'll be back in a couple of days I promise and then you'll have my undivided attention."

When Jimmy hung up the phone he headed for the Ultimate Ace Casino and walked away with $25,000. He had his money in a brief case and deposited it in the bank. When he finished, he went to one casino after the other and by the end of the day, he had won about a hundred thousand dollars.

Jimmy arrived at Jessica's house on a late Friday night. He knocked on the door and Jessica came out. She took his hand and said, "You look tired sweetheart. Are you going to be okay?"

Jimmy had bags under his eyes and he looked pale. He was a bit thinner than when she had seen him a few days earlier. Jimmy put his hands over his face and said, "Yeah, I'm gonna be alright."

"You need to call your family. They are worried about you. Mrs. Turner called and wants you to call her. She says that the team…"

"I'll call in the morning. I just need some rest."

Jimmy sat on the couch and closed his eyes until he drifted into a peaceful sleep.

When Jessica got up the next morning, Jimmy was gone. She looked around for a note but there was none. She sat on her couch and began to cry.

THE FINEST MOMENT

FIGHTING DEMONS

Jimmy spent the next few days hopping around from one casino to the other. He deposited his money in the bank. Jimmy decided that he would go home after one more day. He was determined to get a million dollars so he started his quest at the Lady Luck Gallery where he had picked up $5,000. After depositing his winnings, he went over to The Foxy Lady and racked up another $2,000.00 which he had deposited as well. At around five p.m. he went to the Queen of Hearts lounge and had himself a nice steak and fries dinner before heading for the casino. When he got to the casino, he took his place at the roulette table. He couldn't do anything wrong and, by the end of the night, he had $20,000 dollars in his hand. He figured now was a good time to exit before the management decided to throw him out. He went up to the collection office and gathered his winnings and put them into his briefcase. As he headed for the exit door, he saw a familiar face heading in his direction. The older gentleman was smoking a cigar furiously. He was accompanied by two lugs.

"Capelli! Mario Capelli. Oh shit. I'm dead." Jimmy thought out loud as he ran for the bathroom: the only place he could think at the time, considering the circumstances. When he got there, he saw the window from which he would make his escape. He heard a loud voice outside the door yell, "He's in the bathroom. We got him cornered. The voice compelled Jimmy to expedite his escape. He hastily grabbed his brief case with one hand and opened the window with the other one. He leaped up and over and went head over heels like a gymnast would. Jimmy, however, lacked the grace of a gymnast, and landed face down in an alley. A voice inside the bathroom shouted, "He got out. Head for da alley and cut him awwf. Don't lose 'im."

Jimmy picked up his brief case and sprinted towards the back of the building. He ran and never looked back until he reached a dead end. Just like in the movies, he lunged for a locked door. He looked around and saw a dumpster that he could step on and hopefully leap for a window. He hurried when he heard the voices of the men getting closer. He reached for the sides of the dumpster and got to the top when he slipped and fell to the ground. "No time for the pain," he thought out loud and heard the voices of his B.U.D. Seal boot camp, instructors. 'Climb up that wall you lazy piece of shit. Get up there.' Jimmy hurled his brief case to the top of the dumpster and climbed to the top. His job was only half finished. He had to get into the window no matter what was on the other side of it. He launched his brief case toward the window, closed his eyes and hoped for the best. He wiped his brow and sighed when he heard the glass break for he knew he had made contact. Out of the corner of his eye he saw 3 men running. Jimmy squatted down and, with everything he had, leaped to the edge of the window sill. As he hung there, he remembered a time when he was running from leftist guerillas and had to climb his way into a window. He was, of course, much younger and more agile then. But now, he had much more to live for—- $100, 000 more than he did way back when. He also had someone waiting for him at home so he was certain to do anything and everything in his power to get back to her.

As he dangled there he willed his left foot up to the ledge, but it had other plans. Finally, he looked down and saw the men standing below him. Suddenly, without warning, he found his left leg up on the ledge. Now, all he had to do was get the rest of his body to follow.

He was more encouraged after seeing one of the men pull out a Colt 44 revolver pistol. Jimmy used all of his strength to pull his body up. As he lay there he heard Mario say, "put away the pistol Gino. We'll get him. We'll get him. He can't go nowhere's. Spread out. I'll go to the front entrance. Al, you go to the back and Gino, get ya ass up there the way he did and chase him." There was a pause as Gino looked up at the window. "Let's go Gino, get up there. I'm goin' out front."

Mario and Al went their own way and Gino attempted to climb the dumpster.

THE FINEST MOMENT

Jimmy finally rolled himself into the window and onto the floor. It was dark and he couldn't see a thing. He felt around until he found his brief case. As he reached for it, he felt something warm and furry dash across his arm. He heard a squeaking sound and followed it to a moon beam that stretched across the center of the room. It was a rat. It wasn't like the ones that he had seen in New Hampshire. This one was bigger than a cat. Jimmy grabbed his brief case and headed for the door. He had entered a dark hallway and put one hand in front of him in lieu of his own eyes. As he snaked his way through the dark maze he was thinking of where he could hide his money. He figured that if he got caught and didn't have any money on him, the men would just beat him a little and let him go.

He continued to run aimlessly down the dark corridor until he found a stairwell. The stairwell was lit a little by the outside neon lights. Jimmy would use the stairwell as a reference point. He had thought of putting his briefcase in the ceiling tile. "But where?" he thought out loud. He frantically reached for a door that was also lit by neon lights. He opened the door and walked forward until he pumped into a desk. He let out a big yelp and leaned over in pain. He jumped onto the desk and reached for the ceiling and lifting up one of the tiles, he carefully placed his bag on top of one of the other tiles. A rat jumped for his throat and then 4 more followed. Jimmy pulled them off and then his feet came out from under him. As he slipped he grabbed for the ceiling frame to hold on to, but a bunch of ceiling tiles collapsed on him. He fell off the desk and tried landing on his feet. His arm was numb and he couldn't move it. He laid there for a few minutes. Then he picked himself up. He couldn't see anything. His briefcase was under the pile of ceiling tiles.

He heard a voice in the distance. "Up there. Did ya hear that? Up there. Go."

Jimmy slithered his way down the stairs and looked carefully at every dark corner to make sure he saw nothing move or make noise. When he reached the bottom of the stairs, he was startled by a bang and a rattling noise in the corner. He dove behind what might have been a crate and listened. He heard the sound of a cat that was being castrated by rats. He waited for a few minutes for the sound to end and then he moved forward. The beam of a neon light had shone in a corner where a dead cat lay. It looked as though a bunch of rats had gotten to him or it. The eyes were chewed out and his anus had been chewed out. The rats had chewed a tunnel into the poor cat.

Jimmy spotted a door that would probably lead him outside. His main objective was to get out so that he wouldn't get caught by Mario and his clan. Jimmy knew for sure that he would, indeed, get caught; but he didn't want any attention drawn to where the money had been hidden. He opened the door with a great deal of caution, yet he moved quickly enough to get outside. As he worked his way down the abandoned sidewalk he heard a voice say, "There he is. Get him."

Jimmy picked his feet up and sprinted as fast as he could until he was knocked off his feet when one of the men tackled him. Jimmy got up and started swinging his fists as hard and as fast as he could at the man's face until he fell to the ground. Jimmy's efforts were nil because Mario had a pistol.

Mario pointed the pistol at Jimmy and helped the man up with his free hand. He motioned for Jimmy to drop to his knees. "Get on ya knees and say ya prayahs. Do it now."

Mario pointed to a black Cadillac that was parked on the side of the desolate street and ordered, "Gino, put him in da trunk. Al get ya' self togetha and get in the ca'" Mario kept his gun on Jimmy as Gino grabbed him.

Jimmy pulled away and grumbled. "You'll never take me alive you 'Rat Pack' wanna be's. You guys aint real gangsters, you're just a bunch of..."

Just then Mario walked over and bitched slapped Jimmy with the butt of his pistol and said, "Get him in the trunk right now."

Gino body slammed Jimmy into the trunk and closed the door. They drove for what seemed like hours until the door opened and Jimmy saw himself looking out at an old junk yard. Gino pulled him out and threw him on the ground.

Mario grabbed Jimmy by the arm and picked him up. When Jimmy got to his feet, Gino grabbed him by the throat and forced him to his knees.

THE FINEST MOMENT

Mario put the gun in Jimmy's mouth and said, "Okay, you've got 2 seconds to tell me where the money is."

Jimmy looked up at him with tear filled eyes. "I don't know. I dropped it in the dumpster."

"Dropped it in the dumpsta." Mario gave Jimmy a backhand and a punch to the gut. "What a ya' think, I'm an idiot. Huh? Where's the loot?"

"I told you I don't have it."

"All right than smart ass, I'll take it out of your head."

Mario backed up but kept the gun pointed at Jimmy and said, "Okay, one more chance. Where is it?"

Jimmy began bawling and sobbing and shaking uncontrollably. He let out a big holler. "Go ahead, you son of a bitch. I've got nothin' to live for." Jimmy gritted his teeth and began hyperventilating. "If I lose the money, I might as well be dead I tell you. I ain't ever going back to that life again. I've probably already lost my girlfriend. I've got nothing to go back for. So kill me, you son of a bitch. Do it for me, it's what I've wanted to do for years, but at least now..." Jimmy put his head down and began weeping like a child who had just lost his mother to cancer. "...at least this way, I'll go to heaven. Do it God damned it. Just fuckin' do it."

He had pissed his pants and was trembling. Mario pointed the gun at Jimmy's head and pulled the trigger. "Click." Nothing came out accept for a click that echoed through Jimmy's head as he shit his pants. He heard another click and then another.

Mario looked at him and said, "You ready to tell me now, you wining little snot nosed punk. You gonna tell me now?"

Jimmy picked his head up and in a low tone said, "fuck you."

"Click, click, click."

Jimmy dove to the ground and put his hands in front of his face and began screaming. "Ah, I don't know where the money is. Just do it now. Just hurry up and do it."

Jimmy closed his eyes in anticipation of the gun blast. "Okay. Okay, asshole. It's up on the second floor in the middle of the building. You'll see ceiling tiles on the floor and rat's. I swear. That's the truth.

Mario walked up to Jimmy and picked him up and said, "Today's ya lucky day kid. Consider this a warning pal. Next time the gun is gonna be loaded. Oh, and by the way, the bullets won't be for you. I'll find that little girlfriend of yours or one of your friends or even your mothah. I'll find out who you love and so help me Gawd, I'll cut them up into little pieces. Kapish."

Jimmy shook his head and wiped his nose. "Yeah, I got it."

"I like you kid, you out foxed my best men. You aren't afraid to die. Most guys would have been beggin' for their lives. Not you kid, I respect that. Now, we're gonna drive on out of here and this was all a bad dream. You breathe this to anyone, I will find your girl and I'll have a little fun with her before I kill her. Get my drift?"

Jessica had called Shawn to see if he had seen his old friend. Fortunately, Shawn answered right away. "Hello?"

"Shawn?"

"Yeah, who's this?"

"It's Jessica."

"Is everything okay Jessica? You sound troubled."

"It's Jimmy. I'm worried about him. He went to Las Vegas. He said he'd be gone for a couple of days, but he's not back." Jessica began crying.

"I'm sure he's okay. Listen, if it makes you feel any better, I'll call some friends in Las Vegas. They might know where he is. Don't worry. He'll be fine. I'll let you go now so I can find out where he is. I'll call you if I hear any word."

"Please find him Shawn."

"I will."

Jessica waited patiently for either Jimmy to show up or for Shawn to call. When he did, he told her that he didn't have any news; but if he did, he'd call her.

A couple of days turned into a couple of weeks and Jessica waited by the phone for a call that never came.

When Jimmy finally did get home, he drove over to Jessica's. She opened the door and Jimmy collapsed in her arms. She carried him to the couch and put a cover over him. She sat next to him and looked

THE FINEST MOMENT

at him as tears rolled down her cheek. Jimmy looked as though he had come back from a concentration camp. His eyes were all sunken in and his face was pale. She could hardly recognize the man she had grown to love.

She stroked his hair and said, "Jimmy, everything's gonna be all right."

She was too worried to be mad so she continued to stroke his hair. "You have to stop doing this to yourself. I know you want to save your business, but you're going to die before you can enjoy the fruits of it."

She fixed him a sandwich and nursed him back to health. She could not understand the extend of his intent to push on with this charade until he explained to her again how his family had struggled and he didn't want them to go back to that life again. He also told her that he'd rather die than to go back to where he was. In fact, he almost did and was prepared to do so, if necessary.

She looked concerned and said, "You can still have those nice things Jimmy, if you'd just sell some of what you own. I'd be happy if you ran a small comfort Inn."

"I know, baby, you just don't know what it means to me to make sure I have enough money in the bank to have nice things. I have to keep this going. I cannot fail."

"Jimmy, you're not a failure. You won't fail, but you don't have to own the world you know?"

"Remember how happy your family was when I flew them all to Disney?"

"Jimmy, my family loves you. They'd be happy with you no matter what you did."

"But don't you like having the fine things in life?"

"Jimmy, it's not everything. I admit I have found myself indulging in your wealth and I'm beginning to feel like a heathen. I just want to live the simple life. And I want to live it with you."

A couple of days later Jimmy left again. This time he was gone for a month. He never called or let Jessica know what was going on. He returned again and stood at Jessica's doorway with a dozen red roses. She looked at the roses and looked at him.

She kept the door open and went back inside. Jimmy followed Jessica to the living room. A thin, young man of about 28 was sitting at her kitchen table. He had bleached blond hair that was fluffed in the front. He wore a goat tee and had bright blue eyes.

Jessica introduced them. "Jimmy, this is Kurt."

Kurt stood and extended his hand. Jimmy shook it with an unbearable death grip. "It's nice to meet you, Kurt. The pleasure is all mine. I'm sorry, Jessica, I didn't know you had company. I should have called."

Kurt headed for the door and said, "That's okay, I have to get going. I'll call you Jess."

Jessica walked him to the door and said goodbye.

Jimmy looked at Jessica and asked, "Who's that? Brad Pitt's brother?"

Jessica rolled her eyes and sighed. "He's only a friend. I've known him since I was a kid. He wants more than friendship; but, I dunno. He's a physical therapist and lives a simple life, Jimmy. That's the kind of man I need right now—somebody who's not more interested in money. Someone who is not so insecure with his life that he has to…" She studied Jimmy's black eyes and asked, "Would you care to explain?"

"No." He paused. "Shawn and I…we were wrestling"

She pointed to the kitchen table and said, "Jimmy, we need to talk." She took her engagement ring off her finger and gave it to him and began crying. She looked at him and said, "I just can't do this anymore. I can't live like this. I just want to live a simple life."

Jimmy's leg began shaking anxiously. "Oh, the simple life is it? You certainly had your hand deep into the cookie jar. My money was good enough for charity. Oh, yeah. I was good enough to give it away to every skid row bum in New England."

Jessica wiped her eyes and sniveled. "I haven't really spent quality time with you in months because you were out trying to make sure that you wouldn't be poor. It wouldn't have mattered to me if you had nothing."

"That is so easy for you to say; but I know that if I were as poor

THE FINEST MOMENT

as I was a few years ago, you'd leave me in a heart beat. Don't give me this, 'all we need is love' bull-shit. You know that if I were a loser again, you would drop me."

"That's not true. You know that's not true." She began shouting. "How can you say that? Don't you know me by now? Don't you know...?"

"Oh save it Jessica. You've found some young buck who will satisfy you. How long has he been coming over to your house? How long?"

"Oh, I've heard enough. Don't get me wrong, I enjoyed our time together; but now I need to put my career first and move on with my life. Oh, Jimmy, it's so complicated."

"Don't you dare. Don't you dare pull that, 'oh, I need to move on with my life' routine.'"

The tears rolled down Jessica's face in steady streams as she put her head in her hands. There was silence for a while as she sobbed. It wasn't the sobbing of a young school girl who had just broken up with her boyfriend. Her emotions were likened to a combination of things: she sobbed like a mother would sob when she saw her young son ruining his life with reckless behavior, yet at the same time her pain was indicative of the absolute sorrow she felt, knowing that she had to say goodbye to the man who mattered most in her life. The feeling of helplessness made her feel trapped like a bear that had just fallen into a well dug trap in the wilderness and could not get out. "We're just two different people. I mean we're heading in opposite directions. I mean, I am...Oh I don't know what I mean. It's just that...You're just..."

"Greedy?"

"I wasn't going to say that."

"Yes, you were. If you only knew what type of life I lived before I met you. If only you knew how people laughed at me for so long because I was a God damned loser."

"Jimmy, I know. I feel badly for how things went for you when you..."

"Oh, you know the pain I suffered. You know it so well...You have no idea what I've been through in my life."

"You're right. I don't know the hell you've been through. That's why I can't relate."

"Oh, you are so right, Saint Jessica. Daughter of a Doctor with his own private practice. Miss field hockey scholarship, didn't have to pay a fuckin' dime. You don't know what it's like to struggle inside and out. You were born perfect."

"Jimmy, why are you being so hurtful? This isn't the Jimmy that I fell in love with. Your words are so hateful. Why are you doing this?"

"I want you to feel the pain that I've been through. I want you to know how painful it was." Jimmy's voice got louder with each word. "I grew up in poverty. I didn't have running water and had to take a shit in a damn outhouse like the mother fucking Pilgrims. I was raped by a' priest. I was prostituted by the Catholic Church." He pounded on the table and gritted his teeth in anger until, by the time he finished, he was hollering. He stood up and towered over Jessica. "You didn't know that did you Jessica? You didn't know How could you? I was raped by God. Then, that wasn't enough. I had to go over to Panama and watch my best friends' heads and legs come off and I had to run around hell, eating river rats and drinking swamp juice. I had to watch little girls and little boys as the soldiers in El Salvador raped them No, that wasn't quite enough torture for me, Jessica. I had to sit back and watch as these little children and their mothers were tortured in the same way I had been and then had their fucking heads blown off. You don't remember me telling you about that, do you? Well to top it off, I lived in a shit hole and worked a piece of shit job for the last six years."

She put her hands over her mouth and began crying and screaming frantically. "I didn't know that Jimmy. I didn't know..."

"You didn't know that I was prostituted by the entire Catholic fuckin' church did you?"

"You never told me."

"Oh, yeah, I was so anxious to share that part of my life with you. I just wanted to tell the whole fuck'n world. Well, the church gave me $50,000 and I'll be God damned if I'm gonna let some prick

THE FINEST MOMENT

of a principal fire me and put me on the street. No, way. I've been paid in full."

"Jimmy, I'm sorry about what happened to you." She reached for him but he slapped her hand away. She put her hands over her eyes and began crying helplessly for him until she could barely breathe. "I'm so sorry, Jimmy that life has been so cruel to you. Please, sweetheart, don't be angry at God."

"Angry? Angry? Oh, I'm not angry at God. No, not at all, I'd just like the opportunity to bring him down here and watch as he gets raped and murdered."

Jessica sat on the couch and continued to cry. After a few minutes, she calmed down a little. "He did. He did. Jesus was beaten and probably raped. They ripped his beard out and then put him on the cross. Jimmy, he took those beatings along with you. When you saw those children raped, you saw Jesus being raped." There was an eerie silence for a moment. Then Jessica continued, "There are a lot of people who have it bad. When I worked with Mother Theresa, I saw things...I saw people who were..."

Jimmy slammed his fist on the table and grabbed the engagement ring and threw it across the room. "To hell with mother Theresa, to hell with the church. What kind of God would take Kayleigh's father from her and then have the entire administration at Lincoln Academy thinking that she was having an affair with her coach? When I was so broke that I never had food in my refrigerator, I couldn't get a girlfriend to save my life. Now, that I have some money, I still can't even...I can't win...I can't even win the state fucking meet." He waved his hand in the air and said "Oh to hell with it." He walked to the door and opened it and said, "You're going to regret taking that piece of shit off your finger. You'll see my true colors. I'll show you the shape of my heart. I'll show the whole God damned world." He slammed the door and ran to his car. He drove around all day to clear his mind and he finally went home.

One night as Jimmy lay in his bed curled up in the fetal position, Shawn came over. He cajoled Jimmy into getting out of the house. They drove down the highway in silence until Shawn pulled over at a diner. As they ate their dinner in silence, Shawn looked at his friend with concern. Shawn's face was expressionless and he was deep in thought. Jimmy just nibbled at his food and his eyes kept opening and closing. He would occasionally look at Shawn and force a smile.

Shawn was the first to break the dreadful silence. "Jimmy, man, I'm not gonna lie to ya, pal. You look like hell. How much sleep did you get last night?"

Jimmy popped up as if Shawn had pulled the covers off him on a cold winter morning. "Ah, I got a couple hours. I've got a lot on my mind."

"Jimmy. Things are going to be all right. We've got things back under control."

"I know that Shawn," snapped Jimmy, "I just need a little bit more money to make sure that nothing else will go wrong."

"Jim, man, things can always go wrong. You just have to take care of them when they happen. You're running yourself ragged to make sure bad things won't happen again, but look at you. Things cannot possibly get any worse than they are now. You're..."

"I know Shawn. I know what the hell I'm doing. Okay? I didn't get where I am today without knowing what I was doing? I'm just putting a few more eggs in the nest. I'm just putting more money into my account in case of an emergency. I'm not gonna fuckin' lose what I have Shawn. Okay? God damned it. It'll be okay in a few weeks. You'll see."

"A few weeks? When's the last time you saw Jessica?"

"Never mind Jessica. She's okay. You'll see. I'll be able to secure a future with her without any worries."

"That's what it's about Jimmy."

"What are you trying to say Shawn?"

"Jimmy, I've known you a long time. You've struggled your whole life and you weren't dealt a good hand. You are afraid of losing everything you've worked hard for. Did you stop and think that all of this trouble happened when you asked Jessica to marry you and you bought the house in Florida?"

"No, I never thought of it." Jimmy spoke with sarcasm and contempt.

THE FINEST MOMENT

"Don't you think that...well, you're getting closer to God now so do you think that maybe he's trying to tell you something?"

"What's he trying to tell me, Shawn?"

"Listen, Jimmy. I do believe that the forces of evil are pretty powerful, but they're not as powerful as the powers of God. Evil always uses situations and people, and demons don't have horns Jimmy. They always come dressed like sheep. Something bad has happened in your life and the devil is tempting you. He's making it seem as though you can gamble and make things right. Don't you see what's happening?"

"Yeah, I suppose, but what do I do?"

"You have to get control of yourself."

"I am in control."

"Well it doesn't seem like you have too much control lately."

"What the hell are you talking about?"

"Jimmy, you're like a brother to me and personally, you're not doing your job at home with your lady."

Jimmy's face turned red and his voice got louder. "Don't you dare. Don't you dare bring Jessica into this! Things are under control pal."

"Are they?"

"Yeah, what are you talking about? Jessica loves me."

"You're right, but she won't wait while you run around the countryside trying to get rich. When is the last time you saw her?"

"Enough. The subject is closed."

"Is it?"

"Yes Shawn, let it go."

"No, brother, you've got a woman at home that any guy would die for, and you've completely disregarded her. I won't sit back and let you do that to her or yourself. You need to go back and get things in order."

"That's enough Shawn. Just because you found religion, you don't need to be holier than thou. I'm telling you. Back off!"

There was silence for a few minutes while the two men finished their meal.

Shawn interrupted the peace with a simple but profound comment. "God is knocking you off your high horse. Can't you hear what he's trying to tell you?"

Jimmy slammed his fork down and wiped his face with his napkin. "What's he trying to tell me Shawn?"

"He's telling you that you are not meant to run off to Las Vegas and have money to start a hotel business. You are not meant to be a wealthy man. I mean, look at what you have. You've got a wonderful woman. You will get a job in Florida, if you just go. Maybe this is a way of him telling you that you're supposed to count your blessings and appreciate what you have. It takes losing something to appreciate it. It's God's way of giving you a chance to reflect upon things. Just go live a simple life and raise children with the woman you love."

Jimmy shook his head. "Now I know what this is about. This is mutiny. You're trying to push me out of here so that I can go to Florida and fail. And in a year or so, I will be a loser again and Jessica will leave me. And she'll come running to you and leave me in the dust. No way, pal. I think that you want to get my woman into your bed. That's what you're getting at, isn't Shawn?"

Shawn laughed and said, "Now you're being a fool. You know that I would never want to use Jessica; but I tell you something, I'd give anything to have a woman with half her caliber. Listen Jimmy, I love you like a brother. You're a loving man and worthy of Jessica but now you're blowing it. You're putting your pride first. Why can't you just get the hell out and move to Florida. Let Jessica work until you get back on your feet again. You'll find a job working with kids and coaching. Jessica can work. It's not like you're gonna go broke again. Just swallow your foolish pride and go on with your life. Get off your ass. Pick yourself up and get on with it. Don't just lie down in front of those assholes. Don't just give up. I know that down deep you want to live the simple life, but you're too damn scared of being poor again. You'll never be poor; you've worked too hard. Why can't you just accept living the simple life? Look, I, too, would like to live a simple life. I'm as high on the food chain as I want to get. I'm happy where I am and don't want to go any further. I don't want to be rich and I don't want Jessica. You're paranoid, just plain afraid."

THE FINEST MOMENT

"I'm not afraid of anything Shawn. I've got everything under control."

"Do you?"

"Yes."

"Then why has Jessica been calling me looking for you?"

"When has she called?"

"She hasn't called in a while but she used to call every other day to see if you had been there. She said you've been spending a lot of time away."

"I knew you had something going on with her. How long have you been talking to my bitch?" Jimmy slammed his fist on the table. "How dare she get you involve with this. This is none of your God damned business. You're supposed to be my friend. You've been taking advantage of this situation to work your way into my old lady's pants. Listen, pal, why don't you mind your own business anyway? If I want to gamble, then that's my business. In fact, wasn't it you who got me turned on to it in the first place?"

"Afraid not. You're like a brother to me, and it's my business to make sure you don't destroy yourself. Listen to yourself. So paranoid that you think I've got something going on with Jessica. For your information pal, she loves you like nobody else could. She was worried about you so she kept checking in on you. Kept talking about how good things were for you guys. You're way off. You've totally lost it now. You don't even realize how well you have it. You're going in the wrong direction pal. Like I said before, it seems strange that everything began falling apart after you began getting close to God. Well, you got close to him and when you develop a relationship with him, you begin to lose everything again. I'm not sure. I think he's trying to tell you to slow down. You need to get back home, simmer down, and stop destroying yourself."

Jimmy got louder and everyone in the restaurant stopped talking and looked over at the two arguing friends. "Nobody's destroying themselves. If anyone's destroying himself, it's you who is planning his own demise by talking to me that way. You keep going on and on like a broken record about what God is trying to tell me. You act as though you know all about God's omnipotent wisdom. As if you have a personal hotline to heaven. You don't know shit. You'd better show me some respect. I've been treated like shit and talked to like a fool my entire life. People bow when I walk by now. People worship me. I am a fucking God. Do you know how I could destroy you Shawn? I could ruin you. Don't forget who butters your toast pal. I inspired you to get out of that piece of shit job. You'd better kiss my ass and shine my purple helmet pal. You owe me. You'd be nothing without me, you fuckin' loser. I put you where you are today, you worthless piece of shit. You'd be nothing without me but a hapless, pitiful dog."

Shawn stood up and pointed at Jimmy. "Come on. Let's take it outside. I'm gonna school you?"

Jimmy stood up and walked by Shawn. "Let's go tough guy. I'm gonna show you some manners."

Shawn followed and when they got to the parking lot they stood toe to toe. Shawn wound his arm back and started punching Jimmy repeatedly in the face. Jimmy fell to the pavement. Shawn picked him up and pinned him against his car.

"Who has been there for you? I treated you like my own brother. And you have the balls to tell me how you could ruin me. Go to hell Jimmy. I hope you rot, you piece of..."

Jimmy put his hand up and reached for Shawn. Shawn watched Jimmy shake uncontrollably as the tears fell from his eyes. He made a cackling sound more like a laugh than a cry. Shawn reached for his brother and held him in his arms while Jimmy's heart and soul came gushing out of his body.

After a few minutes, Jimmy spoke with his head in Shawn's shoulder. Although his voice was muffled, Shawn understood him. "I'm sorry Shawn. Oh my God, what have I done. Oh my God, what have I done. I'm afraid, okay? I'm so damn scared. I just don't ever want to be in poverty again. I had no respect. I was a piece of shit that everyone kicked. I just want my respect Shawn. I just want the good things. Oh, Lord, Shawn, I might lose Jessica. Oh, I don't know what to do."

That night, Jimmy called Jessica in hopes to work things out.

THE FINEST MOMENT

"Jessica? This is Jimmy."

"Jimmy where are you?"

"I'm at home. I. I wanted to tell you that I'm finished with my shenanigans. I'm done. I just want to get outta here. Let's go to Florida and get married. I'll find a job. I know I will. I just need to get out of here, sweetheart. I still love you with all my heart."

"I still love you Jimmy and I care about you but I've just grown so disgusted with you. I'm so angry right now. You were crazy the other night. You scared me. I've never seen you that way."

"I've been under a great deal of stress lately. I am going to get help with dealing with all the pain I feel inside."

"That's a good idea."

Jimmy began crying for he wanted to reach out to Jessica and somehow plug into her soul, the remorse, the love, the fear that he was feeling. He wanted so desperately to set things right. "I miss you so much. Jessica. I'm willing to live in Africa in some hut in the missionary and give it all up for you. I just need to be with you. I love you so much."

"I still care about you Jimmy. I miss you too and I love you. I've just been so worried about you. When you left the other night, I wasn't sure where you were going. I mean, you were...I miss you too." She paused for a moment and couldn't say anything, as her emotions got the best of her. "Give me some time. Please. I'll call you when I'm ready. I just need time to think."

"Okay. I love you."

"Okay Jimmy, I have to run."

"Goodbye."

Jimmy woke up the next morning with an overwhelming feeling of despair and impending doom. He had no hope of anything good happening for him again. He knew that everything between him and Jessica were over and she would never come back to him. Before hopelessness and despair could set in too deeply into his thoughts, he went outside, jumped in his Jeep and headed north to a river where he and Shawn had often gone fishing. Along the way, he pulled into a county store. He had simply wanted to feel the warmth that an ice cold beer could give him. He didn't really want to get drunk. He simply wanted all of the tension to go away for a while. He filled his tank with gas and walked up the creaky, wooden steps. A bell rang when he opened the door. The smell of fresh bread and deli meat met a sweet aroma of bubble gum and candy in the air. As Jimmy worked his way to the beer cooler, the old wooden planks below his feet creaked gently with each step he made. He grabbed a six pack of Budweiser and went to the counter where a woman of about 70 years was standing. She looked at him and then looked down at the beer.

"How ya doin' today?"

"Good. How are you?"

"I'm doin'. I'd be all right if 'twern't fa my ahhthritis."

"I'm sorry to hear that."

"'Salright. It's the damned cold weathah we've been havin'. Yuh, it's the damned cold."

"At least the really cold weather is over. It'll be warm in a month or so."

"Yuh. It was wicked cold the loohst few months. My ahhthritis tells me that the winta's nowt ovah yet."

"We'll probably get a couple more storms before it's over."

"Yuh. I imagine we will. We been thinkin' ah movin' to Florider ta get away from this mess. Yes Sa."

"Florida is nice. Ever been?"

"We used ta go down when I was little. Had an aunt who lived theyah. Lived in Tamper. Went ta visit a lowt."

"If you got yourself a more comfortable stool to sit on, you would probably not be in so much pain."

"I don't usually work heyah. Nohhh. Gave it up many yeaahs ago. My son and my grandchildren run the stoahh now. We bought it 50 yeaahs ago. Me and my husband. Them Massholes…Them rich ass Massta'ds used to come heyah alowt. To see the Old Man of the Mountain. Then that Gawddd damned CITGO opened up down the road a piece."

"You mean you own this store?"

"Ayuh. Shoah do. Me and my husband. We had five kids and

THE FINEST MOMENT

they helped us ovah the yeaahs. Shoah did. Then they all moved away but one of my sons stayed and helped and his kids help out now. Theyah on Spring Break. Went to Daytoner. Spring break my ass. They should be heyah lookin' aftah things. Ya know? My son is gonna lose this business with all the competition. He's gonna have to expand. We've worked to ha'd fa him to just lose it. I'm gonna have to talk to him 'bout addin' on. We've just got to hold on to this…It's what we've put our lives into."

She looked down at the beer. "Is that it?"

"Yes. Oh, wait. Do you have worms and crawlers?"

"Ayuh." She pointed to the back of the store. "Should be right theyah. In the back. Next to the ice."

"No. There isn't any. I looked."

"Well, I sawrrr them theyahh. Probably out."

Jimmy continued with the conversation, "Everyone needs a vacation from time to time."

"Go on, will ya. I nevah took no vacations. Had to mind the stoaahh. Otha wise we would have lost it."

An elderly man walked out from the back and went behind the counter. "Ma'tha chewin' ya eaahh awwff, young man?"

"Oh, I don't mind."

"Now, why ya want ta botha this young man. Ya hahhdly know him."

"Oh, go on, Chestah. Befooahhh I fo'get, go down cellahh and get some crawlahs and some wewwms fa this heyah young man?"

"Crawlahs. What foah?"

"Well, what else? Fishin'."

"It's Ma'ch. It's still wicked cold out. Too late fa ice fishin' and too early for regulah season. Haven't even stocked the rivahs owah lakes yet. Theyahs no good fishin' yet. 'Tis colda than a Basta'd out theyah."

Jimmy smiled and chuckled. "It's more or less just to sit and relax. I just want to catch a little buzz and clear my mind."

Martha leaned over to Jimmy. "What's on ya mind, son?"

"My girlfriend and I. We."

"Ya broke her haahht. Didn't ya?"

He looked down shamefully and played with the top of the beer can. "Something like that."

"You just get back in ya ca' and go find that girl."

"Ma'tha," Chester interrupted. "You ain't got no business inte'fering with his affayahs."

"Wait a minute, now. I know this young man has got a girl that he wouldn't give up for all the tea in Chiner. Now, go on. Ma'ch you'self back home and tell her that ya love huh."

"Jesum Crow, let the man go fishin'."

She turned around and shouted, "Ya said soww ya'self, Chestah. It's too Gawd damned cold to fish. It's like an ice arener out theyah on the lake. He needs to be with this girl. I'll betcha she's a keepahh. What's huh name? In fact, I don't even know yoahhh name."

"My name is Jimmy. Her name is Jessica."

"Jessicer. 'Tis a sweet name. Betcha she's as sweet as her name."

"Yes, ma'am."

"You go ahead and cleaahh ya mind down rivah. Think a somethin' goowd to say and get back home."

"Yes ma'am. I appreciate the advice."

"No problem. Now go on will ya. Haven't gowt all day. Get the hell outta heeyahh."

It was chilly when Jimmy got to the stream. The wind blew causing the water to ripple. As the trees swayed back and forth, Jimmy looked around at his surroundings and saw the early spring buds everywhere. The sounds of the birds and the gentle whisper of the stream had soothed his soul. He pulled out the beer and opened one of the cans. The smoke from the cold beer worked its way upward and so did the smell. Jimmy thought about the woman and the man at the store. They reminded him a great deal of his own grandparents. He thought about the woman who was so dedicated to her store that she ignored the pain of her arthritis to run it. He admired her dedication. Most of all, Jimmy thought about the love she and her family shared. Jimmy put the can down on the ground and walked backwards a few yards. He looked at the can and ran towards it, kicking it like a foot-

THE FINEST MOMENT

ball, towards the river. He left the rest of the cans there knowing that another fisherman would happen upon it. He walked over to the edge of the lake, took out his pole, baited his hook, and threw the line in. As he sat waiting for a trout to bite, he pondered everything that had happened and prayed to God for forgiveness. He didn't pray to get Jessica back or anything else. He just wanted his heavenly father to forgive him and put him back on whatever course it was that he was supposed to be on.

"Oh, Lord," he begged, please just let all the pain end. Please God forgive me for all that I've done. I've really messed things up, but you Lord can fix it. I have confidence. I really believe that you can put me back on course. Just please lead me in the right direction. Let me do something wonderful in this terrible world. Please let me do something that everyone can be proud of. But most of all, oh Lord, let me do something that I can be proud of." Jimmy continued to pray and meditate for a couple of hours. He didn't catch any fish, but wasn't disappointed. He nibbled on a sandwich and drank a cola. Then he packed his gear and headed up to his Jeep.

On the way back home, he was driving behind a school bus on the Kancamangus Highway. The bus was going along at a slow speed and Jimmy couldn't pass because the road was too narrow and curvy. He was patient and just enjoyed the ride. Suddenly the bus picked up speed and was now moving along when—- kaboom. The two back tires of the bus blew out causing it to swerve. It fishtailed and ended up going over the side of a hill. Jimmy immediately picked up his cell phone and called 911. He grabbed his bungee cord from the back of his car and ran to the scene. He looked down the hill and saw that the bus was resting on some rocks at the top of a steep ledge. Jimmy saw a car coming so he motioned for it to pull over. He assessed the situation and knew he had to act quickly. After he tied the bungee cord to the guardrail, he ran down the hill to where the bus was. He tried to open the emergency door, but it was stuck. He continued tirelessly trying to unlatch the door until finally it opened.

THE FINEST MOMENT

THE FINEST MOMENT

As soon as the door opened, a couple of elementary school children began jumping out. The bus was resting on an unstable rock and he knew that it was ready to give way at any moment. He had to work quickly, but had to be careful so that the bus would not shift in the wrong direction. He latched the bungee cord hook to the bumper of the bus. Then motioned for the man who had stopped to come down and help.

As soon as he came down, Jimmy gave him directions. "Listen carefully. When I throw the kids out, you guide 'em up the hill. Tell them to grab the bungee cord to help them out. Okay? The short, burly man who was about 50 or so nodded his head in cooperation. He looked frightened but insisted that he would help.

Jimmy jumped gingerly into the bus and started grabbing kids. They were all screaming and had their faces and hands glued to the windows. They were all frightened but not half as scared as Jimmy was. He grabbed one boy who had a death grip on his seat.

Jimmy looked at the little boy and said, "Hey, little man. I'm gonna get you home, chief. Do you want to go home and see your mommy?"

The little boy shook his head and jumped up and wrapped his arms around Jimmy. Jimmy led the little boy to the door but the boy would not let go. Jimmy had to talk to him some more.

"Okay, brave, man, I have to help your friends so that they can go home to their mom so you have to let go of me. Okay?"

The little boy was crying. "I want to go home. Please don't let me die. I'm scared. Please. I'm not going to die am I?"

"No, chief, you're home free, pal. Just let go and jump into the man's hands. Come on. I gotta help your friends. Okay? Time to go home."

The boy jumped out and the man helped him to the rope. Jimmy headed for the next kid. She was calm and quiet. Jimmy grabbed her and led her out. As he walked forward he felt the bus shift some more. The children all screamed in unison as if going down a roller coaster. Jimmy knew that if the boulder gave way, they would all plummet down the cliff to their death. He thought for sure that he would piss his pants but kept pushing on. The next kid was a tough one. He was tiny but held on to the bar at the bottom of the seat and would not let go. Jimmy had a clear vision of his good friends being shot to death in Panama. He could here them crying for their lives so he knew now that he had to save these children in order to compensate for his helplessness on the infamous air strip.

He grabbed the boy and said, "Did you see how I helped your friend? Your friend is okay. He's going home now. Do you want to be safe?"

The boy looked up at Jimmy. The poor little guy had a runny nose and his face was full of tears. "I, I, I, amm, am, am, sc, sc, scarred." He was hyperventilating and continued to cry.

"Hey big guy, I'm scared too but I want to get you out of here. Okay?"

The boy continued to cry and held on to the seat.

"Listen, pal, I have to get you out of here, buddy. This bus is going to go sliding and then we'll have to swim out of here. Don't you want to save all that trouble and get out of here? I do because I'm not real good in the water. I'm not much of a swimmer. I tend to sink. Also, that water is real cold pal. So, what do you say?"

"I wanna go home. I want to be with my parents." The boy let go and held onto Jimmy.

Some of the other children had no problem whatsoever bailing out of the bus. Jimmy headed toward the front and saw a young lady talking to a little girl. She must have been one of the other teachers. There were two more teachers that were trying to get some of the more frightened ones out. Jimmy went over to another little girl who was curled up in a ball.

He tapped her and said, "Hey beautiful, I've come to save you. Okay? I'm gonna get you out of..."

THE FINEST MOMENT

Just then the bus shifted again and then swayed. The boulder broke free and the bus did a 180, submerged, and crashed into another boulder. Jimmy had to move fast. He didn't have time for child psychology any more. The rear of the bus was hanging over the side of the cliff. Jimmy had to break open a side window to throw the kids out.

He yelled to the teachers, "This thing is going to go. You gotta force these kids out. You may hurt them when you pry 'em, but it'll be nothing compared to the fall. As soon as you get them out, get your asses out of here. Okay? Don't delay. Move, move, move!"

The teachers started yanking the children and throwing them out. There was one little girl left. She was in a corner shaking. She was pale and expressionless. Jimmy grabbed her and put her on his back. As soon as she did that, the girl threw up all over him. Jimmy led her to the window and dropped her. She landed safely in the arms of one of the teachers. Jimmy looked around to make sure that he didn't forget anybody and spotted the driver in her seat. Jimmy walked slowly to the front. She was half conscious and was bleeding on her forehead. Jimmy felt the bus shift again and it began to slide. He saw that she was in a seat belt so he threw himself on top of her to act as a shield when the impact came.

All at once, the boulder that the bus was resting on came loose and Jimmy held on to the bars in the front for dear life. The bus bounced around on the ledge of the cliff. Luckily, the cliff wasn't a straight drop. There were other rock shelves for the bus to bounce around on. Jimmy lost his grip and began ricocheting around the bus until it hit the ground. When it did, it bounced some more and then went into the icy waters of late March.

By this time rescue workers had gotten there and anticipated the fall, so they were already in the water. Divers were ready to act. The bus floated down the river and was headed for the rapids. Jimmy mustered every ounce of strength he had to get the driver out of there. He ignored the blood that was flowing rapidly from his mouth and nose. He grabbed the driver and put her into a fireman's carry and led her to the exit door. The door was stuck so Jimmy had to kick it with all his might. He finally got it open and threw the woman into the water. A rubber Zodiac boat was right there waiting and the men in it grabbed the woman. Jimmy was ready to jump in when all of a sudden—- Lights out, here we go. Like a ride at Disney, the door slammed shut and threw Jimmy back into the bus. He and the bus were now traveling down the rapids. The bus bounced around as Jimmy grabbed one of the seats and started kicking the emergency exit window open. He failed at first but he persisted until the plastic window was out. Jimmy slid through the hole and was now in the water. He knew he'd be under for a long time so he took in a large gulp of air and began swimming at an angle toward what seemed to be the direction of the shore. Boy was he wrong. He surfaced and gasped for air. He found himself in the middle of the river.

He was bumping into rocks and scraping every inch of his body. He angled himself and began pushing himself toward the shore. He finally surfaced and hit land; but he had to climb up an embankment. When he got to the top, he collapsed.

At about 5:00pm that night, Jessica was in the nurse's office at the hospital doing paperwork when Betsy, one of the other nightshift nurses, barged in. "Jessica, I think. your boyfriend...he's, you'd better come out and watch the television with us."

Jessica looked puzzled. "What's wrong?"

"Come on."

Jessica went to the lounge where she found the night staff glued to the television. A news 9 reporter was talking about an accident. "Just minutes before the bus plummeted to its watery grave, James O'Neal, a former Navy Seal, used his talents that he learned in the military to evacuate 30 first grade students who were on a field trip. Unfortunately, he was unable to save himself." The reporter pointed to the river and said, "Somewhere in these icy waters is James O'Neal. Rescue workers are diligently trying to find him. The bus driver was..."

Jessica put her hands over her mouth and said, "Can't be Jimmy. How do they know who is in that bus?" Jessica became frantic and started screaming. "I mean, what. What did he do—yell out to them, 'my name is James O'Neal'?"

THE FINEST MOMENT

Betsy, put her arms around Jessica and consoled her saying, "I don't know sweetie, I don't...They might have gotten the info from his license plate or saw a wallet. The news team is usually certain about things like that before they go public." A few minutes later the phone rang and Betsy ran to answer it. She came back and said, "Jennifer is on the phone."

Jessica hastened to the phone. "Hello?"

"Jessica, this is Jennifer. I got a call at about 3 o'clock from the state police. They said that at 1:00 there was a bus accident. Jimmy was helping. They can't find him."

Jessica began running her hand through her hair nervously. "How do they know it's Jimmy?"

"They said that he had called 911 and they asked him for his name. They told him to stay away from the bus as it might go into the water. So, he told them that he had been trained in the Seals for this sort of emergency. Oh, Jessica. I don't know what's going to happen to him."

Jessica's chin began to tremble. "What are we going to do, Jennifer?

"We have to wait."

"I can't, Jennifer, I can't just sit here and..."

"Why don't you come over here? I'll wait with you."

"Okay, just give me an hour or so and I'm on my way."

Jessica hung up and stood there helplessly crying into Betsy's shoulder. "It can't be him. I know it's not him. I just saw him the other day. He's all right. I'll call him now. I just know he's all right."

Jessica went to the phone and called Jimmy's number but only got his voice mail. She grabbed her coat and went to her house. She grabbed some clothes and some toiletries because she knew it would be a long couple of nights. As she was stumbling around her house, she saw something shiny in the corner of her living room next to her television. It was her engagement ring that Jimmy threw across the room and had been presumed lost. Jessica grabbed it, fondled it and put it on. As she put it on, she recalled the time when she first met him. She smiled as she thought about all the corny jokes he had told her. Jessica sat on her couch for a minute and thought about how gentle Jimmy was. She looked up at the ceiling and remembered how good he had been with his and her nieces and nephews. She drifted into a daydream of how good Jimmy would be to their children, when, not if, they had them. Jessica had always respected Jimmy's allegiance to his friends, especially Shawn. Images of Jimmy running around on the beach and acting like a schoolboy deluged her mind. Tears began to flow from her eyes as she thought about the wonderful times they had shared and how Jimmy had been the perfect gentleman by respecting her, Jessica's, need to be pure and chaste before marriage. Finally, the thoughts of Jimmy coming back from a 3 week gambling bender haunted Jessica. She remembered how he had just passed out in her arms. She began trembling as her hands absorbed the tears that were now flowing generously as she thought about their last conversation. She felt helpless as she thought about what he had said in regards to being raped by a priest. When he said it, Jessica wanted to comfort him and take away the pain but was unable to. Jessica didn't know what was going to happen but she did know that she did not tell Jimmy how much she really loved him, when they last talked.

The cool breeze from her slightly opened window chilled her. She immediately called Shawn to tell him what had happened. He wasn't there so she left a message explaining what had happened and left her cell phone number. When Jessica hung up, she called her mother to let her know where she'd be, then drove to Jennifer's. On the way there, she got a call from Shawn. She told him what had happened and told him where she was going. When Jessica got to Jennifer's house, the two women held each other and cried.

Jennifer held Jessica's chin up and said, "We're gonna find him. God knows, if anyone can survive a bus crashing into the river, it would be Jimmy."

The women waited and waited. Becca and Anita held onto Jessica's hand and comforted her. Jon went out to the garage and worked on his old truck to keep himself busy. The phone rang and everyone jumped. Jennifer ran to the phone and answered it. "Hello? Hey, Rachel. No, still no word. Yeah, yeah, call mom and dad. I can't get hold of Charlene, but I left a message. Love ya. Bye.

THE FINEST MOMENT

They continued to sit and wait and pray. It was about 8 o'clock and still no word. They were beginning to give up hope when the phone rang. Jennifer jumped up and grabbed it.

"Hello? Yes, this is she. Yes. Okay. Um hmm."

Jennifer put her hand over her mouth.

"Okay. Yeah. No. No. Where?"

Tears started rolling down her face.

"Okay. Okay. I'll get there as soon as I can."

Jessica was standing next to Jennifer and was anxious to find out what was going on. "Did they find him?"

Jennifer kept her hand on her mouth. Then she looked down and ran both of her hands through her hair. She looked at Jessica and said, "Yes he's alive."

Jessica put her head in her hands and began crying. "Oh thank God, thank God.

"Is he okay?"

"Jessica, it doesn't look good. They med-evaced him to Dartmouth. He's in serious condition." Jennifer paused and took a deep breath. "The doctors don't think he's gonna make it."

Jessica began crying again. "What's wrong with him? What's wrong...?"

"He's broken his ribs and one of his lungs is punctured. He has pneumonia and hypothermia." Jennifer started to cry. "He's bleeding inside and the doctors can't stop it. We have to get to the hospital."

Jennifer called Rachel and told her where Jimmy was. When she hung up, she, Anita, Becca, and Jon jumped into their van and Jessica followed.

THE FINEST MOMENT

THE FINAL BATTLE

When Jessica and the others arrived at the hospital, they went to the emergency room and told the nurse on duty who they were. The nurse pointed them to where Jimmy was. Jessica entered the small room where her worst nightmare awaited. She saw the only man she truly loved with all her heart lying helplessly in a bed. Everything that had recently happened between them was no longer important to her. Rachel and Charlene were standing at the foot of the bed and Jimmy's parents were at either side of him, looking at their loved one in disbelief. They were crying—- mostly sobbing. The real tears were hindered by their denial of the catastrophe.

Jimmy's eyes were swollen shut. He had thick, dark bruises and deep cuts on every part of his body. Blood was seeping steadily from his nose and mouth. An oxygen mask was carefully placed on his swollen lips. He was breathing heavily like a woman who was in tough labor. Periodically he convulsed and trembled and he let out a painful groan after each episode.

Jimmy's father stood up and motioned for Jessica to come over to where he was. As she moved slowly toward her battered soul mate, she did not take her eyes off him. She reached for the chair and sat down and took his throbbing hand. Although Jimmy could not see, he knew who it was that was holding his hand. For this hand was not only familiar to him, but also imperative to his sense of belonging in this world. Her touch was warm and gentle, and he knew that it belonged to the person that was most important to him. Jimmy was overwhelmed by an unspeakable feeling of rejuvenation and strength that he would not have normally possessed. He turned his head toward her and reached out his other hand and held on to her other hand with what little bit of strength he had. He tried laboriously to smile, but fell short with a slight grin of relief.

Jimmy ran his index finger along Jessica's engagement ring and a feeling of joy overcame him for he knew that there was hope for their relationship after all. A feeling of helplessness overcame both of them. He was not able to see her and he didn't know if he'd pull through. She wanted more than anything to take his pain away; to just heal him and have her husband to be walking and talking again but she could not. She could only rely on her faith. It was difficult to believe in anything when something like this was sitting heavily on her shoulder. She did, however, know without a doubt that her heavenly father had plans for her and Jimmy.

She began stroking his hair gently. She spoke in a compassionate, low, tone of voice—- the way a mother would talk to her young child after he had fallen from a swing and was hurting all over. The words she spoke were reassuring to Jimmy.

"It's gonna be okay, sweetheart. I'm here now. I'm here baby. You're going to be okay. Just relax. I'm here with you."

Jimmy's breathing got a little bit better and his trembling subsided with each word that Jessica uttered. One of the doctors, a young Jordanian man, came in to check on his patient. He walked over to where Shawn was standing and looked at Jimmy.

"Hang in there my friend. We're going to take care of you." He looked around at the exhausted family and friends and sighed. He introduced himself. "My name is Doctor Asaad Hasid Mustaffa, I am going to be taking care of Jimmy."

Dr. Mustaffa wiped the sweat from his forehead and sighed a deeper sigh than before. "Before I go...there's something you need to know. Look, now, I'm not going to sugar coat anything. I'm not gonna lie to ya. Things are grim. One of his lungs has collapsed. Some of his ribs are broken and he has internal bleeding. He also has hypothermia. And the least of my worries are some fractures on his legs, arms and hands. Frankly folks, I don't know how he'll make it through the night. I've seen much milder cases in equally strong individuals who don't make it."

His family and friends began to mumble and the real tears began to flow. Jennifer and her daughters all held on to Jon for strength.

THE FINEST MOMENT

Jennifer let out loud wails and leaned into her husband's shoulder. Rachel's cry sounded more like someone who was laughing at a funny joke, but her sounds were far from festive.

Shawn and Mike just looked at Jimmy as if they could not believe what they heard or saw. They remained expressionless almost stoic as they watched their dying brother.

Roland O'Neil, Jimmy's father, put his head up and said a quick prayer and then he spoke to the others. "Jimmy's going to be fine. We have to be strong. We must pull ourselves together." He put his hand on Jennifer's shoulder and reassured her. Then he went over and consoled Rachel and Charlene who were standing there shaking uncontrollably.

Jessica kissed Jimmy's forehead and continued to stroke his arms. She tried to be strong for his sake but was unable to swallow the frog that was in her throat. The flood gates opened and she began to cry. "I'm sorry sweetheart, If only I, I, would have only...called." Her voice got louder and bolder as she pleaded with Jimmy, God, and everyone around him. "PLEASE...PLEASE...JIMMY, PLEASE BABY... GOD, I BEG YOU...JIMMY, STOP BLEEDING. WE'VE GOT TOO MUCH TO DO. WE HAVE WAY TOO MUCH TO DO. OH, GOD, PLEASE WE'VE BEEN THROUGH SO MUCH TOGETHER. I LOVE YOU JIMMY. OH GOD...JIMMY I LOVE YOU SO MUCH."

She buried her face in his arm and pleaded with him in a muffled voice. "Please don't leave me. Not now Jimmy. Don't leave me. Don't go away." She continued to kiss his hands and rub his hair. "Oh, baby, we still have so much more to do. We have babies to raise, places to go. We still have things to..."

Suddenly the EKG began to pulsate at a quick rate. It sped up and got faster and faster with each moment. Jimmy had flat lined and the endless beep echoed in everyone's ears.

Jessica yelled louder than she had ever yelled before in her entire life. "JIMMY? JIMMY? Oh, Jimmy. NO, NO, NO, NO. DON'T GO AWAY. DON'T GO. OH GOD, PLEASE DON'T TAKE MY..."

Although Shawn had remained quiet and motionless prior to this moment, he suddenly jumped up and put his arms around his friend and held onto him tightly and hollered, "NO, JIMMY, PLEASE." Shawn began crying like a child would when his mother left him at nursery school for the first time. "OH, GOD, NO. PLEASE DON'T GO. BE STRONG, HOLD ON. COME BACK, PLEASE COME BACK." Shawn continued to cry and shake like a person who had just fallen into an icy lake.

Mike put his hands on his head and screamed. "AHHHHH-HHH!" He raised his head to the sky and continued to yell out.

Jennifer and Rachel continued to cry and Ellen put her head in Roland's chest and began crying. The tears rolled down Jon's face and his mouth opened, but no words came out.

The nurses and doctors came in and told everyone to get out as they placed the electro shock paddles on their patient's chest. Jimmy's family and friends went to the lobby and held each other and listened as the medical team tried to save him.

Dr. Mustaffa wiped the sweat from his brow, took a deep breath and said, "Okay, put the paddles on. Let's shock his heart. Ready, 1,2,3," POP! "Come on, do it again. 1,2,3," POP! The team persisted desperately to no avail. Jimmy was not responding. The team began shooting adrenaline in Jimmy's arm and continued shocking his heart; however, he did not respond to the treatment and the EKG flat lined. Jimmy's eyes rolled and he stopped breathing.

"Shock him again."

The team tried one more time to put the paddles on his chest. POP, POP.

Jimmy drifted into a dream of being in a large field. The sun was shining and it was warm. He was near a lake, and when he looked out, he saw a man walking on the water. Jimmy felt good. His pain was gone and he was at peace. Without warning, he found himself in the middle of the ocean on a raft that was slowly deflating. The wind was blowing heavily and the waves were about 40 feet. It was raining and the thunder and lightning frightened him. Suddenly, he looked up and saw a giant Naval Destroyer approaching. On the bow a signal

THE FINEST MOMENT

light was flashing. It was almost speaking, as if it were alive. The light was signaling in Morse code. "I've come to save you. I've come to save you."

Jimmy looked up at the deck and saw a man standing there unaffected by the lighting that was crashing around him. The man threw out a line with a buoyant tube attached and pulled Jimmy toward the ship. After Jimmy had wiggled his way on board, the stranger pulled him to his feet and hugged him. He held Jimmy close to him like a brother who had been gone for many years and had returned. The man spoke with great authority and compassion. "You're safe now. You're safe. Everything's gonna be all right."

Jimmy wept and shook. "Please forgive me. Please Father forgive me."

In an instant, Jimmy was standing on a mountain looking down at the ocean when…kaboom, a tidal wave hit the shore. He saw a man walking on the ocean. It was raining and lightning was dancing on the ocean's surface. The man yelled out. "You must cast your troubles into the sea."

Jimmy had a giant rock in his hands and threw it into the ocean. The rock had turned into a flock of doves that flew away.

Before Jimmy knew it, he somehow found himself in an office. A man in an expensive suit was looking at something on his desk. The man looked at Jimmy and said, "I see your resume, it looks good; but, I have no openings. There is no room for you here just yet."

Jimmy found himself standing on a sidewalk near a large house. He saw himself teaching a little boy how to ride a bike. Then he saw himself playing catch with the little boy. Jimmy looked at the front door and saw Jessica coming outside with a baby in her hands. She sat on the front steps and watched. Jimmy heard the boy yell, "Look mommy, did you see that catch I made? Daddy's tho'ing me da bawl."

Jessica smiled and said, "Yes, sweetie, I see."

Jimmy saw a German shepherd running around chasing them. He ran frantically and Jimmy threw a stick out for him to catch.

Jimmy heard a loud voice saying, "Go back. Go back." Another voice said, "Come back, come back. Let's try it one more time. Okay? 1,2,3," Pop.

Jimmy woke up and heard the medical team talking amongst themselves. "He's back, okay, let's stabilize him. Okay. He's breathing again. Let's get him into Intensive Care."

Jimmy was brought to Intensive Care where Jessica spent every waking moment with him for the next couple of weeks until he was healthy again.

EMAIL ROBERT W. BRITT AT *robbie6440@yahoo.com*

Made in the USA